A Whisper from the Edge of the World

K.N. Salustro

NOVA DRAGON STUDIOS, LLC

For David

A champion among humans, and a hero among friends.

The World
as known to Aurora Renglade

Forbidden Sea

Solkyria
Sunthrone City

Western Siren Territories

Atlantic Dragon Islands

Coral Chain Islands

Spider's Nest

Vertha

The Pod

Aurora Sea

Frozen North

Common Sea

Leviathan Sea

Gambeart Islands

Contents

Prologue: What Was Taken

Rori never expected the river to betray her, but it did, the day after a rainstorm when the air was clogged with heat and humidity.

It was supposed to be a rest day for her and Charlotte, no school or work other than their household chores, and it would have been another unremarkable but happy day in Rori's life. But when Rori met her friend at the field on the eastern side of the village, Charlotte was staring at the ground with her nose wrinkled and chin upturned in an affronted expression that would have been hostile on anyone else. Charlotte wore it with comic exaggeration, and Rori giggled as she approached.

"The gods hate us," Charlotte declared the moment Rori was within earshot. "Our perfect flower heaven is nothing but mud."

Rori surveyed the field. It wasn't quite as terrible as Charlotte was making it out to be, but the wildflowers that had bloomed earlier that week were now missing many of their petals, and there were brown puddles surrounding the survivors. That was enough to foil Charlotte's plan to weave flowers into each others hair and then ambush a few of the village boys, one of whom was Charlotte's favorite of the week.

Rori hid her relief; that same boy had caught her own attention nearly six months ago, and she hadn't found the courage to tell Charlotte about it. Maybe she would, once her friend's eye had moved on to someone else, but for now, Rori was content to take this small gift for what it was, and find something else to occupy their time.

"It's hot today," she noted, glancing up at the clouded sky. "Let's go for a swim."

Charlotte brightened at the suggestion, but frowned again almost immediately. "The river is going to be swarming with boats and people making up for yesterday," she said. "We'll never find a good spot."

She was right, but Rori wasn't ready to give up on the idea so easily. Added to that, the air was heavy against her skin, making it difficult to think about anything else.

"I know another river," Rori said. "It's not the easiest to get to, but we'll have it to ourselves."

Charlotte pondered this, her eyes still fixed longingly on the ruined flower field, and then agreed.

So Rori took her friend north, through the forest to the secret river she'd found years ago.

Maybe it wasn't really a secret. Surely someone else from the village knew about it, but in all the time Rori had been coming to its banks to practice her magic, she had never seen another soul. That was good; the isolation meant she was safe. At the small river, Rori could open her heart to the magic in her body, feel the pulse of the river as steady as her own, and simply be the truest version of herself. She had to hide that from everyone else, including her family.

Their warnings echoed in Rori's ears as she led Charlotte through the trees, but Rori pushed them away easily enough. She wouldn't be practicing her magic today, just swimming with a friend. Her parents couldn't possibly object to that. It was what any normal Solkyrian girl would have done on a hot day, after all.

But when they reached the river, their clothes plastered to their backs with sweat, Rori began to second-guess the whole idea.

The storm had left the usually small river swollen, pushing the water far up the banks on both sides. The river was murky with churned dirt, and it was Rori's turn to wrinkle her nose.

"It's usually clearer than this," she said apologetically to Charlotte. "Maybe we shouldn't."

Charlotte scraped a lock of hair off of her forehead, taking a decent amount of sweat with it. She grinned at Rori. "We absolutely should," she said. Then she ran full tilt at the water and jumped in with a heady splash.

Rori gasped and followed after her, stopping at the edge of the bank and searching frantically for her friend in the murky water. Charlotte's head popped up a few moments later, and she gave a breathy laugh.

"The water is *wonderful*," she called, treading lazily in place as she flashed another smile at Rori. In spite of the rain, it seemed the river was still flowing gently, and Charlotte was easily holding her own against the current. "What are you waiting for?"

Rori gave her friend a dramatic eye roll, then bent to strip off her shoes and socks.

"Oh fine," Charlotte teased from the water, "be all proper about it."

"You're going to wish you'd been, too, when you have to walk back in wet clothes," Rori pointed out.

Charlotte laughed and flipped in the water, nimble and comfortable as a fish. She began swimming towards the center of the river, where it ran deepest.

Rori felt an excited shiver run through her, and knew it was her magic eager to touch the water once again. Her magic wasn't quite a living thing, but ever since her Skill had manifested, it had been a steady presence inside her body just as much as her heart or her lungs, and just as vital. She quickly tugged one sock off and stretched her leg towards the river, letting her toes dip into the water.

That was all she needed to feel the full force of the river, steady and reliable as it had always been. It was stronger after the storm, yes, but not dangerous. It was never dangerous. Not for Rori. Smiling, she bent to undo her other shoe, and let the river's pulse whisper in time with her own as the water brushed past her bare foot. Her fingers stilled when she felt an unfamiliar surge ripple through her chest. Then she shot to her feet and screamed for Charlotte.

Her friend jerked to a stop near the center of the river, starting to turn to face Rori back on the bank, but that was when the hidden current hooked itself around Charlotte and pulled her under. One moment, Charlotte was there, her mouth and eyes both wide with confusion and surprise, and then she was gone, pulled beneath the surface.

Rori was moving before she even realized it, splashing into water up to her hips. She felt the undercurrent more strongly now, running in a deadly line right through the core of the river. Rori reached with her magic, plunging herself deep into the river and taking a firm grip around that treacherous ribbon in the middle.

Rori pulled, and the river bucked against her.

They'd done this before, countless times, Rori coaxing and guiding pieces of the river on to new paths, sometimes even stopping it altogether. She had never been as rough as she was now. The river responded in kind, fighting her with all the power of that vicious undertow. It wanted to flow downstream, taking Charlotte with it, and it would not give her back until it had washed her life away and filled her back up with water.

Rori would not let it.

She pulled again, and again, and again, until the current shuddered and softened in her grip. Then she dragged it all back, calling the water against its nature. Pain flared at the base of Rori's skull as her magic strained against the undertow, but she couldn't stop, not until she had Charlotte back.

Her eyes were closed, and Rori felt rather than saw the way the river twisted back on itself, rolling into a wall as the downstream water returned. There was so much of it, and Rori couldn't tell how much more she needed to pull back before she found Charlotte again.

If she found Charlotte again.

She can't be gone, Rori thought desperately, and pulled again.

There was a sudden splash, and Rori heard gasping and coughing from the center of the river. Cracking her eyes open, Rori saw that Charlotte had fought her way back to the surface.

Relief flooded Rori as she tugged on the river again, directing the current to bring her friend back to the bank. She was harsher than she should have been with her magic, and Charlotte was dunked beneath the surface twice more before she was deposited on the muddy ground, vomiting water. Rori kept hold of the river just long enough to spread the gathered water further downstream, and then she let it go. It roared away, sloshing up the banks, but it wasn't long before Rori felt the river's natural rhythm return.

Exhausted, Rori slogged up the bank and collapsed into the mud next to Charlotte. Her friend's breathing was ragged, but she was alive, and for a beautiful moment, that was all that mattered.

The moment ended.

"You," Charlotte panted, coughed, tried again.

"You're Skilled?"

Rori glanced up to see her friend staring at her. Charlotte's wide eyes were streaming with tears as she recovered her breath, and they shone with fading panic, mounting awe, and something else that made Rori flinch away.

Charlotte's hand shot out and wrapped around Rori's wrist. "You're a *tide worker*," she breathed.

Rori tried to speak, but her voice failed her. The warnings from her parents and grandmother that she had so easily pushed aside before came swarming back, and every instinct Rori had screamed at her to lie.

But Charlotte hadn't put a question in her last words. She was alive, and she knew the truth, and there was nothing Rori could do except tremble and nod.

For a long moment, they were frozen like that, Charlotte's hand gripping Rori's wrist as they stared at each other, neither one so much as blinking. Then Charlotte pulled Rori into a fierce and desperate hug, and she sobbed and laughed against Rori's shoulder, and whispered, "Thank you," over and over again in Rori's ear.

Rori sagged against Charlotte, too stunned to say anything herself, but it wasn't long before she was smiling and crying, too.

When they pulled apart, Charlotte wanted to know everything. How long Rori had been a Skilled. Why she was still in the village, and hadn't gone with the enforcers on a Collection Day. How Rori could *do* what she could to the river, where her magic came from, how it felt to use it. Her questions buzzed through the air faster than Rori could answer them, but there was a long afternoon ahead of them, and when Rori finally started talking, she found that she did not want to stop.

"My grandmother had a brother," Rori said when Charlotte paused for breath. "He was a tide worker, same as me. The only one in my family that I know of."

"Was he strong?" Charlotte asked eagerly.

"I don't know," Rori admitted. "Aside from what kind of magic he had, the only thing I know about him is that he never should have gone to the tide working academy." She shrugged. "That's what Gran always says, anyway."

Charlotte frowned at this and pushed up on to her elbow. The sun had started to peek between the clouds, and she and Rori had spread themselves along the riverbank, trying to convince the sun to dry their clothes despite the humidity. They were both streaked with mud, but Charlotte wasn't keen on going back into the water any time soon.

"Why would she think that?" she asked as she studied Rori. "The academy is where her brother would have learned to control his magic. They're wonderful places, and the Skilled are lucky to have them." She frowned then. "Isn't it dangerous if you don't go?"

Rori did not like the direction Charlotte's questions were taking. "I figured things out well enough on my own," she said defensively. "And I haven't hurt anyone."

"True," Charlotte said after a moment. She settled down next to Rori again. "Do you think you're a Goodtide or a Malatide?"

"I think I'm Rori Redglade, and that's not going to change."

"Hmm." Charlotte was quiet for nearly a minute. "How come there aren't more Skilled like you?"

"Tide workers?" Rori asked.

"No," Charlotte said, "I mean, Skilled who can control their magic. That's why they go to the academies when they're young, isn't it? So they don't hurt anyone?"

Rori made a noncommittal noise and gazed up at the cloud-spattered sky.

All of her lessons on the Skilled at school had certainly told Rori the same thing. In part, that was why she'd started sneaking off to the secret river; it gave her a place to practice without putting anyone else in danger, when her growing magic had steamed through her veins and demanded to be released. It hadn't taken long for the river to become so much more, though; teacher, nurturer, friend. Rori's magic had grown in its currents, the shifting seasons bringing their own quirks to the water and opening new possibilities for her to explore, until Rori had finally admitted to herself something dangerous and exhilarating: she loved her magic.

That was something she couldn't even tell her family, who had been horrified when a much, much younger Rori had shown them how she could make the running water in the sink dance, and who had begged her to keep quiet about her Skill and never use it again.

But she could tell Charlotte now, who may as well know all of Rori's secrets if she was going to carry the biggest one.

So Rori told Charlotte about her love for her magic, how she couldn't tell her parents or grandmother that, how she hated keeping secrets. That led to a few more questions that ended with Rori blushing fiercely as she confessed her feelings for a certain boy. Charlotte nearly shrieked with delight.

"You're not mad?" Rori managed to ask. She'd buried her face in her hands, and it was a wonder any of the words had gotten out.

"Of course not!" Charlotte beamed and tugged

Rori's hands away from her face. "Oh, when those flowers are back, I am going to make you the most *magnificent* crown. You'll look even better than the empress!"

Rori shushed her blasphemous friend and giggled, and everything felt bright and perfect as the morning slid into afternoon. They spent most of it talking, but Charlotte wanted to see what else Rori's Skill could do, and Rori was happy to oblige. It was wonderfully freeing to finally show someone what she could do with her magic, and she felt so many surges of pride as Charlotte clapped and demanded more.

Under Rori's hand and Charlotte's awestruck gaze, the river slowed to perfect stillness. Then it rushed along with the speed that only came in the middle of a heavy rainstorm. It parted and reversed its flow, danced with waves and flattened out to a glassy sheen. A small whirlpool even appeared in the middle of the river, when Rori managed to draw that vicious under-current into a loop. But that last trick was the hardest, and Rori could only hold it for a few seconds before pain started to nibble at her edges.

Sweating and breathing hard once more, Rori eased the river back into its natural flow, and then turned and gave a flourishing bow. Charlotte applauded madly.

"Oh, I can just *see* the boys' faces when we show them this," Charlotte said gleefully. "They'll go mad, watching you work the river with flowers in your hair—"

"No," Rori cut in quickly. "This is a secret. *Our* secret."

For a moment, Charlotte looked ready to protest. She had that same defiant gleam in her eye that Rori had seen whenever her father forbade her from doing something, the gleam that said Charlotte would find the very edge of that imposed line and poke it until it moved. But something like fear must have shown on Rori's face, for Charlotte's gaze softened and she only said, "All right."

They went back to the village not long after that, scheming for their next rest day and what they would do if the weather was too cold to swim, although they both doubted it would be. They parted ways with a hug, giggling at the mud on each other's clothes and the hell they knew they'd catch from their parents when they returned home.

Charlotte lived on the east side of the village, where the houses were larger and almost looked like they could belong in Sunthrone City, if they'd been made completely of stone. Rori's family was on the west side, where the homes were smaller and wooden but just as well-kept.

This time of afternoon, the day after a fierce rainstorm, Rori knew that both her parents were likely to be out, either assisting the village's imperial-trained doctor or easing ailments on their own. Her mother and father were both healers. Neither had the education of the medics that came from Solkyria's capital, but they had extensive, generational knowledge of herbs and salves and cures for all sorts of common maladies. They'd likely be in demand today, and Rori felt a small thrill at the thought that she just might be able to get herself and her clothes clean before they came home.

That hope died when she walked through the back door of the house into the kitchen, and found herself face-to-face with her grandmother.

The old woman eyed Rori up and down as she came in, her lips pressing into one more thin line across her wrinkled face. Rori winced and waited for the scolding.

But her grandmother only snorted and turned back

to the pot she was tipping chopped vegetables into. "I certainly hope you won," she said.

Rori stopped halfway across the kitchen, confused.

"Your fight with the mud creature," her grandmother explained. "Can't think of anything else that would've gotten you so dirty. Although, from the looks of you, I'd say you lost."

Rori grinned and ran forward to give her grandmother a quick, tight hug around the waist, then jumped back before the old woman could slap her with the wooden spoon she held.

"Away, fiendish imp!" her grandmother squawked. "I will not be a casualty in your war against cleanliness!"

Rori laughed and retreated towards the washroom. "You should see Charlotte, Gran, she's *much* worse."

Her grandmother chuckled. "That's one way to describe that girl. Where did you two go, that you brought back half the empire's mud with you?"

"To the river," Rori said, keeping her voice light.

The spoon stilled in the pot. Gran's voice was very low when she asked, "To do what?"

For a moment, Rori considered letting the truth spill out of her, the way it had with Charlotte. *My friend knows about my magic,* Rori wanted to say to her grandmother, *and* nothing *bad is going to happen.*

Instead, she said, "It was too rough to swim, so we just stuck our feet in the water and sat talking on the bank. That's all."

Her grandmother turned to look at her, dark eyes roving over Rori's dirty clothes once again. "All that from talking and sitting?"

Rori gave her a small shrug and a lopsided smile. "We may have also discovered that it's a lot of fun to throw mud at each other."

Gran did not return the smile. She stared at Rori as

though she knew that was not the truth.

Rori felt her nerves start to crawl under that penetrating gaze. She forced herself to hold still, and keep looking the old woman in the eye.

Finally, Gran turned back to the stove and gave Rori a dismissive wave over her shoulder. "Just get yourself cleaned up before your parents get home."

Relieved, Rori retreated.

In the washroom, she stripped down and freed her hair from its braid. She ran a bath, leaving her soiled clothes in a puddle on the floor, and focused on getting herself clean first. Sitting in still water was nothing like standing or swimming in the river, and baths were always mechanical things for her, her magic lying dormant and uninterested. Dirt and sweat sluiced off of her and clouded the water, and Rori scrubbed her skin until she felt like she would glow under the sun. When that was done, she stood over the tub, watching the water drain while she toweled her hair dry, and thought about the great-uncle she had never met.

"They took him when we were young," Gran had told her at least once a week since Rori's magic had bloomed. "He was honest about his Skill, and the empire took him away for it and I never saw him again, but I still remember how people looked at him when his magic started to show. They were afraid of him, and they hated him, and everyone was relieved when the enforcers came and took him to the academy down the coast, but my mama and papa mourned for him, and I did too. None of us want that for you, little imp."

Well, Charlotte had not been afraid when she'd seen Rori's magic. Charlotte was *alive* because of Rori's magic, and Charlotte did not hate her, and the world hadn't stopped and life was stretching out before Rori, only now it was even more open than it had been just that morning.

Rori watched the tight spiral of water at the mouth of the bathtub drain for a moment, then reached out with her hand and her magic, and gave them both a light flick. The bath water jittered and splashed as the element responded to her command, and she couldn't help but smile as she released the tiny current and sent pleasant ripples lapping against the sides of the tub.

She loved her magic.

Once she was dry enough, Rori dressed in fresh clothes, and then set to scouring the old set clean. When the last traces of mud were finally gone, she took the clothes outside and hung them to dry. She poked her head into the kitchen to see if Gran needed any help fixing dinner. The old woman said no, and Rori went off to enjoy what remained of her rest day.

Yawning, she decided part of that would involve a nap. Now that the adrenaline had fully left her, she realized how tired she was after using her magic to save Charlotte and then show off, and she collapsed on her bed. She shut her eyes, intending to rest for just a little while.

When she next opened her eyes, twilight had claimed the world. Rori had slept far longer than she'd intended, but it had been a wonderful nap, and she was not going to complain. She stretched and stepped out of the bedroom to find candles already lighting the home. Her mother and father were both back, and dinner was nearly ready.

"The slumbering princess has risen," Rori's father noted as she slipped into the kitchen. He gave her a sidelong look that sparked with humor. "Your grandmother tells us you went to war with a mud monster today."

Rori looked at the old woman, who was sitting at the table looking perfectly pleased with herself. "Traitor," Rori murmured, and was answered with an unapologetic grin.

Rori helped her mother set the table, insisting that yes, she was perfectly fine and had not scraped herself and gotten mud into the wound. "No, Mama, I don't need any herbs," Rori said exasperatedly, but she was happy and submitted to her mother's fussing for once, allowing her mother to check her head and the back of her neck for any injuries Rori might have missed.

"You slept an awfully long time," her mother said as she finished her inspection. "You're certain you're feeling all right?"

"I'm wonderful," Rori said, and gave her mother a light kiss on the cheek before taking her seat at the table.

There was a knock at the door.

Her father rose to answer it. "Probably Mary, wondering if we've got her poultice ready yet."

"I told her twice it will take the full night to brew," Mama said tiredly.

"I'll tell her to come back in the morning," Papa said. He disappeared around the corner, and Rori helped her grandmother begin to portion out food.

Rori was only half-listening when her father answered the door, and it didn't fully register in her mind when a firm voice ordered him to step aside. She only looked up from the plate she'd just finished piling high with roasted meat and vegetables when she realized it was a man's voice, not the gentler pitch of the woman they'd been expecting.

"What's this about?" she heard her father say. Then he yelped and started to yell, "You can't—" but there was a crunching noise, and then the heavy sound of boots storming across the floor.

Confusion washed through Rori, trailed by a rising tide of alarm. Her mother started to stand, but she was only half out of her chair when the enforcers flooded into the kitchen. She had just enough time to flash Rori a single panicked look and shout, "Run!" before the first enforcer grabbed her by the arm, and swung her out of the way. She hit the wall and started screaming.

Rori dropped the plate, and even over her mother's screams, the sound was impossibly loud. She flinched as the other enforcers turned their attention on her.

"There she is," one of them said, and then all three of them were stalking forward.

Rori jumped when her grandmother smacked the back of her hand. "Your mother told you to run," Gran said calmly, but with that same commanding tone that Rori had obeyed since childhood.

Almost reflexively, Rori shot to her feet, her chair falling to the ground behind her. She turned and bolted for the back door, but she felt as though she were covered in molasses or something equally as sticky, her movements slowed to a fraction of their usual speed even as her terrified heart hammered in her chest. Her fingers had just closed on the doorknob when a gloved hand snatched the collar of her shirt.

Rori screamed as the enforcer dragged her back through the kitchen, her mother's howls answering her own. She saw her grandmother sitting frozen at the table, the blade of an enforcer's sword resting across her throat.

"You know the law," the enforcer standing behind her told her gravely, the same one holding the sword. "Do you understand the penalty for keeping a Skilled from the empire?"

Gran answered him with a defiant silence, her dark eyes raging with fury. They softened when they swiveled to Rori for the last time.

"You be brave, little imp," her grandmother said as the enforcer holding Rori yanked her away. The sword pressed closer against her throat, and small ruby beads bloomed under the steel blade's touch. "You hear me?" Gran called as Rori was pulled through the door. Somehow, Rori heard her over her mother's screams as well as her own. "Be brave, Rori!"

Then there were no more screams from the kitchen, and Rori did not have time to wonder what that meant before the enforcer had dragged her outside, and she saw her father's crumpled body lying on the ground. There was a dark red puddle under his head, growing steadily larger.

"Papa!" she shrieked.

Her father did not move.

"Let me go!" Rori howled.

She redoubled her efforts against the enforcer, trying to break his grip. She managed to twist around enough to take a swipe at his face. He ducked his head aside, then stopped and tugged Rori in front of him. He hit her hard across the face, nearly sending her sprawling, and it was only his hand still locked around her arm that kept her from falling. "Be quiet," he said, and he almost sounded bored.

Rori stumbled after him as he pulled her along again. Her head was ringing, but when she looked up, she saw Charlotte standing on the side of the road, next to her father. Rori's hope surged, and she called out to her friend, but Charlotte bit her lip and looked away. Her clothes were clean now, but her face was red and streaked with tears. Her father stood over her, watching Rori with none of the familiar warmth he'd shown throughout the years of Charlotte's and Rori's steady friendship. His gaze was cold now, his jaw set, and he gave the enforcer holding Rori a firm nod as the officer dragged her past.

"Charlotte," Rori whimpered, reaching for her friend. Her fingers almost brushed Charlotte's sleeve.

"Help me."

Charlotte's father slapped Rori's hand away and pushed his daughter behind him. "You'll never come anywhere near her again," he growled, "you magic-tainted monster."

Rori did not understand, and anger rose with her confusion. "She almost drowned today!" Rori shouted at Charlotte's father, twisting in the enforcer's grasp. "I'm the one who—" The hand on her arm tightened, and Rori lost the rest of the words to pain.

"So you admit it, then?" the enforcer demanded. "You took that girl to the river and tried to kill her."

Rori gaped at him. "What?"

The enforcer looked at her with pure disgust, and then resume dragging her down the road.

"No!" Rori shrieked. "I saved her!" She twisted again, fighting against the shooting pain in her arm, and looked back up the road. "Charlotte, tell them! Charlotte!"

But Charlotte still would not look at her, and her father's eyes held nothing but scorn.

Desperate, Rori looked around, noting all the people opening the doors of the small houses that lined the dirt road leading away from Rori's home. People she knew and had grown up with, whose children she had played with, who had come to her parents for medicines when the local doctor was too busy or too expensive. Not one of them came forward or so much as breathed a word of protest. They all watched impassively as the enforcer took Rori away, their faces blurring into unforgiving uniformity as she began to cry.

That did not stop their words from reaching her ears.

"Did that Redglade girl really try to drown poor Charlotte?"

"Always knew there was something not quite right with her."

"All the Skilled go mad if they're left to run wild."

"This is why the academies break them while they're young."

When the horse-drawn wagon reared up in the road ahead, Rori found her voice again.

"I didn't hurt her," she sobbed. "Charlotte is my friend! I *saved* her!"

"That's not what she said," the enforcer snapped. "Poor girl was shaking all over when her father brought her to us." He gave Rori a slow, menacing look as he pulled her towards the wagon. "Did it make you happy, when you tried to drown her?"

"I didn't!" Rori insisted. "She's alive because of my magic!"

The enforcer's lip curled. "Your *magic*," he snarled, "is dangerous. Your magic is why the Redglades are lying dead in their house. Gods only know why they wanted to keep a monster under their roof."

"I'm not," Rori breathed. "I'm not—"

"All you Skilled are monsters," the enforcer said. "It's by the grace of the emperor that we try to tame you instead of killing you like they did in the Goldsun days." He tugged Rori over the last few steps and flung her into the wagon. She was crying too hard to resist when he bound her hands and feet with rope. "Ask me," he said as he finished a savagely tight knot, "we should go back to that, even with you weather workers."

Terrified, Rori did not answer. She just sat huddled on the hard floor of the wagon, shaking with quiet sobs as the horses were whipped into a light trot. She felt her life unspool across the ground with each creaking turn of the wheels, and watched her home fade away forever into the darkness of the night.

CHAPTER ONE

Promises and Warnings

NATE LEANED BACK ON the rope, pulling it tight alongside the riggers. It felt wonderful to be up and moving again after sleeping off the exhaustion of the dragon hunt. His muscles burned with the effort of drawing the rope back, but it was a low, familiar burn, one that came with the satisfaction of hard work paying off. Overhead, the sail snapped taut, catching more of the steady wind blowing in off the stern and sending the *Southern Echo* gliding over the waves. It felt like the ship was flying more than sailing these days, though whether that was thanks to Nate finally and fully adjusting to life on a ship or the warmth he still felt whenever he thought of the *Southern Echo* as his home, he could not say. He also did not care. His spirit felt as light and free as the black flag flying bravely overhead.

As the riggers secured the sail, Nate shook his dark hair out of his eyes, squinting up at the flag. Its motion in the sea winds made the white dragon emblem look like it was closing its jaws around the golden sun, and Nate felt a fresh surge of joy and pride. It wasn't just the symbol of his crew, but of the new life Nate had been given a chance to live. He couldn't wait to see how it unfolded.

The days were growing cooler as winter settled in, but the sun was still warm and the winds were stable, and Nate could feel his magic like a steady hum in his chest, ever present but finally at ease.

He did not use his Skill much these days. Not since the dragon hunt. He'd been up the shrouds earlier that day to work with the lower sails, and although that was nowhere near as high as the riggers climbed, it had been enough to place him in the path of an uninterrupted breeze and stir his magic. He had not pushed his Skill further than that, but the height above the deck and the glittering sea had been dizzying and exhilarating, and even without flexing his magic, Nate had never felt so alive.

Someday, I'll get all the way up there, Nate thought as he glanced at the topsail, where Liliana and Xander worked. They were so far above that the two looked nearly indistinguishable from each other, but Nate could tell from the quick, acrobatic, and almost reckless movements of one dark body against the sky that it belonged to Xander Grayvoice.

Xander made climbing look so effortless, and as far as Nate knew, the Grayvoice had yet to define *too high*. He showed no fear and if he ever looked down, he did it with purpose and excitement.

Nate envied that. He still couldn't climb higher than the first sail without fear clenching around his heart, but he badly wanted to see the world from the very top of the mainmast, with the wind all around him and nothing but the open sky above him. Until he could convince his arms and legs to take him further up the lines, however, he'd have to settle for the lower masts and endure the teasing of the riggers who found his tendency to stay close to the decks so amusing.

With the sail secured, Xander and Liliana began to descend from the topsail. The Grayvoice quickly outpaced the other rigger, nearly sliding down the shrouds before landing surefooted as a cat on the main deck. Xander stretched and rolled his shoulders, pausing when he found Nate watching him. Nate offered a smile, but Xander's eyes were cold as he turned away.

Nate felt a twinge of irritation, but he smoothed the feeling down before it could flare into anything more.

He knew that Xander was disappointed that the crew had voted to release the dragon. They'd given up the legendary beast that possessed both the map and the magical fire that would have unlocked the lost treasure of Mordanti the Thief, all to save Nate from the Solkyrian navy. He knew that Xander had voted to keep the dragon, which still stung to think about, but Nate understood why Xander had cast his lot in favor of continuing with the voyage. It fit, too, that Xander was taking a while to come to terms with the crew's decision.

It had been a few days now since the release of the dragon and Nate's rescue. Nate had slept through most of them, his body and mind recovering from the severe magic drain, but that had been enough for nearly everyone to move on from the hunt. While there were a few other than Xander who still grumbled about losing the black mimic dragon and Mordanti's map, the majority of those who'd voted to continue the treasure hunt had managed to leave the past behind in favor of the future. Even sour Jim Greenroot was almost pleasant to be around these days, going so far as to dip his head in a sort of respectful acknowledgment whenever he and Nate passed each other. Nate still couldn't quite believe the man had been part of his rescue party. He couldn't say that he would have done the same for the gunner, if their positions had been reversed.

Nate felt more than a little ashamed of that, but he thought he'd had good reason to be wary of Greenroot, given the gunner's open disdain for the Skilled at the start of the voyage. That was a sharp contrast to the man who'd put his own life in danger to sneak aboard a navy ship and save one of them.

Nate had never expected to see the day when he'd think favorably of Jim Greenroot while Xander Grayvoice scorned him, but here it was, and it was confusing.

At least Nate could count on Marcus and Eric to be consistent. He spied the two Darkbends near the bow of the ship, deep in an animated discussion that had Eric looking more and more despondent with each passing moment.

Nate started towards them, already grinning in anticipation of whatever ridiculousness Marcus was pushing, but he was tugged to an abrupt halt and spun around by a rough hand.

"Here, see, he'll tell you," came Jim Greenroot's voice from Nate's side. The gunner clapped his hand on Nate's shoulder and gave him a firm shake before releasing him, leaving Nate with a sore spot that almost certainly would bruise. "Good to see you finally steady on your feet, Lowwind," Greenroot said. "Now go on and tell her."

Nate blinked. He was too disoriented from the sudden spin to even begin to guess what the gunner was talking about, and the impassive stare he was getting from AnnaMarie Blueshore offered no clues.

Greenroot gazed expectantly at Nate, round spectacles perched at the tip of his nose. "Tell her about the captain's plan for the dragon," he insisted when Nate's silence continued.

Nate frowned, and Greenroot gave an impatient huff before turning back to Blueshore.

"We're gonna restock and then go find the dragon again," the bespectacled gunner declared.

That was certainly news to Nate, especially in light of the conversation he'd had earlier with Captain Arani, when she'd sworn to Nate that she did not intend to seek out the black dragon again, unless he *and* the crew were fully ready and willing. Nate did not think that he would be either of those things for a long time, and after the deaths of so many by dragon fire and the navy after, the crew wasn't keen on following Arani into a dragon's lair again. Most of them were just glad to be close to Spider's Nest once more, Nate and his friends included.

Jim Greenroot, however, either had a very different conversation with the captain at some point, or was sorely misinformed. Nate desperately hoped it was the latter.

AnnaMarie Blueshore seemed to agree. "Captain made it very clear we're not going after the dragon again," she said, her tone flat and unimpressed.

Greenroot made a disbelieving noise and jostled Nate closer. "Arani had to release the dragon, but if she was going to give up the Thief's treasure that easily, you think we would've bothered getting this back?"

It took Nate a moment to realize what—or rather, who—Greenroot was talking about, and it only clicked in his mind when Blueshore's attention flickered to Nate and she winced a little. Something ugly stirred in his gut.

"*This* has a name," Nate said, gently but firmly pushing Greenroot's hand off of his arm. "And as far as I'm concerned, that dragon can spend the rest of its life on that island. If I never see it again, it'll be too soon."

Greenroot shook his head, still directing his words at Blueshore. "Nah, you'll see, we'll get more sleeping draught, *a lot* more, and then we'll follow that map. That's the whole reason we got the Lowwind back."

The ugly feeling in Nate's stomach grew, but his

confusion pushed it down. Nate frowned and glanced between the two gunners. "You voted to release the dragon, though," he reminded them.

AnnaMarie Blueshore took a sudden interest in the deck beneath their feet. Jim Greenroot had far less tact.

"The crew did," the bespectacled gunner said, "but *I* voted to keep it. Same as the rest of the sane ones on this ship, plus the Sheep Lips. Even he knew that was the smart thing to do."

Nate felt his mouth gape open. "But you volunteered for the rescue crew. You *saved* me."

"Well, of course," Greenroot said. "How else are we going to find the dragon again after we get rid of the people who don't want to take up the Thief's treasure hunt?"

Blueshore covered her eyes with one hand.

"Are you telling me," Nate said slowly, "that you expect me to use my Skill to track that dragon again?"

Greenroot stared at Nate over the rim of his spectacles. "Why else would you be here, Lowwind?" he asked. "Gods above know you're not good for anything else."

Nate's heart went cold. "I'm not tracking that dragon," he spat through clenched teeth.

Greenroot snorted. "We'll see," he said. Then he grinned and turned back to Blueshore. "I'd put money on Arani picking that hunt up again, if she wouldn't have my left hand for gambling on the ship."

"She'd take your tongue, too, if she knew what you were saying," Nate growled, but the gunners were already moving away, clearly done with him now that he'd served his part in their conversation. And Greenroot was still grinning.

Nate no longer felt guilty over the thought that he would have voted to leave Jim Greenroot to the navy if their places had been switched, but that brought him no comfort. Once, he had ravenously dreamed of what it would be like to have a Skill that was so desirable, people would fight for it. Now that he had it, all he felt was repulsed.

Arani promised I wouldn't have to do that ever again, Nate reassured himself. But he paused as a small bit of doubt wormed its way into his mind. *Unless I said I wanted to,* he remembered. *Is she expecting me to change my mind?*

He squinted up at the black flag once more, hoping it would give him an answer that he wanted to hear, but all it did was flap in the wind.

Greenroot's wrong, Nate told himself. *There's more that my magic can do. That I can do.*

As he brought his gaze down from the flag, he caught sight of a small group of sailors gathered at the starboard rail, feeding a long spool of rope into the sea and calling numbers across each other as the knotted rope played out and marked the *Southern Echo*'s speed. Among them was Rori, taking quick notes in her navigation journal. A light frown of concentration adorned her face, made more intense by the deep blue Goodtide tattoo that wove across her left brow and down her cheek. There were dark smudges beneath her eyes, but they were nowhere near as intense as they'd been a few days ago.

Like Nate, Rori was still tired from the trials of the dragon hunt, her wild use of her own magic having drained her almost as much as Nate's Skill had done to him. But they were both back on their feet, and the fading marks beneath her eyes were the only signs of Rori's weariness.

As though sensing Nate's scrutiny, Rori suddenly lifted her attention from the journal and locked her gaze with his. She gave him a quick smile that immediately warmed his heart, and then ducked back to her work.

Rori had helped Nate so much on the dragon hunt, even when he'd scorned the small gestures. She was a good friend, maybe even Nate's best friend, despite her pet bird Luken's fondness for attacking his head at every possible opportunity. She also was the first person who had ever suggested to Nate that he could exist outside of his Skill. He remembered that now, and Jim Greenroot's words faded from his mind.

Nate also remembered that, according to Eric, Rori had been inconsolable when she'd learned that Nate had thrown himself on to the navy ship in order to disrupt the Highwinds and give the *Southern Echo* the chance to escape a battle that could not be won. Nate wasn't certain if that meant what he secretly hoped it did, and he quickly turned away before Rori could look up again and catch him blushing.

By the time he'd crossed the deck to where Marcus and Eric were, his mood had considerably improved from where the gunner had left it.

The Darkbends were arguing about something as Nate came up, which was fairly standard for them, although it was rarely anything serious. Nate was pretty sure that held true this time, too, as Eric was shaking his head exasperatedly and saying, "Because I don't think you could fit a siren in a bathtub."

"Not with that attitude, you couldn't," Marcus returned.

Eric threw his hands up and turned away, which Marcus smugly took to mean that he had won the debate.

Nate raised an eyebrow as he settled in next to his friends. "Do I want to know?" he asked Eric.

The tall, elegant man sighed and massaged his temple, distorting the white tattoo on his brow. "No," he said, "you really don't." Without opening his eyes, he held up his other hand, stopping Marcus just as the stouter Darkbend opened his mouth. "And don't you tell him, Marcus, or I swear to every god I can name, I will tell the captain what really happened to her tea when we were coming back from the Gemheart Islands."

Marcus closed his mouth so fast, his teeth clicked.

Nate laughed, but it was cut short by the quartermaster's deep voice ringing out across the ship.

"Full crew meeting," Daxton Malatide called. "Gather on the main deck now."

Nate and the Darkbends shifted back towards the center of the ship, and he nudged Eric on the way. "What do you think Dax wants to say?"

"Oh, the usual," Eric answered. He ticked off each point on a calloused finger. "We're coming up on Spider's Nest soon; everyone will have their turn ashore; try not to kill each other before we get there; don't be too disappointed when we can't afford what we want." He looked at Nate sidelong. "Someday, you'll be able to have some proper fun on the Nest. Can't do much without any money, sadly." He shrugged apologetically.

Nate waved him off. "So long as I don't have to spend the entire time standing on a beach while someone throws shells at my head, I'll be happy."

Marcus snorted. "Like you'd mind if it was just Rori throwing the shells again." He smirked when Nate gave him a startled look. "If you two wanted some privacy, Eric and I could distract Luken for a bit. Probably. Actually, no, that bird is mean. You can deal with him yourself."

"Marcus," Eric said. "Shut up."

The stout Darkbend only grinned wider, and Nate felt his face heat.

He was spared from any further teasing by a loud whistle from the quarterdeck, where Dax stood ready to address the crew. Captain Arani was a few steps off to his side, looking as calm and dangerous as Nate had come to expect of her. Light from the setting sun bathed the two officers in fiery gold, and for a moment, it was easy to forget that they'd come back from the legendary treasure hunt battered and poorer. Or simply just battered in Nate's case, given it had been a long, long time since he'd had more than a single copper mark to his name.

"We'll reach Spider's Nest a little after nightfall," Dax said, his deep voice projecting easily across the ship. "We know you're all anxious to have your feet on land again, and you can trust that you'll have your chance to get into trouble, but try to keep your patience and avoid stabbing your fellows before we put into port, even if you are sick of their faces."

Nate gave Eric a quick smirk, impressed by the accuracy of his prediction. The Darkbend winked.

"As you may have guessed," Dax continued, "we won't be there long. The captain means to sail again before the week is done."

A few murmurs went up across the crew. None of them sounded particularly happy.

Dax turned his head to Arani before the disappointment could rise further, opening the moment for her to speak.

"Gods above know that we all could use a proper rest," the captain said, her voice clear and strong. "I mean to do everything I can to see that you each have some coin to spend on the Nest. I only regret that it won't be what you deserve, especially after this last voyage."

A few people turned unhappy gazes on Nate at this, but he stood tall. It was easy, with Marcus and Eric both shooting challenging glares into the crowd, and the clear support from the rest of the crew. Quickly, the resentful stares broke away, and Nate could not quite manage to keep himself from smiling. He couldn't believe he'd let Greenroot sow doubt in him earlier. It wouldn't happen again. This was Nate's crew and his life, and he was only going forward.

Arani waited until the crew's attention had fully returned to her before speaking. "I've made my intentions for the future clear, but to say it again, I intend to sail east and get us away from the Solkyrian navy." She gave them a sharp grin. "I think it's time we see for ourselves just how fat those Votheinian merchant ships are."

Some laughs went up in response, but the majority of the crew remained silent, and several people shifted uneasily.

That was not lost on the captain. "I understand if not all of you will want to come with me. I hope that you will, but know that you will be free to leave the *Southern Echo* once we reach Spider's Nest. Find yourself a new crew, or even form one of your own, if that's what you want." Her smile turned dangerous. "Just pray we never cross blades over a prize in the future."

Silence was the crew's answer this time.

The quartermaster stepped in again before the moment could stretch. "Whatever you decide to do on the Nest, and regardless of whether or not you choose to sail with the *Southern Echo* again, there's one thing you *need* to do." Dax swept a stern look across the crew, his dark eyes intensified by the twin tattoos that curved out from his brow along the sides of his shaved head. They disguised his Malatide mark, but Nate was familiar enough with the designs to pick the Skill symbol out at a glance. "Keep the previous voyage a secret," Dax said, slow and deliberate. "As far as anyone outside of this crew knows, we went after a prize, same as always, and ran into bad luck with the Solkyrian navy. Now we've decided to see if there's better luck waiting for us in Votheinian waters, just as other ships and crews have done before us."

"Aye, but none of them have come back," a sour voice called out.

Nate did not try to hide his disdain as he looked around at Jim Greenroot. *We're going east,* Nate shot silently at the gunner. *Stay on the Nest if you don't like it.*

Dax was unruffled. "Plenty of ships never come back from voyages, even in familiar waters," he said. "If the idea of sailing into something unknown terrifies you, Mr. Greenroot, then you are not in the right profession."

The gunner opened his mouth to say something more, but a jab to the ribs from AnnaMarie Blueshore cut him off. He massaged the sore spot, but grumbled something under his breath, and shot a look towards Nate that may as well have been a shout to take up the dragon hunt again.

"I say again," the quartermaster continued, "keep your wits about you and keep the black mimic a secret. Few will believe the story as it is, but there's no sense in looking for trouble. Stick to the pleasure house and the gambling rings if you can afford them, and the cheap ale from the tavern if you can't."

This time, Nate's voice was among the disappointed murmurs, but Eric nudged his shoulder.

"Don't worry," the Darkbend whispered. "Marcus and I know how to stretch a coin."

Nate's smile returned just long enough for it to fall away when he saw Captain Arani staring right at him.

She had tried to dissuade Nate from going ashore at all once the ship reached Spider's Nest, believing it too unsafe. Nate had balked against the restrictions, but it was only when Eric and Marcus had sworn to look out for him *and* confirmed that Rori was likely to stab anyone who so much as glanced at Nate funny that Arani had relented, as long as Dax could sway the crew to secrecy on the dragon hunt and Nate's wind reading Skill.

Nate met the captain's gaze now, and he could see her weighing the crew's reaction against his desire to go ashore, and the danger that could pose if anyone learned the truth. He held her stare, willing her to trust that he could hold his own, especially with his friends at his side.

I'm not that scared, helpless boy anymore, Nate thought, and he raised his chin defiantly.

Arani did not look away, but she did step forward once more. "One more thing you all should remember is that while everyone saw the map on the dragon's wings, most of you lack the necessary knowledge and experience to follow it, even if you could reliably replicate it from memory. And even if you could piece it together, how many of you think you could capture another dragon without losing your life?"

No one answered.

Satisfied that she'd made her point, Arani nodded for Dax to continue, and then moved down the stairs as the quartermaster began to run through the usual rules and expectations for the crew once they reached the Nest. It wasn't long before he dismissed them to return to their duties or to dinner, depending on their rotation, and Nate started to head for the galley with Marcus and Eric.

A call from the boatswain stopped them.

Nate and the Darkbends turned to meet Nikolai Novachak as he stepped up to them, eyeing Marcus and Eric warily.

"I know you two are excited to get Nate here into all kinds of trouble, but remember the captain's orders to—"

"Always remain with someone who will watch my back," Nate finished, but he was smiling. His grin only broadened when Marcus slung an arm around his shoulder.

"Not to worry, sir," the stout Darkbend quipped, "we've got our eye on him. He's still a bit of a Nest virgin, after all."

Novachak rolled his icy eyes skyward. "Frozen goddess give me strength," he murmured before focusing on Nate. "Maybe you could do *me* a favor and watch these two. They have a bad habit of 'accidentally' getting into trouble whenever they find themselves with too much time on their hands."

"Sir, I can assure you," Eric said, affronted, "it always is purely coincidental and entirely accidental."

"I'll sleep easier if I pretend to believe that," Novachak groaned. "Just don't do anything, accidental or otherwise, until the captain's finished her meeting with Spider. We need that to go well."

Then he dismissed them, and Nate and his friends laughed as they went off to eat and get ready for Spider's Nest.

CHAPTER TWO

Broken Faith

TRUE TO THE QUARTERMASTER'S prediction, the *Southern Echo* slid into the Nest's harbor just after nightfall. It was a near thing, as if they'd been an hour later, it would have been too dark to navigate the coral mazes that surrounded the island and kept it so well protected from idly passing merchants or navy ships. The reefs were so dense and dangerous in some parts of the Coral Chain that they'd been given the nickname the Gauntlet, and the ones surrounding Spider's Nest were notoriously difficult for anything larger than a brigantine to pass through. The nimble *Southern Echo*, riding light in the water, had a much easier time, although the ship's ability to sail straight over some of the deeper coral was a bitter reminder that her stores were near empty, and there was no treasure in her hold.

Nate tried not to think too hard on that as the *Southern Echo*'s anchor splashed into the harbor, even as he caught Jim Greenroot eyeing him speculatively. But then Marcus grabbed Nate and swept him into a rowboat, somehow securing them a spot on the second one heading to shore. Eric and Rori managed to scramble aboard, too, and they chatted excitedly about what Spider's Nest would have for them at this time of year.

"This close to the Dancing Skies Festival," Eric said

as the rowboat laboriously crossed the dark water, "there ought to be at least one puppeteer on the island. Those are always good for a laugh."

"I liked those acrobats that were here last year," Rori said. "Think they'll be back?"

"Definitely," Marcus said. "This time of year, the whole island will be drunk, and that's a great time for them to earn a pretty coin or two."

"Aren't most people usually drunk on Spider's Nest?" Nate asked. "I didn't think the holiday had much to do with that."

"Oh, aye," Marcus agreed, "but the difference now is they'll be merrily drunk instead of belligerently, and the performers know that. They come at the Dancing Skies Festival because they know there's a better chance they'll be tipped instead of robbed."

Nate chuckled, but stopped when he saw the tight look on Eric's face. "Is something wrong?" he asked.

The elegant Darkbend pursed his lips.

Marcus's expression clouded, and then he abruptly burst out laughing. "I forgot," he gasped, "Eric has a *history* with one of the contortionists."

Nate exchanged a bemused look with Rori before turning back to Eric again.

"I'd rather not talk about it," Eric said primly.

That earned him a tap on the shoulder from Liliana, who was sitting next to him in the crowded rowboat. "That story was true?" the pretty rigger asked. "You really did go off with that twiggy troll-man?"

Eric's lips pressed into a thin line. "He was a very talented contortionist," he said stiffly. "And I was... curious."

"Oh," Liliana said, clearly disappointed. Then her frown shifted into thoughtfulness. "Was he any good?"

"A very. Talented. Contortionist," Eric repeated.

"That you had to spend the next day hiding from,"

Marcus cut in, "because he was absolutely love struck and kept shouting terrible poetry every time he caught a glimpse of you. I bet this time, he proposes."

Eric glowered at the other Darkbend. "I will throw you overboard."

The laughter kept them occupied until the rowboat bumped against the sand of the beach. Nate splashed ashore with the others, pausing just long enough to push the rowboat back into the water and send it on its way back to the *Southern Echo* to collect more eager sailors. The sea was cool as it soaked into Nate's trousers, almost unpleasantly so. It wouldn't be long before the islands as far south as Spider's Nest felt winter's bite and wading through the surf became agonizing.

With the stars and the twin moons bright overhead, Nate and his friends ran across the beach, passing a few groups of pirates from other ships gathered around driftwood fires, their voices sending blurry songs and stories up into the night. In the morning, Nate knew, the beach would be full of vendors peddling everything from blacksmith services to roasted meats to those with the coin to spend, but at night it belonged to anyone who sank their boots into its sands, no matter if their pockets were empty or full.

"Where to first?" Nate asked as he came up alongside Eric and Rori a short distance away from one of the fires. The pirates around it were deep into a raunchy song and paid their small group no mind.

"Tavern," Marcus said before anyone else had the chance to open their mouths.

"We just ate," Eric said, exasperation clear in his voice.

"Ship food," Marcus countered. "This is *real food* we're talking about now."

Eric rolled his eyes. "And do you have *real marks*

to pay for it? Gods above know I'm not lending you another copper until you've paid me back the last five."

The stout Darkbend was undeterred. "Captain said she'd be getting us what she could after the meeting. Spider does all his business at the tavern, so we may as well be there when they're done. That way, Arani can pay us straight away."

"How is it you only ever demonstrate flawless logic when it comes to filling your stomach?" Eric asked.

Nate laughed softly, and turned to see Rori smiling in the faint light from the fire. His heart stuttered a little, thrilled at the prospect of spending some time with her when neither of them had pressure on their shoulders.

Rori caught him looking at her, and her smile widened just a little bit more. "I'm not sure I want to spend the whole night waiting around the tavern," she said. "I think I'd like to scout the island a bit, see if those performers really are back or if there's anything new. Anyone want to come with me?"

Nate swallowed past the sudden lump of nerves in his throat, and that was all the time it took for Eric to seize the invitation before he could.

"I want to make sure I see those acrobats before they see me," the Darkbend said as he hooked his arm through Rori's and led her away. "Last thing I need is a whole troupe ambushing me on the beach."

Rori glanced back once as she and Eric drifted away, offering Nate a small shrug. Luken twittered on her shoulder, and Nate had the distinct impression that the bird was snickering.

Marcus's hand slapped down on Nate's back before he could begin to sulk too much.

"You and me to the tavern, then!" Marcus proclaimed, already pulling Nate along without waiting for an answer. "They'll meet us there when they realize they've made a terrible mistake."

Nate managed to stifle a groan of protest. He told himself that there would be other chances for him and Rori, especially since she was still angry with Xander. That thought brought on a pang of guilt. He'd never been clear on the relationship between the Goodtide and the Grayvoice, but Nate was fairly certain that getting closer to Rori would only make it harder for him to reconcile with Xander. Nate had more friends now than he'd had at any other point in his life, but he didn't have so many that he was ready to start throwing some of those friendships away. He was still mulling over this when he and Marcus reached the tavern.

They weren't the only ones who had headed straight there. Many others freshly delivered from the *Southern Echo* were already inside, and the dining area was stuffed to bursting with people from other crews. One table was already full of *Southern Echo* sailors, but some people had drifted off to connect with acquaintances from other ships. Nate spied AnnaMarie Blueshore and Jim Greenroot sitting with a group of very burly men and women, most likely other gunners from the look of them. They laughed and shoved tankards together in a toast, yelling something about cannonballs and gunpowder. It was too loud to make out anything else.

Marcus nudged Nate's shoulder and nodded to the far corner of the tavern, where several faintly familiar men lounged like they owned the building.

"*Dragonsbane* crewmen," Marcus said, nearly shouting in Nate's ear to make himself heard. "Watch yourself around them."

Nate's memory flashed back to the duel he'd stumbled into on Solkyria, where he'd first met Captain Arani. She'd been fighting the quartermaster from the *Dragonsbane*, a giant bear of a man named Ed. Nate eyed the massive form of one man at the *Dragonsbane* table sitting with his back to him and Marcus, and had the feeling that was Ed the bear man. The faces of the people around the quartermaster came into focus from there, and Nate thought that he recognized almost all of them from that duel.

He also remembered that Captain Arani had a special dislike for them.

"What happened between the *Southern Echo* and the *Dragonsbane*?" Nate asked.

"It goes a ways back," Marcus answered, still almost shouting. "See, their captain, Blackcliff, he tried to race Arani for a prize once, back when they were both a bit green. He had a different ship then, and it couldn't keep up with the *Southern Echo*, so he waited for her to come back after she'd taken the prize. Then he tried to board her to take the treasure for himself, and when that didn't work, he tried to sink her. Way I heard it, he did enough damage that Captain Arani had to dump most of the haul into the ocean to keep the *Southern Echo* afloat, so neither of them really got anything out of that whole mess."

"And they've had a rivalry going since then?" Nate asked.

Marcus gave him a lopsided grimace. "Let's just say Blackcliff made sure to get himself a faster ship after that, named it the *Dragonsbane*, and then changed his flag to a dragon getting gutted by a spear. Not exactly subtle."

Nate snorted in agreement. He let his attention linger on the table full of *Dragonsbane* sailors for a moment longer, feeling even prouder of Captain Arani for winning that duel on Solkyria against Ed the bear man, and angry on her behalf that someone from the *Dragonsbane* had shot her despite the clean victory. It was strange, to feel such strong emotions over something he had not been involved in, but it also left a warm feeling in Nate's chest, and a small bubble of excitement at the thought of someday outdoing the *Dragonsbane*. He'd love to help his crew achieve that for their captain.

For the moment, though, Nate knew that the only thing he'd accomplish by glowering at the *Dragonsbane* pirates was stirring up their own ire, so he turned his attention elsewhere.

After a short while, Nate and Marcus decided to wait outside, where the air was cooler and there weren't so many voices hammering against their ears. They settled against the side of the tavern, Nate leaning against the wall and Marcus sprawling carelessly in the dusty road, and Nate got the full story of Eric's amorous encounter with the acrobat.

He learned that the contortionist had been smitten with the Darkbend from first sight, but all his attempts to seduce Eric had been clumsy at best. Marcus still didn't fully understand why Eric had agreed to spend a night with the man, given that he was rather homely, although Eric had confessed afterwards that it had easily been one of the best nights of passion he'd ever experienced. That, however, did not make up for the obnoxious poetry and proclamations of love that immediately followed.

"Is Eric going to be safe, if this man is here?" Nate asked once the story of the acrobat's obsessive infatuation was finished.

"I think so," Marcus said, "considering I heard the contortionist say the exact same things to a gunner from the *Red Siren* two days later." He gave a thoughtful frown. "So that means all his awkward attempts at seduction worked on that gunner, too." He was quiet for a long moment. "Is this acrobat a lot smarter than we all think he is?"

Nate laughed and shook his head. He was about to ask Marcus another question when he caught a quick movement out of the corner of his eye, and looked around just in time to see a familiar figure disappear around the edge of the building.

"Where's he off to?" Nate wondered aloud.

Marcus made an inquisitive sound.

"Xander just went around to the back of the tavern," Nate said. "Looked like he was alone."

"Odd," Marcus said. He pushed himself to his feet. "Come on, let's go see what he's up to."

Nate started to protest, but Marcus was already walking off around the building, brushing dust from the seat of his trousers. Nate considered staying back, but remembered his promise to Novachak to always stay with someone who would watch out for him. The rest of the crew was either still on the ship or inside the crowded tavern, and Nate didn't feel like dipping back into the heat and the noise just yet, so he followed the Darkbend.

They picked their way through the shrubs and trees that grew alongside the tavern, leaves and plant stalks crunching under their boots. Nate shushed Marcus, and then immediately stepped on a twig that burst with a loud snap. Marcus eyed him, and then they both snorted with laughter before bolting forward.

They came up short when they stepped around to the back of the tavern. There were more trees, stretching up to blot out the night sky and cast everything into an even deeper darkness. It took several minutes for Nate's eyes to adjust, but that only revealed that Xander was nowhere to be found.

Marcus moved through the trees, peering around each one as though he expected to find the Grayvoice hiding behind the trunks. "A man doesn't just evaporate," Marcus grumbled. Then he cursed as he thumped his head against a low branch.

Nate stepped forward to join the Darkbend, but stopped when his foot knocked against a boot left at the base of one of the larger trees growing closer to the tavern, almost directly against the wall. Nate glanced up, and saw Xander staring back at him. The Grayvoice was barefoot and settled in the higher branches, light spilling across him from an illuminated window of the tavern. Nate thought that he heard faint voices, but they were drowned out by another thud of a head colliding with a tree appendage and Marcus cursing again.

What is he doing up there? Nate wondered. He reached out and put a hand against the tree.

Xander's eyes narrowed, and he gave a slow shake of his head.

Nate went to pull away, but Marcus came blundering out of the darkness, and Xander tensed at the noise. Nate quickly shushed the Darkbend, pointing up to the Grayvoice. Marcus frowned in bewilderment, but dropped his voice to a whisper when he asked the same question Nate had asked himself a few moments earlier.

Nate strained to hear the voices Xander was so intently listening to, but he couldn't hear them clearly from the ground. "Keep watch," he instructed Marcus.

"Why?" Marcus asked, but Nate was already climbing the tree.

Xander tensed again, this time with anger, but Nate did not shrink away. Instead, he fixed the Grayvoice with a defiant stare. Xander answered it with his own before rolling his eyes and pressing a finger to his lips. Then he turned his attention back to the open window. Nate quickly took the invitation and kept climbing.

He did not get as high as Xander. More than a few

leaves were shaken loose from the branches by the time Nate found a spot he was mildly comfortable with, but he could see the open window now, and hear the voices spilling from inside along with the candlelight.

He blinked in surprise when he recognized Captain Arani's voice.

He's listening in on her meeting with Spider, Nate realized with a jolt.

He couldn't ask the Grayvoice why he was eavesdropping without drawing the attention of the people inside the room. Nate did not want to be caught by Captain Arani or one of the other officers, and he could not fathom why Xander would take such a risk. He glanced up at the Grayvoice again, willing Xander to understand the question on his face.

Xander pressed his finger to his lips once more, and then pointed at a branch a little higher than Nate's current position. It was right below the level of the windowsill, and would let him clearly hear the meeting between Arani and Spider.

Nate wanted nothing to do with that exchange, and would have been perfectly content to climb back down the tree and never know what was said that night. But this was the friendliest gesture the Grayvoice had made towards Nate since the dragon hunt, and Nate didn't want to throw it away. Then he thought about Jim Greenroot insisting that Arani meant to pursue Mordanti's treasure again, and his resolve wavered even more.

Nate eyed the branch Xander had indicated. It looked sturdy enough, and if he kept low, they'd never see him over the sill unless they came right to the window and looked down. He bit his bottom lip, then looked to Xander again. The Grayvoice watched him impassively.

Nate let his breath out in a quiet sigh, then slow-ly climbed to the higher branch. It took him longer than any rigger would have considered acceptable, but Nate focused on keeping his grip firm and footing sure rather than increasing his speed. He felt Xander's unimpressed gaze on the top of his head as he finished the climb, and Nate tried not to panic too openly when his boot slipped and he had to cling to the trunk to get his balance back. By the time he was settled on the branch, Xander had looked away, his interest back on the meeting. Nate poked his head up just enough to peer over the edge of the window.

Spider's office was a decently sized room, with crowded bookshelves lining two of the walls and plen-ty of candles to illuminate the titles. Captain Arani sat in a wooden chair in front of a large desk. She'd set her hat down on top of the numerous papers that flooded the desk's surface, and her coat was thrown open to reveal the saber belted at her hip and two pistols tucked into the red sash around her waist. Nate was fairly certain she was carrying more guns than that, but those were the only ones he could see.

Behind the captain, Dax and Novachak stood quiet-ly, their own jackets removed and shirt sleeves rolled up. Nate could feel the warmth seeping out of the room through the open window, and wasn't surprised to see that the handkerchief the boatswain was using to pat his brow and neck dry was already damp and limp.

All three officers were looking to the side wall, where Spider stood with his hands clasped loosely behind his back as he regarded a massive map painted across its surface. Even from his odd position beneath the window, Nate could see that Spider was the only one unaffected by the stuffiness of the room, not even with his long-sleeved shirt and vest buttoned all the way up to the collar. He was frowning, however, and it was intense enough to make the air from the room feel even hotter.

Abruptly, Spider turned from the painted map and focused his glare on Arani. "Tell it again," he ordered.

Novachak and Dax both groaned, and even Arani looked like she was fighting back one of her own.

"It's not going to change on the fourth retelling," the captain said tiredly.

"Indulge me," Spider growled.

Arani shook her head and held the man's gaze. "Which part, exactly, are you still having trouble with?"

"The part where *you let the dragon go.*" Spider strode forward and slammed his hands down on his desk, sending a neat stack of papers tumbling to the ground and nearly upsetting a pot of ink.

Nate flinched below the window, casting a quick glance up at Xander, but the Grayvoice only looked intrigued. Nate gathered his courage and lifted his head again.

"You had Mordanti's map and a dragon to burn through the magic of the Ice Hook," Spider growled, "and you *let it go.*"

"Yes," Arani said, and nothing more.

Spider and Arani stared at each other for a long moment, their silence weighing heavy in the still air. Candlelight danced over their faces, darkening the shadows and making both people seem like vengeful spirits gleaming in the dark.

Finally, Spider heaved a massive sigh and sank into his own seat behind the desk, his back to the window. He scrubbed a hand over his long, narrow face. "Years," he said quietly. "We waited *years* for this chance, and you threw it away on a Lowwind who'd already served his purpose."

The words flew like a knife, and Nate winced as they landed. He glanced to Xander again, but the Grayvoice's attention was riveted on the meeting. Nate swallowed and looked back to the captain, suddenly afraid of her answer.

"My crew voted, and I acted as a captain should," Arani said coldly. "And regardless of what *you* may think, Nate is part of that crew."

The fear loosened its hold around Nate's heart. It retreated further as he watched the captain push her coat aside and lean forward, giving her easier access to the saber at her hip. The small but dangerous motion was not lost on Spider, who swayed away from the sheathed sword.

"And what," Arani continued, her voice low, "is this 'we' you mentioned? If memory serves, *I* was the one who brought the black mimic to your attention in the first place, and *I* was the one paying *you* to keep track of the Court of Sirens, which you barely did. I lost a good man in bargaining with them, and another eleven people to the dragon. Where were *you* during all of that?"

Spider's hand went from loosely gripping the arm of his cushioned chair to curling into a tight fist. "Those were risks you and your crew agreed to take when you—"

"The navy wasn't," the captain snapped. Nate could feel the anger radiating off of her, filling the room with even more heat. "Twice now, you've sold me the promise of safety from Prince Trystos's pirate hunters, and twice, they've caught us in open waters."

Dax nodded silently over Arani's shoulder, somehow looking menacing even while sweating. Novachak did not move, but the stare he pinned Spider with conveyed more than enough.

The weighted anger of the three officers broke

through Spider's defenses. His shoulders tensed, and he turned his head away from Arani to contemplate the map that covered a full wall of his office once again. Nate followed his gaze to examine the map for himself.

It was a beautiful painting, he saw, done directly on the wall rather than parchment or canvas, and showed the known archipelagos in stunning detail. But all around the islands, open waters sprawled, and Nate got the sense that Spider was actually a little afraid of those unknown spaces and the things that could come out of them.

"It wasn't my fault," Spider murmured, more to himself than anyone else in the room. "Those ships never should have been there."

"And yet they were," Arani said as she leaned back in her seat. "You're slipping, Spider."

Nate braced himself for another violent outburst, but Spider only shook his head and deepened his frown. "Both of those ships were operating outside of my informants' networks. Trystos is up to something, and I don't like it."

"None of us do," Novachak grumbled, but if Spider heard the boatswain, he ignored him.

"Until your informants can get a handle on the royal brat's plans, the Common Sea is no longer safe," Captain Arani said. "Can we agree on that?"

Spider was still and silent for a long moment before nodding reluctantly. "Not for you, at least." He swung around to face Arani and the two officers again. "So what do you plan to do?"

"Sail east," the captain said. "We'll try our luck in Votheinian waters, where they don't know the *Southern Echo* and Trystos's pirate hunters can't follow us. That's the one good thing about the Vothies, isn't it? They'll obliterate any ship flying Solkyrian colors."

Spider made an unamused noise, and Nate heard a huff come from the branches above him. A quick glance up showed him that Xander apparently agreed with Spider.

That surprised Nate. He himself wasn't bursting with excitement to go east, but Nate understood that the dogmatic dangers of the Solkyrian Empire outweighed the hostility of the Votheinians. He'd thought that Xander and the rest of the Skilled among the crew would feel the same, but evidently, he was wrong. And any one of them could walk away, now that they'd put into port.

Nate did not like the thought of Xander leaving while there was still a rift between them.

He had to find a way to fill it, before it was too late.

But Spider was speaking again, and Nate's attention was drawn back into the room.

"I suppose this is going to be one of the last of these meetings between us," Spider mused. He gave Arani a humorless grin as she nodded. "Can't say that I'll miss you, you Veritian bastard."

"The feeling is mutual," Arani assured him.

"Well," Spider said, easily sliding into his calculating business tones, "in light of your recent return from open waters, I'd say the *Southern Echo* is in need of a restock." He reached for a ledger on his desk and began to thumb through the pages. "You have nothing to buy the supplies with, but I'm willing to accept a trade."

Nate frowned, wondering what Spider could possibly mean, but Arani stiffened in her seat.

Spider ran his finger down a column of neat numbers in the ledger. "If I know you," he said without looking up, "you've got a copy of Mordanti's map somewhere on your ship. It's useless without a dragon, of course, but the map alone could conceivably offset the costs of most necessities, provided the detailing is in place." He raised a questioning gaze to Arani then.

"The map is not for sale," the captain said firmly.

Spider tilted his head. "But you do have a copy?"

Arani said nothing, but Dax and Novachak exchanged a knowing glance behind her.

The gesture was not lost on Spider, but he seemed to know better than to pry too far. "What about the boy, then?" he asked. "If you're not going after Mordanti's treasure, he's of no further use to you, but I could do something with a Skill like that."

Something cold unraveled in Nate's stomach, even as Arani's anger boiled behind her eyes and she hissed, "Nate is a person, not some tool for you to take."

"Then how about I borrow him?" Spider asked, as calmly as if he was discussing a breeding bull for cattle.

"No," Arani spat.

Nate suddenly understood why the captain would have preferred for him to remain on the ship. She'd been right when she'd warned him about being a target on Spider's Nest.

Spider sat back in his seat. "So you *are* going after the Thief's treasure again?"

Nate's spine tightened, and he heard the leaves over his head rustle as Xander leaned forward. Dax fixed an uneasy stare on the captain, but he and Novachak remained silent.

Slowly, Captain Arani shook her head. The motion looked like it pained her, but she held herself firm.

Spider let out an exasperated breath, which almost covered Nate's gasp of relief. He tensed, but none of the officers appeared to have heard him, and Spider spoke again.

"Why keep the map and the Lowwind, then? You have no use for either of them."

Arani lifted her chin and stared at Spider with pure

defiance burning in her eyes. "I won't have Captain Mordanti's legacy spoiled by some greedy fool who'd trample all over her history just for the chance to sell a piece of it." She leaned forward once more, and the fire behind her gaze flared even hotter. "As for Nate," she said quietly, "I promised that boy his freedom and his life, and I won't let anyone take that from him. Not even me."

Nate's heart swelled in his chest, and his eyes burned as tears sprang up. He quickly wiped them away, but he was smiling, and so, so happy he had stepped aboard the *Southern Echo* all those months ago.

The branch he perched on shook suddenly, and Nate turned to see Xander descending.

"Where are you going?" Nate whispered.

"I've heard enough," Xander answered, his voice clipped. He dropped down into the darkness, Marcus's surprised yelp the only indication that the Grayvoice had reached the ground.

Nate's joy faded. He was certain that Xander was going to leave now, along with several others from the crew. Nate could not stop them, but he felt a small spark of determination as he decided that, if nothing else, he would make amends with Xander before the Grayvoice walked out of his life. Nate almost climbed down after him, but he knew that Xander needed some time to process everything, and come to terms with it on his own. Nate would give him as much of that as he could afford. It was the least he could do.

For the time being, he turned back to the meeting, and some of his happiness returned as he watched the officers of the *Southern Echo* spar with Spider.

"How exactly do you intend to pay for your new supplies?" Spider was asking now.

"I don't," Arani answered calmly. "You're gifting us

the supplies."

Spider was silent for a stunned moment. "And why, exactly, am I being so magnanimous towards a crew that's failed to come back with any sort of prize for the better part of a year now?"

"It's your way of apologizing for your failure to issue proper warning of threatening naval activity," Dax put in firmly.

"Twice," Novachak added.

Captain Arani bared her teeth in a dangerous smile at Spider. "And, of course, as added thanks for your generous gesture, we won't tell the rest of the island about your unraveling web of spies."

Spider stared at her. "You really are a horrible Veritian bastard."

"And you're a coward who hides behind ledgers and coral mazes," Arani returned.

To Nate's surprise, the man actually chuckled.

"A rich coward," Spider said. "And one that's certainly going to outlive you."

"Even if you do," Arani said, "you'll keep our capture of the black mimic a secret."

Spider gave another deep sigh. "In spite of what you may think of me, I am a man of my word. I will not sell your secrets." His shoulders rolled as he tilted his head again. "Do you trust your crew to do the same? I doubt there are many captains out there who would believe you actually found the black mimic and Mordanti's map, but there are those that will, and it will only take one loose set of lips to break the seal."

Arani nodded grimly. "It's why we've sworn the crew to secrecy, though I know it won't last. I expect some of them will choose to remain on the island instead of going east, and it won't take much for them to start talking." She offered Spider another pointed smile. "Be awfully good of you to squash any rumors you may hear about black dragons carrying treasure maps in their wings and boys who can track flying things against the wind."

Spider sat back in his chair. "I see no way to profit from it without the map, and I'd rather not have a bunch of captains get the wild idea to chase you into the east instead of going after the merchant ships I'm working so hard to find for them."

Arani nodded with mock sympathy. "It certainly would be a shame for you to lose such a large portion of your main source of income."

"Indeed." Spider stood up from his seat, and then abruptly turned around to face the open window. Nate froze as the man's gaze caught on him, and Spider came to a surprised halt as they stared at one another.

"Something wrong?" Captain Arani asked.

Spider cocked an eyebrow at Nate, then shifted ever so slightly to fully block him from the sight of everyone else in the room. "No," Spider said. "I only thought there was a breeze finally coming in, but there's nothing at all." He reached out and pulled the window shut.

Nate sank down below the sill. He was fairly sure he owed Spider a favor now, and knew the man would come to claim it at some point, but after listening to Captain Arani, Nate felt as though he'd been wrapped in armor. His main concern now was his heart, which he was certain was drumming loudly enough in his chest for the whole island to hear. He took a few breaths to steady himself, then glanced once more up at the window. Spider was gone, and he could no longer hear anything Arani or the others said.

Slowly, Nate climbed down the tree. His heart did not slow, but the rhythm took on a new meaning as he began to understand that he had just skirted around a horrible amount of trouble. He felt dangerously alive now, and he was grinning wide enough for Marcus to see his teeth as he dropped down from the last branch.

"You look like you're in a considerably better mood than Xander was when he came out of that tree," Marcus remarked. "He stomped past me without a word."

"He didn't like what Arani said about the dragon hunt," Nate said, his happiness snagging on that small thorn before tugging free and flaring again. "We're not doing it."

"Thank the gods above for that," Marcus murmured. He clapped his hand on Nate's shoulder and gave him a firm shake. "Told you not to worry about the nonsense Greenroot spits."

Nate nodded and started to lead the way through the trees. "It sounded like the meeting was coming to an end, so Captain Arani should be out soon." Something gurgled behind him, and Nate paused to glance back at the Darkbend. "Was that your stomach?"

"It knows what it wants," Marcus returned.

Laughing, he and Nate picked their way back to the tavern's entrance. Good-humored voices spilled into the night, bolstered to greater heights by the food and drink. Nate breathed in deeply as he stepped inside.

The scent of too many people who'd gone too long without a proper bath crowded against the more pleasant smell of the food, but Nate was used to that odor by then, and nothing could disguise the aroma of the meal. Spider's fishers had brought in a sizable haul that day, and the various pirate crews were feasting on grilled fish, vegetables grown on the island, and chunks of dark bread, all washed down with generous helpings of ale and beer. Nate's own stomach gave a small rumble, and he was glad the din of the tavern was too loud for anyone but him to hear it.

Peering through the crowd, Nate scoped out the tables in the corner that the sailors from the *Southern Echo* had claimed. Rori and Eric weren't there yet, but their absence wasn't the only one that Nate noticed.

Ed the bear man and several people from the *Dragonsbane* had left while Nate had been listening to Arani's talk with Spider, and Nate felt a wash of relief at that, buoying his spirits even higher. Everyone else in the room may have been a pirate, but they posed no direct threat to Nate or anyone else from the *Southern Echo* for the time being, and he and Marcus slipped between people from the *Red Siren*, the *Sea Demon*, the *Gryphon*, and several other ships without trouble as they made their way to the *Southern Echo* tables.

They settled in to wait, but it wasn't long before a door on the second floor of the tavern opened and Captain Arani came striding out, looking quite content with the bargain she'd struck with Spider. Novachak seemed equally pleased, and even Dax was smiling as Spider stepped to the railing of the balcony and waved to one of the servers. He called for food to be brought to the *Southern Echo*'s crew, courtesy of Captain Arani, and Nate cheered alongside the others as the server dipped her head in acknowledgement and went to bring fresh plates from the kitchen. Before long, Nate and the others were carving into smoky fish and tearing at hunks of soft bread, and all felt right with the world.

With fresh food and drink in their hands, several people from the *Southern Echo* had drifted off once more to join other tables, catching up with the very few outside friends they had. Nate saw Anna-Marie Blueshore and a couple other gunners standing around a table where five people played cards, and past them, some of the riggers banged mugs against those of another crew and laughed over a shared joke. And there, in the dead center of the room, his face flushed after emptying what must have been an extraordinary number of tankards of ale, was Jim Greenroot, gesturing wildly as he told a story to a ring of pirates around him. Some of his listeners were shaking their heads and smirking to each other, but others had their rapt attention on the gunner, and there was a distinct sense of awe among them.

Nate was about to turn away when Greenroot threw back the rest of his drink, spied Nate over the top of his tankard, and then sputtered and pointed.

"Tha's 'im," Greenroot slurred loudly to his audience. "Tha's the boy who—" he interrupted himself with a belch, loud enough to cut through the din of the crowd and earn him a few glances from the other tables. He swayed on his feet, gathered himself, and finished, "The boy who tracks dragons!"

CHAPTER THREE

A Bird in a Cage

A LARGE NUMBER OF eyes turned to Nate. Their hungry, calculating gleams were something that had not been focused on him very often, but he recognized them as the same looks the other Lowwinds and Highwinds back at the academy would get, when merchants and captains were seeking new wind working Skills for their ships as intently as they would pick over new supplies from a dubious seller. Nate felt heat rise to his face, driven by anger and panic both, and he braced himself for the fight he knew was coming.

Arani had sworn that she would not make him hunt the dragon again, and Nate was not going to let Jim Greenroot tell a room full of pirates otherwise.

Then that room erupted into laughter, and the eyes turned away. The pirates' laughter was underscored with jeers and scoffs, none of them willing to believe that Nate's Skill could do what Greenroot claimed, or that Arani's crew had nearly found the lost treasure of Mordanti the Thief.

Nate slumped in relief. For a moment, he'd been sure that he would have to battle his way out of the tavern, dozens of pirates snapping at his heels as he ran all the way back to the *Southern Echo*. Instead, he just needed to smile and shake his head, as though the whole thing were ridiculous, even if he knew better.

Thank the gods for nonbelievers, he thought.

Jim Greenroot, however, had other ideas. "He can do it," the gunner insisted, stumbling over the words and his feet as he blundered his way to the table.

Nate shrank back, but the wall of the tavern was right behind him, offering no escape. Greenroot nearly missed Nate's arm, but managed to grab it and tug Nate forward. Drunk or not, the gunner was incredibly strong, and Nate was hauled along like a rag doll. Protests rose from some of the people around them, and Marcus put himself in Greenroot's path, but the gunner barreled past him and dragged Nate to the center of the room.

"'S anybody got a bird?" Greenroot slurred, and a cloud of alcoholic breath flooded Nate's nose as the gunner swayed unsteadily next to him, one hand still locked around Nate's arm, the other clutching his half-full tankard.

Nate tried to pull away, but Greenroot only tugged him closer and slung his arm around Nate's neck.

"C'mon," the gunner said, "s'mbody's got a birdie." He squinted through his spectacles at the chuckling crowd. "You," he said, pointing, "tha's one on yer head."

"Gods below," Nate growled at the gunner, "that's the man's *hair*, not a bird."

Greenroot frowned and squinted harder.

Nate took the opportunity to duck under the gunner's arm and slip free. Most people had turned away by then, but there were a few gazes lingering on his Lowwind tattoo like so many fingers. He did not like the quiet thoughtfulness in their eyes, but he gave them a sideways smile and a shrug. "You'll have to excuse our gunner," Nate called to them. "He's a bit of an idiot." The watching pirates smirked, and Nate turned to head back to the table, forcing himself to stay tall as he walked.

Even though he was relieved, there was a small part of him that had rankled at the laughter that had so readily greeted the proclamation of his true Skill. It was easy, though, for Nate to smooth it down as he reminded himself that he had done something incredible, and it wasn't his fault if a room full of pirates didn't want to believe it. And Greenroot could hang for all Nate cared; Nate's Skill was his own, his *life* was his own, and whether he tracked a dragon again or found something new to do with his magic was completely up to him. His smile was genuine as he reached the table, the tension gone from his shoulders and his mind.

That was why he felt it clearly when something heavy cut through the air, sailing straight for his head.

Nate turned and threw up his hands to block the object a moment before Marcus's warning came. He caught it, but that did not stop the cheap ale from splashing into Nate's face. He grimaced as it dripped down his nose and chin, wiping furiously at his eyes to get the stinging stuff clear. People were laughing again, and Nate's anger was back when he finally looked down to see what he was holding. It was a pewter tankard.

Across the tavern, a very smug Jim Greenroot lowered his now-empty hand. "See?" the gunner said. "He *can* do it."

More stares clawed at Nate's face between the ripples of laughter, but the skeptics were still there.

"The Darkbend warned him," one man scoffed. "Anyone can block something they know is coming."

"How'd he manage to aim that, anyway?" a woman from the card table mused as Greenroot drunkenly swung around, nearly losing his footing as he went.

"He tracks stuff in the air," the gunner insisted, now adding wild arm gestures to underscore his statements, or maybe just to keep his balance. "S'meone throw s'methin' else."

"How about we throw you out?" was the response, which earned a few more laughs and nods of agreement.

Nate released his breath in a slow exhale of relief, but it caught in his throat when he saw the same knot of pirates watching him closely, and without a trace of amusement. There were far too many of them for comfort. His gaze rose to the balcony, to where Captain Arani stood, one hand on the railing and the other gripping the hilt of her sword. She watched the curious pirates with a stony expression. Spider was next to her, murmuring something in her ear that only made her eyes narrow further, and Nate felt his heart sink.

This was as bad as he thought it was, and it was no longer safe for Nate to be on the island.

As if to prove the point, a hand suddenly clasped Nate's bicep, and Novachak leaned in to say, "Why don't we get you cleaned up?"

Nate had not seen the boatswain descend the stairs and push his way across the room, but there was no sense in arguing with him, especially with Dax just over his shoulder, already scoping out the best path from the table to the door. Nate sighed, but he did not protest or try to pull away. He followed the quartermaster through the crowd, the boatswain still gripping his arm as he brought up the rear. Nate felt the gazes of the quiet pirates follow him all the way out the door.

Dax and Novachak turned Nate towards the harbor the moment they broke free of the tavern. The boatswain did not even spare a glance across the road at the pleasure house as he ushered Nate along, the threat of an unhappy Captain Arani for once outweighing his mysterious fear of Madame Silverdale.

"You know you're going to have to stay on the ship,

right?" Novachak murmured into Nate's ear.

Nate grunted, the rising swell of anger in his chest blowing away his words.

One thing. Captain Arani had asked the crew to be discreet about *one thing*, and Jim Greenroot had spilled the secret the very first night.

Nate spent the entire journey from the island back to the *Southern Echo* thinking of more and more creative ways for the gunner to meet an unfortunate end. None of them lifted his mood in the slightest, and as the rowboat carried him over the last few waves, the ship loomed before him like a prison.

He felt a little ashamed for thinking of the *Southern Echo* as such, but he could not shake the idea as he climbed up the rope ladder from the rowboat. The few people who'd been unlucky enough to draw shifts on the watch looked at him quizzically as he came over the railing, but Nate was in no mood to answer any questions. He left that task to Dax and Novachak.

Nate stalked up the stairs to the poop deck, not bothering to take a lantern with him. The twin moons were nothing more than slivers on the horizon, but the sky was heavy with stars. Nate did not look at them. All of his attention was on the warm glow of the lights on the island, its promises of joy and time spent with his friends once again beyond his reach.

May the gods below give you an agonizing death, Jim Greenroot, Nate thought bitterly.

It wasn't long before footsteps thudded up the stairs. Nate did not bother turning around as the person came and joined him at the railing, looking out at Spider's Nest.

"Personally, I've never much cared for this island," Dax said after a thoughtful silence. "Too many people, too few inhibitions."

Nate sighed. "I wouldn't know," he said.

"You're not missing much," Dax said gently.

Nate glowered at the cheerful lights of the town.

The quartermaster lingered by his side for a few minutes in what Nate supposed was meant to be a companionable gesture, but it was clear that Nate wasn't interested in continuing the conversation. Finally, Dax turned to go. "You'll be all right," he said. "Disappointment has never killed a man."

Nate wasn't so sure about that.

When Dax was gone, Nate lay down on the warm boards of the ship's deck, letting his bones press against the wood. He remembered the story Dax had told him during one of Nate's first days with the crew, about a dryad being fused with the *Southern Echo*. Nate pretended that he could feel a faint pulse through the ship, some small sign that the dryad's spirit was keeping him company as he stared up at the wild stars dancing across the sky. They seemed closer than the lights of the town.

Nate thumped his frustration against the deck, pounding out an uneven rhythm with his fists. He could still feel the eyes of the quiet pirates on his skin, but the laughter still ringing in his ears was louder. He reminded himself again that he'd done the impossible, and had gotten nearly everything he'd once wished for. It was just strange that it was nothing like what he had wanted.

A little while later, a soft call from one of the night watchers sounded out, and Nate sat up to hear a muffled answer come from the sea. He stood up and stretched before moving back to the railing of the poop deck, watching with only mild interest as the rope ladder was tossed over the side of the ship once more. He expected Arani to climb up, eyes and sword flashing as she ordered him pointblank to stay on the ship. Instead, the bright starlight shone on three

achingly welcome faces, catching on their Skill tattoos. Nate straightened and waved to Eric, Marcus,
and Rori, and all three of them immediately moved to
join him on the poop deck.

"Marcus told us what happened," Eric said as he led
the way up the steps. "I can't believe Greenroot just
announced all of that in the middle of the tavern."

"I can," Marcus said, following close behind with a
lantern in his hand. "He could barely stand, he was so
drunk. Still don't know how he managed to throw the
tankard right at Nate's head."

"I think he's one of those people whose aim gets
better the drunker he is."

"How'd he get the money for that much ale, anyway?" Rori asked darkly.

"From how chummy they looked when we got
there," Eric mused, "I think the gunners from the
Gryphon were treating him."

"Lucky bastard," Marcus grumbled.

Nate felt a relieved smile tug at his lips as the two
Darkbends stepped on to the deck. It grew when Rori
came up after them, shuffling a deck of cards in her
hands.

"Starlight's bright enough that we almost don't need
the lantern to play," she said as she stepped up next to
Nate. She cast an appreciative glance up at the night
sky. It flickered when her gaze snagged on the lights of
the island, but she turned away. "Nicer out here than
in that old tavern, too."

"It's all right," Nate said, "you don't have to pretend
that you want to be here."

The Darkbends paused in their speculations on how
Jim Greenroot had managed to become such good
friends with anyone, let alone people from another
crew.

"We're not pretending," Marcus said. "You're here,

so we're here."

Nate's smile returned, his heart growing warm in his chest. "Thank you," he murmured.

"Of course," Rori said. "Also, it really does smell better than in the tavern."

"Especially since Greenroot vomited not long after you left," Marcus agreed.

"Mouthy demon-spawn deserved his drink coming back to bite him," Eric declared, "though I'm not sure the rest of us did." He nodded eagerly at the playing cards Rori had brought. "Now come on, the champion of Liar's Farm would love to see what sad little strategies you all have been cooking up in your spare time."

Rori sneered good-naturedly at the Darkbend, and then they all sat down in a ring on the deck and began to play. Nate was too distracted to put up much of a fight, his thoughts wandering between the potential trouble Greenroot had stirred up on the island and his gratitude towards Eric, Marcus, and Rori. Nate finished behind Marcus in a few of the early rounds, but as the night wore on and he and his friends talked and teased each other over the game, some of his unease loosened.

Maybe Nate's life was never going to be normal by anyone's standards, but that did not mean it couldn't be a good one.

The next morning saw Eric called away to assist the master carpenter with repairs to the ship. Marcus and Rori stayed with Nate for a while, passing idle time on the deck and playing card games that were decidedly not Liar's Farm, now that Eric was gone and there wasn't much competition left for Rori, who had handily stolen the champion's title away from the Dark-bend the previous night. By midmorning, though, Nate knew that his friends were restless, and they were only staying behind for his sake.

"It's all right, really," Nate finally told them. "Go have fun, and bring me back some stories."

Marcus and Rori glanced at each other, and then at the island. They could not hide their wistfulness.

"We don't want to leave you alone," Rori said.

Nate waved her off. "I'll be fine. Maybe I'll help with the repairs on the hull, if they'll let me. They must have use for an extra pair of hands somewhere."

Rori worried her bottom lip between her teeth and Marcus shifted guiltily, but Nate ushered them both off of the *Southern Echo* and on to the last rowboat heading to shore for the day. He waved cheerfully to them, and tried not to slump too despondently on the railing as he watched them go.

They'll be back soon enough, Nate told himself, but that felt like a lie.

It turned out to be one, too. Hard as he tried to keep himself distracted, there simply wasn't much for Nate to do on the *Southern Echo*. Eric and the master carpenter Tim Whitebranch were ashore, cutting and sanding wood to the measurements they'd already taken for patching the holes in the ship, which fortunately did not require beaching the *Southern Echo*. The damage was all well above the water line, and none of the holes were devastatingly large. The carpenters had the repairs well in hand, and that left Nate with the monotonous tasks of stitching a few minor tears in the spare sailcloth, swabbing the deck clean of the last traces of the battle with the navy, and polishing the ship's weapon stores until the pistols and cutlasses gleamed. Even working alone, he was done by late afternoon, and boredom threatened to gnaw a hole through his skull. He spent a little time lying in the sun on the deck and fighting the urge to use his Skill to explore the patterns of the wind around the island.

He gave into the temptation.

Still remembering the pain and exhaustion from the dragon hunt when he'd overworked his magic, Nate moved cautiously through the winds, but they were steady and gentle. It wasn't long before he was jumping from one salt-stained ribbon to the next. He did not go far, even though the winds kept nudging him towards the open sea. When he came back from the element, the gold ring on his hand was a little warm against his skin, but nowhere near the burning level he'd felt when he'd pushed his Skill so hard, the magic had nearly killed him.

Nate held his hand up and squinted at the gold ring. He'd meant to trade it on Spider's Nest for a good stock of agate, or maybe some Solkyrian silver that did not bear the sun crest of the empire. Eric had promised to take him among the beach vendors and find him a good trade, as well as a weaver or a metalsmith who could fashion whatever kind of bracelet or necklace he wanted to use for his new anchors. Nate had been looking forward to that. Now, he'd have to ask Eric to take the ring on his behalf and see what he could get, but Nate worried that the Darkbend may not come back with the right kind of anchor. He trusted Eric to get him a fair bargain, but Nate's Skill was considerably more complex than Eric's, and it could burn through an anchor far quicker than the light bender's.

Maybe Rori could go with him, if she's willing, Nate thought. Her Skill was the strongest of any of them, and even if she didn't fully understand wind reading, she'd know what would and would not work as an anchor for Nate. He'd have to ask his friends for the favor when they returned for the night.

But that still left him lying on the deck with a gold ring on his hand and nothing to distract him from the sun crest stamped into the metal. If he was honest with himself, Nate still felt a few lingering pangs of guilt for turning pirate. Maybe not for the empire, but for his parents, who had given everything to try to secure him a legitimate life. The gold ring was the last thing his father had given him. It felt wrong to ask someone else to trade it away on his behalf. If he was going to throw off the last of his parents' kindness, he felt that he should do it himself.

Too bad Greenroot had gotten drunk and Arani had forbidden Nate from leaving the ship.

Nate pushed himself to his feet and made his way belowdeck, heading for the berth. Moping in the afternoon sun had at least made him a little drowsy, and he could nap away some more time before his friends came back.

"Untangling rope, polishing cutlasses, and napping," he grumbled as he descended the steps. "Won't they be jealous when they hear how I spent my day."

It took several moments for Nate's eyes to adjust to the gloomier light of the lower deck, but he knew the way and he stepped confidently through the ship. By the time he reached the gun deck, his sight was clear again, and it actually hurt a little when he caught sight of an open gun port and the blazing blue sky outside.

He stopped, frowning.

None of the other gun ports were open. The cannon in that spot had been pushed askew, creating a space just wide enough for someone to wriggle through. Nate knew that, because he'd done the same thing when Arani and the others had rescued him from the navy frigate.

He had just enough time to feel a surge of alarm before a rope closed around his neck.

Nate gasped and clawed at the rope, but the rough noose squeezed tighter, and then a wad of cloth was stuffed into his open mouth. Someone grabbed his hand, and Nate felt the scrape of more rope against his skin. He thrashed and threw himself backwards as hard as he could. He collided with his assailant and sent them stumbling, which released some of the tension in the rope around his neck. Nate's throat opened up and a deep breath rushed into him. He coughed on the gag in his mouth and heard someone grunt as they tried to regain their footing. Nate pushed into them again, and he heard a meaty thump and a growl of pain as they fell into the cannon behind them.

"Gods below, get his feet!" someone hissed.

Nate caught a glimpse of his attackers then. There were three of them, and they all had the brown skin and dark hair of Solkyrians, but they were not from the *Southern Echo*'s crew. Nate did not know them. In that moment, he did not care to. He thrashed again and tried to kick the man who dove at his legs. He jerked his knee into the man's jaw, but the rope around his neck tightened again and pulled him off balance. The third assailant moved in to grab his arms, and Nate felt his feet leave the deck as the man got ahold of his legs and lifted them. Nate struggled and tried to shout, and the sound that escaped around the gag was muffled even to his own ears.

"Hurry up and tie him!" the man with Nate's legs growled.

"I'm trying," another answered. "This bastard Skilled won't—*aaugh!*"

He cut off when the heel of Nate's hand slammed into his nose. Any satisfaction Nate would have felt at the blow was drowned out by the panic surging through him, and he struggled harder against his attackers.

It wasn't enough. He had no purchase with his legs crushed in the one man's arms, and the rope around his neck was too tight. He clawed at it, but his vision was turning dark even as his arms were pulled together and wrapped in rope. The angry whispers of the assailants were going softer and softer, and Nate's vision deserted him entirely as he was lowered to the deck.

He heard it, though, when one of the attackers suddenly shouted, and then something warm hit Nate's face at the same moment that the rope around his neck went totally slack. He nearly choked on whatever had doused him, but he rolled over and cleared his nose in time to draw in several deep breaths. They brought with them a coppery smell, and as Nate's senses returned to him, he realized with horror that his face was covered with someone's blood. It was seeping into the gag, and he struggled free of the ropes to reach up and tear the gag out of his mouth. He spat out the terrible taste of a fading life, and his stomach heaved.

Gasping, Nate wiped his face on his sleeve and turned to see the light leaving the eyes of a man lying next to him, a wide slash across his throat. Nate looked away just in time to see a cutlass rip free from the gut of his second attacker, and then the third was stabbed viciously before he could scramble away. All three assailants lay on the deck, leaking blood from their wounds and dying quickly.

Nate stared at them numbly, forgetting the blood on his face and ignoring the growing pool of it soaking into his trousers.

His savior kicked at the sole of his boot. "Get up, Nowind."

Xander.

Nate's throat was ravaged, and he only sat there, looking shakily at the dead men.

Xander scoffed and moved away, his cutlass dripping dark blood on the deck. Then footsteps were hurrying towards Nate and voices were asking him questions, but Nate's skin was becoming sticky with someone else's death, and his arms felt too weak to even try to raise his hands to wipe away the blood.

CHAPTER FOUR

Cracks in the World

"YOU THINK NATE'S DOING all right?" Marcus asked as he and Rori wandered among the vendors set up on the beach, looking for one that sold Solkyrian agate.

"It's the best thing for him," Rori said softly. Luken chirped an agreement from her shoulder, his weight a light reassurance. "Between Spider's laws and Captain Arani's flag, he's safest on the ship."

"Safe and bored near to death," Marcus grumbled. "Not sure I'd call that the best thing for anyone."

Rori gave him a sidelong look, which he did not meet. They were nearly of the same height, although Marcus was considerably broader and stronger than her, with a muscular build that belied his ability to play the fiddle with graceful ease. It was one of the many contradictions that made up Marcus Darkbend, and though it had taken her some time, Rori had learned to appreciate them all. His one consistency, however, was his uncertainty around her. Rori had never figured out if that was due to conditioning from his academy training as a light bender that had positioned weather workers as superiors to be treated with the utmost respect, or if it was because Eric wasn't there to act as a buffer between them. The two light benders were easily best friends, something Rori had always envied but never tried to breach. She liked both of them well enough, although if she were being truthful, she'd say that she preferred Eric's company as he was cleverer than Marcus. They all knew that, but that did not stop Marcus from occasionally having a surprising bit of insight. One more contradiction to the blunt persona he usually put forth.

Case in point: their hunt for a vendor with Solkyrian agate, which had been Marcus's suggestion.

"Nate will be thrilled if we can bring him something to replace that ring," Rori reminded him. "This was a good idea."

Marcus quirked a smile but kept his eyes on the displays around them. "I do sometimes have them."

If Eric were with them, Rori knew he would have declared this situation an omen akin to the moons colliding, but she kept the thought to herself. She was glad she did when Marcus's expression brightened suddenly.

"Over there," he said, pointing. "Looks like a jeweler."

He took off, and Rori hurried after him, Luken balancing easily on her shoulder.

It was a pleasant day, the sun warm but gentle with the onset of winter, not that an island like Spider's Nest would ever experience the full season. With a soft pang, Rori remembered the biting chill of winter descending over her home village in northern Solkyria. The cold had made the hearth fires so much sweeter, and the soft blanket of snow that always fell just before the Dancing Skies Festival was beautiful and serene. But Rori had not been back to that village in a long, long time, and the memory and the pain receded under the tropical sun.

As Rori and Marcus approached the jeweler, she noticed the Darkbend turning his head to let his gaze linger on a few of the stalls. The beach vendors were much the same as they usually were, with weapon smiths and tailors set up close enough to eye each other's wares and run shrewd calculations in their heads as they sized up every potential buyer. The roasting pits had boars and some wild fowl turning on spits over their flames, some of which had already been sold back to the tavern to serve as dinner over the next few days, but the right coin could buy a fresh cut of sizzling meat with a special bit of seasoning. These were the things that Marcus gazed at with naked longing, despite the cheap meal they'd shared at the tavern less than an hour earlier.

Rori couldn't help herself this time. "Gods below, are you ever not hungry?"

"Usually when I'm sleeping," Marcus said without any ire. "Although, once I had this nasty stomach ache and I didn't eat for a full day. When I went to bed that night, I dreamed of a spectacular feast. Meats and fish and sugared fruits and fresh bread. I gorged myself on all my favorites. When I woke up, I was chewing on my pillow and absolutely famished."

Rori stared at him. "So that's a no, then?"

"That's a no," Marcus agreed as he stepped up to the table covered in a variety of stones and beaten metals. Rori gave a small huff of laughter before joining him to poke through the offerings.

There wasn't much by way of agate; the jeweler was one of the permanent residents of Spider's Nest, and she made a living by selling pretty trinkets to the more successful crews who had the money to spend on such things. None of the jeweler's raw materials were worth trying to steal, so she rarely had trouble, but her creations were valued for the effort and skill she put into them. She smiled at Rori and Marcus and suggested custom pieces for them, combinations of semi-precious gems and metal or woven hemp that would make fine earrings and bracelets, but none of which were suitable anchors for Solkyrian magic. The bits of agate that the jeweler did have were small, chosen more for the beauty of their colors and patterns than their potency, and Rori knew at a glance that they would not work for Nate.

Perhaps if they were all gathered and stacked together on a single bracelet, they could serve, but Rori knew the jeweler would not let that much agate go at a low price. She stepped back from the table and fished a dried berry out of her pocket and fed it to Luken while she waited for Marcus. He lingered a little longer, considering one of the larger pieces of agate, but when he touched it lightly with his finger and felt the cooling steadiness of the stone, he shook his head and pulled away.

"I don't think any of these are strong enough for Nate," he mused.

"They're not," Rori confirmed. "He burned clean through most of my reserve pieces, and some of them were as big as this one." She pulled up her sleeve to show Marcus one of the larger bits of agate that she wore on the woven cords along her arms. It was about the width of her forearm, and was gray and oblong with small holes on the sides where the cord looped through. It was not particularly eye-catching, but the stone was one of her strongest anchors, often staying cool and steady even when the others had grown uncomfortably warm to the touch.

Marcus frowned at the gray agate before looking dubiously back at the jeweler's table. "Do you have anything... bigger?" he asked.

The jeweler gave him a flat look before waving them away in favor of another customer better suited to her wares.

Rori and Marcus made their way further down the beach, but they didn't find much until one of the last stalls, where a vendor was selling and repairing tools along with a few larger pieces of raw agate. They studied the stones for a few moments while the vendor watched them, making no effort to hide his interest in their Skill tattoos.

"A Goodtide needs something strong," the vendor said. "You won't find anything better than what I've got here."

Rori doubted that, but there really wasn't much else to choose from. "It's not for me," she said, "but we do need a strong one."

The vendor pointed at the second largest chunk of agate, banded with blue and white but spiderwebbed with cracks along its face. "I can give you a good price for that one."

Which certainly meant that he would charge them double what it was worth, but that hardly mattered when the agate was so damaged. Rori did not bother with a response, although Marcus gave a disbelieving snort before picking up one of the other pieces and weighing it thoughtfully in his hand.

"This one feels all right."

Rori peered at the rough, unpolished stone dubiously. "We'd have to get it cut for him," she said, "and that's going to cost us."

"I could do that for you," the tool vendor offered. "For an added fee, of course."

Rori gave him an unimpressed stare before walking away with Marcus in tow.

"I thought it'd be easier than this to find an anchor," he said.

"Not for a Skill like Nate's," Rori said quietly. Luken chirped and lightly nibbled at her earlobe. Absently, Rori gave the bird another dried berry.

Marcus frowned at the sand beneath their feet as they walked back along the beach. "I swear I've seen that cracked agate before," he said.

Rori smiled ruefully. "I'm pretty sure it came from Captain Arani's cache. I think she sold it to Spider the last time we were here."

"Why's that vendor got it, then?"

"He probably bought it for twice what Spider paid, and now he's waiting for someone desperate enough to buy it from him."

"So how are we going to get it?"

Rori looked at him sidelong.

"Not the cracked piece," Marcus said, "one of the better ones. Although we probably can't even afford the cracked one."

"No," Rori agreed with a sigh, "we can't."

"Should we steal it?" Marcus asked after a moment.

Rori snorted. "And break a Nest law? Personally, I like having both of my hands attached to me."

"Maybe we could get Greenroot to do it," Marcus suggested. "Penance for running his mouth and all." He smirked suddenly. "And we could make Xander help him."

"I don't think we could make Xander do anything," Rori said mildly.

"Sure, but imagine the two of them having to work together, and be sneaky while they're at it."

"They'd likely set something on fire," Rori mused.

Marcus's grin widened, and Rori answered with a smile of her own, although her thoughts were darker as she remembered the unhappy look Xander had given her the day before, when she'd told him no, they were not going to be continuing on as they always had. His vote to keep the dragon and abandon Nate hadn't surprised her, but it had still disappointed her, and she couldn't look at Xander without a knife stroke of revulsion in her gut.

She wanted to convince herself that she was okay

with the anger alone, that a twinge of sadness and regret didn't come on the tail end of that revulsion, but in spite of everything she knew of Xander, she still felt them.

Maybe she'd wanted to believe that there was more to him. Whether on purpose or by accident, he'd shown her that he could be hurt. She knew that he sometimes had nightmares that left him sweating and breathing hard. Never screaming, because he'd learned as a young boy that his silence was more likely to keep him alive. No one would come to help him if he screamed.

It had never stopped surprising her, then, that Xander was extremely patient and attentive when it came to physical pleasure. The first time they'd lain together, he'd been confident and sure of himself, but he'd still watched Rori's face carefully, and asked her what she liked. Every time since then, he'd preferred going slow, every touch a tease across her skin until she was gasping with need, and only then would he take her to her climax. Then he'd take his own with a hard, savage force, as though time were suddenly running out and that was his last act alive.

He did not murmur sweet words in the aftermath, nor did he try to linger by her side, but he never strayed far, either, and if there was ever so much as a whiff of trouble around Rori, Xander could be counted on to appear with a blade in his hand and a snarl on his lips.

Maybe that was why she had not wanted to believe that Xander could have voted to leave a friend behind. But that had been her mistake.

"You all right, there?" Marcus asked, jolting Rori out of her thoughts.

She nodded absently. "Trying to think where else we could find some agate."

Marcus swallowed the lie easily, and he started to

gesture towards another stall on the beach, but a shout interrupted him. He and Rori both turned, only to see people abandoning the market and hurrying towards the dock.

"What's going on?" Marcus asked, putting the question to no one in particular. No one answered, and Marcus turned a confused look on Rori.

She shook her head and began to follow the crowd. Luken's talons tightened on her coat, and he gave a small chirp that echoed the uneasiness settling in Rori's stomach.

The feeling only grew when they reached the dock and found a tight ring forming up around a box placed in the sand, ready and waiting to elevate the bearer of important information. On Spider's Nest, that could only mean bad news. Rori glanced around, trying to pick out the person who was about to speak. She was surprised when her gaze alighted on Spider himself, and she knew that he would only have come out of his fortress of ledgers and money for something terrible.

Is the navy here? she wondered, and craned her neck to look for deadly sails on the horizon.

The heels of Spider's boots cracked down on the wooden crate as he stepped up, and the crowd went silent. There was pure wrath in Spider's eyes as he swept his gaze over the gathering. Rori recoiled slightly as his attention passed over her, even though she knew that she'd done nothing wrong.

Beside her, Marcus shifted uneasily. "I was only kidding about stealing the agate," he whispered.

Rori touched him lightly on the wrist, and Marcus fell as quiet as the rest of the crowd.

Spider began to speak. "You are all pirates," he boomed out, his deep voice carrying clearly over everyone. "Men and women who have thrown off the yoke of the empire and come here seeking freedom."

His dark eyes flashed across the crowd. "Freedom I give you, but in exchange, there are codes that you must not break. Codes that are meant to protect you from *each other* as much as the empire, and that I and everyone on this island trust you to uphold. When you break those codes, you destroy so much more than just my trust. None of it can be rebuilt."

Rori felt a chill wash down her spine.

Someone had broken a Nest law.

Marcus tensed next to Rori, and she gripped his arm before he could say anything. He'd only been joking, earlier. They hadn't done anything. This was something else. Something far more serious than petty theft. Rori knew it because she saw the young boy in Spider's employ come running, a bundle of black cloth in his arms. He handed the rolled flag up to Spider, and then hastily retreated.

"Today," Spider continued as he shook the cloth loose, "someone has chosen to strike against their peers in my protected waters, and for that crime, they will pay."

He snatched up the corners of the black flag, and let the crowd see the emblem of the gryphon holding an hourglass in its claws. Rori wasn't the only one who drew in a sharp breath. Two more of Spider's aides came forward, and they took the flag from him and held it taut as he drew a long, wicked knife from his belt.

"Captain Charles Bluecape's ship *Gryphon* and all his crew are hereby exiled from this island," Spider snarled as he plunged the knife into the flag, piercing the head of the gryphon. "From this moment forth, they will receive no aid from here. They have no allies here. If any of them ever dare to return to these waters, even under a new flag, they will be blasted into oblivion by every ship and cannon ported here." The knife slashed down, tearing through the fabric and cleaving the gryphon in two. "For the *Gryphon*'s attack on the *Southern Echo*, this I decree."

A murmur went up among the crowd, but Rori barely heard it over the sudden roaring in her ears. She could only think of one reason why anyone would have struck against her own crew. She felt like the ground had dropped away beneath her feet, and she grabbed Marcus's arm again, this time for support.

"Gods below," Marcus muttered as he helped steady her. "Why in the six hells would they...?" He trailed off as he realized the same thing Rori had.

"Nate," she breathed.

Then they were both running for the rowboats.

Nate was all right. That was the important thing.

He was badly shaken and kept jumping at small noises, but Marcus and Eric had him laughing weakly before too long. They all stayed with him the rest of the day and into the night, and Nate finally seemed to relax as he came to understand that his friends were not going to leave him again.

Most of them, at least. Xander was nowhere to be seen, but he'd still defended Nate against three men from the *Gryphon*. He'd probably saved Nate's life; the *Gryphon*'s men had not been gentle, and that rope had left a visible ring of raw flesh around Nate's neck.

The scars on Rori's back itched whenever she looked at the wound, and it was all she could do to keep the memories out of her eyes whenever she and Nate looked at each other. He needed his friends to be strong now, to buoy his spirit, not remind him that the world was a cruel, terrible place for the Skilled.

Rori was determined not to do that. If Xander could step up and save Nate's life, Rori could at least put on a brave face. But her mind kept trying to return to the decks of another ship, to the locked rooms of the tide working academy, to the village road an enforcer had dragged her down while others had watched and done nothing as her world collapsed.

She couldn't be the emotional anchor that Nate needed, so she regretfully held back as Marcus and Eric soothed him, and tried to convince him that he really was safe.

It helped that few people from the *Southern Echo* were willing to leave Nate vulnerable again. As word of the attack spread, most of the crew came back to the ship of their own accord, flooding the watches with volunteers to the point where Novachak actually had to turn people away and ask them to wait until morning.

Jim Greenroot was especially protective. He took up arms and stood sentry as close to Nate as Eric's glower would allow.

"You know this is your fault," Eric growled at Greenroot at one point.

The gunner had the decency to look abashed, but all he said was, "He's *our* wind worker. No one else can have him."

Rori could have stabbed Jim Greenroot in that moment. It took a conscious effort to remove her hand from the cutlass at her hip. Even then, she knew she couldn't trust herself not to attack the gunner and break the crew's code. But she had to do *something*. So she gave Nate's shoulder a gentle squeeze when she caught him darting nervous glances into the shadows, handed Luken over to Eric and received a knowing nod in return, got Marcus going on his story of the time three rats banded together to outwit him and steal his breakfast, and then went to find the captain.

Rori's blood seethed as she made her way through the ship. Of all people, she should have known better. She knew what the tattoos on their faces proclaimed to the world, and she'd seen the curious way some of the people in the tavern had looked at her and Eric when they'd met up with Marcus, after godsdamned Jim Greenroot had spilled the secret of the black mimic. But all the same, she had trusted Spider's laws and the warm, sturdy wood of the *Southern Echo* to protect Nate.

If it hadn't been for Xander...

Rori cursed herself for her own stupid complacency, and everyone around her for their deadly greed.

Even Captain Arani had proven that she was not immune to temptation, with the hunt for the dragon nearly consuming her. The captain had almost killed Nate when she'd pushed him to use his Skill so far past its limits, and then she'd ordered Rori to break the vow she'd made to herself and use her magic again.

Rori paused, one hand braced against the curved wall of the ship. The sea was calm beneath the hold, but she could still feel the susurrations of its currents against the keel, and her fingers itched to reach for the raw power waiting in the water's gentle waves. She'd gone so long without touching the tides that she'd forgotten how much she'd loved her magic, but Arani's orders had brought it all back in a flood of joy and fear, and now Rori couldn't sleep through the night without reaching for the sea and feeling the pulse of its currents tangle with her own, the agate on her arms warm against her skin and phantom whispers in her ears.

She shook her head violently and made herself walk forward again.

Captain Arani had steered them headlong into this

mess, and she needed to fix it. And she needed to do it soon.

When Rori reached the captain's private quarters, she squared her shoulders and knocked firmly on the door. She did not hear anything from the other side for so long, she began to think that she'd been wrong about the captain's whereabouts. Then there were footsteps, and the door swung open to reveal Dax, his gaze stern beneath the twin designs that swept along his skull and disguised his Malatide tattoo, but Rori could always see the Skill mark clear as Luken flying on a sunny day.

"It's not a good time, Rori," the quartermaster began, but there was a shuffle from inside the cabin and Arani called, "Let her in."

Dax turned to glance back at the captain, revealing Arani standing hunched over the long table in the center of the room, pouring over a massive spread of papers. Rori recognized them as charts from the navigation room. Her heart quickened as she wondered why Arani would need so many. Rori said nothing, but she quickly stepped inside when Dax gestured her through. He shut the door behind her with a firm snap.

"You may as well hear this now," the captain said, not looking up as Rori approached the table. "I'm sure you'd figure it out soon enough on your own."

Rori halted next to the captain, but she did not look at the charts. Instead, her gaze was locked on the resigned slump of Captain Arani's shoulders and the tired hang of her head. The saber was gone from her hip, and Arani wasn't wearing her hat or her coat, shirtsleeves pushed sloppily up her arms. Wisps of hair had come loose from the hasty bun tied at the nape of her neck, as though she'd been raking her hands through it in frustration.

Or worse, Rori thought, *resignation*.

The captain did not meet Rori's eyes. She gestured at the charts with a slow wave of her hand. "I don't know where to go," she said softly, and the world cracked like glass.

I didn't hear that right, Rori reassured herself after a stunned moment. *The captain always knows what to do.*

Maybe Arani had simply forgotten about the plan to leave the Common Sea after the attack on Nate and all the chaos that had followed in its wake.

Rori threw a look at the sea charts with their islands and currents so painstakingly drawn out, sometimes by her own hand. "East," she said, thrusting a finger towards one of the rougher, incomplete maps that showed Votheinian territories. Secondhand knowledge had filled in that particular chart, but it was better than nothing, and there was no reason to change their plans other than to hasten them along. Strange that both the captain and the quartermaster had forgotten that. "We spoke of going east, away from the Solkyrian Empire."

"We did," Arani agreed. She reached out to touch the cluster of islands that made up the Coral Chain, with Spider's Nest gathered safely inside its Gauntlet Reefs. "But that was before the *Gryphon.*"

Rori frowned. "By the time Spider finished cutting their flag, that ship was nearly out of the harbor. They're gone."

"I don't think they are," the captain murmured.

Rori's frown deepened. "You think they're waiting to ambush us?"

"I think that they have nowhere to go, and nothing to lose," Arani said. "It would be stupid of them *not* to try, but they won't do it here. There's a lot of ocean out there, but they know as well as we do that there are only so many places we could go that are beyond Solkyrian control." She traced a current inked across the Common Sea that lead into the eastern hemisphere, hitting nothing for several weeks' worth of travel in good weather until one of the islands near the equator. "If we go east, they only need to wait for us."

"And the *Gryphon* has more firepower than the *Southern Echo*," Dax put in.

Rori jumped. She had not heard the quartermaster come up on her other side, but he did not look the slightest bit amused at catching her off guard. There was a grimness in his eyes that she liked even less than the bleak tone of Arani's voice. She wanted both of those things gone.

"So we wait them out, then," Rori said. "They can't stay out there forever, and we have everything we need on the Nest."

"We can't afford it," the captain said. "I convinced Spider to supply us for our next voyage, but he won't be pleased if we camp out in his harbor. He may try to drive us off, and he'll show no mercy when he does. If he lets us stay and the crew doesn't have the money to enjoy the Nest, they'll want out as it is, and I don't know if we'll even be able to hold out that long before someone else attacks us. I don't have a choice. I have to dissolve the crew."

Arani kept speaking, but for Rori, the world suddenly went quiet as death.

Memories flooded Rori's vision, and instead of the captain's face, she saw her mother's, twisted with anguish and pain as the imperial enforcer held her back. She saw her father, lying facedown on the ground, blood pooling around his head. She saw her grandmother, angry and defiant and telling Rori to be brave, but how could she, when the world kept falling apart?

Rori tried to tell herself that this was not the same,

that the breaking of one pirate crew was not her life being ripped to pieces all over again, but she'd been alone and afraid for so long after the enforcers had come, all the way through the tide working academy and the burning sting of her Goodtide tattoo, to the cold decks of the *Godfall* and the tearing touch of the whip and the violent currents of the western seas. The *Southern Echo*—captain, crew, and all—had saved her from that, and Rori couldn't bear to lose them. Even if she found another ship, another captain would only see the Goodtide brand on her face, and want her for her magic. Would want her to use it.

She'd tapped into that power on the dragon hunt, and again in the fight with the navy, and one final time when she'd helped bring Nate home, but she'd been holding back, never going into the true depths of her magic and the horrors that lurked there, the lives she'd let it claim.

When she'd been a monster.

All at once, Rori's magic surged forward with a roar, and it was all she could do to stamp it down. The ship rocked as a larger wave swept by. Dax shot her an alarmed look, but Arani only shifted her weight with the motion of the deck beneath her feet and brushed a lock of hair off of her forehead.

Rori ducked her head in shame as the ship settled, but she couldn't stand by silently while this happened. "What would it take to keep this crew together?" she asked. Her throat felt clogged with fear, but the words still managed to slip out.

"A miracle," the captain answered, voice soft but completely serious. "The crew has gone far too long without payment."

"What about a legend?" Rori asked, thinking of the dragon map with a lightning strike of clarity. "Sell Mordanti's map."

Dax turned to her sharply, and Rori knew she'd overstepped. It was the simple and elegant solution to all their problems, and surely the officers had already discussed it, but it wasn't her place to suggest selling the map, not after everything the crew had gone through to get it, and especially not in the face of what that map and its promises meant to Captain Arani.

But it was too late for Rori to take the words back now, and she could not stand the thought of losing the life and the freedom and the family she'd found to this defeated stranger that was currently impersonating her captain. This was not how things ended. Not for them.

"Spider will pay a good price for the copy I made," Rori forced herself to say, even as Dax's glare screamed for her to stop. "Do you still have it?"

Arani said nothing, but her gaze flicked to the sturdy sea chest tucked into a corner of the room.

"Sell it," Rori urged. "Even just half of it."

Silence was the answer.

"Gods below take you and Mordanti both," Rori snapped, unable to take the strain of her fear and budding anger, "because if you don't do it, I will." She heard Dax draw in a sharp breath, and she braced herself for Arani's inevitable wrath.

The captain only gave her a mild look. "And put Nate in even greater danger, not to mention yourself?"

Rori's anger slowed from a surge to a trickle.

"Even if I was willing to sell that map to Spider or anyone else," Arani said gently, "it's useless without a dragon. How many people do you know who could reliably find one?"

The rage drained out of Rori as quickly as it had come, leaving her cold.

Captain Arani sighed and offered a tired, lopsided smile. "If we stay on Spider's Nest, the best I can hope is that the crew will leave me peacefully. I think we all know that's not going to happen. Their hearts belong to the sea, and they'll want a captain who can take them after a new prize. Even if they don't vote me out, someone will likely challenge me for captainship. They may even try to take the *Southern Echo*." Something dark flickered across Arani's face. "They won't have her. As long as I live, this ship is mine. I've spilled blood for her before, and I won't hesitate to do it again."

Rori believed her. She was almost relieved to see the anger in place of the grim resignation.

But the moment passed, and Arani faced the charts again with a sigh. "So, we can't go east until the *Gryphon*'s crew has grown tired of waiting for us, along with anyone else who decides to head us off before we can get anywhere, and we can't stay here. If we hunt around these waters, we contend with the Solkyrian navy looking for us, along with any other captains who heard last night's story and decided to wait until we're beyond Spider's laws to attack us." She shut her eyes and breathed, "I don't know where else to go."

Another wave of panic washed up and down Rori's spine. She raked her gaze wildly over the sea charts, not believing that there was nowhere in the world the *Southern Echo* could sail, and that this life Rori had learned to love would not fall apart around her, taking the remaining people she'd come to care about with it.

"What if we struck out southeast?" Rori suggested, moving to trace a new path across the paper. "We can't head into Votheinian waters, but if we can get past the doldrums and into the Leviathan Sea, we'd have more options."

"And a lot of very large, very hungry sea serpents to contend with long before we hit the southern islands," Arani said without opening her eyes. "Not to mention the independent traders who won't welcome us if we're not there to barter. And don't forget that it's now the sirens' mating season, and no one really knows how far their territory ranges at this time of the year. Spider certainly doesn't, and I highly doubt we could survive long enough to map it."

"North, then," Rori said. "There's another pirate island up in the Aurora Sea—"

"That Prince Trystos flushed out nearly five years ago," Arani cut in. There was no ire or exasperation in her words. She simply stated the fact. "And the imperial navy controls those waters all the way up to the edges of the Frozen North. There's nothing there for us." She cracked open her eyes and nodded at a chart pushed off to the edge of the table. "And in the west, there is only Solkyria. There is nowhere we can go."

Rori stared at the heart of the empire, and the empty stretch of the Forbidden Sea beyond. Her heart pounded in her chest, and with each heavy beat, she could hear the cracks in the world splintering out, growing larger and larger, threatening to shatter her whole life.

Even after forcing Rori to use her magic and driving Nate beyond exhaustion, even after all the deaths that had come during and after the dragon hunt, Rori had never once considered leaving the *Southern Echo* or Captain Arani. This ship and this crew were the only home and family Rori had left after the empire had torn her early life apart and sold her into service. And Arani, for all her faults, had always seen *Rori*, not the Goodtide tattoo on her face or all the ways her magic could benefit the ship. Arani had allowed Rori to simply be, just as she'd done for Daxton Malatide and Xander Grayvoice and the rest of the Skilled, too.

That included Nate, when she'd finally ended the hunt for Mordanti's treasure. Arani had willingly released the dragon to rescue one of her own. That was the captain that Rori had chosen to follow and build a new life around. This couldn't be the end of all of that.

Rori wouldn't let it. But she couldn't do that with nothing.

A voice in Rori's head echoed her own earlier words: *What about a legend?*

She drew in a sharp breath and stared at the discarded western chart without seeing it. She did not need to. She knew what they needed to do to leave all their pursuers behind, come back with treasure in the *Southern Echo*'s hold, and repair the cracks in the world. All she had to do was say it.

But fear had taken hold of her voice, and Rori wasn't sure that she should even try to wrestle it back.

Then her ears opened just as Captain Arani told Dax to summon the crew one final time at dawn tomorrow, so she could formally disband and release them to whatever fates they'd choose for themselves.

"We'll go west," Rori blurted. "Past Solkyria, into the Forbidden Sea."

The captain and the quartermaster both turned to stare at her. They seemed to wait for her to declare that she had been joking, or at least assert that yes, she had, in fact, gone completely mad and they should probably take her sextant away before she found a horrifically creative use for it. Rori swallowed hard, balled her hands into fists to keep them from shaking, and turned to meet the officers' gazes.

"There's nothing out there," Dax finally said. "Just the empty sea and a lot of lost ships."

Rori shook her head and shoved the next words out. "It's not empty."

Dax frowned and opened his mouth to say something, but the captain stilled him with a touch on his arm. There was something strange in Arani's gaze that Rori could not place, but it wasn't hostile, and she took that as encouragement to continue.

She needed it, for the next bit.

"There's an island," Rori said, her voice tight. "Far out west, in..." She swallowed past the lump in her throat. "In the Rend."

Dax was visibly startled, and Arani's gaze solidified into mild horror.

They both knew the stories, of course, of the Vanishing Island that flickered just beyond the edge of the world. Legends said that those who survived the voyage to its beaches could approach the black temple and beseech the gods themselves to grant their greatest desire, if they proved themselves worthy. The stories claimed that of all the hundreds of ships that had dared attempt the voyage, only six had ever returned, each one bearing a glorious artifact that formed the centerpiece of several cultures' myths and folklore, not just those of Solkyrians. The last ship said to have successfully returned from the Rend had sailed over two hundred years ago. It had come back with a crown of gold so pure, it almost gleamed white in the sunlight. The crown was still said to reside somewhere in the palace of Sunthrone City, locked away from common eyes but always anchoring the empire as a land blessed by the gods and worthy of conquering the world. No one could say for certain if that was true or not, and history and folklore tended to blur together around the time when the Goldskye family had usurped the original Goldsun emperors, but in the last thirty years alone, only a handful of the most stubborn or foolish of captains had dared turn their ships into the sunset. They'd scoffed at the stories and gone chasing after the Rend, hungry for a glimpse of what lay beyond the horizon. None of their ships had ever returned.

"The Forbidden Sea is not an option," Captain Arani said.

"It's the only option," Rori countered. Her voice was still reluctant, but the truth was putting strength behind it. "*Our* only option. It's not a miracle, but the Vanishing Island is real."

"How would you know that?" Captain Arani asked. She managed to keep her words gentle, as though she were addressing a scared but dangerous animal. "When we found you floating on the wreckage of the *Godfall*, you said that a storm had destroyed the ship before it could get very far into the Forbidden Sea. Dax, Novachak, and I got the truth out of you later." She reached out and placed a cautious hand on Rori's shoulder. "Not one of us would have done any different, if we'd been in your position."

"But I lied," Rori said.

Arani frowned. "You didn't tear the *Godfall* apart?"

"I did," Rori said, "but we'd gone far into the Forbidden Sea by then, far enough to reach the Rend."

Captain Arani did not remove her hand, but then, she did not move much at all, not even to blink.

"I've seen the Vanishing Island," Rori said. "I swear to you, it's all real."

Her gaze wandered to the chain around Arani's neck. It had remained tucked inside the captain's shirt while they were on Spider's Nest, but Rori and everyone else from the crew knew that there were two black dragon scales hanging from its links, both taken from a living legend. The place Rori spoke of was more of a myth, or so she had believed until the *Godfall*'s crew had followed the signs nearly to the end.

And Rori had stopped them.

Memories of that day began to burn behind Rori's

eyes, and phantom feelings of raw, untethered power twisted through her blood. Her magic had responded to that place the way so many had tried to answer the sirens' call on the *Southern Echo*'s last voyage. It had been intoxicating and terrifying, and Rori had nearly broken herself in her desperation to get away. Now she was asking her captain to take her back, and she was even more scared than she'd been when the boots of Solkyrian navy sailors had thundered over the *Southern Echo*'s deck and their swords had cut through the crew.

But if this was what it took to keep the crew together and the *Southern Echo* sailing, Rori would take them to that island a hundred times over.

And maybe it would be better this time, if she went of her own free will, with a captain of her choosing and friends to help her through. And this time, no one would drown because of her, a monster with magic in her veins.

She could do this. She could save them.

"Rori," Arani finally said, clearly ready to do the sensible thing and refuse.

"I can get us there," Rori said before the captain could go any further. "Legend says you can ask for your heart's desire, and the gods will grant it to the worthy. We could get a treasure that even Mordanti would have envied."

That made the captain pause, which drew a disbelieving glance from the quartermaster.

"You're not actually considering this?" he asked.

Arani hesitated only a moment longer before shaking her head. "This is too much, Rori," she said, still using that gentle tone. "Even if by some miracle we convince Spider to give us enough provisions for a voyage like that, the Forbidden Sea is dangerous." A shadow came into the captain's eyes. "And I promised you I would never force you to use your magic again."

Rori shook her head. "I don't need my magic to find it. I know the signs. I'm probably the only living soul who's seen them firsthand." She looked between the captain and the quartermaster, surprised at her own desperation to make them believe her, but the cracks were widening, and Rori had to fix them before they swallowed her whole. "No one would follow us if we went into the Forbidden Sea. I'll lead us to the island, and we'll find a legend, and when we come back, you'll pay the crew and we won't fall apart."

There were tears in Rori's eyes by then. She hated that they were there, and she ferociously wiped them away. When she looked at Arani and Dax again, the quartermaster's gaze had softened, as though he had finally realized what Rori was really pushing for. He exchanged a slow glance with the captain.

"The crew would never vote for it," he said softly. "Even if they don't want to disband, they'll never vote to sail west."

"No," Arani agreed, and Rori's heart started to sink, until the captain said, "but there may be a solution to that." She pressed her lips into a thin line and looked at Rori again. "You know that, even if we agree to this, the crew may break regardless?" Her gazed clouded for a moment, and her sigh was somber. "Sometimes, things just run their course. You can't stop it, no matter how badly you may wish otherwise. If they want to leave, you have to let them go."

Rori hesitated, but even through her distress and desperation, she knew the captain was right. Not everyone would want to sail into the Forbidden Sea, no matter what kind of treasure was waiting at the other end of it, and Arani was not the kind of captain who would force her crew. The woman had ultimate authority on a hunt, but only because the crew gave it to her, when they voted to sail. If anyone was going to go with Rori into the Forbidden Sea, they had to do it of their own free will.

But maybe *that* would be the best thing of all. Because those who went would trust her, and they'd be willing to believe the truth.

"The right people will stay," Rori said.

Arani gave her a pitying look, and Dax crossed his arms over his broad chest.

"Don't promise yourself that," he said gravely. "You'll only end up disappointed."

Rori did not have a response to that, so she turned to the captain instead. "Will you propose this to the crew?"

The quartermaster looked to the captain, waiting.

Captain Arani frowned again, this time at the charts behind her. "Before I answer that," she said, "there's a lot that you need to tell me about your time aboard the *Godfall*." She settled her weight against the table, crossing her arms in a mirror of Dax's pose. "So talk."

Rori nodded. She steeled herself with a deep breath, and then she began to speak.

CHAPTER FIVE

The Cleaving of the Crew

DESPITE HIS FRIENDS' BEST efforts, Nate spent the night with his eyes wide open and his pulse jumping at the smallest of sounds. Luken was settled into his cupped hands and would peck at Nate's fingers if he startled too badly while holding the bird. Part of Nate wondered why Eric had insisted he hold the feathered demon-spawn, but everything felt worse if he did not have Luken's slight weight in his palms, the long pennant feathers of the bird's wings tickling his wrists. As the night wore on, Luken drifted in and out of sleep, and when the bird did not jolt awake at creaks and footsteps, Nate managed to bring his own panic under control.

Marcus and Eric stayed with him, although both Darkbends eventually nodded off. Nate did not blame them. He was exhausted himself, but every time he shut his eyes, he felt rope around his neck, and then he'd jerk awake and Luken would deliver a sharp jab to his fingers.

Rori did not come back for Luken. That did not worry Nate until it occurred to him that, as the navigator, Rori was just as much of a target as Nate was, especially if he was the only one under guard. He thought about going out to look for her, but the shadows of night were thick and heavy across the ship.

I couldn't do anything if she was in trouble, anyway, Nate thought, ashamed. *I couldn't even protect myself.*

If Xander had not saved him...

It should have been comforting, to think that the Grayvoice had cared enough to help, but Nate kept remembering Xander's scornful glance. He thought Nate weak, and he was right.

Nate may have helped the *Southern Echo* escape from the navy, but he'd be a fool not to recognize that the victory had relied almost entirely on luck and surprise. If he had to fight again, *when* he had to fight again, it would likely go the way of his battle against the *Gryphon* sailors, and there very well might not be anyone to save him then.

Nate wore the night away with that thought circling in his head. Under it, he squirmed and worried and agitated Luken enough to send the bird flapping over to Eric's shoulder, which was a much quieter roost. By the time dawn came and the ship's bells rang out, echoed by the other ships anchored in the harbor, there were dark circles under Nate's eyes and he'd gnawed his lower lip bloody.

But with the rising sun came Captain Arani and quartermaster Dax with Rori in tow.

All three of them looked as exhausted as Nate felt, but their eyes were bright, and Rori actually smiled a little as Luken flew to her shoulder and settled into his usual place. It was brief, and the light fled her face almost as quickly as it had come, but Nate felt his heart lift. He should have known that Arani never would have embraced defeat so easily; that Dax was too steady and dependable to allow one crisis to throw them into chaos; that Rori was clever and strong and would guide them all as sure as the stars. Nate felt a sharp stab of guilt for letting his fear lock him in place while those three had spent the night coming up with a plan, but that fear was receding as the sun rose, and Nate swore then and there to never fall into inaction again.

I'll get stronger, Nate promised himself. *For them.*

As soon as Arani had set foot on the main deck, she called for all hands to assist with stocking the ship for the next voyage, which was to be followed immediately by a full meeting of the crew aboard the *Southern Echo*. "If you have any lingering business on Spider's Nest," the captain informed everyone present on the ship, "see that you finish it before noon. Anyone not on the ship by that bell will be considered self-removed from the crew." A murmur went up at this, and Arani held up her hand. "I know it's not a lot of time, but you'd all do well to remember that this was never meant to be an extended stay." Her gaze narrowed, becoming that sharp, cutting glance that preceded her real anger. "You also would have had more time here if you'd been able to keep a certain secret."

Nate wasn't the only one who turned to look at Jim Greenroot. The bespectacled gunner was huddled miserably near the mainmast. From the looks of him, Greenroot hadn't slept much the previous night, either, but Nate felt no sympathy for the man. Instead, Nate was glad to see Greenroot flush and duck his head as the crew's attention focused on him.

"And *I'll* remind you," the deep voice of the quartermaster boomed out, "that none of you so much as lifted a finger to stop that secret from spilling last night. There's a lot of blame to be had here; not all of it falls on one man's shoulders."

Nate wasn't sure he believed that, and from the looks he caught across the ship, neither did a good part of the crew, Captain Arani and Rori included. But Dax's point managed to stand, and no one so much as muttered a word as they turned away from Greenroot.

The morning meeting broke into a swarm of confusion as people jostled for places on the rowboats waiting to take them back to shore. The Darkbends both went, Marcus to help with the gathering and loading of the supplies and Eric to assist the master carpenter with final assessments and repairs to the ship. Nate moved to secure himself a spot on the next boat, determined to help the others get the *Southern Echo* ready for her next voyage, but his gaze caught on the bright sand of the beach and the people walking across it. In spite of his promise to himself only minutes ago, Nate's toes curled in his boots as he swallowed a fresh bit of blood from his lip.

"I know you had your heart set on making bad decisions and getting into all sorts of trouble on that frost-touched island," said a gruff voice from over Nate's shoulder, "but unfortunately for you, I've got use for you here on the ship, and I won't be letting you out of my sight."

Nate turned to Novachak, and could not keep the relief out of his expression.

The boatswain's wind-weathered face was creased into a stern frown, but his icy blue eyes had thawed under knowing sympathy. "Don't thank me, you'll be bored out of your thick skull soon enough." He waved a hand, and Nate followed him down to the hold.

Novachak and Nate started by moving the few crates and barrels that had remained on the ship before the boatswain pointed out where the new supplies would go, and how they were to be arranged. "We'll make the strong ones do all the lifting," Novachak said, "but we'll check everything they bring aboard, and make sure they go to the right places. A tidy hold is the one thing the captain, quartermaster, and I can all agree on, and the cook likes it when the potatoes aren't stored next to the gunpowder."

"Does that improve the flavor?" Nate asked absently.

"No, but one incident of exploding potatoes was enough for everyone." The boatswain shrugged. "Personally, I thought that particular meal was one of the best the cook has ever produced, but the frying method is a bit too dangerous for a small galley on a wooden ship. So that's one reason the gunpowder stays far away from everything else, and why we're going to check those particular casks three times over."

Nate quirked a small smile, but it twisted into a grimace. "Is there ever a time when there isn't any trouble?" he asked. "Even just a day, when everything goes right and you don't have to worry about anything?"

Novachak did not say anything for a long moment. "Not when you're a pirate," he finally murmured.

Nate released a hard breath and drew himself up. "I need to get stronger," he said.

The boatswain paused and fixed him with a quizzical frown.

"I've been part of this crew for months," Nate said, "but I spent most of that time training my Skill. I can barely fight. I want to change that, so that the next time I'm in a bad spot, I can defend myself."

Novachak raised one bushy eyebrow. "You say that like you're planning on getting into trouble. Have Marcus and Eric already corrupted you that much?"

Nate gestured at the pale blue Lowwind tattoo over his brow by way of answer.

"Ah," Novachak said. He studied Nate critically for a long moment. "I suppose it's not the worst idea I've ever heard."

"Will you help me, then?" Nate asked, hope rising in his chest. "Anything you can teach me, *anything*, I'm ready to learn."

The boatswain made a thoughtful noise. "You are in sore need of practice with a sword," he remarked. "And we could see about putting some more muscle on those bones."

Nate nodded eagerly. "Thank you, sir," he said. "When can we start?"

Novachak chuckled as he leaned against the wall. "Right now." He gestured into a corner of the hold. "Go get that barrel. No, don't roll it, *lift* it. And use your legs, new blood, not your back."

The morning passed at a steady pace, Nate bringing Novachak every crate, barrel, and cask that came on to the *Southern Echo* to open and examine before sliding them into their proper places. It would have been much easier to do the inspection ashore, but no one made the suggestion. Anyone who looked like they were so much as thinking about it earned a glower from Novachak, and then they quickly ducked their head and went back to work. For Nate, that meant more lifting and pushing than he'd ever done before. By the time they were finished confirming that all of the supplies were accounted for and stored away, Nate's muscles were burning from the effort. Worst of all, his back and shoulders were aching from so much bending and reaching, even Marcus took pity on him.

"I had to help carry heavy cargo to the beach and then row it to the ship and haul it up, and Eric tried to patch the hull in record time without losing one of his fingers in the process, which he only barely managed—" this earned a grunt from Eric, who had a fresh bandage wrapped around his left thumb, "—but somehow, I think you had the worst time of us all."

Nate groaned and rubbed his knuckles against his spine, trying and failing to chase the pain out of his back. "Novachak said he'd help me get stronger, but I think he enjoyed that a little too much." His back creaked under his hands. "Word to the wise," he advised the Darkbends, "if Novachak ever says he has a special assignment for you, just throw yourself overboard and start swimming."

Eric chuckled darkly and Marcus flashed him a broad grin.

"We could have told you that long before today," Marcus said. "At least it's all done." He winced before turning to Eric. "Well, on our end. How much longer before the ship is fully repaired?"

The taller Darkbend frowned at his bandaged hand. "We're finished," he said. The words were slow, as though he were confused by them.

"Devastating news, to be sure," Marcus quipped. He reached over and gave Eric's shoulder a light shove. "You don't have to risk your fingers or cover yourself in sawdust for the foreseeable future. Why aren't you happy?"

Eric's frown did not lighten. "Six days ago, Whitebranch said we'd need a full week to repair the ship. Three days ago, when we went to confirm the measurements, we found that we'd somehow taken them all wrong. We both thought that was odd, but the good news was we'd need less wood and less time for the repairs. Yesterday, the measurements were wrong again, and it only took the better part of the day for us to repair the worst of the damage." He turned his frown from his hand to the railing of the *Southern Echo*. "It's as if the ship was repairing itself."

Nate and Marcus exchanged a glance.

"Did you maybe get a little too much sun yesterday?" Marcus asked.

"I'm serious," Eric said. "Some of the holes were completely gone, like they were never even there, and the big ones had all shrunk. I've never seen anything like it before."

Nate wasn't sure if he was concerned about Eric's perception of reality, or if there was something to the story. He remembered two nights ago, when he'd lain on the deck and pretended he could feel the presence of a spirit in the wood. "Maybe it's that dryad," Nate suggested, only half-joking. "There's supposed to be one fused with the ship, right?"

"That's what the captain and the quartermaster say," Eric said, "but that's just a story to go with the figure-head."

It was Nate's turn to frown. "Dax seemed pretty convinced it was real," he said.

"It's not," Eric insisted. "If it was, then we would have seen something by now to confirm it."

"Like the ship repairing itself?" Nate asked.

Eric hesitated, and then shook his head. "The *Southern Echo* has been damaged before, and nothing like this ever happened." He squinted thoughtfully up at the sky. "Maybe having the dragon aboard did something. It's a creature of pure magic, right?"

"Maybe," Nate said, although that did not seem right to him. Aside from leaving behind a few loose scales, the dragon had not done anything to the ship, except take an extended nap on the main deck.

"Maybe it was the navy fight," Marcus suggested. "All that blood spilled and soaked into the wood. Maybe the dryad drank it."

"That's stupid," Eric snapped, "and disgusting, and shut up before you give me nightmares."

Nate managed a chuckle, glad to know that, whatever had happened to the ship, it wouldn't be long before the *Southern Echo* left the harbor. He glanced about the deck, taking in the agitated faces of the rest of the crew, and knew that he wasn't alone in those thoughts.

The full crew was gathered just before the sun reached the peak of its climb into the sky. As the bells rang out to announce the noon hour, everyone turned expectantly to the quarterdeck, where Captain Arani stood overlooking the crew. Dax was at her side once more, and so was Rori.

Nate hadn't seen much of the Goodtide that morning. She'd sequestered herself in the navigation room, and had only come out once to retrieve a map from the captain's cabin. He had not gotten a good look at her then, but seeing Rori now, Nate had the feeling that she had been working nonstop since the captain's announcement. There were dark smudges under her eyes just like Nate's, and there was a tired slump to her shoulders that even Luken's small weight exaggerated, posed as he was with one brilliant blue wing raised as he preened the feathers underneath. But despite her obvious exhaustion, there was an anxiousness about Rori, as though she could not wait to set sail, or maybe dreaded it. She stared out at the horizon and twisted a quill pen between her fingers, and did not notice when the feather broke in half in her hands. She went right on fiddling with it.

It was never a good sign when the navigator was nervous about the voyage, Nate knew, but he did not have long to dwell on the thought.

Arani raised her hand, almost unnecessarily, as very few people were still talking. "We have not had the kind of hunts I've promised you," the captain began. "It's not for lack of trying, as I think you all know. Certainly, you know that I'm often too stubborn to give up, even when my pursuits are at odds with what the rest of the world accepts as reality. Another crew might have voted such a captain out by now. I thank you for your faith in me."

A few grumbles went up at that, but they died quickly when heads turned to seek out the dissenters.

"I come before you now with a new journey in mind," Arani continued, "but before I tell you what that is, there are certain facts that you all should be aware of.

"First, I can't pay you for our last voyage." Her hand went up again, quelling the considerably louder rumble of discontent. "That should not be a surprise. You all know what I did to give us a chance at Mordanti's treasure, and what we decided regarding the black mimic. I won't apologize for that. As a crew, you voted with me on both counts."

A few people in the crowd shifted and exchanged dark looks, but no one spoke again.

"Second," Arani said, an odd note of resignation creeping into her voice, "the Solkyrian navy is looking for this ship. I don't know if it's the *Southern Echo* herself or my flag in particular that's caught their fancy, but either way, these waters are no longer safe for us."

More glances were exchanged across the crew, some resentful, others regretful but accepting.

The captain took a moment, and when she spoke again, her voice was once more clear and carrying. "Until yesterday, I intended for us to sail east, out of the Common Sea and into Votheinian waters. It would have been dangerous, but it was an open route for us. That is no longer the case. The exiled *Gryphon* will have gone east, as will anyone looking to chase us down the moment we're out of Spider's waters and out from under his protection.

"The *Gryphon* left the harbor yesterday," Arani continued, "and six other ships have since lifted their anchors and departed. None of them were stocked for an extended voyage of any sort, and Spider confirmed that there are no merchant ships nearby." Arani's voice was steady, but her gaze was grim. "The only prize around here worth taking is us. Those captains know that, just as they know that I intended to sail east. They'll be waiting for us, and Spider can't and won't do a thing to help us.

"The whole island knows that we found the black mimic, and whether we're ready for it or not, another crew is going to come for us. I doubt they'll be looking to forge an alliance. With the exception of the few among this crew who could safely navigate the Court of Sirens or track dragons, we're more likely to get steel through our hearts than invitations in our hands. Even then, there's no guarantee that those few would live to see the end. We cannot go east."

A few murmurs of agreement went up this time, and Nate's nerves eased a bit when he saw that even those who had voted against releasing the dragon were nodding.

"The south is closed to us because of the danger posed by the sirens, and the north belongs to the Solkyrian Empire. That leaves one last direction on the map. One that I myself am wary of, but that our navigator swears she'll see us safely through."

Nate felt a bubble of dread form in his gut. He had time to exchange one bewildered look with Eric and Marcus before Arani spoke again.

"Rori and I intend to lead this ship to the Vanishing Island."

A stunned silence fell as all eyes went to Rori, who still turned the broken pen in her hands, but had finally brought her gaze down to the crew. She met their stares with remarkable calm for someone who was sailing west, into the Forbidden Sea, where she'd destroyed a ship and nearly lost her life, all without the assistance of the deadly waterspouts and cyclones said to plague those waters, not to mention the monsters.

Nate waited for Rori or the captain or even the quartermaster to crack the tension with a smile, to say that they were only joking. It was the only logical next step. But they were all silent, and it slowly dawned on Nate that they were fatally serious.

That was pure insanity, and the crew erupted to let the three people on the quarterdeck know that.

Nate tried to catch Rori's attention, but his voice was lost among the shouts and curses. And yet, even over all of that, Arani managed to make herself heard.

"I know this is not what many of you would choose," she called out, "so I'll tell you this: if you wish for a new captain, I will not stand in your way." That brought a fresh wave of stunned quiet over the ship. The captain did not once flinch from anyone's gaze. "You are free men and women," she said, "and you may do with your lives as you see fit. But know that even if you vote me out now, I will not give up the *Southern Echo*. This ship and all that choose to remain with her will be sailing west. You may leave, you may stay, you may even challenge me if you so desire, but no matter our history, no matter who you are, you will need to fight me for this ship, and you had better be prepared to kill me, because I'll only let her go in death."

At Arani's shoulder, Dax shut his eyes, and for a moment looked much older than his thirty-odd years. When he opened them again, he gazed sidelong at the captain, but he did not move to interrupt her.

"If I must sail without a crew for the rest of my days," Arani said, "then I will. Take yourself, take your fellows, forge a new crew or join another. I'll hold no ill will against you for that. I understand what I am asking of you now, and I will not rob you of your choice as I did before." For a fleeting moment, Arani looked ashamed. Then her hand went to the saber at her hip.

"But know that if you try to come for this ship, I will meet you with my sword drawn."

Silence reigned in the wake of those words. Nate felt the intake of anticipated breath as everyone waited to see if anyone would step forward to challenge Arani. Several people looked to Dax, but the quartermaster had his eyes turned to the sky now.

All around Nate, his own confusion and fear was mirrored in others' faces. Even Novachak stood with his mouth open and his gaze frozen on Arani. Part of Nate wanted to laugh at the absurdity of it all. There was nothing in the Forbidden Sea but monsters and madness, and he could not believe that Arani, that *Rori*, would ever willingly sail into it.

But Arani had taken them on a dragon hunt, and had already shown them where one legend lived. Who was to say she couldn't do it again?

"You have one hour to decide if you will stay aboard the *Southern Echo,* or make your own way forward," Arani said into the stunned silence. "Anyone who wishes to leave will be seen safely back to shore." Her grip on her sword tightened. "If you mean to challenge me, do it before the hour is up. I'll go with you to the beach and fight you there if you desire, or we can settle the matter here on the ship, but I'd prefer not to re-stain the decks with blood so soon."

Nate could not help but drop his gaze to the boards below his feet. The rusty patches had long since been scrubbed away, but there were places on the deck that still seemed darker and redder than the rest. He remembered Marcus's joking suggestion about the dryad and the spilled blood of the dead, and shifted uneasily on his feet. He heard both Darkbends do the same beside him.

"One hour," Arani said. She reached into her coat pocket and withdrew a small hourglass. She flipped it, and placed it on the railing of the quarterdeck so all could see the fine white sand begin to run. "Make your choice." Then she turned and climbed up the last few steps to the poop deck, where she settled in to watch the crew and meet any challengers who dared come for her.

One of the crew's few Veritian sailors that had survived the navy attack was the first to break the stunned silence. He called up to Arani, asking if she was serious, a high edge of panic cutting into his voice. When the captain only looked placidly back at him and nodded once, his skin paled to a nauseous olive-yellow, and then Nate lost track of the Veritian as people began to move.

There were shouts of Arani going mad underscored by creative curses on her and her entire bloodline, but those were followed by howls of protest and insistence that the captain would never really lead them into danger like this, never mind that they had just come from a dragon hunt. Nate tried to stay out of the way of what looked to be several fights brewing, but the chaos pulled him away from Marcus and Eric. He lost sight of his friends as the crew seethed and turned their shouts on each other rather than the captain, and his memory flashed to the very first day he'd met the sailors of the *Southern Echo*, when he'd accidentally wandered into a duel. That day, he'd been awestruck by the absolute unification of the pirate crew behind their captain. Now, he watched as that same crew began to tear itself apart.

Most people did not want to go into the Forbidden Sea, and Nate did not blame them. To his shock, however, he came across a few sailors who had thoughtful frowns on their faces and the same gleam in their eyes that they'd had on the dragon hunt.

"They say some real treasures came from the west,"

one of the swabs murmured to Kai the cabin boy.

"Hundreds of years ago," Kai shot back, his face twisted in disgust, "if you even believe those old stories."

"We all believe in the Thief's dragon now," the female swab returned. "Why not the stories of the Rend? Maybe the emperor's crown really *did* come from the Vanishing Island."

"You'd go into the Forbidden Sea for a crown?" Kai asked, visibly stunned.

"It's a *really* nice crown," the swab said.

"Aye," one of the riggers cut in, "said to be made of sunlight, and gifted to the first emperor from the gods themselves. And before that, the Silver Fleet and its haul of rubies, and before that was Captain Bartholomew and the Sword of Judgement."

"And four of his five ships sank trying to get that sword, and half his crew died!" Kai snapped.

The rigger shrugged. "But he got it, in the end, and he didn't have any Skilled in his crew. What do you think *we'll* find?"

Kai shook his head and stalked off, leaving the swab and the rigger to their dangerous fantasies. It wasn't long before someone else joined them, and then they were all under a loud, verbal attack from one of the gun crews that doubted the gods even existed at all, let alone kept an island flickering on the boundary between their realm and the mortal world.

But the louder the shouting matches grew, the more the crew divided itself, and the more the supporters' arguments took on a fevered pitch, fueled by faith founded on their finding of Mordanti's dragon as well as their own unshakeable religion, which said the gods still looked with favor upon mortals who could prove themselves worthy. It wasn't hard to imagine the crew coming to blows over this.

With his heart thudding loudly in his ears, Nate skirted around the worst of the fighting, trying to find Eric or Marcus again. He saw Jim Greenroot and AnnaMarie Blueshore arguing with their respective gun crews behind them, and Kai and the other two cabin boys looking mystified as the chaos unfolded around them, and Xander watching one of the riggers with cold calculation as she tried to gather the courage to go up the steps and challenge Captain Arani.

Up on the quarterdeck, Rori regarded the commotion with a bleak expression, but she hung back and kept on twisting the broken quill in her hands.

A few paces away from her, Dax leaned over the railing and spoke with Novachak. The quartermaster was stoically calm, but the back of the boatswain's neck had gone even redder than its usual sunburned color. Abruptly, Novachak made a violent gesture, to which Dax shook his head. The boatswain snarled something that made the quartermaster frown, and then Novachak turned on his heel and stormed towards the steps that would take him down into the ship. Nate had never seen the man look so angry.

Desperately, Nate cast about for his friends once more, and finally spied them at the port railing near the bow. Nate hurried over to them, but his steps slowed when he saw their faces. Neither of the Darkbends were speaking, but Nate knew what they were thinking long before he stood in front of them. They both looked at him with sad, scared eyes.

"You're leaving?" Nate asked.

Marcus and Eric exchanged a glance.

"This ship has been good to us," Marcus said, just slowly enough for hope to surge in Nate's chest. "But the Forbidden Sea... I can't." He gave Nate a bleak look, and the hope died. "Who could?"

"Arani, apparently," Eric said, "and Dax and Rori,

which is what I don't understand. I could see one of them going mad enough to suggest this, but for the other two to agree with it?" He shifted uneasily against the ship's railing. "It's just an elaborate form of suicide."

Nate shook his head vehemently. "You know Rori wouldn't do that," he said. "She's fought too hard for her own life. And I don't think Arani or Dax would throw theirs away, either. Not after everything we've been through. I don't know what they're really planning, but it can't be so simple as us going west."

Marcus did not say anything, but Eric had caught the "we" and the "us" that Nate had reflexively slipped in.

"You're staying, then?" the taller Darkbend asked.

Nate hesitated, not sure if he was surprised by the question, or the answer that presented itself so readily. "There's nowhere else for me to go," he said.

"That's a lie, and you know it," Eric said, but there was no malice in the words. "No one else in the world can read the wind like you. Even if you don't want to go after the dragon again, you could find a captain who would love to make use of that kind of Skill." When Nate did not respond, Eric gave him a lopsided smile that did not manage to detract from the elegance of his features, or the graceful sweep of his Darkbend tattoo. "You have options, Nate. You know that."

Eric wasn't wrong, but he wasn't right, either. If Nate left, the entire world would only ever see the Lowwind mark on his brow, and demand his service and his magic. His memory flashed to when Rori had stood before Nate and the others on a starlit night with a sleeping dragon chained to the ship's deck and said that, because of the magic in their blood, she and Nate would never be safe. Deep down, Nate had known that she'd been right, but he had not expected to have to admit that to himself so soon. But maybe if he could find a captain who at least let him work his Skill on his own terms...

Well, that had been Captain Arani. Nate doubted that he'd ever find someone else like her.

He recalled the way the other crews had looked at him in the tavern the other night. Phantom ropes coiled around his neck and arms, reminding him of his own weakness and inability to protect himself. How would he ever grow stronger, if the place he felt safest fell apart?

"What about you?" Nate asked, trying to deflect away from his own squirming unease. "What are *your* options? Your Skills aren't—" He cut off the rest of the thought before he said something he would immediately and forever regret, but Marcus bristled all the same, and Eric stared at him coolly.

"I've learned carpentry," Eric said. He nodded towards Marcus. "He plays the fiddle, and he's actually very good at it. Those are valuable skills to anyone, even if they're not magic."

Marcus's rising anger gave way to discomfort, and Nate remembered what the stout Darkbend had said about why he could play the instrument to begin with. Imperial instructors had taught him, to make him attractive to Solkyrian nobles when his plainer looks would fail. Eric had been given no such tutoring. He was handsome enough that the empire had not felt that he needed to supplement his appearance. Prospective buyers would have wanted him just as he was.

Nate flushed with shame for forgetting that, even for a moment. Marcus and Eric were his best friends, but he kept losing sight of them when his own problems reared up.

"I didn't—" Nate began, but abandoned the attempt to explain. "I'm sorry," he said instead. He looked between the two Darkbends, wishing he could protect them too, and felt a deep well of sorrow open in his chest. "I don't want either of you to go," he said. "I know that's selfish, but..." He shrugged, unsure of what words, if any, could follow.

Marcus's expression softened. "You're really going to stay with Arani?" he asked.

Nate drew in a breath and glanced about the ship, taking in the fall of the rigging lines and the furled canvas sails that would swell so proudly with a good wind behind them. The deck was warm and sturdy beneath his boots, and every curve and corner of the ship had become as familiar to him as his own body. Against all odds, Nate had found a home somewhere between the edges of the life he'd left in Solkyria and the new one he'd begun to forge under a black flag. A flag that belonged to a captain who was currently watching her crew seethe and dissolve, but who also made no move to stop anyone from making their own choices.

Nate turned his gaze back to his friends. "Captain Arani was the first person who saw something in me when the rest of the world only saw the Nowind," he said. "She wanted to use my Skill, but she also gave me hope, and then she gave me my life back, and the chance to live it how I want. I'm going to take that chance, and I want to do it on the ship that's become my home." He offered the two Darkbends a sad smile. "Even if that means that I have to say goodbye to my friends, when they make their own choices for their own lives."

Marcus gave Nate a long look, his thoughts visibly churning in his head.

Eric sighed. "But Nate, the Forbidden Sea..." He cast a bleak look to the quarterdeck, where the hourglass tracked the unstoppable. Abruptly, Eric pushed away from the railing. "I can't," he murmured as he walked away.

Nate watched him go, but before the sadness could fully bloom in his heart, Marcus's hand closed on his shoulder.

"I'll talk to him," Marcus said.

Nate nodded. "At least tell him I'd like to say a proper goodbye. And to you, too, if you decide to leave. Please don't go without that."

Marcus bumped his fist lightly against Nate's arm, and then followed Eric.

By then, the shouting had subsided across the ship, but there was no sense of calm. A few people were already coming up from the berth with their possessions in tow, and those that had not gone down to collect their things were either arguing at a lower volume, or staring out to sea with torn, anguished expressions. These were the people that Nate knew had been on the *Southern Echo* the longest, and were weighing their loyalty to Arani and their faith in the old stories against their fears. A few of them broke away from the horizon to join the small crowd gathering around Dax, who had come down from the quarterdeck to answer questions and hear grievances. Arani was still on the poop deck, unmoving and unchallenged. And Rori had finally discarded the broken quill in favor of absently petting Luken as she watched everything unfold. Several people threw her uneasy looks, but no one approached her, and it was easy for Nate to get to her side. Luken chirped a greeting, and Rori tilted her head to listen, but she did not take her eyes off of the people moving across the main deck.

"Are you all right?" Nate asked.

"Why wouldn't I be?"

Nate flicked a glance up at the captain, but her attention was locked on the crew. He still kept his voice low when he said, "Because Arani wants to sail into the Forbidden Sea, and she said you'd be leading the way."

Rori nodded.

Nate studied her for a long moment. She was tense and clearly nervous, but she wasn't screaming or trying to stab Arani with her sword, both of which Nate would have considered perfectly reasonable given the current situation. "You're disturbingly calm right now," he said. "It's scaring me."

Rori quirked a small, dry smile. "It shouldn't. Going into the Forbidden Sea was my idea."

The shock of that statement actually pushed Nate back a step. "Gods below, why would you want to do that?" He did not mention the *Godfall* or the things she'd told him of her past, but he knew she understood the question perfectly.

"I couldn't let the crew fall apart," she said with a shrug.

Nate looked out over the arguments and anger and despair that had gripped the ship, threaded through by wild hope that was becoming almost fanatical. "It doesn't look like it's staying together."

Rori shook her head, idly running her fingers along Luken's back. "The right ones will stay. That's better than nothing."

"I'm not so sure about that," Nate murmured.

Finally, Rori turned to him, and he saw how exhausted she looked. "After the *Gryphon* attacked, Captain Arani didn't know what to do," Rori said with a strained edge in her voice. "She was getting ready to dissolve the crew. There was no other choice."

"That can't be true," Nate said.

"You weren't there," Rori returned. She looked out over the ship again, and Nate wondered if she meant in the meeting with the captain, or on the *Godfall*.

"Do you remember when you told me not to lose myself in my Skill?" he asked after a moment.

"This isn't the same thing," Rori said curtly.

"I think it is," Nate said.

She blinked and opened her mouth to say something, only to close it again without a word.

Nate had spent so long convinced that he had to give his life in service to others. Rori hadn't, but Nate recognized in her the same desperate, wild drive that had caused him to plunge himself into the wind, and nearly let it untether him from his life. Rori may have insisted that this was different, but the danger was the same, and Nate could not stand the thought of her collapsing under the traumas of her past in the name of an uncertain future.

But he also knew that he wouldn't be able to talk her out of trying.

He'd have to watch out for her, just as she had for him on the dragon hunt.

"Promise me you'll be careful?" Nate asked.

"I'll be all right."

"That's not what I asked."

Rori huffed a sigh, but the smile she gave him this time was a bit more genuine. "I promise."

"I'm not leaving, you know, so I'll be here to yell at you if it turns out you're lying."

She breathed out a soft laugh and dropped her hand away from Luken. "I'm glad," she said, and then her fingers brushed against Nate's for a moment. She pulled away before he could wonder if that had been an accident or not, but then an argument by the foremast escalated into shouting again, and there were other things to worry about.

As the promised hour drew to a close, more than half of the crew waited by the railing, packs and small chests filled with possessions held in their arms. Novachak reappeared then, a heavy bag slung over his shoulder and his footsteps slow as he made his way to the railing. He kept his eyes on the deck as he went, and Nate felt his heart give a cold, tight squeeze. From the looks on their faces, Dax and Arani felt much the same way, but neither of them moved to stop the boatswain.

Nate, however, couldn't stop himself from taking a few steps after the man.

Novachak looked up at the sound of his footsteps. His gaze skimmed over Nate, taking in his distinct lack of a traveling pack, and his icy eyes went even colder. "Better find someone else to teach you how to fight, new blood," Novachak told him gravely. "You'll need it, where you're going."

Then Novachak stepped over the railing, and began to descend the ladder to the boat waiting in the water. He glanced up one last time, at the flag flying off the stern of the *Southern Echo*, and then grit his teeth and disappeared from sight. The rest began to follow, and Nate shrank away from the press of bodies.

Many of the people leaving looked darkly at Arani and Dax and even Rori as they departed the *Southern Echo* for the last time, but everything had already been said, and minds were made up.

Among those leaving were master carpenter Tim Whitebranch, an entire gun crew, and Davy the rigger, who had been quiet and withdrawn after his cohort Ethan had bled out following the navy fight. Nate did not have any particularly strong ties to any of them, but he was a little sad to see young Kai and another cabin boy waiting for their turn to head back to Spider's Nest.

More importantly, and to Nate's immense relief, both Marcus and Eric had decided to stay. Eric did not look particularly happy about the decision, but Marcus leaned in and whispered, "He thought about what you said about Captain Arani for a long time, and he's not ready to walk away from someone like that, either." Then the stout Darkbend grinned. "Plus, with Whitebranch leaving, he's up for a nice promotion."

Nate clasped his friends' arms and tried not to look like he'd been personally blessed by the gods above. Marcus answered by slinging his arm around Nate's neck and jostling him affectionately. Eric did not smile, but he did promise Nate that he'd be around to see what kind of fresh stupidity the crew threw themselves into.

It surprised Nate, in the end, to see who else stayed. For one, there was AnnaMarie Blueshore, who'd taken up a lounging position against one of the cannons on the main deck at the start of the chaotic hour, crossed her muscled arms, and not moved since, even when her own gun crew had begged her to change her mind.

"I've sailed with three captains," AnnaMarie had said at one point. "Arani has been the best, and she hasn't led me astray yet. I think she's mad, but a little madness makes for a more eventful life."

"She's going to get you killed," one of her underlings had growled back at her.

"So could every other captain," AnnaMarie had said. "At least with Arani, I know she'll show me something interesting before I die."

That had set a few more arguments into motion, by the end of which, two more gunners and most of their respective crews had decided to stay as well.

Looking over at the cluster of people around AnnaMarie and her chosen cannon, Nate nearly tripped when he saw Jim Greenroot. The bespectacled man did not look at all happy to be staying on the *Southern Echo*, and he threw one long, wistful glance at Spider's Nest before adopting his usual sour expression and turning away from the island with clear resentment and regret.

"Greenroot can't possibly be staying," Nate said.

"He has no prospects outside of this crew," Eric responded. "He's a decent enough gunner, but anyone can become decent enough if they practice. He has no special talents that would endear him to another crew, unless you count getting drunk and spilling your mates' secrets." A deep frown creased Eric's brow, its severity dampened by his white Darkbend tattoo. "He's lucky Arani hasn't keel-hauled him for that."

"Maybe she's waiting until we're out to sea," Marcus suggested.

Nate snorted. "If only."

That begged the question of what Arani did plan to do with Jim Greenroot. Nate could not imagine her letting that kind of a transgression go without punishment, although the act of carrying it out would have fallen to Novachak. Nate cast about for the boatswain, and felt a stab of pain in his heart as he reminded himself that Novachak had already gone over the railing, into a waiting rowboat. It was going to take a long time to get used to the ship without Nikolai Novachak aboard. Nate started to turn back to Marcus and Eric to say as much, but his attention caught on Xander.

The Grayvoice had taken up one of his favorite positions in the rigging, leaning back against the ropes with a loose one coiled almost carelessly around his arm as his one concession to the dangers of being up so high. Xander surveyed the crew like some bird of prey scouting out its next meal, and he clearly had no intention of leaving. Nate was bewildered by Xander's choice until he remembered something the Grayvoice had said on their last voyage, about how he'd follow Captain Arani to the end of the world if she'd caught the trail of a legendary treasure. It seemed he was making good on that promise once more.

If the legends held true, and if the *Southern Echo* could safely cross the Forbidden Sea and slip through the Rend into the realm of the gods, and if they were found worthy, they could be granted their heart's strongest desire. For Xander, that would easily be the weight in gold of an entire fleet of imperial men-of-war. There were a lot of *ifs* to overcome, but if anyone could lead them through the uncertainty to a legend, it would be Captain Arani and Rori Goodtide. It seemed Xander's faith was holding strong in them, too.

Maybe this was what the Grayvoice needed to finally put the dragon hunt behind him.

Either way, Xander's decision to stay had clearly influenced the riggers, as more than half of them chose to remain with the *Southern Echo*. Nate was relieved to see that, as he would not have been able to make up for their absence with his magic, and the whole ship would have suffered under that level of imbalance.

He was glad, too, that no one had challenged Arani for ownership of the *Southern Echo*. Several people had thought about it, and then they had thought better of it. Nate had seen the woman duel firsthand, and while he had every confidence that she would have defeated each and every challenger, enough blood had already been spilled. All things considered, this was a surprisingly peaceful way for the crew to break.

It remained that way as the rowboats filled.

When the last person was over the railing, Captain Arani gave a heavy sigh, and turned to face those who had stayed. There was an uncomfortable amount of room on the *Southern Echo*'s deck now, and Nate couldn't help but shiver as the wind passed through all that empty space.

"Well," the captain said, her gaze sweeping quickly over her crew's thinned numbers, "you won't be getting nearly as much time to rest between your shifts, but we have enough sailors to see the *Southern Echo* through her next voyage. Dax will distribute work as fairly as he can, but be ready to be exhausted. That said, I thank you all for—"

She broke off when a gruff shout came from over the railing, followed by some muted words and a soft thump, and then someone came scrabbling up the side of the ship.

Nate took an involuntary step away from the railing, his ears filling with the scrapes and scuffles of the fight that had nearly seen him kidnapped from the *Southern Echo*, but his heart gave a joyful leap when Novachak's face popped over the railing. The rest of the boatswain clambered back on to the ship in a hurry, as though afraid he'd change his mind and go back down to the rowboat.

The boatswain swung heavily over the railing and landed on the deck. His face was set in a glower as he turned and headed to the stairs that led down into the berth, shooting everyone on the main deck a nasty look as he went, although he saved the worst one for Arani.

"Northern winds freeze you where you stand, Captain," he spat as he stepped past her, but he paused all the same when Arani gently touched his shoulder and murmured something to him. Nate saw the boatswain's expression soften for the briefest of moments before he secured the scowl once more and stalked off to reclaim his hammock.

Novachak was the only one who came back.

When the rowboats had gone to shore and returned, the anchor had been lifted, and the sails were in place, the *Southern Echo* left the harbor. With nothing between the ship and the horizon but the open sea, Arani addressed the crew once more. This time, Novachak stood a few steps off to her right, and though the boatswain still glared daggers at her, Arani's smile was genuinely happy.

"As I was saying earlier," she said, her voice rough with emotion but still strong and steady over the rush of the wind, "I thank you all for staying. It's a brave thing you do, sailing into the Forbidden Sea, but even braver is your willingness to trust me. I swear to you, it has not been misplaced. Now that we've left the harbor, there's something more I can tell you.

"We will be sailing west, yes, but only for one month. Those who left us today will take back to Spider's Nest the story of us sailing off to seek the Vanishing Island, and that one month will allow that story to fester and grow in our wake. That alone should be enough to scare off anyone who has thought of coming after us and free up the eastern waters, but we go west for more than simply keeping up appearances."

The captain paused, and Nate was surprised to see her take a deep breath, as though she needed to steady herself for what she was about to say next. In that silence, Rori stepped up next to her and gave Arani a solemn nod. In spite of his trust in his friend, Nate felt a curl of unease deep in his gut.

"I want you all to know that there will be a vote to determine whether or not we turn around and head into Votheinian waters. I will not try to sway your decision when the time comes, and it will not matter what we have or have not seen, nor what has or has not happened. The vote will come after one month on the Forbidden Sea. That is all I will ask of you, and it is what I've promised our navigator. No more, but no less, because there is one more piece to this that she will now explain." The captain stepped back then, and it seemed to Nate that she did so reluctantly.

Rori moved into the vacated space at the center of the quarterdeck, Luken a blaze of color on her shoulder. It took her a moment to speak, but when she did, her voice was calm and steady.

"The *Southern Echo* found me floating in the sea, clinging to a piece of wreckage from a ship called the *Godfall*. You all know this. Most of you were there when Captain Arani pulled me out of the water. A few of you thought that I was a siren come to lure you to your doom." Her mouth twisted into a wry smile. "But now you've seen sirens with your own eyes, and I think you know by now that I'm nothing like them."

No one laughed, but Nate did hear a few soft *hmm*s across the ship.

Rori licked her lips and continued. "You also know that the *Godfall* was sailing west when it was destroyed. Caught out by a bad storm that sank the ship and killed the crew, with me as the only survivor. What most of you don't know is that there was no storm, and I was the only survivor because I'm the one who tore the *Godfall* apart."

The murmurs were louder this time, and several people exchanged uneasy looks. Nate answered them with a glare. Rori had saved their lives in the navy attack as surely as he had, and the crew owed all of that to her and her Skill. They had no right to judge her for what she'd done with her magic earlier in her life.

"The *Godfall* was a very different ship from the *Southern Echo*," Rori pressed on, raising her voice to carry over everyone else's. "Not just in design, but in captain and in crew. When I was on the *Godfall*, I was beaten, and I was whipped, and I..." She faltered for a moment, and Nate dared anyone to so much as utter a syllable. He may not win the fight, but for Rori, he'd try. The whole crew was quiet, though, and Rori's next words carried clearly to everyone. "I was in chains. I didn't expect to survive. So when I saw my chance to destroy the *Godfall*, I took it. Gods above only know how the *Southern Echo* found me after that."

Behind Rori, Arani and Dax shared a brief glance, and Nate had the feeling that there was something that was being left unsaid.

Rori continued before anyone could question her. "As I'm sure you've guessed, the *Godfall* wasn't sailing into the Forbidden Sea on a whim. Its captain was searching for the Vanishing Island." Her eyes skimmed across the crew, touching even on Xander and Liliana up in the rigging before she said, "He found it."

The only sounds in the wake of that simple statement were the breath of the wind and the rustle of the sails. Even Nate's heart had fallen quiet, and he was vaguely aware that his mouth had dropped open as he stared up at Rori.

"The *Godfall* never made landfall," Rori said, suddenly speaking quickly as though she was afraid someone or something would stop her before she could finish. "But I saw the island with my own eyes, just as I saw the five signs that led us to it. Then I destroyed the *Godfall* before it got anywhere near the beach. I never intended to go back into the Forbidden Sea, but I'll do it now, for a captain and a crew of my own choosing, and I'll lead you to a treasure that makes the Thief's pale in comparison, and then I'll lead you safely home. I swear by my life and my family's name—gods above keep them close—that I, Aurora Redglade, will see you through." Her voice broke on the last syllable, and her final words came in a murmur that carried nonetheless. "Please trust me."

Silence answered her, until Arani stepped forward.

"If not her, then trust me," the captain said. "One month, and then no matter what, you will be the ones to decide if we continue on, or turn back." She drew a dagger from her belt and pressed the tip of the blade into her thumb. "This I swear, by my blood and my life." Arani turned and smeared her blood against the ship's wheel, leaving a scarlet oath for everyone to see. "What say you?" she called as she turned back to face the crew.

Nate did not know who was the first to call *aye*, but he quickly added his own voice to the subdued agreement, along with Marcus and all the people immediately around them, save for Eric. Nate looked at his friend, and Eric glanced away. He did not speak.

But it did not matter, for the *Southern Echo* was already turning west, her black flag snapping in the breeze.

CHAPTER SIX

Closed Doors

THE FIRST FEW DAYS of the voyage were uneventful, but with the crew's numbers cut so low, everyone was too busy to spend much time ruminating. Combined with the good eating of the early days of a voyage when the supplies were still fresh, that helped keep spirits higher than they might have been otherwise, even if everyone was exhausted by the end of their work shifts.

The ship caught a good tailwind that filled the sails and saw them swiftly out of the Coral Chain. They had to skirt further north than anyone would have liked to ensure that they completely avoided the territories of the western sirens, which put them within striking distance of Solkyria. Rori kept a constant vigil over the *Southern Echo*'s speeds and positions, never once letting them drift off of that fine line that passed safely between the Court of Sirens and Solkyrian naval patrols. Her vision was blurry after pouring over sea charts and calculations for so long every day, but as the *Southern Echo* slipped past the imperial island, her heart eased a little. The empire did not care about the sea where the sun set. No ships ever came out of the west. Not since the retrieval of the Sun Crown, if the legends were to be believed.

You saw the Vanishing Island with your own eyes, Rori reminded herself firmly. *There's no room for you to doubt the stories now.*

Especially not if she wanted to soothe the thought scratching at the back of her mind, telling her that there was more to all of this than even she remembered.

Rori had tried to bury that thought, but it kept worming its way back to the surface, powered by her own trepidation and her much, much stronger curiosity. She'd always wondered where her magic had come from, first with awe, and then with bitterness. Maybe there were answers in the Rend, along with absolution for what she'd done.

And, if she was brutally honest with herself, Rori had to admit that she wanted to see what kinds of treasures were worthy of legends. She knew the stories of the Sun Crown and the Flower of the Frozen North, and of course the stolen treasure of Mordanti the Thief, but this would be something new. Something entirely of and for the *Southern Echo* and her crew, and they wouldn't have to capture and drug a dragon to get it, or force the Skilled to nearly kill themselves with their magic, or face off against the warring navies of Solkyria and Vothein, or even flee from the black flags of the ships in Spider's harbor. All they had to do was sail off the edge of the map, and survive.

I've done it before, Rori thought, *and I will do it again. We all will.*

She was afraid to return to the Forbidden Sea and all of its dangers, to the Rend and its primal magic, to the Vanishing Island and all of its terrible promises. But she knew that she could guide the ship to that place, and she could think of no one more worthy of the gods' favor than Captain Arani, and when this was all over, Rori would get her own wish of keeping the crew—her family—together.

What was left of them.

Rori shook her head. She was still trying to accept how many people had left, and her heart was heavy with the loss, but the right ones really had stayed. They would be with her. Maybe not forever, but at least a little further into an open future.

Buoyed by the thought, Rori held her head high when she next stepped out of the navigation room, Solkyria firmly left behind in their wake.

Of course, that meant that the crew of the *Southern Echo* suddenly had nothing but the Forbidden Sea before them, and Rori's confidence wavered as she saw that even some of the supporters of the voyage were frowning at the horizon, their expressions clouded with second thoughts. She offered encouraging smiles to anyone who would look her way as she walked across the deck, but while a few returned them earnestly, their eyes sparkling with excitement, many of the others either dropped their gazes, or pointedly turned away.

Rori's ears caught the murmurs not long after that. The excited ones spoke dreamily of rubies as large and dark as a gryphon's heart and ships with sails made of silver and other wonders, certain that endless riches awaited them. The rest tracked the sun's progress through the sky and muttered to each other, "Less than one month now."

They were counting the days, Rori realized, like they were bits of glass with jagged edges, waiting to cut the first person who handled them too carelessly. And when they looked at her, they saw the fool who had broken the glass to begin with.

Fool was better than monster, but how long until those expressions changed? How long until they looked at her the way the people from her village had, that night the world had shattered and the enforcers had taken her away?

Rori had the feeling that her presence would only accelerate the shift, so she retreated back to the navigation room, and settled in to wait.

She fully expected people to come and ask her about the signs of the Vanishing Island, and she was prepared to answer all of their questions. Captain Arani had said that there was no room for secrets on this voyage, and Rori agreed. She gathered herself to tell them everything.

What she was not prepared for, however, was for Eric Darkbend to be the first, or for the violence of his fury. He came with the intensity of a rogue wave, slamming open the door to the navigation room and blasting her with disapproval so sharp, it should have drawn blood.

"Did you lose your mind somewhere in the Common Sea," he barked the moment he'd stepped inside the navigation room, "or are you actually a very well-disguised siren trying to take us all to our deaths?"

Rori was startled enough by his entrance to upset a pot of ink on the table, although she managed to right it before more than a small black smudge was left on the lower corner of a sea chart. She dabbed at the spilled ink with a rag and answered Eric calmly. "I addressed that very question already."

"I think you lied."

Rori faced him, frowning as she realized that he was genuinely angry. "About being a siren," she asked, "or seeing the Vanishing Island?"

"About leading us safely through," he snapped.

"I'm going to do my best," she said.

"That's what I'm afraid of."

At a corner of the table, nestled in the battered hat he'd pilfered from Nate, Luken gave a soft chirp, the same uneasy note the bird used when he knew that a storm was coming.

"I would never do anything to harm this ship or its crew," Rori said quietly.

Eric's hands were balled into fists at his sides, but he did not raise his voice. "Haven't you already?"

"*Never*," she said again.

"Then give up this pursuit of the Vanishing Island."

"Captain Arani promised me a month to—"

"Gods below, you're going to lead us all to our deaths before a month is up."

The words stung worse than if he'd slapped her.

"Do you have so little faith in me, Eric?" Rori asked softly.

Eric shut his eyes and breathed a hard sigh through his teeth. "I have every faith that you're going to find exactly what you're looking for, and that's what terrifies me. Out of all those stories about the treasures that came from the Vanishing Island, there isn't one where everyone comes home safely. Sacrifices have to be made. Someone always suffers for the grandest treasures."

"That's not true," Rori protested.

"Yes, it is," Eric insisted. "You ever see *The Ballad of the Sun Crown* performed?" When she shook her head, he recited, "'And lo, when the sunlit favor of the gods was placed upon the emperor's brow, it shone forth with such brilliant purity his wife and eldest child did weep and die, so moved were they by the light, their hearts did overfill and burst with serenity and joy.'" Eric scrubbed a hand over his face, suddenly looking exhausted. "They made me recite that thing so many times at the light bending academy. You hear it enough, you speak the words enough, you start to catch all of the pieces in between the wonder and the reverence.

"In that story, the emperor got his godly crown, but

the queen and the heir to the throne both perished for it. It's such a strange part of this epic, triumphant tale. Why is it there? Why did they really die, if the story is true?"

Rori hesitated, unsure how to answer him. She wracked her brain, trying to remember the full story, but she hadn't studied it nearly as much as Eric had, if he could recite pieces on a whim. She did not remember anyone dying in *The Ballad of the Sun Crown*, but then, she'd been more interested in concrete history during her time at school, and she hadn't paid that story or the ones like it much mind until she'd seen the Vanishing Island with her own eyes. Even then, she hadn't had much time or motivation to seek out texts on the matter. Maybe she should have.

Maybe this was all a terrible mistake.

You paid the blood price, Rori thought. *The gods accepted the sacrifice.*

That was the last secret she was keeping, the one of the whispers in her ears after she'd destroyed the *Godfall* and drowned the crew. The one where something not of this world had gleefully said the blood price had been paid. Rori had tried to swim as far and as fast as possible away from that island, but she'd been exhausted from magic use, and she'd only made it to a floating piece of wood with *Godfall* painted across its surface in curling, black letters. It had been difficult to read under that red sky, but Rori would never forget the sharp pain of splinters in her hand and the sting of salt water in her eyes as a current came and carried her away, the pleased voice in her head fading but promising that the price had been paid, and she was welcome on the island's shores whenever she saw fit to return.

And now she was going back to that place, trusting that her payment was still good. There were only the lives of everyone left in the world that she cared about in the balance.

My magic is dangerous, Rori thought bitterly. *It always has been, and always will be.*

It had been so easy to drown the crew of the *Godfall.*

Maybe that was the missing piece, though, since *The Ballad of the Sun Crown* certainly had never made any mention of the emperor paying a blood price. Perhaps the queen and prince had died because the price had not been paid. Rori, however, had paid it the last time she'd been to the Rend, but that did not strike her as the kind of thing that would soothe Eric at that moment. She stayed silent.

Eric rubbed his face again and turned to leave. "No matter what you find out there," he said, "when the month is up, I'm voting to turn around."

"Understood," Rori said, turning back to the table and the sea charts.

"I hope you fail," he murmured.

Rori stiffened and whirled to face the Darkbend once more. "This is how I save the crew," she said.

Eric gave a humorless bark of laughter as he stepped to the door and gripped the knob. "You mean the one that broke?" He twisted the knob and pushed the door open, but he stopped before slamming it closed, and gave Rori a half-apologetic look. "How will you save anyone if we're all dead?" he asked softly.

Rori swallowed hard. "I'm not going to hurt anyone," she promised.

Eric's eyes swirled with pity and fear. "It may not matter if you do," he said, and then gently closed the door.

Rori ran to turn the lock, hot tears in her eyes. She stood with her back pressed against the door and tried to calm the frustrated tide rising within her chest.

"He's wrong," she said, looking to Luken for support.

"We can do this. *I* can do this."

The bird tilted his head to regard her with one bright eye. Then he chirped and nestled further into the old hat.

Rori allowed herself another few moments to collect herself, and then she dove back in to the navigational calculations. Her mind wanted to wander, however, and she started wondering if Eric was right, that even if she did everything right, she would be leading the ship and the crew to their doom.

"I made it once before," she reminded herself, "and they said I could return."

Luken twittered softly, and Rori pulled herself out of her own thoughts with a shudder.

But she kept hearing Eric say *I hope you fail*, and she wasn't so sure that he was wrong to want that.

Some time later, just as she'd managed to lock her attention on the numbers again and fall into the rhythm of scratching her calculations out on paper, there was a knock at the door. It proved to be the boatswain, come to rattle some sense into her frost-touched brain, as he so eloquently put it. Rori refused to open the door, and told him to speak with the captain if he still had objections this far into the voyage. Novachak was not impressed with this refusal, but left her alone after reiterating that he thought that she was mad.

"Yes, you and everyone else," Rori muttered, and then bent her head back over her work.

AnnaMarie Blueshore and Jim Greenroot came after that, arguing about the voyage and looking for Rori to settle it, but she refused them, too, and advised them to take their dispute to the quartermaster. The gunners reluctantly left, but Liliana Blackriver came on their heels, and Rori gave the rigger flat, one-word answers until she huffed and went away. Marcus and

Nate came after that, and Rori almost opened the door for them, but she made herself sit still.

"Rori," Nate called softly through the door, "we want to help."

"You can't," she answered, too softly for either of them to hear. "And what if I hurt you, too?"

The boys tried again, but were forced to give up when they were both called to help the riggers as the wind shifted.

She was being childish, she knew, and she would have to face everyone when she inevitably left the navigation room, but she wanted to put that off for as long as possible. She leaned back in her chair and covered her eyes with her hand, and tried and failed not to think about the cold wreckage of a ship floating in the water.

When the next knock came, Rori ignored it, even when it persisted. It occurred to her that it could be the captain or quartermaster come to discuss the voyage, but neither of their voices rang out, and it wasn't too long before the knocking stopped and soft footsteps creaked away.

A few minutes later, there was a tap on the window.

Rori opened her eyes, and surged out of her seat when she saw Xander, barefoot and clinging to what could only be some very narrow hand and footholds as he smirked at her through the glass.

"Gods below, what is wrong with you?" she snapped as she ran to the window. "Get back on the ship!"

"Will you let me in?" Xander said, his voice muffled by the glass between them.

"These windows don't open," Rori said, not even trying to keep the frustration out of her voice.

"Neither will the door," he remarked.

She stared at him, but Xander only offered her a flat, pointed look in return.

"Just climb back up," she finally said, and then held her breath as Xander scampered up and out of sight, moving as though this was the most natural thing in the world for him. When he did not plummet past the window, she went and opened the door to find him standing there, holding his boots in one hand and looking disgustingly pleased with himself. "You're going to get yourself killed someday," she told him.

"Not today," he said with a shrug, and then stepped past her into the navigation room.

Rori glared at his back as she shut the door again.

"You've been spending a lot of time in here," Xander said idly as he tugged his boots on, giving the charts spread across the table only a cursory glance. He'd never taken her up on her offer to teach him to read, claiming he had better ways to waste his time. He showed no remorse for that decision now.

"It's part of my job," she responded.

Xander made a thoughtful noise, and then spied Luken at the corner of the table. He approached the bird familiarly, and to Rori's annoyance, Luken let Xander stroke his feathers. Rori did not think that she would ever forgive Xander for how he'd voted at the end of the dragon hunt, but she had not found a way to communicate that to Luken just yet. The bird cooed and leaned into Xander's touch.

"What do you want?" Rori asked acidly.

"To know why you've been cowering in here with your head up your own ass," Xander answered calmly, as though she'd just asked him about the weather.

Rori blinked.

Still petting Luken, Xander turned to face her. "The Vanishing Island was your idea, wasn't it?" He waited for her to nod. "Then stop acting like a child who just discovered that the gryphon she's been secretly trying to feed ate her cat instead of the pie she left out."

"Once again," Rori said after a moment, "I have to ask, what is wrong with you?"

"A lot," Xander said, "but you don't see me trying to hide from it."

"Sometimes, I wish you would," Rori grumbled.

He smirked. "So why are you hiding?"

Rori crossed her arms and leaned heavily against the wall. "Because I'm probably sending us all to our deaths, and maybe I should think about telling the captain to turn the ship around."

"Don't you dare," Xander said. "I want to see the Vanishing Island."

"I don't give a damn what you want," she growled.

"I know that," he said, and the simplicity of the statement startled her.

Rori watched him coax Luken on to his wrist, gentle as the sea on a calm night.

"You somehow convinced Arani to sail her beloved old boat into the Forbidden Sea," Xander said as he lifted Luken, letting the bird's long pennant feathers trail through the air. "You wouldn't have done that if you didn't believe in it."

Rori sighed. "It's not a matter of believing. I know it's out there."

"Then take us to it."

"It's dangerous."

"So is everything else we do," Xander quipped. He gave his hand a shake, and Luken wobbled precariously before jumping off and fluttering over to perch on the back of the room's sole chair. "Who convinced you otherwise?" Xander peered at her narrowly from beneath the black Grayvoice tattoo on his brow. "Was it the Nowind?"

"Don't call him that," Rori snapped.

"Why not?" Xander asked. "It fits, doesn't it? A special name for the special boy with the special Skill."

"Jealousy is an ugly thing, Xander."

He actually laughed at that. "I promise you, I'm not jealous of a boy who couldn't figure out his own magic."

"That's not fair," Rori protested.

"It's true," Xander said. "But if you're so fond of him, how come he's not in here with you?"

Rori stared at him for a long moment. "Maybe he should be."

The mirth fell out of Xander's eyes, and Rori watched him visibly struggle to control himself. She might have been impressed by the effort, if she wasn't still mad at him. But Xander had saved Nate's life, hadn't he? Rori remembered that with a small flush of guilt, although she couldn't quite bring herself to apologize.

Once he'd calmed his irritation enough, Xander turned his head and skimmed his gaze over the charts once more, clearly not interested in them. "Saw Marcus and the Nowind come here earlier."

"What of it?"

"You didn't let them in, either."

"No," Rori said after a beat, "I didn't."

"Why not?"

"Because they can't help."

"That's right," Xander said, suddenly focusing on her again. He came towards her, and did not stop until he was less than a hand's breadth away, gazing down at her with enough intensity to make her press herself even harder against the wall. "Nate can't help you, and neither can Arani, or Novachak, or even me. It's all up to you this time, and if you fail, we all go home with nothing." He leaned in closer, until their noses were almost touching. "So are you going to grow up and do your job," he murmured, "or are you going to be the scared little child crying under the table?"

Rori raised her hand to Xander's chest, and shoved him away.

"There she is," Xander laughed as he stumbled back. "There's that Goodtide bitch." He pulled his shirt straight and shook his hair out of his eyes. "I missed her."

"You'll be seeing a lot more of her if you don't get out of here," Rori growled.

"Is that a promise?"

"A threat," she countered.

"Even better." Xander moved to the door, and Rori stepped out of his way. He paused before turning the handle, and his eyes danced mischievously. "What animal do you think I can speak to?" he asked.

She considered not answering, but the old joke was hard to resist. And after everything, it was nice that Xander still wanted to share it with her.

"Unicorns," Rori said flatly. "But only the brown ones."

Xander smirked again. "You got it." Then he left, and Rori slammed the door behind him.

No one could infuriate her quite like Xander, and he knew it. Why else would he have come to the navigation room? But as much as she did not want to admit it, Xander had managed to help her, or at least goad her into getting out of her own head. She gave a frustrated huff that somehow turned into a quiet laugh before she returned to her calculations, and finally worked out the *Southern Echo*'s position.

Over the next few days, whenever she emerged from the navigation room to personally take readings of the ship's speed and position relative to the sun and the stars, more and more people asked her if she was certain that they should be doing this. Rori answered yes every single time.

A little less than one month, she thought as she

noted down the reading from her sextant. *Let's make it worth something.*

CHAPTER SEVEN

Into the Forbidden Sea

THERE WAS NO GRAND, dramatic thunderclap from the sky or abrupt change in the color of the water to mark the moment the *Southern Echo* passed into the Forbidden Sea. Most people, Nate included, did not even notice that the ship had made the crossing until Jim Greenroot accosted Dax on the main deck, trying to needle the quartermaster into convincing the captain to turn around before the ship entered dangerous waters.

Dax looked calmly back at the man and said, "Too late by half a day."

He'd made no effort to keep his voice down, and Nate wasn't the only one who froze at the quartermaster's words before turning a wary eye on the blue waves around the ship. There was a bone-rattling thud as Liliana—who'd just begun the climb for an adjustment to the mainsail—missed a step and fell back to the deck. She limped for a few days after that, but aside from a couple of bruises on her knees and her ego as a rigger, she was unharmed.

For a while, that was the only issue the crew faced. The winds held steady and the sea was calm under bright, clear skies, and some began to wonder if the Forbidden Sea would actually live up to its name.

"Maybe they just call it that to keep people from sailing into it," Marcus mused a few days after the crossing.

He and Nate stood at the railing, both glad to have a little time to rest after a morning spent scrubbing down the decks and hauling on the sail lines. They peered down into water that looked like any other seawater.

"Do you think there are even any monsters in there?" Marcus asked.

"Probably," Nate answered. "There were sirens back in the Common Sea. Who knows what's out here?"

"So far, a lot of nothing," Marcus said. He squinted out at the blue line where the sky met the sea. "At this rate, the only real risk is that we'll all die of boredom before we get anywhere near the Vanishing Island."

"Rori doesn't seem to think that's going to be the case," Nate pointed out mildly.

She was coming out of the navigation room more regularly now, and sometimes even ate with Nate and the others, but there was a worried line on her forehead that only deepened as the days wore on. Nate tried to draw out her anxieties, but she only offered him thin smiles and remarks about how none of her worries would matter if they did not find the signs of the Rend and the Vanishing Island.

"So does Arani," Marcus said. "Doesn't mean they're right."

As one, Nate and Marcus both turned to look up to where the captain stood on the poop deck, a spyglass raised to her eye as she scanned the horizon. She was frowning, and her expression did not clear as she lowered and folded the instrument.

"Doesn't mean they're wrong, either," Nate remarked. "If they're both this worried, we probably should be, too."

Marcus made a noise of agreement, but he turned back to the railing and drew in a deep, contented breath. "Hard to be when the weather's this fine," he said.

Nate had to agree with him, and he turned his face to the sun as the wind played gently over his skin.

A hand suddenly clapped down on his shoulder, and he stumbled under its force.

"Just what I've been looking for," Novachak boomed as he turned Nate and Marcus around. "Two able-bodied young men with time on their hands."

Nate wasn't certain if he or Marcus groaned louder, but that only earned them a wicked smirk from the boatswain as he marched them off to a new task.

The good weather continued to hold, giving the crew easy sailing and a reason to release more of their apprehension. For his part, Nate spent a good portion of his severely diminished free time sparring with Marcus under Novachak's watchful eye, and sometimes with the boatswain himself when he could spare the time. Nate couldn't turn aside every blow, but his arms were growing stronger, and the strikes were becoming easier to take against his cutlass. His muscles protested loudly and persistently each day, but Nate knew that his progress was being helped along by the additional shifts he took with the riggers, learning how to handle the lines and the sails. His abilities did not match up to what the other riggers could do, as Liliana bluntly pointed out to him one afternoon, but with the pleasant weather and nearly the full crew in good spirits because of it, Nate was too, and he did not mind Liliana's teasing.

Nearly half the month was gone by then, and so far, the worst that was happening was the expected start of the decline in the quality of the ship's stored food. People were learning to relax again during their few off hours, and Marcus even began to bring out his fiddle in the evenings. There was no dancing as most everyone was too tired for that, but there was clapping and singing and laughter, and Nate was thrilled when Eric enthusiastically joined in.

"I'm still voting no when the month is up," the elegant Darkbend informed Nate over the music. "It's been perfectly pleasant so far, but I have no desire to extend our vacation out here."

"Is *that* what we've been doing?" Nate asked, turning his palms to show Eric the rope burns he'd managed to acquire that afternoon, which had only aggravated the callouses from his sword fighting lessons.

Eric gave a low whistle. "You're a terrible rigger, aren't you?"

"Liliana said the same thing," Nate said. "Then she told me I should get some tutoring."

Eric did not immediately respond. When Nate glanced over, he was surprised to see the Darkbend fighting back a smile.

"Nate," Eric said, "what exactly did Lily say to you?"

Nate thought back to the exchange between him and the rigger earlier in the day. He'd just finished tying what he had thought was a perfectly serviceable series of loops. Liliana had looked critically at the arrangement, and then plucked lightly at the center. The entire thing had come unraveled, and she'd turned a pretty, teasing smile on him.

"She told me that I could use a bit more practice tying knots," Nate remembered. "Then she asked me if I fancied some private lessons."

Eric shut his eyes and shook with silent laughter.

"And what did you say?"

It finally dawned on Nate what Liliana had really been proposing. Mortified, Nate told Eric, "I said I'd see if Novachak was available."

Eric nearly fell to the deck, he was laughing so hard. Nate's face burned with embarrassment, but he couldn't help laughing, too.

"Don't tell Marcus," Nate said once Eric had managed to contain himself again.

"No promises," Eric said with a wink. He nodded across the deck, to where Liliana was visibly sulking. "Between you and me, that poor girl is having the worst luck finding a paramour."

Nate gave another nervous laugh, but his attention had slipped past the rigger and landed on the two people standing in front of the navigation room: Dax and Arani.

Dax was leaning in to say something into the captain's ear. Whatever it was, it was only deepening Arani's frown, and she abruptly drew away and shook her head. Dax gave her a grim look, but he nodded when Arani whispered something back. The two stood watching the singing crew for a few moments, neither of them smiling. Then Arani turned and headed for the stairs leading down into the ship. Dax remained topside, watching the crew for the rest of the night, and whenever Nate glanced in his direction again, the quartermaster looked troubled.

The next day began much the same, calm and cheerful, although Liliana made a point of avoiding Nate whenever she could. This suited him fine as he was still embarrassed by both her proposition and his response, although the rigging work was constantly threatening to bring them together. Nate was glad that the others, especially Xander, were too absorbed in their own labor to notice their awkwardness.

But even then, the storm shouldn't have taken them by surprise.

Nate was hauling back on a rope, his mind divided between keeping his balance and trying to follow how the riggers were shaping the fore and mainsails to best counter the soft but steady headwind blowing in from the northeast, when the warning sounded out from the crow's nest. Nate and the others paused, making sure to keep their grip on the rope as they turned to look southwest.

A low bank of clouds had formed on the horizon, surprisingly dense and dark against the open blue of the sky.

Nate wasn't the only one who frowned.

"How long has that been there?" asked Theo Yellowwood, one of the older sailors among the crew. He squinted hard at the distant clouds, fighting for a better look against his age and years spent on the bright, glaring seas.

Nate couldn't say for certain, not even with his younger and sharper eyesight. He'd spent enough time on the *Southern Echo* to know that such clouds could usually be spotted from a much greater distance, long before the eye could discern the dark curtain of rain falling from their underbellies. He wondered why it had taken so long for the lookout to spot them, but then, with the calm weather and no real danger of them being followed, Nate couldn't blame the lookout. It must have been easy to dose off up there, with the sun shining down and very little to see.

Nate shrugged, turning back to the mast and the rigging work. The lookout hadn't seemed alarmed when she'd given the warning, and with the way the winds were blowing, the clouds and the rain would be keeping well away from the ship. Theo Yellowwood and the others moved to help Nate, but they all froze when the boatswain's orders to stop cracked over their heads like a whip.

The rough fibers of the rope burned Nate's palms as his grip slipped and then caught again. Behind him, Yellowwood cursed and tugged against the rope.

"Hold it steady, Lowwind," Theo grunted.

"Quiet," Novachak snapped.

Nate, Yellowwood, and all the others turned to see the boatswain watching Captain Arani. She stood at the port railing, spyglass raised and shoulders rigid against the gentle breeze that played with the feather in her hat. Several long moments crawled past before she lowered the spyglass.

"Furl the sails," she said. Her voice was calm, but there was a hard edge to it that Nate did not like at all.

He glanced at the distant storm again, just in time to see a flash of lightning flicker in the clouds.

"Do it now," Arani said. "And then get everyone below deck."

Novachak did not hesitate. He roared out the orders, and Nate snapped to work alongside Theo and the others. Nate wasn't quite as swift and fluid in his motions as the experienced riggers, but Theo kept close to him and told him which lines to hold and when to pull or release.

Before long, every sail on the *Southern Echo* was secured tight against the yards, and the last of the riggers were climbing down the shrouds to the main deck. Nate would have been impressed by the speed and efficiency of it all, if he wasn't shivering in the cold wind that had come blustering out of the southwest. It was harsh and sharp against his skin, and he felt his magic stir unpleasantly in his chest, as though in protest. When Nate looked at the clouds again, his heart leapt into his throat when he saw how quickly they'd swollen. They were easily triple the size they'd been only minutes ago, and they were boring down on the *Southern Echo* fast. Beneath them, the ocean churned angrily, stirred into white foam by the hardest rain Nate had ever seen.

"Get below!" Novachak shouted. He ran across the deck, pushing everyone he came across towards the steps that led into the ship's interior.

Nate did not need to be told twice. He made it to the stairs with time to spare, but as he began to descend, he caught sight of Captain Arani at the helm, teeth bared in a silent snarl as she turned the great wheel and swung the bow of the *Southern Echo* into the storm.

"What is she doing?" he breathed.

"Pointing the strongest part of the ship at the brunt of the danger," Novachak snapped, descending on Nate's heels and nudging him further into the gloom below. He paused to throw a final look at the looming storm. The boatswain swore quietly. "Frozen Goddess, spare us all," he muttered. Then he grabbed Nate by the arm and bundled him down the steps. "Come with me, new blood, and do exactly as I tell you."

Nate nodded mutely as Novachak steered him into the berth. Several people were already in their hammocks in anticipation of the violent rocking of the ship. Nate expected Novachak to send him into his own bunk, but the boatswain started grabbing blankets off of the few empty hammocks and shoving them into Nate's arms. Then he ordered Nate out of the berth and back across the gun deck.

They passed Dax on their way, the quartermaster looking harried even as he called for everyone to stay calm and keep away from openings. He frowned at Novachak, Nate, and the conscripted blankets. "Where are you going?"

"To save that frost-touched woman's life," the boatswain growled back. He ushered Nate up the first few steps to the main deck before Dax could respond. "Take those to the helm," Novachak barked as he gave Nate a final push. "Spread them over yourself and the captain. I'll be right behind you."

Nate bit down on his questions and protests, even as the sky boiled angrily over the ship and his magic stirred again at the blasting touch of the cold winds. Rain began to fall as Nate stepped on to the deck, hard and stinging, and he winced at the pain as he ran to the helm.

Arani gave him a startled look as he skidded to her side, but she eyed the blankets and did not protest as Nate shook them loose and flung them over the captain and himself. They only provided meager protection and the wind threatened to tear them away, but the fabric blocked the worst of the rain, if Nate kept his head down and his back to the wind. Captain Arani had her hands locked on the ship's wheel, holding the course steady, but at least her head and neck were more protected now, and she did not seem to care that it came at the expense of her vision. She struggled to hold the wheel still as the sea turned choppy, and Nate moved to help, placing his hands were she instructed and bracing the wheel alongside her.

Novachak came slipping across the deck moments later, a coil of rope around one arm. He moved to lash the wheel into place as Arani and Nate held it, working quickly despite the cold. Nate's teeth chattered as he huddled miserably beneath the wet blanket, straining to hear over the storm for any further orders from Novachak or Arani.

The rain hammered the ship and all three of their bodies with equal abandon, growing even more intense as Novachak finished. The sound of it hitting the deck changed, shifting from the steady rumble to an even angrier clacking, and Nate felt the intensity of the impacts through the blanket. Small chips of white ice bounced against Nate's boots, and he shuddered from more than just the cold this time.

He'd never seen a hailstorm before, but he'd learned about them at the wind working academy. Mostly, those lessons had boiled down to "take cover and wait it out," but he and the other young wind workers had been assured that hail at sea was an incredibly rare phenomenon, and it was unlikely they would ever need to face it.

If he wasn't so busy grimacing against the pain of the hail striking his back, Nate might have laughed at the sheer number of things he'd found himself facing as a pirate that the academy instructors had sworn would never come up over a career as a sailor.

The thought was cut short when the door to the navigation room banged open and Rori shouted to them over the roar of the storm.

With the ship's wheel secured, Arani and Novachak did not hesitate. They dove for the shelter of the small room, and Nate followed on their heels, his boots slipping on the hail-rattled deck. Rori slammed the door closed behind them, and Nate nearly sobbed in relief as the wind cut off and the tightness in his chest eased. He was still cold, but at least his magic had calmed.

"Stay away from the windows," Novachak advised. The drumming of the hailstones nearly drowned out his voice.

Arani nodded, wincing as she massaged her hands. There were red splotches across her skin where the hail had pelted her, promising to deepen into bruises.

Novachak had a few similar spots, and Nate examined his own skin for the telltale strike marks. He'd faired better than the two officers, even with the scattering of sore spots on his back that would likely linger for a few days. He listened to the hail grow louder and marveled that a few bruises were the worst they'd walk away with.

He swallowed that thought as he realized that the ship still had to survive the storm.

Over the sound of the hail, a distressed bird cry pierced the air. Despite his dislike for the bird, Nate felt a pang of sympathy for Luken. The poor animal must have been scared out of his mind by the storm. He flapped and screeched, and Rori was there immediately, trying to push soothing sounds through the endless thunder and coax Luken into the pseudo-nest he'd made out of Nate's old cap. Nate couldn't help but smile; he had yet to replace the hat, but seeing Rori's bird take comfort in the worn cap brought some warmth back into Nate's chest.

It faded when a voice cut through the storm, just over his shoulder, "Aren't you supposed to sense these things, Nowind?"

Nate barely managed to avoid jumping out of his own skin as he spun to face Xander. The Grayvoice's mouth gave an amused twist, but his eyes were flat as he looked at Nate.

"What are you doing here?" Nate blurted.

The hail grew even louder, slamming against the ship with such force that Nate barely heard the end of his own question. Xander did not bother to respond, but his dark eyes flickered past Nate to settle on Rori, and that was answer enough.

Arani and Novachak both looked surprised to see Xander inside the navigation room, but they motioned for him, Rori, and Nate to settle near the center of the room, putting the sole table between them and the windows of the stern. They waited out the storm without speaking, Luken's cries drowned out by the hail. Nate peered around the table to watch through the glass as the ice fell from the dark sky, pelting and churning the sea into a sickly gray. Lightning flashed again, and the ship shuddered against the winds. A hailstone struck and cracked a window, and Nate swallowed and retreated back behind the table.

He did not know how long he sat there, huddled with the others on the floor of the navigation room, but the hail ended with an abrupt crash into silence and a flood of sunshine.

They all sat frozen for a stunned moment, Luken's sad chirping the only sound in the room. Then Captain Arani was on her feet and opening the door. She held up her arm against the light as Nate and the others filed in behind her, giving the sky a wary and thorough scan. Over her shoulder, Nate saw nothing but sheer blue.

Arani's confusion was plain on her face as she took a few cautious steps outside. Hailstones ranging in size from small pebbles to Nate's fist crunched beneath her boots, but she ignored them as she turned to take in the full sweep of the horizon. Her frown deepened.

Nate understood why as soon as he was out of the room. All around the ship, the dome of the sky was clean and unbroken, the sun shining as merrily as it had been before the storm had appeared. The air was already warmer, the sea calm and deep blue all around, and if it weren't for the hailstones littering the deck and the many dents and gouges they'd left in the wood, it would have been easy to believe that the storm had never happened. When Nate turned to look for the receding clouds, he could not find them, nor was there any trace of the wind that had woven so much tension through his chest.

Luken gave a sharp chirp and burst out of Rori's hands in a violent spray of wings and feathers, angling into the clear sky and circling around the masts. Nate heard Rori breathe out a sigh. He turned to her at the same moment the captain did.

"I thought you said the waterspouts would be the worst we'd need to watch out for," Arani said tightly.

Rori nodded.

The captain stared at her. "So then, that was...?"

"Not the worst," Rori said in a small voice. Her gaze dropped to the deck. "Not by a long shot."

Arani was the one who sighed this time, deep and bone-weary. She turned her face to the sun, as though seeking comfort from its warmth.

Nate glanced out at the horizon again, in the direction he'd expected to see the retreating storm clouds. There was still nothing but smooth and open sky. Absently, he touched the gold ring on his hand, wondering if he should use his Skill to range out and try to pick up the freak storm, or anything like it. He opened his mouth to suggest as much.

"I say that's a good thing," Xander cut in before Nate could get a single syllable out. "This cruise got boring a week ago, and the riggers were starting to look a bit complacent. Things like this will at least keep us on our toes." He tilted his head towards Nate. "Especially since our special wind worker couldn't be bothered to tell us that this one was coming."

The words cut, and Nate started to protest. He broke off when the captain's hand came down on his arm.

"Xander," Arani said warningly. "I'll not hear that kind of talk from you."

The Grayvoice shrugged and folded his arms. "Greenroot talks like that all the time."

"Yes," Arani said, "but I expect better of you."

Xander did not respond, other than to give the captain a sidelong look and another shrug.

"I could do it," Nate interjected. He was sure he only imagined the ring on his hand growing warmer at the mere suggestion, but a tightness came back into his throat as he remembered what the dragon hunt had done to him, what it had nearly cost him. Still, it was a way he could help the crew, and he already knew just how strong he was when it came to his magic. "I could range out on the winds and see what I can find."

Arani's hand stiffened before she released him. "And which direction will you go?" she asked. "The winds out here don't play by the rules of the rest of the world, if that storm is anything to go by. It came out of nowhere, and then it vanished. How do you plan to search for something like that?"

Nate did not have a response.

Xander smirked, but it was not lost on Novachak.

"And what were *you* doing in the navigation room, exactly?" Novachak demanded. "I don't remember seeing you up the lines before the hailstorm came."

Xander looked at the boatswain coolly. "Talking to our navigator about the kinds of weather patterns the riggers should expect this far west."

Novachak looked faintly displeased by the logic of this answer, and he turned to Rori for confirmation. She nodded. Nate glanced between her and Xander, and tried to ignore the ugly feeling that stirred in his gut.

The captain sighed again into the quiet and kicked at one of the larger ice chunks on the deck. "We need to get this cleaned up and the ship back on course," she said.

"What course?" the sour voice of Jim Greenroot put in. Nate turned to see that he and several others had climbed up on to the main deck and were looking about with as much bewilderment as the captain had shown a few minutes earlier. "We don't have a course," the gunner said. "We're just wandering around out here, looking for nothing."

"As was voted, Mr. Greenroot," Arani put in mildly. "And we're going to continue the journey until the month is up. We've gone through far worse for the chance of much less, and this ship can handle a little unexpected weather." Her gaze shot to Rori, heavy with a meaning that Nate did not understand. "Right, Miss Rori?"

The Goodtide met the captain's stare and drew herself up straighter. "Aye," she said. "I'll see us through."

Greenroot snorted and turned away. Nate shot a dark look at the gunner's back, and was glad to see it mirrored by a few of the sailors who had willingly voted in favor of the voyage into the Forbidden Sea. That included Dax, who seemed more than a little relieved to have discovered the captain alive and well.

It was going to take a lot more than a surprise storm to shake the crew of the *Southern Echo*, Nate realized. His heart swelled with pride at the thought.

The feeling stayed with him even as Dax and Novachak doled out orders for the riggers to unfurl the sails and everyone else to shovel the hailstones off the deck before they melted. The cleaning efforts weren't entirely successful, but they did manage to fling the majority of the ice overboard. It struck the surface of the water and sank below the waves, and Nate did not see any of it rise again.

Two more freak storms took the *Southern Echo* by surprise in as many days, appearing out of nowhere with no warning or preamble. The first was only rain, and though it fell in iron-colored sheets, it did not cause any harm. They were even able to refill one of the water barrels, although Dax insisted that barrel be marked and its contents boiled twice as long before the water be used for anything, particularly the captain's tea.

The second storm, however, came with a vengeful fury to rival that of the gods themselves. Several people were left with deep bruises after they failed to get belowdeck in time. Theo Yellowwood ended up with a particularly nasty gash on his forehead from a large hailstone, and the blow left him dizzy in his hammock for the rest of the day, a dark and weaving trail of dried blood droplets leading from the stairs to his place in the berth.

Nate helped with the cleanup of the main deck again, the hailstones heavier this time and adding so much weight to the bucket he used to scoop them up, his arms threatened to pop off. He wasn't the only one who struggled, as even the gunners were grunting with the effort, but he took no satisfaction in that. He tipped the last of a bucketful over the side of the ship and slumped against the railing, stealing a few moments for a break.

The hail had hammered the ship again, leaving dents and scars in the wood. Nate pressed his hand against the railing, feeling the uneven bumps, and a bubble of regret formed in his throat. The *Southern Echo* was a beautiful ship, well-cared for and meticulously maintained, and Nate hated to see these blemishes on her.

His thoughts wandered back to the damage the ship had sustained during the battle with the navy frigate, and how Eric had marveled over what he'd sworn were shrinking holes.

Nate curled his fingers over the railing, feeling the warmth of the wood and wondering if Dax's claim was true, that a dryad still lived within the ship.

Be a really nice story if it was, Nate thought wistfully.

He stretched until his back gave a satisfying crack, then picked up his bucket and braced himself for another load of ice, but his gaze caught on an odd shape on the horizon, tall and thin and clearly moving closer. He cried out at almost the exact same moment as the lookout, and then Captain Arani was there, spyglass raised and locked on the thing.

"Gods below," she growled as she snapped the spyglass closed. She rounded on the crew and bellowed, "Riggers, top speed from those sails!"

Xander Grayvoice's answer came from the base of the foremast, for once formal and without any trace of a challenge. "We're already getting the best we can from this wind, Captain."

Arani swore again, and Nate's heart began to beat fast and hard as the shape bore down on them, resolving into a massive funnel of mist between the sky and sea. Nate felt the shift in the wind, and his magic answered again, groaning and reluctant. He backed away from the railing, unconsciously grabbing at the ring on his hand. He wore it with the sun crest facing in towards his palm these days so he did not have to look at it, but his thumb traced the Solkyrian symbol now, seeking even a shred of comfort as the waterspout lunged towards the ship at an impossible speed. Between one blink and the next, it was almost on top of them, the winds howling through the sails and drowning out the terrified cries of the crew.

Without warning, the ship lurched under Nate's feet, and he fell to the deck as a massive wave picked the *Southern Echo* up and carried her forward. Another wave came, and then another, and Nate rolled over to see Rori on the main deck, her arms whipping almost as fast as the waves were rising, her face flushed with the strain of magic use and panic.

Nate clung to the deck, his nails digging into the wood as the waves called up by Rori's Skill shoved the *Southern Echo* on. The waterspout bore down, wind roaring and water churning at its base, and then it was past, barely skimming across the ship's wake and completely unaffected by Rori's waves. It tore off as quickly as it had come, barreling into the horizon and leaving the ship and her crew rocking in the water, sick with fear.

Nate pressed his forehead against the warm wood of the deck and shut his eyes, trying to stave off the nausea that rolled over him. People were still screaming, and from the sound of it, not everyone had managed to keep their breakfast down. Someone was violently ill over the railing, and Nate tried to block the sound out before his own body answered in kind.

When he finally lifted his head again, the screaming had stopped, although many people were visibly shaken. Even Xander's eyes were wide, his chest and shoulders heaving as he stared after the waterspout. Nate spied Marcus huddled near the mainmast, arms wrapped tightly around his own bucket like it was a precious memory. Beyond him, Rori was on her hands and knees, panting hard and looking faintly sick.

Nate stumbled to his feet, but he was far from the first person to reach the Goodtide.

"What was that?" Liliana shrieked as Jim Greenroot howled, "We're going to die out here!" and a half dozen others demanded to know why in their right minds they'd come out here in the first place.

Rori took a deep, steadying breath, and then stood up. "The waterspouts are the worst of it," she grimly informed anyone who was listening. "But they're pretty rare, and they won't bother us after we find the first sign of the Rend. I don't know why, but they don't come back after that."

"*If* you find the signs!" Theo Yellowwood pointed out acidly.

Nate's heart squeezed when he saw the dark looks several people traded, and the nods they directed at Rori.

The Goodtide shut her eyes for a moment and took another long breath. "We'll find them," she said. "And I promise, I'll keep you safe."

Liliana made a disbelieving noise, and more uneasy glances were traded around Rori.

Nate couldn't take it. "She saved us!" he called out, pushing his way to Rori's side.

She was still panting shallowly as she looked at him sidelong, but there was a spark of gratitude in her eyes.

Nate gave her a reassuring nod, and then faced down her harassers. "Like it or not, we're out here now, and Rori's the one who's been guiding us so far. We're sailing the Forbidden Sea, and we're *still alive*, and she's going to keep it that way."

"What makes you so sure?" Jim Greenroot growled.

Nate drew himself up to his full height and stared the gunner down. He wasn't anywhere near as broad as Greenroot, but that was not going to stop him now. "Did you see what her magic just did?" Nate demanded. "Her Skill is incredible, and she used it to carry us out of the path of that monster. If she hadn't, we'd be a wreck at the bottom of the ocean right now." He took a step forward, his confidence bolstered by the way the others leaned back. "Rori saved all our lives, and this is how you thank her?"

Liliana and a few others had the decency to look ashamed. Jim Greenroot, though, only shook his head.

"From what I understand," he said, "we're only out here *because* of her. That makes her a bigger monster than anything we've seen so far."

"Enough!" Dax shouted. He and Novachak came bearing down on the small knot, intending to break them up. "Mr. Greenroot, Miss Blackwater, you two can take the first watch for more waterspouts. One of you at the bow, the other at the stern. Relief will come at the top of the next hour. The rest of you, get back to work."

Nate and Jim Greenroot glowered at each other for another moment, but the gunner had to turn away and obey the quartermaster's orders.

Nate wasn't satisfied with the way that confrontation had ended, but he had to let it go for the moment. He took a beat to release his anger, and then turned back to Rori. "You all right?" he asked.

She nodded. "Thanks," she murmured.

"Any time," Nate said, "although I think Eric would've given a better speech."

Rori smiled and huffed a soft laugh, and Nate walked with her back to the navigation room.

"Is Luken okay?" he asked before she stepped inside.

Rori nodded again. "He's been refusing to leave the hat you gave him, which is probably for the best." She paused, and they both heard an agitated twittering from the other side of the door. "I don't think he liked the waterspout."

Nate grimaced. "I promise you, none of us did."

To his surprise, Rori winced and dropped her gaze, as though ashamed. "I know," she whispered.

A surge of concern washed through Nate. "We all came out here willingly," he reminded her. He took a moment to brace his next words with a confident grin. "We're going to beat the Forbidden Sea, and all of its monsters."

Rori blinked at him, and the smile Nate had expected to receive in return never came, not even a ghost of it.

His own began to fade.

Rori opened the door and stepped inside the navigation room.

"I'm proud of you," Nate blurted, unsure of what else to say.

Rori paused and cocked her head.

"For using your Skill again," he clarified. "It really is amazing. You shouldn't hide from your own magic."

For a brief moment, something like raw pain flashed across Rori's face. She looked like she was about to say something, but with a visible effort, she swallowed the words and her emotions. "I've got work to do," she said instead, her voice flat. Then she closed the door softly between them.

And Nate stood there for a long time, not quite sure what he'd said to upset her, but certain it had been the wrong thing entirely to say.

He spent the rest of that day replaying his conversation with Rori in his head, agonizing over every moment of it. He could not figure out what he'd said or done to hurt her, except praise her for the strength of her magic. On the dragon hunt, Nate had seen how much she'd feared her own Skill, but he hadn't understood why. He still didn't, but he knew that he'd hurt her, and he had to make up for that.

Somehow.

He had no idea how.

So Nate sought out first Eric, and then Marcus when

he couldn't find the elegant Darkbend. Of the two of them, he trusted Eric to give him sounder advice, but Marcus might have a decent idea, provided he'd been properly fed. Arani had beaten Nate to the stout Darkbend, though, and asked him to take up his fiddle in hopes of restoring some of the crew's spirit after the brush with the waterspout.

Marcus sat on a crate on the main deck, tuning the instrument between nervous glances at the surrounding sea. He wasn't the only one hunting for signs of another waterspout, but he'd been excused from the official watch in exchange for playing music for the crew.

"It'll help," Marcus confirmed to Nate. "A little music will keep everyone distracted from their own dread."

So Nate had to let the Darkbend be, and watched as Marcus's songs soothed away the worst of the crew's anxieties. People were still clearly nervous, but the familiar music brought them back from the edge of panic, and some even began to sing along to a few of the shanties as they worked. An hour passed, and Marcus was just getting ready to wind down when Eric came hurrying up from the hold, his face ashen.

Concerned, Nate started towards his friend, but Eric gave a single sharp shake of his head, and then went straight to Marcus. The smile on Eric's face was even more wooden than the ship itself, but no one but Nate seemed to notice as Eric leaned down and said something to Marcus just as he started to put away his fiddle.

The stout Darkbend made a displeased face. "Really?" he whined, but then he caught Eric's expression. After a moment of startled hesitation, Marcus hitched a false smile of his own and said, "All right, I can play one more."

He pulled the fiddle back out of its case, stood up,

positioned the instrument carefully on his shoulder, and then played a few lively chords punctuated by the stomping of his foot. Eric joined him with clapping and stamping of his own, and then he began to sing.

> *Oh, out we sail to the open sea,*
> *Armed with blades and hope are we.*
> *Our flag is black against a sun that's risin'.*
>
> *And our captain says,*
> *"Trust in me, sail with me*
> *Over the next horizon."*

The crew cheered faintly and took up the song, perhaps more out of a desire for Marcus to keep playing than for any enthusiasm over the choice in music, and Eric let them have it. As they sang of a glorious ship setting sail, Eric threaded his way over to Nate, looking like his face was going to split open under the weight of maintaining that false joy.

"What's going on?" Nate murmured when Eric was finally close enough.

"I just had a very disturbing conversation down in the hold," Eric said softly. "Try to look like I'm telling you something interesting."

"You are," Nate said.

"Interesting and amusing," Eric amended. "I need there to be smiles so that they don't know I'm trying to warn Arani."

Growing more confused by the moment, Nate nonetheless decided to play along. "What do you need me to do?" he asked, twisting his mouth as though he'd said something sarcastic.

"Nothing," Eric said. "The song is enough."

Nate listened to the thin voices of the crew sing about a pirate ship finding and taking a prize so rich, the crew nearly drowned in gold. At the end of every chorus, the song's captain asked for the crew's trust to sail over the horizon once more, and the few singers would cheer, their growing enthusiasm making up for what they lacked in numbers.

"You're warning her that this voyage is going to be a huge success and the crew is going to love her?" Nate asked as Marcus spun in a tight circle, and then began the song once more. This time, more voices joined in.

Eric laughed as though Nate had told a wonderful joke. "I'm warning her that there may be a mutiny."

Nate's grin slipped, and it took considerable effort to hitch it back into place. His bewilderment rose as he listened to the crew repeat the lyrics. "This song has nothing to do with a mutiny."

"This version doesn't," Eric agreed, "but there's a companion piece that does. Same melody, same chorus, very different outcome."

"What happens in that one?" Nate asked.

"The captain takes the crew after an impossible prize and nearly gets them all killed. So the crew turns on the captain and executes him."

Nate nodded towards the considerably happier crew as they sang of riches beyond dreams. "And you think Arani is going to get that from this?"

"She's no fool," Eric said firmly. "She knows this is premature."

"Doesn't everyone?" Nate asked.

Eric laughed again, and Nate had to admit that his friend's acting skills were disturbingly good. "Turns out, some of us think that it would be best if we left the Forbidden Sea sooner than later."

This time, Nate did not try to disguise his frown. "Aren't you one of those people?"

"Aye," Eric said, "but unlike the two people who just approached me in the dark, I don't want to go after the black mimic again."

Nate went cold.

"Smile, try to smile," Eric reminded him, his voice going high and reedy.

Nate twitched a panicked grin back into place. "I thought everyone who wanted that stayed on Spider's Nest."

"No, just the ones who refused to sail west." The Darkbend cheered along with the rest of the crew as the song came to a close, and then turned to face Nate as Marcus struck up a different tune to appease the cries for more. "Best possible outcome, Arani calls all of this off, we go east, and we find a prize before this turns into anything more."

Nate lounged against the ship's railing, bobbing his head along to the music. Every movement was stiff and unnatural. "And the worst possible outcome?"

"Things get bloody."

"Arani would never let anyone take this ship from her."

"I know," Eric said. "That's why it's going to be bloody."

"And no one is going to know that you just tried to warn Arani with a song?"

Eric leaned over the railing then, finally letting his worry show now that he was turned away from the crew. "Most people don't know about the second version of the song."

"But Arani does?"

Eric nodded. "She's the one who taught it to me and Marcus. We were both desperate for something to distract us from the fact that we had just run away from Solkyria to be pirates, and she offered to teach us a secret song."

"Interesting choice," Nate mused.

Eric shrugged. "It worked."

"Why did they approach you?" Nate asked after a long moment. "Those people, down in the hold?"

"They know that I'm going to vote 'no' at the end of the month, no matter what." Eric sighed and ran a hand through his hair. "They were also hoping that I'd be able to convince you to willingly track the dragon again."

"No," Nate said immediately. "Willing or otherwise."

"Good, because I'm not feeling particularly charitable towards whoever it was that accosted me, and then shoved me into a crate so they could run off and disappear like spirits fleeing the dawn."

"Sounds like something Jim Greenroot would do," Nate growled, remembering the gunner's refusal to fully give up on the prospect of the dragon hunt.

"I don't know who it was," Eric frowned down at the water. "They spoke in whispers, and pitched their voices strangely. Whoever it was, they knew better than to let me hear what they really sound like. Honestly, that's a little too smart for Greenroot."

Nate had to agree. He released a hard breath and turned to lean against the railing beside Eric. They stared out at the dark sea.

"I don't know," Nate finally said, "if I want us to find the signs of the Vanishing Island or not."

Eric buried his face in his hands. "I hope not. Gods above and below, I hope not."

CHAPTER EIGHT

Monsters

RORI SAT IN THE navigation room, listening to the music and the singing from the main deck. She should have felt lighter, with the crew rallying around the songs and proving that they were far more resilient than they were sometimes given credit for, but she only felt a dragging heaviness.

Jim Greenroot had not been wrong. They were only in the Forbidden Sea because of Rori, and she was the one keeping them there.

She should not have wanted to come back to this side of the compass. She had every reason to stay away. But her world and her family had been breaking again right in front of her, and this time, she'd been able to do something about it.

Now they were here, deep in the Forbidden Sea, and there was nothing but danger waiting for them on all sides.

Rori knew that. All the way through her soul, she knew that. And yet, she still wanted to push on.

Keep going, a voice whispered to her in the silence of the navigation room. *Find the Rend. Find your answers. Take this crew to a legend worthy of them, and them alone.*

But she had to find the signs to do that, and if she couldn't, then she'd brought them all into the Forbidden Sea for nothing.

Nothing, save the chance they break apart even more than they already had. She'd so badly wanted to keep them together, to prove to them that she could be trusted and there was still a path forward for them, one forged through fire if not blood. She should have known better. Her true family was dead, just like the sailors on the *Godfall*.

Because of her magic.

How long until she broke the fragile lives aboard the *Southern Echo*? Not even Captain Arani could survive the full fury of the sea, and Dax Malatide's Skill wouldn't be able to stop Rori if she lost control, not even if his power had been over water instead of blood. So easily, everyone she knew and loved in this life she'd built from the shattered pieces of her old one could be taken away, sent to water-filled graves by her magic. She'd used her Skill to save the *Southern Echo*, but it had taken so much effort and willpower to stop her magic from surging to destructive heights every time. Her magic *wanted* to capsize the ship. Her magic *wanted* to drown everyone.

She thought of those people from the *Godfall*, but their faces changed, became the faces from the *Southern Echo*, became the captain and the quartermaster and Eric and Marcus and the boatswain and Nate. Sweet Nate, who still thought of Rori's magic as something to be looked upon with reverence and wonder.

How horrified he'd be if he ever learned how badly that magic wanted to destroy him.

Rori couldn't let it hurt him, or anyone else. Not ever again.

But she'd brought them all out here just the same.

The simple fact reared before her: the *Southern Echo* and her crew did not belong in the Forbidden Sea.

Maybe Rori did, though. Maybe she belonged in the

Forbidden Sea, with all its other monsters. Maybe she should put herself over the side and leave the crew in peace. Just let the currents and the mercy of the gods decide if she was meant to return to the Rend again or not. Float in the sea and give herself over to her magic and let it consume her before it thrashed out of her control.

Keep going, that persistent voice said.

Rori took a deep breath, ready to plunge back into the snarled calculations she'd been trying to work through, but her hand stilled, the end of the pen not quite touching the paper, and she could not bring herself to make the next mark.

The music suddenly swelled as the door opened and someone's quick footsteps came into the room. Rori turned, almost relieved to have Xander interrupt her, but she froze when she saw that it was Nate who had come through the door, not the Grayvoice.

"What are you doing here?" she asked, more surprised than anything, but Nate still hesitated at her tone.

"Sorry," he said. "You didn't answer when I knocked."

Rori blinked. She hadn't even heard his hand against the door.

Nate fidgeted awkwardly when she did not respond. "Do you want me to leave?"

"No," she said after a moment. "You can stay."

Nate nodded, closing the door more firmly behind him. He drifted to the table, his gaze roving over the few maps and crumpled sheets of calculations spread out before her. His mouth twisted into a wry smile. "There's a lot less paper here than there usually is," he noted. "I think this is the first time I've actually seen the surface of this table."

Rori shrugged, glancing at the mess. "This part of

the world isn't exactly charted out. I have to make do with what we've got."

Nate made a thoughtful noise and picked up one of the crumpled balls of parchment. He smoothed it out against his thigh, then frowned down at the scrawled numbers that had been crossed out and rewritten over and over.

Rori watched him as he studied her work, not certain what he hoped to gain from it, but she found that she didn't mind. It was nice to have Nate near her again. It had been a while since they'd last talked, and it struck her that his shoulders and arms had filled out a bit since the beginning of the voyage. She'd heard he was working hard alongside the riggers, and training with Novachak and Marcus when they all had free time, but she hadn't really *looked* at Nate for a while. He still had a long way to go if he aimed to be as strong as someone like Marcus or Xander, but it was hard to believe that this was the same skinny boy Captain Arani had picked up from Solkyria.

"You've been working really hard on these," Nate suddenly said, breaking her train of thought.

Rori blinked as she came back to the present moment, then she shrugged again.

Nate turned the paper to face her, showing Rori her own calculations. For some reason, he looked cautious as he gazed at her. "Have you let yourself rest since we've started this voyage?"

Rori turned her attention to the table, where Luken sat dozing in his pilfered hat-nest. "There's a lot to do," she said mildly.

Nate made an unconvinced noise and set the paper down. She gave it a cursory glance out of habit, then paused when she saw just how violently she'd slashed out her own work, scarring the paper with ink and even a hole where the nub of her pen had torn through.

That must have been when I broke the fourth one, she realized. Her gaze skimmed over the broken quills lying on the floor next to her chair, and then the blotches of ink on the papers as well as her own fingers. *I wonder if there's any on my face,* she wondered. She almost laughed at the thought, but the last thing she needed was for Nate to think she was starting to crack.

"I'm all right," she told him, even as her heart roiled in her chest. "Do you need something?"

Nate's frank stare told Rori that he did not believe her, but he let it pass. "No," he said, "but there is something I wanted to tell you." He took an unsteady breath, suddenly looking afraid. "I don't know if you heard the song Marcus played earlier, but—"

A solid knock on the door interrupted him, this time loud and clear in Rori's ears.

She hesitated, gazing at Nate for a moment, then rose from her seat. She opened the door to find Xander on the other side, already eyeing her critically.

"You're still hiding in here?" Xander asked, stepping inside before Rori could stop him. "How many times do I need to—" He broke off when he saw Nate, his spine going rigid. "Nowind," Xander breathed by way of greeting.

"Don't," Rori said, abruptly exhausted. She was not in the mood for any kind of fight, and swore aloud that she'd throw them both out if they started.

Xander snorted, clearly amused by the idea. "I don't think you could," he remarked before turning to Nate and looking him up and down. "And I *know* you couldn't."

Nate frowned, the fear Rori had seen in him earlier completely gone now, but he did not rise to the bait. Instead, he leaned against the table and regarded Xander coolly. "I was about to speak to Rori about something," Nate said. "Do you mind giving us a minute?"

"Yes, I do," Xander quipped.

Rori groaned softly.

That was enough for the Grayvoice to round on her. "Don't tell me he's convinced you to give up?"

"What?" Nate asked at the same moment Rori said, "Of course not."

"Good," Xander said, ignoring Nate entirely. "So, where are the signs?"

"Xander," Nate growled warningly.

Rori waved him off. "I'm still looking," she answered.

"Look harder," Xander said.

Rori gave the Grayvoice a tired look. She knew he was trying to get a rise out of her; it was the best—and only—way he knew how to encourage her. This wasn't the time for it, though.

But before Rori could speak again, Nate had stepped towards the Grayvoice and grabbed his shoulder. "Enough!" he barked as he tugged Xander around.

Xander threw Nate's hand off like it was nothing before sliding his feet into a fighting stance and sinking into a partial crouch. His fists came up, ready for a brawl, but thankfully, Nate had already backed away. Xander hesitated, as though confused not to already be trading punches, then gave another dismissive snort as he straightened. "That seems about right."

Nate flushed, but did not retreat further. "Leave her alone," he said quietly.

Xander was not impressed. "I could say the same to you," he said. "She needs to find the signs. Let her concentrate instead of making her worry about you for a change."

Rori started to protest, but as far as the boys were concerned, it was as though she was no longer in the room.

"She needs to rest," Nate insisted.

"She *needs* to find the signs of the Rend," Xander returned.

"She's trying!"

"Not hard enough, if you ask me."

"No one is asking you," Nate snapped. "She's been doing far too much on this voyage."

"Then where are the signs?"

"Who cares? Haven't you seen what she's been using her magic to do for us?"

"I don't care about her magic," Xander spat.

"You should!" Nate shot back. "It's incredible. Imagine what she could do if—"

"Stop!" Rori shouted, her anger surging through her. Her magic rose in answer, but she stamped it down before she could pull another wave out of the sea. "I'm not going to do *anything*, Nate. Get that through your head."

Xander smirked, and Nate gave her a wounded look.

"You don't have to be afraid," Nate said, and Rori's fury became a riptide.

"Yes, I do," she snarled, "and you should be, too. And *you*—" Xander had the courtesy to look startled when she rounded on him, "—start accepting that maybe there really is nothing out here, or maybe that I'll kill us all before we find it."

Silence roared in the wake of those words, broken only by a distressed twitter from Luken. Xander and Nate both stared at her, their mouths slightly agape, and Rori's anger receded into shame.

"What?" Xander asked after several long moments.

Rori sighed, and weariness ran deep in her veins. "I thought this voyage could save us," she confessed, "but maybe I was just being selfish. I asked Captain Arani for a month, because I thought that would be more than enough time to find the signs, and I thought the crew would be able to hold out that long while I tried. But I haven't found anything. Maybe there isn't anything to find, after all. Maybe I just brought us all out here for nothing. Or maybe my magic wants to do to the *Southern Echo* what it did to the *Godfall*. Gods below, it feels that way." She shut her eyes, and the next words came out as a whisper. "Maybe I am a monster."

"Rori, no," Nate said, achingly gentle.

But Xander cut in. "So what?" he snapped. "You're not the only one here with magic."

Rori cracked her eyes open and saw Nate glowering at the Grayvoice. Xander, however, had turned away from them both to stare out the windows at the back of the navigation room. She followed his gaze, only to have hers catch on the cracked pane. Her throat tightened at the sight of that scar from the first hailstorm.

"You have magic," Xander went on, "and that means that no matter what you do, someone is always going to hate you for it. You can't change that. But you don't have to let it stop you." He leaned on the navigation table, his hands pressed on top of the sea charts Rori had been trying and failing to wrap her attention around before the boys had come into the room. "If that makes us monsters, so what? If we have to be monsters to take back a little dignity, then I'll be the biggest monster this world has ever seen." He smiled at Rori then, sharp and cutting. "I'll make you look like Luken next to a dragon."

Nate shifted, clearly uncomfortable, but Rori ignored him, her attention locked on Xander now.

The Grayvoice's smile broadened when he saw that her thoughts were beginning to spiral around what he was telling her. "You brought us to the Forbidden Sea, full of big dangers and scary monsters." He took a step towards her, spreading his arms wide. "So be bigger,

stronger, and scarier than anything else out here, because we're not going to find the Rend if you're not."

"That's enough," Nate said.

"Shove off, Nowind," Xander said flatly. "This
doesn't concern you."

"It absolutely does," Nate growled.

They turned back to each other, but Rori had had
enough by then.

"Get out," she said. "Both of you."

Xander blinked at her in surprise, and Nate started
to protest. Rori opened the door of the navigation
room by way of response, and waited.

Nate slumped, but nodded and stepped through the
door, pausing just long enough to murmur, "You don't
have to push yourself." He shot Xander one last glower, and then set off across the ship, his steps clipped
and agitated.

Rori turned back to the Grayvoice. "You, too," she
said. "Go."

Xander shrugged and sauntered forward. "Stronger
and scarier," he said as he drew level with her. "That's
the only way you can keep us out here, and keep
what's left of the crew together. I know you're capable
of it." He leaned closer, his gaze and voice both steady
and firm. "Don't prove me wrong."

Then he was gone, and Rori shut the door behind
him with a firm click. She let a breath out, hard and
shaking, and pressed her forehead against the door.

A sea of monsters, she thought. *Do I really need to
be the biggest one?*

Keep going, the voice in her head answered.

CHAPTER NINE

The Weight of a Promise

NATE WENT TO SLEEP that night thinking of Rori. He'd told Eric that, thanks to Xander's interruption, he had not had the chance to warn her about the possible mutiny, and Nate was starting to question if they even should tell her at all. She had a lot on her mind. He'd seen that clearly in the violent ways she'd discarded her own calculations, slashing the paper with ink as if it were a sword drawing blood from a hated foe. And then Xander had come in, and Rori had called herself a monster, and the Grayvoice had *encouraged it*. Worst of all, she had listened.

Nate was becoming more and more certain that if he told Rori about the mutiny, she'd blame herself. He didn't want that for her, but he still felt that he should warn her. He wondered if he wanted her to know for her own sake, or simply to ease his own burden. His sleep that night was troubled.

The next day, no one came to Nate to talk about the dragon hunt. That should have counted as a good thing, but it left Nate peering suspiciously at almost everyone, especially Jim Greenroot and his gun crew. Every day since the start of the voyage, Greenroot had sought out Dax and used everything from begging to outright demands for the quartermaster to tell Arani to turn the ship around and sail out of the Forbidden Sea. Every day, Dax had said no, and pointed to the tally that Novachak was keeping in plain sight of the entire crew, marking each day as it passed. And every day, Jim Greenroot had not been appeased.

When Nate found Eric again that morning and asked if it was Greenroot's people who had approached him, the Darkbend considered it for a long moment before shaking his head.

"I honestly don't know who it was," Eric said. "So don't run to Arani to make the accusation. There isn't enough proof for her to act."

"Someone tried to convince you to join a mutiny," Nate pointed out.

"Not in so many words," Eric said, reluctantly. "They talked about convincing Arani to leave the Forbidden Sea and hunt the dragon again. They implied that they were not willing to accept 'no' as an answer, but they never outright said they'd mutiny."

"Then why did you bother having Marcus play that song?"

Eric's gaze narrowed. "Because having a captain on their guard over nothing is better than an unprepared one being keel-hauled by an actual problem."

"So what do we do, then?" Nate demanded. "Just wait for things to get worse?"

"I spoke to Arani last night," Eric said. "She knows to be on the lookout, but she did remind me that if I or anyone else were to come forward with such a serious accusation, we'd better have absolute proof. If she tries to act without that, she could lose the support of the crew, and give power to the very thing she wants to avoid."

Nate turned this idea around and around in his mind, only growing more frustrated with each new way he looked at it. "This is a mess."

Eric shrugged. "This is how we do things aboard the *Southern Echo*. If you wanted a captain who acts with iron-fisted authority and doles out punishment on a whim, you should have sailed on a merchant ship."

"They wouldn't have me," Nate reminded him.

"Then count yourself lucky, and keep your eyes and ears open."

So Nate tried to do just that, but the matter only grew more complicated as the ship sailed deeper into the Forbidden Sea.

Three days after Marcus played the warning song, the unpredictable storms had calmed and the last waterspout they'd seen had been well off the starboard railing, heading in the exact opposite direction as the ship. But the western edge of the compass was not showing them mercy. The steady tailwind that had carried them all the way from the Common Sea broke, becoming messy and unpredictable. No matter how hard the riggers worked, they could not catch the wind, and even the strongest among them were being ground down to weariness as they chased the breezes.

Nate thought of how Rori had shut down when he'd told her that he was proud of her for using her magic again. He still did not understand her fear of something that was so integral to herself and could do so much good, far more than his own magic could. She'd called herself a monster because of her Skill, and Xander had said they all were monsters with their magic. But Nate knew that wasn't true, and he knew that he could help his crew.

He flexed his Skill to read the winds in the immediate area, helping the riggers pick out the cleaner streams that would carry the ship forward, but they were always muddled by new winds coming in off the bow. The rigging work became more and more complicated as the sails had to be adjusted for the constantly shifting winds, and despite their best efforts and Nate's, the ship slowed. Nate quickly became wrapped up in his Skill as he tried to remedy that. There was no need for him to venture far beyond the *Southern Echo*, so he was not at risk of burning through his anchor as he had on the dragon hunt, but he was constantly dividing his attention between the tailwind and the headwind, trying to find the points where the one overpowered the other. Mental exhaustion crept back in, and although Nate made sure to keep well away from the edges of actual pain, he gave Marcus permission to dump a pail of water over his head if he seemed to be falling back into that pit. The Darkbend agreed, and designated a bucket for that exact purpose. He and the bucket were never far when Nate did his Skill work.

Thankfully, blessedly, the skies remained clear as the ship sailed on, and even with the unpredictable winds, it seemed the worst was finally behind them. Moods began to cautiously lift, and Nate wondered if they'd rise high enough to destroy the mutiny before it could even begin. Then the sea began to answer the nightmarish challenges thrown down by the sky.

The first things that came from the water were long, needle-shaped fish that broke the surface and skipped along the waves surrounding the ship. At first, Nate and several others thought this a boon, as the fish were plentiful and easy to catch, but up close, the creatures were bony, narrow things with milky eyes and jagged teeth. When the cook cut one of them open, the flesh inside oozed black blood that burned when touched and gave off a foul stink that permeated the entire ship. Novachak advised against anyone trying to eat the fish, and the entire catch was thrown back into the water without protest. Then the crew watched in horrified silence as the living fish swarmed around their returned fellows and devoured them, leaving bloody foam in the *Southern Echo*'s wake. Most people kept away from the railings after that, and everyone was relieved when the jumping fish disappeared as the sun set.

That, however, brought on a new problem, as something slow and massive came drifting up to swim beneath the ship. It seemed sedate and gentle at first, nothing more than a large, dark shadow that glowed with a faint bioluminescence along its sides as the creature easily undulated through the water. Even with that sickly light, it grew harder to see the underwater giant as the night settled in, until it was lost beneath the waves.

"Did it dive back down?" AnnaMarie Blueshore asked after nearly an hour had passed without anyone seeing the creature.

"Could have," Novachak answered her. "Maybe it was looking for food earlier, or just interested in the ship as something new in its territory."

The boatswain had barely finished the last syllable when the *Southern Echo* suddenly heaved under their feet, sending Nate and several others sprawling across the deck. The ship nearly rolled with the sudden force against the keel, and Nate caught a dizzying glimpse of black waves glinting with moonlight before the ship crashed back into the water, rocking violently back and forth.

Liliana had been on watch up in the crow's nest when the ship was hit, and she was nearly flung out to sea, saved only by one rope and her rigger's reflexes. AnnaMarie Blueshore had rent the night with a scream when she'd seen Liliana almost fly to her death, but that was cut short when a massive patch of light suddenly flared in the blackness, and the giant burst from the water some distance from the ship, edged in otherworldly blue.

The creature's body was thick and heavy, with wickedly pointed fins and a massive tail that lashed the air. Its head came to a sharp point, with a gaping mouth opened to reveal a large number of serrated, glowing teeth that were currently digging into a smaller, stockier creature that thrashed in panic or agony or both as the massive jaws closed around it. The giant crashed back into the water, once more becoming a patch of brightness beneath the waves. It turned and headed straight for the *Southern Echo*, its lights fading as it drew closer. It dove back beneath the hull, and then the light faded completely, leaving nothing but dark water all around the ship once more.

Jim Greenroot wasn't the only one who asked to turn around that night, and the captain and the quartermaster both came forward to hear what everyone had to say.

To Nate's surprise, Arani actually looked like she was entertaining the idea. She looked at the stars rather than the black water beneath them, but her hands were locked on the saber at her hip and the pistol tucked into her sash, as though she expected the heavens themselves to suddenly pose a threat. Still, she nodded when Greenroot reiterated his strong desire to turn around; and when Eric expressed his own trepidations; and when Blueshore admitted that the giant, bioluminescent predator had unnerved her enough to make her reconsider her original support for the westward voyage.

"We must have thrown off anyone pursuing us by now," Greenroot put in. "There's nothing out here for us. We should turn back before we tempt the gods any further."

There were several murmurs of agreement, and Nate found himself hoping that Arani would listen.

Surely, that would quell any brewing mutinies, and so long as she retained her captainship, she would not force Nate to track the black mimic again. They could go east, and leave the worst of their troubles in the Forbidden Sea, where they belonged.

"What say you, Captain?" Dax asked. He gazed at Arani steadily, but by the set of his jaw, Nate knew that the man was ready to act on behalf of the crew, even if that meant challenging Arani right there and then.

Captain Arani brought her gaze down from the sky and met the unblinking stare of the quartermaster. "I'm willing to put this to a vote," she said, and there was a collective sigh of relief from everyone around her.

"One month!" a voice rang out from the back of the crowd.

Gazes rippled towards the speaker, and people stepped aside to reveal Rori standing ramrod straight, her hands curled into fists at her side. Her entire body looked exhausted, as though she were barely keeping her feet, but her eyes were bright, and Nate felt his heart tighten with concern.

The Goodtide raised her chin defiantly. "You promised me one month to find the signs of the Vanishing Island before you let the crew vote on whether we turn around or not."

Arani ran her thumb across the pommel of her saber. "Circumstances have changed," the captain said.

"They have not," Rori insisted. "The Forbidden Sea is full of monsters, but we all knew that going in. Just because we've seen a few doesn't mean that we'll succumb to them."

"Doesn't it?" someone asked.

"What do you mean 'a few?'" someone else called.

Rori ignored them. "Those who were unwilling to

risk the Forbidden Sea were left back on Spider's Nest. Everyone on this ship came willingly, knowing full and well what we were going to do." She turned from the captain then, letting her gaze sweep over the crew. "You already voted to try. I have one month to find the signs."

"Are these monsters not one of those signs?" a woman shouted—Liliana, Nate thought.

Rori hesitated for a moment longer than was comforting. "No," she said. "Just... locals."

That sent a groan rippling through the crew.

"I've survived these waters once before," Rori called out, somehow finding the confidence to make herself heard. "If the *Godfall* made it, so can the *Southern Echo*."

"The *Godfall* didn't make it," Jim Greenroot spat as he pushed his way towards the front of the crowd. "It was destroyed!"

"By me," Rori snarled as she rounded on the gunner. "I said I'd see the *Southern Echo* safely across the Forbidden Sea, and I aim to keep that promise. I can protect us because I can be stronger and scarier than anything we find out here." Nate's heart clenched at Xander's mirrored words, but he kept quiet as Rori stepped up close to Greenroot, thrusting her face at the gunner's and glaring at him with enough anger to make a dragon turn away. "Do you mean to test me?" she growled.

Jim Greenroot flinched and dropped his gaze.

In that moment, Nate wasn't certain if he was more proud of Rori, or terrified of her.

"One month," she repeated, once Greenroot was sufficiently cowed.

"Eleven days," the rough voice of the boatswain called out. When he stepped forward, Rori was the one who shrank back a bit. "There are eleven days left in your promised month," Novachak said, pitching his voice to carry to the rest of the crew beyond Rori. "If you insist on all of them, fine. But that's all you have, and we will not go a moment further into this frost-touched madness without the vote."

Nate watched Rori meet the boatswain's icy stare. He saw her swallow hard, but she still drew herself up and nodded.

"Not a moment less, either," she said.

Novachak glanced at Arani, who gave a slow nod.

"Eleven days, Rori," the captain said, "and then we vote."

Though the crew was far from pleased by this decision, no one stepped up to challenge it, especially not with Rori there to glare daggers at anyone who so much as glanced in her direction. That included Nate, and he thought it best to leave her be.

I can't tell her, he decided.

It would be too much on top of everything already piled on Rori's shoulders. Letting her know about a potential mutiny would do nothing but strain her even more.

Nate could keep that burden from her, and protect her from at least that much.

In the small hours of the morning, Nate woke suddenly to a strange noise. Panic rose in him as he thought of strangers stealing aboard the *Southern Echo*, and he felt phantom ropes around his wrists and throat, but then he remembered that they were deep in the Forbidden Sea, and no one was following them, and he was as safe as he could be.

He lay in his hammock in the darkness of the berth,

listening to the familiar snores and grunts of the sleeping people around him. He waited for weariness to take him again, but his heart was still pumping adrenaline through his veins, and sleep eluded him.

After a few minutes of unsuccessfully lying still with his eyes closed, Nate climbed out of his hammock and reached for his boots. He half expected Luken to come soaring out of the dark, now that Nate had presented him with an easy target, but the bird's perch was empty, and so was Rori's hammock.

He found them both topside, at the bow of the ship. They were completely alone. Those on the night watch were clustered near the stern, sitting well away from the railings and keeping only a cursory eye out for more trouble from the sea. There was no one up in the crow's nest or the rigging, not after Liliana's near-death experience. Dax said they'd go back up in the morning if the giant was gone, but not while it still lurked beneath the ship. Everyone was to remain either below deck, or as far from the railings as possible if they were on the watches.

Rori was clearly ignoring that order. She had Luken in her arms, and was petting the dozing bird idly as she stared out at the dark horizon. Gazing uneasily at the churning water below the ship, Nate approached Rori slowly, and gave a soft call to let her know that he was coming. She tilted her head towards his voice, but did not turn around. He took that as a good sign, and moved to join her.

"It's not safe to be out here," he said.

Rori reached down and tugged lightly on the lifeline she'd secured around her waist. "Safe enough."

Nate did not agree, but he did not want to fight her on the matter and push up her defenses. "Have you slept at all tonight?" he asked as he stepped up next to her.

Rori shook her head. "I'm not the only one. A few people have been poking around the lower decks. Probably too nervous to close their eyes."

Nate felt a flare of irritation on Rori's behalf. The vast majority of the crew had already made their opinions on the voyage clear. They did not need to keep telling her that. But he looked at Rori again, and knew that wasn't what was weighing on her.

"What is it?" he asked. When she did not answer, Nate gently nudged her shoulder with his own, which earned a disgruntled twitter from Luken. "You know that you can tell me if you want to, but I can also just stand here with you if you'd rather enjoy the silence." He waited a few moments. "Or I could leave you alone," he suggested, a little pained, but sincerely.

Rori shook her head. "I don't mind the company."

Nate nodded, and the two of them spent a few minutes contemplating the night, the conflicting winds lifting their hair and dragging it in and out of their faces. Despite that annoyance and his desire to stay with Rori, sleepiness began to steal back over Nate, underscored by the raw exhaustion he was constantly feeling with his work-intensive schedule and extra training. He was about to tell Rori that he was going back below and suggest that she try to get some rest, too, when she suddenly spoke.

"I don't know if I can do this."

Nate drew in a deep breath of the salt-stained wind, letting it chase his tiredness away for a few minutes longer. He had an idea that he knew what she was talking about, but he knew that she needed to say it more than anything. "'This' being what, exactly?"

Rori's sigh came out in a hard, sharp line. "All of it," she said, waving her hand at the darkness in front of them.

Nate did not point out that she had seemed sure of

herself a few hours earlier. Instead, he moved a little closer, putting more of his back between her and the wind. "For whatever it's worth," he said, "I think you *can* do this. All of it." He was relieved when she gave the smallest quirk of a smile. "But it's okay if it's too much."

Rori tore her gaze away from the horizon and looked at Nate in silence.

"You saw that dragon hunt almost destroy me," Nate said, "and I didn't have a history weighing down on me."

Rori's eyebrow took on a pointed arch, pushing the top half of her Goodtide tattoo towards her hairline. "I'd call the legend of Mordanti the Thief a fairly heavy weight."

Nate huffed a soft laugh. "Fair point," he said. "But what I meant was that I didn't have a history with where we were going."

She turned wordlessly back to the night sea.

"It's a lot, Rori," Nate said. "You're trying to go back to a place that's haunted you, and you're trying to be brave because gods above know the rest of the crew is openly admitting that they're scared, but that would be too much for anyone, really." Hesitantly, he reached out and touched her shoulder. When she did not pull away, he rested his hand more firmly against her, hoping she took some comfort from the gesture. "I know better than to ask you to give up," he said softly, "but just promise me that you'll remember that if you don't find the signs of the Vanishing Island, it's going to be okay."

Rori shut her eyes and breathed out another hard sigh, but her voice was quiet when she said, "I don't think it is."

"It will be," Nate insisted. "We'll go east, and find prizes in Votheinian waters. It'll take time, but we'll find a way to make it work."

We have to, he added silently.

But Rori was shaking her head, and when she opened her eyes again, the moonlight gleamed strangely off of them.

"Can I ask you something?" Nate said, and then waited for her to nod. "Why did you want to come out here?"

Rori's breathing tightened. "It was the only way I could stop the captain from disbanding the crew."

"I understand that," Nate said slowly, gently. "But we don't need to stay out here. We could go back."

"And have all of this be for nothing?" she spat, and Nate was startled enough by the savage edge to her words to take a step back. Rori took a moment to visibly compose herself. Luken twittered in her hands, alarmed, but he fell quiet again as Rori let out a few shaky breaths. "The crew split because of me, and I've put you all in so much danger by bringing us here. If we turn back now, we leave with nothing, and I'll have let you all down."

It was Nate's turn to shake his head. "You've kept us safe this long. No one would blame you if you agree that we should turn around."

"It can't have been for nothing," she said, desperation coloring the words.

"It wasn't," Nate said. He stepped back to her side. "Anyone who would have pursued us has to have given up by now. You opened the way for us again. That's not nothing."

Rori's shoulders hunched and a shiver ran through her body. "It was too big a sacrifice."

"We haven't sacrificed anything except our time," Nate said. "And we all came willingly."

But Rori shook her head again. A single tear slid down her cheek, following the dark curve of her

Goodtide tattoo. "All those people on the *Godfall*," she whispered. "I killed them. I really am just another monster who came from the Forbidden Sea." Her voice hitched, and she began to shake.

"No," Nate said firmly. He put his arm around her shoulder. "You're not a monster."

She turned into him, releasing Luken to wrap her arms around Nate's waist. "I have so much blood on my hands," she murmured, her head pressed against his chest.

Nate pulled her closer, letting the displaced Luken settle on his shoulder with a concerned twitter. "You did what you needed to save yourself," Nate said. "That's all."

Rori stiffened against him, and he felt her shake her head again. "I didn't need to tear that ship apart," she said. "I didn't need to drown them all."

Nate did not have the words to answer that. Instead, he held her tight, letting her breathe through all the things that still haunted her. She sobbed once against him, and then was quiet for several long minutes before finally pulling away.

"I'll be all right," she said, scrubbing away the trails her tears had left.

"You will," Nate agreed. "We all will."

She gave a heavy sigh, but she nodded. "Ten more days now," she said, turning to look back out to sea. Luken hopped off of Nate's shoulder and settled on hers, and she idly reached up to stroke the bird's feathers. "And then it's over."

Nate shifted on his feet. He knew that Rori wasn't ready to see their departure from the Forbidden Sea as a victory. Maybe she would in the end, but if not, he resolved to be there for her no matter what. Until then, it would do no good for either of them to waste the time they had to rest. Nate turned to start back to the stairs that would take him down to the closed, safe darkness of the berth. Rori did not move.

"Get some rest?" Nate asked her gently.

"In a minute," she said. But she did not turn around, not then, and not when Nate finally left her alone once more with only Luken for company.

CHAPTER TEN

The First Sign

RORI WANTED TO BELIEVE Nate, that she'd done what she'd done to the *Godfall* and all its sailors to keep herself alive, but the longer she spent on the Forbidden Sea, the more clearly she remembered thinking, *Drown them all.*

It had been so easy, with power surging through her blood in that space between two worlds. The past couple days, at sunset, she'd thought that she could hear their screams as she waited for the sky to turn red.

But the world was silent and empty around her, and the sunsets were golden and burnt orange but never the bloody spill she was looking for, and she wasn't sure if she was relieved or devastated that she hadn't found that first sign yet.

She remembered those red sunsets leaking into the *Godfall*, penetrating the ship's gloom with an unnatural scarlet that lingered far longer than any sunset light should have, until the sky broke open and the world went completely red. The Vanishing Island had been just on the other side, and Rori's Skill had stormed in her veins.

If she couldn't find those red skies now, then she really had put her entire crew in danger for nothing.

Bigger and scarier, Xander had said.

That was the easy part. What happened if the sky

did break open, but there was nothing that could stop Rori?

The price was paid, the voice in her head reminded her. It was stronger these days, more of a murmur than a whisper. That should have been terrifying, but strangely, Rori found it comforting. It was like an old friend returning to talk her back from an edge, gentle and encouraging.

I don't need to use my magic for this, Rori reminded herself. The blood price had been paid with the lives from the *Godfall*, and all the *Southern Echo* had to do was keep sailing. With the waterspouts gone, she did not need to use her magic again.

But gods above and below, how she had missed it.

Remember the river, the voice in her head advised.

Rori's heart caught in her throat as countless days spent standing in its shallows unspooled across her memory, its waters familiar and steady and almost laughably weak compared to the currents she'd encountered in the ocean. And before it had betrayed her, the river had been Rori's teacher. It had taught her how to control her wild magic in its depths, even when the entire empire insisted that was impossible, and she should have gone mad.

She hadn't. Instead, Rori had saved a life.

Was it so far a leap to believe that she really could control that same magic enough to help her new family, her rowdy pirate crew?

Keep going, the voice in her head agreed.

So Rori put Luken down and stood alone at the bow of the ship, in the middle of the ink-black sea. She took a steadying breath, and called upon her Skill.

The magic came all too easily, boiling up in her blood and surging through her in its eagerness to snag the currents and bend them to her will. Rori clenched her teeth and stamped it down, keeping the power locked inside herself. The last time she'd truly let it loose, it had been during the fight with the navy, and she'd nearly capsized the *Southern Echo* with the sheer size of the waves she'd called up. That was still nothing compared to what she'd done to the *Godfall*. She wouldn't let herself do that again. Not now, not ever.

Rori focused her magic inward, until she could feel the flow of the sea around the ship as surely as the blood in her veins, just as she'd done with the river. The currents were firm and steady, and while her magic strained to morph them, Rori forced herself to let them be.

Good, she thought.

She held the magic there for a few moments, simply letting it be. It shivered and rippled through her, but it did not try to lash out of her control. When she was ready, Rori reached for the currents, feeling their own untapped power alongside her own. They did not resist her or shy away, but seemed to almost welcome her touch, and Rori felt that surge of joy she'd left behind on Solkyria so many years ago.

Keep going, the voice said.

I will, Rori answered, and then wondered how best to do that.

It would be so simple, she knew, to twist the water element and speed the ship along where the wind was failing, but she had not figured out the right heading, and could very well send the *Southern Echo* into something far worse than a few carnivorous fish and one lazy sea giant. The skies may have calmed, but for all Rori knew, she could push them straight into a whirlpool, or across the path of another terrifying column of wind come screaming down from the sky to pull the sea into a deadly cone. The *Godfall* had encountered and barely escaped each of those perils, mostly thanks to Rori's magic, but she knew that the *Southern Echo* was avoiding them through luck now.

Or maybe the fact that they had stopped finding such dangers meant that Rori had them on the wrong course entirely.

She tried to remember what had happened on the *Godfall*'s voyage, but the time she hadn't spent locked belowdeck had been stained with terror, and it was hard to focus on the details she needed rather than the ones that still gave her nightmares.

It had not taken the *Godfall* a full month to find the first sign of the Vanishing Island, that much she knew for certain. That ship had sailed recklessly, but Rori had felt the tug on her soul when it had found the right current. She had not been alone; the wind worker who had gladly served aboard the *Godfall* had felt the pull as well, and then pushed the ship straight through to the end.

She wished she could do what Nate could, and run her awareness along the currents until they brushed up against something, anything out beyond the horizon.

Stop wishing, she told herself firmly, *and keep going.*

But Rori found nothing in the currents that night, or the next night, or the one after that. She spent her days pouring over the sea charts and her own calculations, refusing to let anyone see her growing doubts and the war that raged within her soul, and she kept returning to the bow after dark to reach out and touch the currents. Her magic was always there when she called for it, but it whispered nothing back to her, and the sea remained silent.

By the time there were only five days left in the promised month, it was a foregone conclusion that the *Southern Echo* was going to turn around. Jim Greenroot and his lackeys continued to call for the vote early, and Rori knew that they'd only gain support the further west the ship went. She thought about giving it all up and telling the captain to stage the vote, but the screams from the *Godfall* tumbled through her mind, and that voice kept urging, *Keep going.*

Rori spent that morning locked in the navigation room, running her calculations over and over again, but every time she finished, she reached the same conclusion: she was not going to find the Vanishing Island unless the gods themselves decided to intervene.

Defeated, Rori slumped in her seat. She was too tired to cry, although she felt like she could have wept for hours without stopping.

"I can't do it," she said aloud.

Luken stopped preening his wing and gave an inquisitive chirp.

Rori clenched her fists, frustration boiling inside her chest, but it dissipated into steam that escaped with her next sigh. There was nothing for it. She had to tell the captain to let the crew have their vote.

It took a few minutes for Rori to convince her legs that she needed to stand up, and a few minutes more to take the steps from the table to the door. Luken had reclaimed his favorite spot on her shoulder at that point, and he nuzzled into her neck with pure affection and trust. Rori felt that she deserved neither, but she reached up to pet the bird all the same. He wasn't the one who had failed.

When Rori stepped outside, the sunlight blinded her for a moment. She started looking around for Arani before her vision had the chance to fully clear, but instead of the captain, she saw a knot of people standing at the foremast, pointing up at the sails and gesturing to each other. She blinked, and recognized Xander and Liliana and the other riggers, along with

Nate and Novachak. They all looked bewildered.

Rori knew she could not help them much when it came to rigging and the wind, but she snatched at the excuse to delay seeking out the captain. "What's wrong?" she asked as she came up to the group.

Nate was the first to look over at her. "It's the wind," he said gravely. "It's not behaving like it's supposed to."

There was a dismissive snort from Xander, which Rori chose to ignore. He was not in the mood to go unacknowledged, however. "So not only do you read the wind, you're now an expert on its behavior," Xander drawled. "You want to try talking to it, see if you can get it to cooperate? Gods above know you can't bend it, so maybe you should annoy it into a new direction."

Nate did not take the bait, but Rori saw the tension flex across his shoulders at Xander's words.

"Enough," Novachak barked before anyone could say anything more. To Rori, he said, "Strong winds like this usually mean there's a storm on the way, but it's been blowing hard from the west for the better part of the morning, and we have yet to see any clouds."

Rori stared blankly at the boatswain for a long moment, memories spilling through her mind. Screams and red skies and monsters from the sea... and a wall of wind that had almost killed the Lowwind on the *Godfall*. Had that been before or after the bloody skies?

I don't know, Rori realized. *They kept me below deck. I don't know which came first, only that they were there.*

Rori's heart surged in her chest. She stepped to the railing and studied the open sea all around them. The carnivorous fish were back, but other than the agitation stirred up by their leaping bodies, the waves were calm in spite of the heavy wind blowing in off the bow. Rori narrowed her eyes as she glanced up at the ship's sails, which had been furled against the headwind. The ship was coasting forward on the currents alone, and she knew that if she took a measure of their speed, the *Southern Echo* would be advancing at a crawl at best.

"Something you'd like to share with the rest of us?" Novachak asked. He'd come up behind Rori and was watching her with cold wariness.

Rori studied the motion of the flags overhead. They looked as though they'd been pulled taut by an invisible hand, showcasing Captain Arani's dragon emblem with steady pride as they stood straight out along the winds. No breezes seemed to come from the other points of the compass to so much as nudge the flags.

"This has to be the wind wall," she said.

She could feel Novachak's frown on her back.

"Thought we were supposed to see the red sky first?" the boatswain asked pointedly, but he kept his voice pitched low so that Nate and the riggers behind him could not hear, interested as they were in the conversation.

Rori swallowed, her stomach filled with a strange mix of hope and dread. "I may have been wrong," she murmured to the officer.

Novachak gave a low, contemplative groan. "That's not what anyone wants to hear from their navigator." He still kept his voice quiet, but his gaze was hard beneath his bushy white brows.

Rori felt it then, that tug on her very being. It was a small touch, light as a feather, but coming distinctly from the west, and something new washed over her: relief.

Keep going.

"We're on the right course," she said. "I'm certain of it now."

Novachak stiffened. "Did you just say, 'now?' What

were you before?"

"Less certain," Rori said as she turned to him. "I'm going to go speak with the captain."

"Good, see what she has to say about that 'now,'" Novachak said before turning back to the riggers and barking new orders that demanded their immediate attention.

Nate lingered, though, watching Rori with an open question on his face. She tried to give him a reassuring smile, but his answering frown told her that she'd failed, so she quickly turned away and headed for the poop deck.

She found Arani on the top level, her raised spyglass pointed west, directly off the *Southern Echo*'s bow. She lowered it when she heard Rori's footsteps coming up the stairs.

"No clouds," the captain mused, repeating what Novachak had said. "If it's a storm, there should be something in the sky by now. All the others were upon us well before we hit any winds like this."

Rori did not need to glance up at the clear, unbroken blue overhead to confirm that the weather was unusual. "I think it's a sign of the Vanishing Island," Rori said.

Arani's frown deepened. "You think?"

Rori swallowed and tried again. "It's the wind wall. It'll keep blowing in from the west. We have to ride the currents until we cross it."

The captain's gaze took on a sharp edge. "If I remember correctly, you said the first sign of the Rend would be the blood sky."

"Your memory is correct," Rori said, feeling heat rise to her cheeks. "Mine wasn't. I got the order wrong."

"You're sure of that?"

Rori drew herself up and met the captain's eye. "I am."

Captain Arani regarded her for a long moment. Rori did not allow herself to squirm.

"If it is the first sign," Arani finally said, "will you allow the crew to vote?"

It's not enough. Keep going.

The thought thundered across Rori's mind, and she knew it was true. "No," she said. "It would be best if they don't vote until they see the sky bleed."

The captain tilted her head. "And do you believe you'll be able to find that before the month is up?"

Rori bit her lip, wondering if she should confess her doubts to the captain. Standing before Arani now, however, she had the sense that the captain already knew.

"There are only a few days left," Rori said. "If I can't find the red skies by then, it won't matter."

"So you don't believe the wind wall is a strong enough sign for the crew?" Arani mused.

"Do you believe it?" Rori asked candidly. "Or do you think it's more likely a storm?"

Arani sighed and looked past Rori. Her gaze caught on something on the main deck, and her frown took on a panicked edge. "Nate," the captain called as she began to descend the stairs, "what are you doing?"

Alarmed, Rori turned to see that Nate had moved to the bow. He was facing directly into the wind, his hands spread and head tilted back. Rori did not need to see his face to know that he had tapped into his Skill, and had already gone off on the winds. Her heart squeezed as she hurried after Arani.

"He said he's not going far," Novachak said as the captain rushed past him. "And he's got Marcus watching him."

"Like that will save him," Captain Arani growled. She called Nate's name again as she crossed the deck in long, fast strides.

Rori had to run to keep up, but she did see that Marcus had appeared to take up a post just off to Nate's side, squatting next to a large bucket and watching the wind worker with the intensity of a silverwing falcon.

"Nate!" Arani shouted again. She sped up when he did not so much as flinch. "NATE!"

Rori did not know if it was the bellow or the heavy strike of the captain's boots on the deck that finally made Nate sway a little on his feet. For a moment, Rori feared that he had gone too far and was about to collapse, but his frown was one of concentration rather than pain, and his eyes blinked open just before Arani's hand came down on his shoulder.

"What in the six hells are you doing, boy?" Captain Arani snarled as she tugged Nate around.

He stumbled, looking from Arani to Rori with surprised confusion, but he was alive and, aside from the captain's hand clutching hard at his shirt, unruffled.

"I followed the wind," Nate said.

"Why?" Arani all but snarled. "Who told you to do that?"

"No one," Nate said, his dark eyes still wide.

The captain's grip tightened, and Rori exchanged a confused glance with Marcus as he slowly rose to his feet.

"I'm all right, Captain," Nate said. "I swear it."

Arani was breathing hard, as though she'd sprinted a great distance, or been dealt a sharp blow to her middle. Rori was unsure of what to make of such a strong reaction, although she herself had felt her heart hammering in her chest only moments before, when she'd thought that Nate had come untethered by the pull of his magic. He'd grown so much from the frightened boy the captain had found on Solkyria, but if this truly was the wind wall, then this was magic from the realm of the gods, and that was nothing to venture lightly into. Rori had felt that raw power in the currents around the Vanishing Island. She had no idea what Nate would find in the wind, but she knew it would not be gentle. Perhaps Arani had feared the same.

Finally, the captain released Nate. She patted his shoulder as she drew in a deep breath to steady herself. "Why did you use your Skill?" she asked. Gently, as though she were trying to reassure a child they had done nothing wrong after coming close to severing their own hand while playing with a sword.

"The wind is not natural out here," he said. "The shape of it is all wrong."

"How do you mean?" Arani asked.

Despite her earlier concern for Nate, Rori felt her heart surge as he answered.

"It's this solid stream just pouring in from the west, and it's the same no matter how far north or south you go. Or at least not from what I could tell. I didn't go very far." He directed this last bit directly at Captain Arani, who did not relax even a little. "There's no changes in it," Nate continued. "It's just... a wall."

Rori looked at the captain, who glared back at her.

"A few more days," Arani finally said, "and then the vote."

Rori nodded, and moved out of the captain's way.

Before she got very far, Arani turned back to Nate. "Don't do that again," she told him. She turned and stalked off without waiting for a response.

"So that was odd," Marcus said after a few moments. He nudged the bucket at his feet, which was filled with seawater. "I'm glad I didn't have to use this, but I'm also a little disappointed that I didn't get to."

"Don't get rid of it," Nate said, still staring after the captain. "Not yet."

"What was it like?" Rori blurted, unable to contain

her curiosity any longer. "Riding those winds?"

Her enthusiasm wavered when Nate grimaced.

"Hard," he admitted. "They're not very strong, but there's something about them that wanted to pull me away. I was fine," he quickly reassured her when he saw the growing horror on her face, "but those winds are... strange." He fixed his gaze on the western horizon, the wind bringing tears into his eyes. "I'd say this is definitely that wind sign you told us about." Then he gave her a quizzical frown. "Wasn't the sky supposed to turn red first, though?"

Rori ignored that and snatched at his hand. She touched the gold ring he wore, feeling the heat of the magic burn in her fingers. "How far, exactly, did you go?" she asked him tightly.

Nate took his hand back. "I promise, I'm all right," he said. "Are you?"

Rori nodded. "Never better," she lied.

That night, Dax spoke to the crew. Arani had shared the news of the wind wall with him, and in turn, the quartermaster passed it on to everyone else. As Rori had feared, not everyone was ready to accept the wind wall as a sign that they were heading for the Rend.

"Seems even the weather is telling us to turn around," Jim Greenroot called. There were loud sounds of agreement.

"Three more days," Dax reminded them all, his voice steady and firm.

Rori felt that deadline crushing down on her shoulders with the full weight of the empty, endless sea.

You'll find it, she told herself. *You have to.*

Keep going.

CHAPTER ELEVEN

A Shadow in the Night

NO STORM CAME, BUT the wind wall persisted, just as Rori said it would. Nate felt the strangeness of it under his skin and through his bones, a pervading sense of wrongness that practically screamed that they did not belong here. And still, the *Southern Echo* pushed on.

The wind wall gave the riggers no respite, constantly tugging on the sails and threatening to rip them where the cloth was even the slightest bit loose. The next morning, Xander, Liliana, and the others had to spend more time up in the rigging than on the deck, and Nate watched them in the swaying ropes with his heart in his throat, Novachak grim and quiet beside him.

"If one of them falls," the boatswain growled at one point, but not even he seemed to know how to finish the threat, other than shooting a dangerous glare at Dax and Arani, who both came to watch the riggers with solemn faces and tense stances. At one point, Arani took a step forward, as though she meant to scale the lines herself, but Dax stopped her with a hand on her shoulder.

"The wind is hard but steady," the quartermaster told her. "They'll be all right, as long as we let them concentrate."

The captain grimaced, but she did not argue.

The morning passed slow and terrified, but the riggers succeeded in fully securing the sails, and the canvases were saved. It was just in time, too. A few minutes after the last rigger had come down from the shrouds, the wind picked up even more, howling out of the west with a vengeance. Dax had the lifelines brought out, and anyone who had to be topside was ordered to secure themselves to the ship the moment they were at their post.

"If we turn around now," Nate heard Jim Greenroot remark sourly to AnnaMarie Blueshore as they checked the locking wedges behind the wheels of the cannons, "we'd fly out of here on this wind."

Blueshore grunted, but did not disagree.

Something unpleasant twinged in Nate's gut, and he spoke up. "Three days," he reminded them. "No less."

Blueshore huffed an exhausted sigh, but Greenroot gave Nate a scathing look over the rims of his glasses.

"No more, either," the gunner snapped. "Don't you or that Goodtide bitch forget it, Lowwind."

There was a gleam in his eye that Nate did not like at all.

Nate's hands curled into fists as he thought about Jim Greenroot openly pushing to return to the dragon hunt, and he could have fought the gunner right then and there, never mind the considerable weight advantage the barrel-chested man had over him. One solid hit, though, and Nate could break his nose, maybe even knock him over the railing and save himself and the rest of the crew a great deal of trouble.

Mutinous trouble.

But he remembered what Eric had told him about acting without proof, and so Nate restrained himself, worked through the afternoon, and then went to find his friend when he had a break.

He found Eric below, taking careful measure of the water levels in the ship's bilges. Despite the nightly battering the keel took from the underwater giant that hunted beneath the *Southern Echo*, the levels were shallow enough that Eric was not concerned, and he divided his attention to listen while Nate recounted his interaction with Greenroot. By the time Nate was done, however, Eric was staring at him, the bilge levels completely forgotten.

"If he's going to mutiny," Nate finished, "he's going to do it soon."

Eric slowly straightened up and wiped his hands on a rag. "That's assuming he's even involved."

"How could he not be?" Nate pressed. "You've heard him talk about the dragon hunt."

"I have," Eric said grimly, "but what I haven't heard is anyone else whispering about trying to take control of the ship."

Nate stared at the Darkbend. "That doesn't mean the mutiny threat is dead."

"No," Eric agreed, but there was a troubled line between his eyes. "But it just doesn't make any sense for a mutiny to happen now. The vote is in a few days. A mutiny is too much risk for something that they could easily get without any bloodshed if they just wait."

"Unless the crew votes to continue," Nate pointed out.

That made Eric pause. "If," he said slowly, "the highly unlikely scenario arises that the crew votes to continue sailing west, then that will have been decided by the majority of the crew. And that means a mutiny would lack the support it needs to guarantee its own success."

"Because mutineers are known for playing fair," Nate said acidly.

Eric sighed impatiently. "Because they'd be trying to ambush Iris Arani, and sneak around Daxton Malatide, *and* risk pissing off Nikolai Novachak, not to mention anyone who voted to continue west." He gave Nate a pointed look. "Do *you* think you could do all that without getting a sword plunged straight through your heart?"

Nate shifted on his feet.

"Exactly." Eric squatted down to examine the curving hull and the seams between the wooden boards, squinting in the lantern light. "Now get out of here, before I put you to work caulking the seams. The smell of the pitch is worse than the bilge water, and I'd kill for an apprentice to take the brunt of the fumes for me."

Nate sighed and left Eric to his work. But he was not as willing as the Darkbend to let the matter go, and he watched Jim Greenroot and his gun crew as close as he could without outright staring at them. He was not as subtle as he thought.

"Did you take a fancy to one of the gunners?" Marcus asked at dinner, when he caught Nate eyeing the people at the other table. "Novachak's going to be so disappointed if you did."

"No, I—" He broke off when he realized what Marcus had said. "I told Eric not to tell you," he whispered fiercely, his face going hot.

Marcus grinned. "He didn't. Lily did."

Nate's embarrassment gave way to horror. "*She* told you?"

"She asked me some interesting questions about you, and I pieced it together from there." He waggled his eyebrows at Nate. "Novachak, huh?"

Nate groaned, but he gave a mild laugh, too. "How long do you think I can pretend that's true before it comes back to bite me?"

"So long as the boatswain doesn't find out, probably a while." Marcus tore off a large bite of salted meat and chewed it thoughtfully. "Might not keep Lily from making another pass at you, though, considering how long she had her eye on Eric." He swallowed and grinned. "But she is quite pretty, so maybe you want to consider setting the record straight with her." His smile took on a sly tilt. "Unless you're still holding out for a certain navigator, but the Novachak rumor isn't likely to help you with that, you know."

Nate felt another flush creep up the back of his neck, and he quickly changed the subject.

That night, Nate somehow felt more at ease as he climbed into his hammock, although he kept worrying over the prospect of a mutiny as he drifted off to sleep, exhausted snores and the unending howl of the western winds against the ship's hull filling his ears.

He woke what must have only been an hour or two later.

The berth was warm and dark, filled with the familiar noises of people sleeping. The wind was still a constant thing against the ship, a sound that Nate had grown accustomed to, just like the lapping of the water against the keel.

That was why the muted thud had woken him.

He lay still for a while, waiting to see if it would come again. It did not, and Nate tried to rationalize it as someone's misplaced footstep on the deck above, or some shifting of supplies within the ship. He could not shake the feeling that there was something wrong about the sound, though, and his heart spun up as he thought about ropes and unseen assailants. He took a few moments to calm himself, then climbed out of his hammock as quietly as he could.

Someone groaned and shifted in their sleep as Nate pulled on his boots and gingerly picked his way out of the berth and on to the gun deck. He squinted into the dark, but nothing moved, and he decided that he'd have to go topside if he wanted to find the source of the odd sound. Carefully, Nate climbed the stairs, wincing whenever one of them creaked under his weight. Quiet as he was, each small betrayal of his movements sounded like a gunshot in his ears.

When he finally reached the main deck, Nate peered about, searching for something out of place in the flickering lantern light that spottily lit the deck. The wind tugged relentlessly at his hair and stung his eyes, but other than the violently swaying ropes, Nate saw nothing out of the ordinary.

That did not comfort him, so he sought out one of the night watches. He found Theo Yellowwood in his assigned position, snoring softly and head lolling with the motion of the ship. Nate shook him awake, and Yellowwood peered at him through bleary, sunken eyes before sitting bolt upright.

"Gods below, was I asleep?" the sailor asked. When Nate nodded, he groaned. "Thanks, boy. Don't tell Dax, yeah?"

"You haven't seen anyone else up here, have you?" Nate asked.

Theo made a noise somewhere between a vocal shrug and a guilty whine.

"I thought I heard something odd," Nate said. "I came up to check."

Theo looked at him blankly and made the noise again.

"I suppose I'll go try to find out what it was," Nate offered after an awkward pause.

Theo bobbed his graying head in agreement. "I'll keep an eye out for anything unusual over here."

Nate did not bother to thank the man. He had the feeling he was going to come back and find Yellowwood nodding off again. Nate couldn't exactly blame him, as the wind wall was demanding extra hands on the rigging lines and everyone was suffering for it. Novachak, even, had needed to call a halt to Nate's fighting lessons, as his attention and energy were needed elsewhere. Nate knew he had made a lot of progress on that front, but it wouldn't do him much good as he prowled unarmed across the ship. Unease rippled through his stomach as he made his way across the dark deck, but he couldn't waste the time trying to find a cutlass.

Something had woken Nate from his own exhausted sleep, and he knew it would be a mistake to ignore the noise.

There had been a thud, and then a quick scrabbling, and then nothing. No splash of anything falling into the water, no creak of the deck or pounding of footsteps, and no voices. If it was something still on the ship, Nate should have come across it by now, or at least heard someone trying to conceal it. But there was nothing but the wind.

Nate hesitated, his thumb idly pressing against the gold ring on his right hand. It was cool and solid, and would be enough to anchor him for a short distance. It had grown a little warmer than he'd expected the last time he'd explored the unnatural winds, but he'd been pushing against them then, trying to find a gap in the wall. This time, he'd let the wind take him, and see if it brought him to anything interesting off the stern.

Picking up the end of a lifeline, Nate tied the rope around his waist as he moved to the railing. He took a few deep breaths of the constant wind, letting it fill his chest and carve its shape along his skin. He double checked the knot he'd tied, made sure the gold ring was firmly against his knuckle, and then cautiously reached for the wind.

It snatched him up in an instant and bore him off on its unbending lines, carrying him far away from the *Southern Echo* in a matter of moments. The ship receded into a dark, blurry shadow, and Nate nearly panicked as he struggled to break free. The wind fought to keep him. It sent his awareness tumbling farther and farther away, and somewhere distantly behind him, the gold ring began to burn.

Nate concentrated on that small flash of pain, a tiny spark of harsh brightness that kept him tethered to his mortal self. Gradually, painfully, he clawed to a stop, the wind cutting all around him in violent blue and wild purple lines. He knew that he wouldn't be able to fight his way back to the *Southern Echo*, but he couldn't let the wind carry him any further. He was stuck.

Come on, Nate told himself. *There has to be a way. Find it!*

But no matter how hard he pushed, the wind wall would not let up. He knew that it ranged further north and south than his stamina could endure, and going east would do nothing except break his anchor and tear him away for good. Desperately, Nate thrashed against the wind, but that only loosened his grip on his body, and panic set in as the wind dragged him forward again.

I should have woken Marcus, he thought bleakly. *Could've used that water now.*

And then he had an idea.

Tentatively, Nate pushed himself down, towards the sea. The strength of the wind only intensified the closer he got to the black water, and he backed off quickly, pulling himself skywards again. The wind howled all around him, far from gentle, but no where near as bad as it had been by the water. Nate went higher, and the wind weakened even more.

He nearly lost himself then, not believing that he had managed to find a way out, but before the wind could rip him away, he sent himself soaring up as hard and as fast as he could, out of the grip of the gods-cursed wind wall. The air was thin now, and the wind was still strong, but it curled more naturally around him. He could see the shapes of the air currents again, and they weren't all hellbent on going east.

Relieved, Nate sought out a gust that would carry him west, skimming him over the top of the wind wall. He'd ride it all the way back to the *Southern Echo* and that burning ring on his hand, a tiny beacon of pain and hope in the middle of raw terror.

Then a wind shadow cut into his awareness, and Nate nearly lost himself all over again. By the time he had recovered his grip, the shadow had passed and disappeared. He had no desire to follow it. Instead, he found the thread of wind that he needed, and traced it back to the ship.

He crashed back into himself, and was completely unsurprised to discover that his body had fallen to the deck. He lay staring up at the stars, breathing hard, and then moaned as his head began to throb. The ring on his hand was so hot, he was sure the skin was going to blister, but he did not care.

He was alive.

"Bad idea," he murmured as his skull continued to try to split itself open. "Terrible, awful idea." His body agreed with him, and he stayed firmly pressed against the deck until the pain in his head had subsided from completely unbearable to merely agonizing.

With a heavy groan, Nate slowly got to his feet, giving himself permission to grab and lean against whatever he needed to achieve the task. He pressed his hand to his forehead, trying to calm the throbbing. The pressure did nothing, but Nate could not let himself rest now.

The wind shadow he'd encountered in the high sky had belonged to a bird. He was sure of that. He'd spent long enough tracking Luken in preparation for the dragon hunt to know that the creature was significantly larger than the pennant-winged bird, and better suited to fighting through harsh winds. But much like it had been for Nate, the wind wall had been too much to contend with, and the larger bird had sought higher altitudes to ease its flight.

All of that made perfect sense to Nate.

But what did not make sense was what a bird—any bird—would be doing out over the Forbidden Sea. It was the only one Nate had seen since the *Southern Echo* had slipped past Solkyria. And if he'd read the bird's trajectory correctly, it had come up from the wind wall rather than flying straight over the top. The bird had risen from the sea and battled its way into the sky, as though it had recently taken off from landing. But there was nothing to land on anywhere in this vast, empty sea, except the *Southern Echo*.

Stumbling a little under the strength of the wind and his own dizziness, Nate made his way back to the stairs. It took him a few minutes to safely descend into the dark hold, even without caring about the creaks and groans of the boards beneath his feet. Once he was out of the unnatural winds, his head began to clear a bit, although that familiar spike of pain continued to reside at the base of his skull. He rubbed at it resentfully as he made his way to the captain's cabin.

Arani answered his first soft knock, looking disheveled in sloppily rolled up shirt sleeves and no coat or sash. From the loose bags under her eyes, Nate guessed that she had not been sleeping particularly well, or at all, given the candles already lit inside the room and the many papers spread out over the central table. She peered quizzically at Nate for a few moments, blinking like an owl caught in sudden sunlight, and then pushed a loose wisp of hair off of her forehead.

"Something I can do for you?" she asked, not at all embarrassed to have been caught in anything less than her usual pristine state.

"I found something," Nate said.

Arani cocked an unimpressed eyebrow. For a moment, she seemed on the verge of telling him to come back with something a bit more interesting, like the ship being on fire or the imperial navy materializing on the horizon. Then she blinked again, her gaze focusing on Nate's Lowwind tattoo, and she straightened in alarm.

"Come inside," she said softly, and shut the door behind him.

She rounded on him the moment they were alone.

"You used your Skill, didn't you?" she asked. Her voice was still quiet, but there was nothing gentle about it.

Nate was very aware that Arani already knew the answer to that question, but he nodded all the same.

"What," she hissed, "in the six hells were you thinking?" She crossed the distance between them and jabbed a finger into Nate's chest, accentuating each angry point. "We're in the middle of the Forbidden Sea, trying to find the realm of the gods. You said yourself that wind coming in from the west is unnatural. *Everyone* can feel how wrong it is, and it's only getting stronger. And you decided to put yourself in the kind of danger *no one* on this *entire ship* can save you from." The captain was breathing hard by then, and with a jolt, Nate realized why Arani had been so unnerved by him using his magic earlier in the voyage.

"I'm not broken, Captain," he said softly.

"No," Arani agreed, moving back a step, "but you so easily could be." She gave a bone-weary sigh before collapsing into a chair at the table and waving for Nate to join her. "What did you find?"

Arani listened intently as Nate described what he'd done, and how he'd found the bird's wind shadow. Her brow creased into a hard frown when he tried to skirt around the way the wind wall had nearly ripped him away. Her gaze slipped past him, and Nate glanced over to see the sheathed saber resting on the far side of the table. For a moment, he was stunned, unable to think of a single time that he'd seen the sword separated from Arani. That was enough to make him recount the dangerous trouble he'd really found within the wind wall, and he was surprised when Arani did not interrupt him. She shut her eyes and dug her nails into the arm of her chair, but she let him speak.

"You're sure the bird came from the *Southern Echo?*" she asked when he had finished.

"Not entirely," Nate admitted, "but I don't know where else it could have possibly come from. It had recently taken off, and there's nothing else around here where it could have landed."

The captain gave a slow nod as she sat back in her seat and turned her gaze to the charts on the table. "That's why I haven't found anything," she muttered.

Nate frowned as Arani drifted further into her own thoughts. "Captain?"

She startled slightly and looked at Nate as though just remembering he was there. "You said the bird was heading east and a little north of our current position?" she asked.

Still puzzled, Nate nodded. That much, at least, he had been able to see without any doubt whatsoever.

Arani was quiet for a long time.

Nate fidgeted in the silence, unsure if he should speak or leave the captain to her thoughts this time. He stole another glance at the charts spread out next to him, but the islands were unfamiliar to him, and he could not read any of the labels or numbers written on the paper. He wondered if these were the islands in Votheinian waters. If they were, then Arani was clearly getting ready for the ship to turn around and sail east.

"Rori really could find the Rend," he murmured. "If she had more time, she could find it."

"I don't doubt that," Arani said. "But that is far from my concern at the moment." She drummed her fingers on the table, the sound deadened to small pats by the papers. "What worries me is that if this bird actually did take off from the *Southern Echo*, then it needed a reason to land here to begin with. If it was migrating from the west, there's no reason it would have stopped, especially if the winds are easier higher up, as you said."

"I don't know of any birds that migrate across the Forbidden Sea," Nate said.

"Nor do I," Arani agreed. "Which leads me to think that this particular bird came from somewhere else, and was seeking out this particular ship." She shut her eyes, looking far older than her thirty-some years, but when she looked at Nate again, her gaze was bright and alert. "You said the bird was larger than Luken. How much larger?"

Nate thought for a moment, then held up his hands a little further apart than the width of his shoulders. "I can't say exactly," he said apologetically, "but maybe a bit bigger?"

Arani nodded grimly. "There are a few species of messenger birds that grow to that size. One in particular is bred to handle strong winds and long distances, although they're useless if one of their lodestones is lost."

"Lodestones?" Nate asked.

The captain waved her hand. "I don't fully understand them, but they're pairs of special rocks that the birds are trained to sense. Something about magnetics, I think. Someone once explained it to me using a compass to illustrate the point, but that was years ago and it honestly wasn't terribly important for me to remember. Regardless, the birds will fly back and forth between any two points on the map, as long as there's a lodestone at each end." Arani tilted her head back and let her eyes fall shut once more. "That means there's one on the *Southern Echo*, and who knows who's got the other one."

Nate was stunned, and silent until outrage crept in, but with it came a way to exploit a weakness in the traitor's plan. "I could find out where that bird is going," Nate said. "At least, we'll know how long it will spend in the air before it lands again and offloads its message."

He could tell from the troubled grimace on the captain's face that she was having similar thoughts, but to his surprise, she shook her head.

"It's far too dangerous for you to use your Skill."

"I'll be careful," Nate said. "I know what to expect now, and how to avoid the worst of the wind wall."

"No."

Nate sat back, startled by the force Arani put into the single word.

The captain kept him pinned with a glare, but her eyes softened after a few moments. "I've seen first-hand what happens to the Skilled when they're push beyond the limits of their magic." Her gaze cut to the table again, back to the saber. The sword was fully sheathed, but the polished leather mimicked the fine, deadly curve of the blade. "The man who carried that before me was a tyrant, cruel and unforgiving, especially to the Skilled. Most of the wind workers that stepped aboard his ship did not survive a year." Captain Arani's dark eyes gleamed in the candlelight. "I swore I would never do that to any of my sailors, but

I almost did it to you on the dragon hunt." She looked at Nate then, her gaze open and haunted. "I'm sorry, Nate. I became the exact person that I've always hated, and you almost died for it. I won't do that ever again. Not to you, and not to anyone else."

"Captain," Nate said after a moment, "you don't have to ask me to do anything. I'm offering, of my own free will. I want to help."

"I know you do," Arani murmured, "but as your captain, I'm ordering you not to."

Nate's mouth fell open, and a million frustrations and protests rose to his lips. "You would just sit back and let someone betray us?"

He regretted the question even before Arani shot out of her seat and loomed dangerously over him, fury practically sparking off of her.

"I would do no such thing," she snarled, "but I will not throw away the lives of the men and women who sail with me on a whim. That includes you, too."

Nate swallowed hard and dropped his gaze to the deck.

Arani sighed and slowly sat back down. "Look at me, Nate." She waited until he did. "I took Eric's warning to heart. I've been looking for evidence of a mutiny, and while I haven't found anything solid, I know what's being said in the shadows on my ship. I know there's a threat here, and I know that it's a dangerous one, but I must serve my crew. Sometimes, that means letting them blow off some steam, or whisper the things they'd never dare say aloud if they knew I was listening. Do you understand?"

"No," Nate said, and he meant it.

Arani nodded. "Truthfully, I don't expect you to. Until you've held the lives of people you love and loathe in your hands, you're not going to." She leaned forward, resting her elbows on her knees. "But I need you to trust me, Nate. Can you do that?"

He nodded without hesitating.

Arani's smile was grim, but earnest. "I trust you too, you know. I don't want you using your magic, but if you're willing, try to find that lodestone."

Nate nodded again.

"You're a smart one," Arani said. "I know you'll keep your eyes and ears open, but be careful who you trust. Until you truly know someone, you'll never be able to see all the things that could turn their heart."

"How do you know when you truly know someone?" Nate asked.

The captain gave another mirthless smile. "People will usually tell you who they are when you first meet them. It's up to you if you believe them or not."

Nate wanted to ask if Arani believed that she truly knew her entire crew, but he held back this time. Instead, he asked if he should share his theories on potential mutineers with her or not.

"Better me than someone else," Arani decided after a moment. "Last thing I want is trouble stirring up where I can't see it. But to be clear, while I will listen, that does not mean I will be able to act."

Nate agreed, and then told Arani about Jim Greenroot and his desire to use Nate's Skill to hunt the black mimic again.

Arani listened, just as she said she would, and then she waved the idea away. "Jim Greenroot is notoriously difficult to please, and the whole crew knows that there's nothing between his brain and his mouth to filter out the nonsense, but he's not someone who would lead a mutiny. He's simply not that kind of man."

Nate wanted to protest, but Arani had pinned him with another level stare that brokered no room for argument, and he felt like he was sitting across from a stranger.

He did not know this Captain Arani, who was scared of the very idea of Nate using his Skill but willing to shut her eyes and her ears against the discontent Jim Greenroot was openly sowing. Maybe Arani was right not to fear the man, but Nate remembered the rough scrape of ropes against his skin and the force of the would-be kidnappers from the *Gryphon*. They'd come after him because of Greenroot's drunken speech the night before. Who knew what other ugly troubles the gunner had stirred up, whether he'd meant to or not? What was more, there was more than just Nate's life on the line now. His friends were in danger, and if a mutiny came to fruition, none of them would be spared. His heart squeezed at the thought.

"I'm scared," he admitted aloud.

"You're right to be," Arani said. "But you are part of my crew, Nate. I will protect you."

Nate nodded, but he did not fully believe her.

The dragon hunt had changed everyone, it seemed, and not for the better. But if Arani needed solid proof in order to accept the reality of what was happening on her ship and take action, then Nate would find it. By every god above and below, he would find it.

CHAPTER TWELVE

The Search Begins

"DAX ALREADY ASKED ME what I've heard," Eric said the next morning. "I told him the same thing I'm going to tell you: nothing."

They were down in the hold, in a small, sectioned off space that had been designated as the carpenter's workshop. The walls were thin and Nate's hands were full of splinters after helping Eric with the raw wood that the Darkbend was busily transforming into braces for the masts, but at least it gave them the chance to talk somewhat privately. Unfortunately, the closeness kept the sawdust in the air. Nate's lingering headache from his battle with the wind wall the previous night may have gotten him excused from working topside with the riggers, but it was doing him no favors now as he sneezed and coughed his way through the carpentry work.

"There has to be something," Nate insisted, his voice thick with the next sneeze coming on. It escaped him in a violent blast that he just barely managed to direct away from the shavings on the floor. "Mutinies don't just die like that."

"They can, if they never really get off the ground," Eric said as he positioned a nail against the brace. "But I think you're right, in this case. The bird is... worrying." He hammered the nail into the wood with three firm, practiced strikes. "If someone really is sending messages off the ship, then we're being followed."

Nate grimaced. "So much for the Forbidden Sea scaring off our enemies."

"I'm sure it did," Eric said mildly, "at least the ones who didn't know we always intended to turn around." He picked up the hammer again and weighed it thoughtfully in his hands. "The mutineers must have had this planned since before we left Spider's Nest," he mused. "None of us would have had the funds to secure a messenger bird like that, so it must have come from someone else. They would have had to make those arrangements before we left the Nest, so all our traitor had to do was bring the lodestone on to the *Southern Echo* and wait." Eric spun the hammer in his hands, frowning down at the metal head. "You said it's not safe for you to track anything in the wind wall, right?"

"That's what the captain thinks," Nate said, "and honestly, after last night, I agree."

Eric nodded, a worried line appearing between his brows. "So you can't use your magic, but that doesn't mean the messenger bird is having the same kind of trouble. If it's following a lodestone on the *Southern Echo*, then whoever is following us can use the bird to track us. Even when they're not sending messages, the bird should point them in the right direction."

That idea landed cold and heavy in Nate's stomach. His mind painted a vivid picture of an enemy ship looming over the *Southern Echo*, casting its shadow across his friends as certain as death. Nate nearly choked on his next breath. He forced the air down, and then let it out in a slow, quiet stream. "This is all pointing to Greenroot."

Eric looked at Nate sidelong, but gestured for him to continue.

"Greenroot was the one who talked about the

dragon hunt on Spider's Nest. He announced it to the whole tavern, but he was mostly talking to the *Gryphon*'s crew. Then three men from the *Gryphon* tried to kidnap me." Nate felt the phantom scratches of ropes against his wrists and throat, and he shuddered. "Maybe they were planning it, and Greenroot tried to make it seem like he spilled the secret by mistake. And then, when the kidnapping didn't work..."

"The *Gryphon* gave him a lodestone so they could communicate," Eric finished. He was nodding now. "It fits, but we can't do anything without proof."

Nate threw his hands in the air. "He's practically screaming it every day!"

Eric motioned sharply for him to keep his voice down.

Nate obliged, but did not keep the heat out of his words. "Greenroot wants to turn around but he doesn't want to go east. He *wants* to go after Mordanti's dragon again. And he thinks of me like some particularly handy pocket knife that can be used for anything from cutting rope to picking the dirt out from under his nails."

"Charming," Eric said.

"I'm serious," Nate snapped.

"I know," Eric said, "and I'm not disagreeing with you, but without something solid that we can hold up and use to show without a single doubt that it's Greenroot behind this, we're stuck."

"Arani said the same thing," Nate grumbled.

"As I told you she would. She knows better than to strike against her own crew without proof."

Nate hefted the brace while Eric slammed another nail into place. "We have to find the lodestone, then," Nate said.

"A message would be better," Eric said.

"It would," Nate agreed, "but not even Greenroot

is stupid enough to leave those lying around, and we don't know how often the bird comes. I can't track it, and the watches are clearly missing it. The lodestone at least gives us a place to start. Maybe we'll even be able to catch the bird, if it comes back again."

The Darkbend made a thoughtful noise. "We're going to need help with this."

"Mmm." Nate lowered the brace to the deck at Eric's command, then picked at one of the splinters sticking out of his palm. He winced at the sharp pain the little sliver of wood sent through his hand. "Arani said to be careful with who I trust. At this point, I'm a little worried about trusting her."

Eric did not glance up from his inspection of the brace, but Nate saw the worry creep into his eyes. "How so?"

"Ever since the dragon hunt, she's seemed... off. Like she's afraid to act." He watched Eric sand down a particularly rough spot on the brace. "Has she ever been like this before?"

"Not that I've seen," Eric said. "Could be the Forbidden Sea making her act strangely, but Marcus told me about her reaction to seeing you use your Skill the other day. I think you're right. Something's off." He blew away the dust and straightened up. "But if we can bring her definitive proof, she'll act when the time comes."

Nate wasn't so certain about that, but he did not see the point in arguing with Eric. If nothing else, Nate would ensure that he himself was ready to act, along with any allies he could collect. If and when the traitor made their move, Nate would be ready. No one was going to hurt him or his friends ever again. "Who can we trust with this?" he asked.

"Marcus, obviously," Eric said without missing a beat. "His skull is thicker than the wood we just cut, but he'll take this seriously." Eric gave the completed brace one last inspection, and then began to put away his tools. "Dax, too, as he already knows about all of this. I'm sure he'd prefer this be resolved peacefully, before bloodshed divides the crew even more."

"What about Novachak?" Nate asked. "He didn't want to come out here, but surely he wouldn't betray Arani."

"He wouldn't," Eric agreed. "I guarantee he lets her know every day that he's not happy, but he's working with Dax to keep the peace. All he wants is a fair vote when the time comes."

They both fell silent for a moment as the closeness of the end of the month weighed down on them. There wasn't much time at all for them to find the lodestone.

"What about Rori?" Eric suggested. For some reason, he sounded almost reluctant. "The last thing she wants is the crew to break apart even more."

Nate quickly shook his head. "She's busy enough as it is. We don't need to add this to her shoulders."

Eric tilted his head in clear confusion. "I thought you already spoke to her about this?"

Nate felt a flare of irritation as he remembered that night in the navigation room. "I tried. We were interrupted, remember?"

The Darkbend made a thoughtful noise at the back of his throat. "And you haven't spoken to her since then?" Eric asked suspiciously.

"I have," Nate admitted. "But she has so much on her mind already. If we add this, it's just cruel. She'll blame herself." Nate sighed, his irritation giving way to conviction. "Let her focus on finding the next sign. If she doesn't, we'll tell her after the vote. Until then, we can handle the mutiny, and make sure she's safe."

Eric made another noise, but did not press further.

"What about AnnaMarie or Liliana, then?"

Nate shook his head. "As of this morning, they're both in favor of turning around."

Eric glanced over his shoulder at Nate. "And that means you can't trust them?"

"It makes me wary of them."

Eric slowly tapped a finger against the wooden chest that held the carpentry tools.

"You're different," Nate said firmly. "You warned Arani about all of this in the first place. And you told *me*, too. But as to Liliana, I don't think either of us could safely work with her. She may be more of a distraction than any help."

"Speak for yourself," Eric murmured.

"As for AnnaMarie," Nate went on quickly, "I think she'd just club Greenroot over the head and ask him pointblank about the mutiny. Subtlety is not one of her strengths."

"That would certainly save us some time, but point taken," Eric said with a shrug. "Who would you suggest, then? More eyes can only be better on a search like this."

Nate thought for a long moment, wondering who else they could possibly trust within the crew. Without Rori, Nate did not have many other friends to turn to.

He found himself remembering his conversation with Arani the previous night. She had not said anything about friendships, just that he could only understand what would turn someone's heart if he fully understood them.

"Xander," Nate said. The name left a bitter taste in his mouth, but Nate knew it was the right choice.

Eric looked at him with open shock. "Xander?"

Nate nodded. "He once said he'd follow Arani to the end of the world if she'd promised to lead him to treasure. I can't imagine him letting anyone come between him and gold in his pockets."

"He voted to leave you behind," Eric pointed out.

"He did," Nate said grimly, "but he did it openly, and he hasn't pretended otherwise since. He's not kind, but he's honest. We know what we're getting with him." He hesitated for a moment. "He also was the one who saved me when the *Gryphon* tried to take me."

Eric screwed up his face as though he'd taken a whiff of something rancid. "I'm not going to be the one to talk to him."

Nate gave a reluctant nod. "It should be me, anyway. He and I have a few things that we need to discuss."

"You already know he hates weather workers. What else could you possibly lay to rest?"

Nate did not say anything, but Eric caught the meaning in his gaze.

"Ah," he said. "The one exception to Xander's rule. Well, gods above protect you when you have that conversation." He squatted down and took hold of the larger of the two braces he and Nate had fashioned. "Come on, help me get these topside before the wind wall snaps the masts in half."

Nate had to wait until Xander's shift was over and he had descended from the shrouds. Of all the riggers, he was the only one still willingly climbing up and down the lines, and he personally handled and re-secured the topsails against the unyielding wind wall. Nate watched in awe as Xander moved confidently through the ropes, never once misplacing his feet or his hands. When he finally came down, he was breathing hard, but his eyes were bright beneath his black Grayvoice tattoo. They went cold as Nate approached.

"I need to talk to you," Nate said before the Grayvoice could turn away.

"And isn't that just a treat for me," Xander said dryly. He moved to step away, but Nate blocked his path.

"It's important," Nate said, firmly enough to draw the attention of those nearby.

Xander's eyes narrowed. He did not offer so much as a mocking smile when he said, "Why don't you go play with those toothy fish off the bow, Nowind? They seem hungry for attention."

Nate couldn't help bristling at the old nickname, but he had far more important things to worry about. They both did. He stepped forward and snatched Xander's arm, pulling away from the others. "Get your head out of your ass," Nate snarled, "and come with me."

"I'd rather go swim with the fish."

Nate's grip tightened, but Xander did not flinch. He stared down at Nate with open contempt, and Nate knew that there was only one way he was going to get the Grayvoice to talk to him.

"It's about Rori," Nate said quietly.

Xander's brow rose, but he did not resist as Nate pushed him towards the stairs at the stern of the ship.

With the wind wall raging, most people were taking shelter belowdeck as soon as their topside work was done. Nate was still getting headaches if he stood in the wind too long, and Xander's hands were chapped after spending so much time up in the rigging. Neither of them protested when they hit the stairs, however. They climbed up to the deserted poop deck, where the wind buffeted them even more but would also whip their words away before anyone else could hear.

Still, Xander hunched his shoulders and turned his back to the wind, trying to keep the worst of it out of his face. "What's wrong with Rori?" he demanded. "What does she need?"

"Nothing," Nate answered. He had to stand shoulder-to-shoulder with Xander for them to hear each other, and he wasn't certain if he or the Grayvoice recoiled more from the touch. "But there's something going on that's about to make things extremely dangerous."

Xander's eyes narrowed again. "For her, or for you?"

"For everyone."

The Grayvoice scowled. "Talk straight, Nowind. What do you want?"

Nate felt a bloom of anger in his gut, but he stamped it down. Rage would do no good here. "I need your help," he said instead.

Xander's scowl turned into a scoff. "The great wind reader has come to *me*, a lowly Grayvoice, for *help?*" He laid a hand lightly across his chest. "Be still, my wild heart."

The anger flared again, but Nate did not try to temper it this time. "What is wrong with you?" he asked, and he meant it seriously.

"Other than the fact that I don't see the need to worship the ground you walk on?" Xander gave a dramatic yawn and scratched at his neck. "Nothing, really, except that my time is being wasted by a half-bit hero who fancies himself a rigger, but can't even tie a noose to hang himself."

Nate glared at him. The wind wall may have halted Nate's fighting lessons, but right then, he felt like he could take down a god with the sheer force of his angry determination alone. "I'm trying to talk to you. Would you prefer I beat some sense into you?"

Xander laughed, and the wind whipped it away in a cruel ribbon of sound. "What are you going to do, Nowind? Breathe on me?"

"Gods below, Xander, there's going to be a *mutiny!*"

To his surprise, the Grayvoice laughed again. "Is

there?" he asked mockingly. "Or do you just need something else to go wrong so you can play the hero and keep everyone's attention on you?"

Nate drew back as though Xander had struck him. "You think I asked for any of this?"

"You love it," Xander growled. "Don't you dare deny it."

"I love people trying to kidnap me and force me to hunt dragons?"

"You love everyone looking at you and actually caring about what you can do with your Skill." His eyes cut deep into Nate's. "You're nothing without it. So, what, you heard someone talking about picking up the dragon hunt again, and you decided to make up a little story about a mutiny with you at the center?"

"No," Nate snapped, "I found a messenger bird."

The laughter died in Xander's eyes. "You what?"

Quickly, harshly, Nate recounted waking up to a strange sound in the night, finding the bird in the wind, and his conversation with Arani.

"I'm not going to be able to sense the bird coming with the wind wall," Nate finished, "and if it keeps coming at night, the watches aren't going to see it. That's why we need to find the lodestone, before it's too late."

Xander had fallen quiet, and turned his calculating stare to the wake left by the slow, staggering passage of the *Southern Echo*.

Nate waited, but his exasperation grew the longer Xander did not respond. He couldn't believe that the Grayvoice would be this petty, but then again, he had voted to leave Nate behind. "If you won't do this for anyone else," Nate said, "Do it for Rori. You know she wouldn't want this."

Xander blinked, but he was still silent for several moments. "You're sure it's Greenroot?" he finally said.

"If he's not leading it, he's heavily involved," Nate said.

Xander made a thoughtful noise that the wind nearly drowned out. "Anyone else?" he asked.

"I don't know," Nate admitted. "If it is him, probably the people from his gun crew."

"And if it's not?" Xander pressed.

Nate gave a reluctant shrug. "I suppose it could be anyone."

He frowned as he thought back to last night. Theo Yellowwood had been on watch, sleeping peacefully as though he wasn't in the middle of the Forbidden Sea. Had he also been on watch that night Nate had woken to another strange noise, and gone above deck to find Rori standing alone in the dark? Nate couldn't remember.

That shadow he had imagined looming over the *Southern Echo* and his friends grew and darkened, and Nate clenched his hands into fists against it.

"There have to be answers somewhere," Nate said. He did not try to hide the desperation in his voice. "If we can find the lodestone, maybe we'll get at least one."

"Fine," Xander said, turning his hard gaze back on Nate. "I'll look for the thing."

"Thank you," Nate said, and his relief was genuine.

Xander scoffed, but he nodded all the same.

"If you hear anything else about the mutiny, report it to Arani," Nate told him.

Xander waved him off. "Whatever you say, Nowind," he grumbled as he turned to go.

Nate felt a deep chasm of regret open up beneath his anger. He'd hoped that he'd be able to reconcile with Xander, but that seemed as unreachable as the Vanishing Island at this point. He'd thought that his time at the wind working academy had hardened his heart, but accepting that he had truly lost a friend cut so much deeper than Nate had expected. Or maybe he was just finally admitting to himself that he and Xander had never really been friends at all.

He turned to the stairs with a sigh, only to stop short when he saw that Xander was still there, looking at him.

"You ever get those private knot-tying lessons from Novachak?" the Grayvoice asked.

Nate frowned, and then blanched with mortification.

Xander's mouth curved into a smile, and some of the coldness melted out of his gaze. "Normally, I wouldn't judge," he said, "but *Novachak*? Really?"

Nate buried his face in his hands. "I'm never going to live that down."

Xander laughed again, but when Nate opened his eyes, the Grayvoice had already descended the steps and started back across the deck, quiet as the night.

The search for the lodestone turned up nothing that first day, and the next morning was equally fruitless, no matter how many times they crisscrossed the decks and checked every possible hiding spot, including inside the cannons and up in the crow's nest. Marcus, Eric, and Xander all shook their heads when they caught Nate's questioning glance, and Novachak also came up empty. Dax was especially troubled by the failure.

"Ship this size, six of us looking, we should have found something by now," the quartermaster said when Nate had a moment to approach him.

Dax had scoured the hold, claiming the need to

check some supplies as an excuse to search every nook and cranny, even inside the crates and barrels. He'd enlisted the help of the ship's one remaining cabin boy, who now slumped against a crate, dead asleep and drooling a little after the overnight search. Dax scooped the boy up like he was nothing more than a bundle of twigs and carried him to the berth.

"Keep looking," the quartermaster instructed Nate as he passed. "It has to be here somewhere."

So Nate redoubled his efforts, rechecking every spot he'd already thought of and bending his imagination until he'd come up with a dozen new ones. He had to stop short of climbing out along the bowsprit to see if the lodestone had been lodged somewhere within the figurehead. Xander found him trying to get a better look at the carving of the dryad. When Nate told him his idea, Xander only paused long enough to removed his boots and socks, and then he climbed out on to the bowsprit with terrifying speed and grace. The Grayvoice pretended to adjust some of the lines that ran from the bowsprit to the foremast, but he lowered himself down far enough to examine the figurehead, and then came up shaking his head. He did all that without once glancing down at the churning waters, where the sharp-toothed fish frenzied and jumped.

Silently, Nate wondered if Xander actually feared death, or had simply been born without that basic instinct.

The afternoon wore into evening, and still the search returned nothing.

Out of desperation, Eric and Marcus took it upon themselves to dive into the bilge water, and they came up dripping, stinking, and empty handed. They received a lot of questioning looks as they stomped their way topside and doused themselves with clean seawater. Nate followed them, Xander close behind, and it wasn't long before Dax and Novachak had joined the small group on the main deck.

"I don't understand where this frost-touched thing could be," Novachak said. He leaned hard into the wind, the gradually setting sun gilding his white beard and hair. "Unless someone swallowed it and hasn't shat it out yet, we've looked everywhere."

Dax gave the boatswain a sidelong look. "But did you actually—?" he started to ask.

Novachak bared his teeth. "*Every*where," he growled.

Dax did not pursue the matter.

"Other than the captain, we're the only ones who know about this, right?" Eric asked. "We're certain the mutineers don't know that we're looking?"

"Unless one of us told them," Dax said grimly, "they shouldn't."

"So they wouldn't be moving it around?" Eric pressed.

The quartermaster began to shake his head, and then stopped, looking dismayed. "They could be," he said. "Precautionary measures."

Novachak slumped further into the wind. "So we actually could have missed it," he groaned. "We're going to have to search *again*."

"Or catch the bird when it returns," Nate suggested.

"If it returns," Dax said ruefully, "and if we're lucky enough to see it coming."

"I'll scout for it," Nate said.

"Not in this wind, you won't," Dax snapped. "The captain told me what happened last time. You're not to use your Skill out here."

Nate wanted to argue, but part of him was relieved, too, and that was the side that won out.

"I say we put up extra patrols," Novachak said.

"With what poor souls?" the quartermaster demanded. "With the size of the crew, everyone is already stretched too thin. Almost no one is making it through their entire watches without falling asleep, and that's during the day, when a sea monster isn't head-butting the keel. You try to put any more of them on night watches above deck, they'll riot."

A pit was opening in Nate's stomach. "What do we do, then?" he asked.

"Keep searching," Dax said. "And start preparing for the worst."

Nate exchanged an uneasy look with the others, but before the group could disperse, a thin, sour voice drifted over the wind.

"Mr. Malatide," Jim Greenroot called as he sauntered across the deck, several people from his and AnnaMarie's gun crews following him. "A word, if I may?"

Dax openly groaned, scrubbing his hands over the intricate twin tattoos that disguised his Skill mark. "Tomorrow is the last day, Mr. Greenroot," the quartermaster said impatiently.

"All the more reason to consider turning around tonight," the gunner said. "The wind is only getting stronger, and the Goodtide hasn't found anything."

"She has a name," Nate bit out before Dax could respond.

Greenroot blinked at him, as though just realizing Nate was there. His gazed wandered over Eric and Marcus, and barely touched on Xander before flicking back to the quartermaster.

"There's nothing for it," the gunner said. "Why waste another day out here, sir?" He added the last word after a pause just too long to be respectful.

Nate did not realize his hands had clenched into fists until he felt a sharp pain in his palms, and saw that his nails had pressed little crescent moons deep into the skin. "Because that's what we voted on," Nate snapped. He stepped forward and pushed past the restraining arm the quartermaster lifted across his path. Nate was angry, and here was Jim Greenroot, speaking brazenly. It wasn't right. "Rori has one more day." He glared at the gunner. "We *all* have one more day."

Greenroot's gun crew shifted behind him, pressing in as though shoring up a defense. Behind Nate, the deck creaked as Xander stepped forward, and then Marcus.

Jim Greenroot peered at Nate over the rims of his round glasses. "Look, boy," he said, in what may have been intended to be a soothing tone, but was nothing short of condescending. "The Goodtide's done what she promised, and seen us safely through these waters so far. Why tempt the gods and go further? What's one more day going to do, other than give that sea monster another chance to capsize the ship?"

"One day could make all the difference," Nate said. His throat tightened, but he forced himself to say the next words. "It did for me, on the dragon hunt. You wanted to turn around then, too."

Greenroot blinked again as his gunners exchanged glances. Then he looked past Nate to Dax and Novachak.

"You don't mean to let this Lowwind decide for us all, do you?" he demanded.

"It'll be for the crew to decide," Dax said firmly. "*After* the month is over."

"It *is* over!" Greenroot snarled. "The Goodtide failed, and the captain's touched in the head if she thinks we're going to let that girl lead us to our doom."

"You followed the Nowind," Xander said from over Nate's shoulder. "Why is Rori any different?"

The look that Jim Greenroot turned on Xander was one of pure disgust. "I don't know why you're talking,

Sheep Lips. Out of all the Skilled on this boat, you're the only one who completely failed to make yourself useful on the dragon hunt."

Nate stiffened, and even over his own mounting rage, he could feel the anger radiating off of Xander. But unlike Nate's, Xander's was cold and silent, heavy on the wind. Nate knew long before Novachak shouted and lunged forward that Xander had his dagger in his hand.

"Drop it!" the boatswain snarled.

Novachak and Xander collided, and they bumped hard into Nate. He stumbled forward, which Greenroot all too eagerly accepted as an invitation. He moved to meet Nate, his fists raised. Nate wished he had a dagger of his own, but he felt his muscles waking and responding with the memory of his sparring sessions with Marcus, and Nate dove closer even as Greenroot began a heavy swing. Dax snatched Nate by the collar of his shirt and hauled him back before either of them could land a blow.

"Enough of this!" the quartermaster roared.

He shoved Nate back into Marcus and Eric at the same time that someone from the gun crew loudly grumbled, "Magic-tainted freaks."

This time, the anger flared in the quartermaster's eyes, and he rounded on the gunners. "Say that again," he growled.

Greenroot shrank back, looking like he would very much prefer to avoid the quartermaster's wrath, but the gunners behind him stood their ground, and he had nowhere to go.

"I said," one of the older men from Greenroot's crew hissed, "Magic. Tainted. *Freaks.*"

By the time Nate had regained his footing, disentangled himself from the Darkbends, and then stepped forward to the quartermaster's side, all diplomacy had bled out of Dax. He stood like a wall, ready to meet whatever kind of force the gunners dared use. At his sides, his fingers twitched, as though trying to reach for his magic.

Novachak appeared in front of them, arms raised and calling for everyone to stand down. No one listened, and heated voices began to rise on the wind. Heads turned towards the commotion, and Nate dully heard the door of the navigation room creak open as Rori poked her head out to see what was happening.

All sound cut off when a pistol shot cracked through the air.

Every head whipped around to where Captain Arani stood, one arm pointed high with a gun in her hand. Smoke from the barrel curled away on the wind.

"*What* is going on up here?" Arani demanded, her voice slicing through the wind and the silence alike. Behind her, heads poked up from the staircase, the rest of the crew drawn up by the shouting.

No one answered her immediately. When her gaze cut to the quartermaster, Dax actually looked ashamed, but he drew in a steadying breath and met her glare.

"Disagreement in opinions, Captain," Dax said.

Arani's sharp eyes narrowed as they roved over the two groups. "I'll not have fighting among this crew," she said. She lowered the pistol and tucked it back inside her sash. She addressed Jim Greenroot directly when she said, "The final vote on the Vanishing Island is tomorrow. Nothing more to it. Do *not* kill each other before then. That's an order." She turned to leave, and Nate felt a fresh spike of anger towards her for letting Greenroot and his gunners go unpunished for trying to provoke a fight, and for her refusal to act on the simmering mutiny before it could boil over.

You absolute fool, Nate wanted to shout at her. He

opened his mouth, but Jim Greenroot spoke first.

"You're going to kill us all, you Veritian bastard," he snapped at Arani.

She stopped, her spine going rigid, and turned back to the gunner.

He swallowed hard and dropped his eyes to the deck, but to Nate's surprise, he kept speaking.

"There's nothing out here, and prospects out east are bleak at best," Greenroot said. "We all know it. Just like we all know that boy—" he pointed a thick finger at Nate, "—is the key to finding the Thief's lost treasure. We have him, and no one else does. That means we're the only ones who can track down the black dragon again and follow the map." Greenroot's eyes came up from the deck, and his voice rose with them. "We may as well use him!"

Calls of agreement went up from the men and women behind the gunner, and Nate felt his blood run cold.

"We're not hunting the dragon again," Dax snarled.

"Shove off it," a burly, sun-bronzed woman yelled back, "you pathetic excuse for a Malatide!"

Novachak gave a sharp shout, and Dax's lip curled back. Arani's hand went to the saber at her hip, Xander's dagger flashed in the light, and Nate braced himself for a fight, Marcus and Eric doing the same at his sides.

Then Rori shouted, "Look!" and came running out of the navigation room, heading for the bow.

She stumbled a bit in the face of the wind, which tangled her hair across her face, but she raked the dark locks aside and sprinted across the deck, her face turned skyward.

The fight went silent once more as Rori blew past. Nate and the rest all looked to Arani, who stood frozen with her sword half-drawn. After a moment, she slowly pushed the blade back into its sheath and followed Rori. Nate exchanged a glance with Marcus and Eric, and then started after the captain. The rest of the crew fell in behind them, until nearly everyone was gathered at the bow, watching Rori stare into the west.

Rori had one hand wrapped around a taut line of rope, and the other was lifted to point at the setting sun, which was round and gold as a polished coin hovering above the ocean. She stayed like that as the sun sank lower, until its edge kissed the water.

"There!" she yelled, and Nate squinted into the light, trying to see what had caught her attention.

It began as a flash of red at the line of the horizon, soft and beautiful as any calm sunset. But then it rippled and split, and a jagged crack ran up the length of the sun, raw and bloody. Red light spilled out from the wound in the sun, staining everything deep red, and the wind roared even louder all around them.

Nate gasped as the gale forced itself into his lungs, and the taste was strange, almost acrid on his tongue. He coughed, and heard the echoes of the sound throughout the rest of the crew as they stumbled under the renewed onslaught of the wind wall, and everywhere was the red, red light from the rend in the sun.

And then, without warning, the wind softened to a gentle breeze, and Nate could breathe again.

He lifted his head to see that the sunset had gone permanently red, and the color spilled across the sky like blood. A stronger wind began to blow off the stern, as though the wind wall had not been rearing before the bow mere moments ago, and the *Southern Echo* pushed forward, towards that crimson sky and the single blistering star that now hung directly over the sun, far too bright and steady to be natural.

And at the bow, the curve of her cheek lit up by the

red light, Rori looked back at the crew, and said, "*That* is the red sky we're looking for."

CHAPTER THIRTEEN

How Deep They Run

RORI'S MEMORIES HAD BEEN so stained by that red sky that she could not recall exactly when the *Godfall* had crossed the threshold and the ship's Lowwind had finally been granted some respite, but she knew that the violent display of the blood sky and their passing through the wind wall was the best chance she had to convince the *Southern Echo*'s crew to vote to continue west. She went to Dax and Arani to arrange for the vote to be held that night, after the sun had fully set and the entire crew had been given the chance to see the sky.

Keep going, the voice in her head urged.

For the first time, Rori really believed they could.

With the wind wall now behind them, Luken was finally feeling brave enough to emerge from the navigation room. He flew easily and stretched his wings, his beautiful pennant feathers a welcome sight against the darkening sky, but he returned to Rori's shoulder quickly and chattered uneasily against her neck, upset by something Rori did not understand. She tried to soothe the bird with gentle pets and an offering of a dried berry, but even when Luken accepted the distractions, he still huddled against her and would not be coaxed down.

At least seeing the blood sky had been an intense relief. Rori had steeped so long in doubt, her entire world had gone bitter with it, but now she knew they were on the right course, and more importantly, she now had the beacon star to navigate by. Even with the little they'd let her see on the *Godfall*, she knew that the star would remain low on the horizon even at midday, and the closer the *Southern Echo* sailed to the Rend, the longer that red color would linger in the sky at sunset. But with that knowledge came a new problem.

Her desperation to find the signs of the Vanishing Island was no longer dammed against her memories, and they came back in a flood.

Chains around her wrists and magic burning in her blood.

Something urging her to break free and drown them all.

Screams and death and surging waters under a red, red sky.

It would be so easy to do it all again.

Rori shudderd and shunted the thought to the side, as far away as she could.

By the time the crew had gathered on the main deck for the vote, a surprisingly large part of her wished that they would decide to turn around after all. But after everything they'd endured, the crew deserved a treasury worthy of its own legend, and Rori could give them that, and they wouldn't have to go east into uncertain waters, with Captain Arani balanced between the crew voting a new captain into her place and a mutiny trying to force her out.

Keep going.

The voice in her head was clearer now, still breathy like a whisper but with steady force behind it, and it was warm and beckoning.

The price was paid, Rori reminded herself. *We can do this.* I *can do this. For them.*

She repeated those words to herself over and over, then schooled her expression into something fierce and confident as she stood among the crew, waiting for the vote.

The captain, the quartermaster, and the boatswain were all on the quarterdeck, standing in a tight huddle with their heads together. From her position near the port stairs, Rori could see the worried frowns on the officers' faces. They persisted even when the three nodded and turned to face the crew.

Captain Arani took up her usual position in the center, but she was acting strange. There was none of her usual easy confidence, and her voice was oddly quiet when she spoke. If the crew had not already been waiting attentively, Rori doubted they would have heard her at all.

"We've agreed to hold the vote on the pursuit of the Vanishing Island tonight," Arani said, and Rori felt her stomach drop. "Would those in favor of continuing west—"

"A flat and glassy sea," Rori shouted, drawing everyone's attention to herself. She swallowed past the lump in her throat and made herself take a few steps up to the quarterdeck. "That will be the next sign we find."

Everyone was looking at her, and no one was moving. Rori had no idea if she was swaying them in favor of continuing on, or convincing them to turn around.

Keep going.

"The worst is behind us," Rori continued. "With the wind wall gone, we can expect much quicker sailing, and then the sea will flatten out until it looks like glass, even with a steady tailwind and strong currents all around. We'll be close then, and we'll reach the Rend far quicker than it took us to journey this far."

She took a breath to gauge the reactions of the crew. Most of them were stoic and silent, but she saw a few who looked somewhat intrigued by what she was saying. She tried to take heart in that.

"The fourth sign will come to us as sea serpents. Small ones," she added quickly, "nothing like the leviathans of the south. They will come to correct our course and escort us forward."

If we're worthy, she added silently, but last time, they'd willingly come for the *Godfall*, when the blood price had not yet been paid. Rori had already established her credit. The serpents would let the *Southern Echo* through. They had to.

"It should only be three or four days of sailing once the serpents come," Rori told the crew. "After that, they'll leave us, and the tear in the sky will open during the day. That will be the final sign, when the blue sky bleeds red and the sea goes dark. We'll be able to see the Vanishing Island then, and it's a straight course to the end."

Glances were exchanged all across the ship, and Rori could see their doubts rising. Her gaze flickered to Jim Greenroot, who stood sullenly by one of the starboard swivel guns. He glowered back at her, and with a sinking feeling, Rori knew that he had already made up his mind, and would not be swayed. He would not be the only one.

Looking past the bespectacled gunner, she saw more people with the same hard sets to their jaws and flatness in their eyes.

"I know it's hard to believe," she said, "but I swear to you, we are already so close to that island and a treasure that will put this ship, this *crew*, into a legend of our own. The storms are past, and there are no waterspouts on this side of the wind wall. There are no sirens in these waters, and no doldrums to drag us to a halt. There are no dragons in the skies to attack and burn the ship." Rori glanced at Captain Arani, who looked grim but nodded for her to continue. "And," Rori said, making herself turn back into the steady gaze of the crew, "there's no navy ship waiting to ambush us on our return. We can get our treasure, and then go back home, because this is the Forbidden Sea, and there's no one in their right mind who would come for us here."

Movement caught her eye, and Rori saw Nate exchange a sharp glance with Eric and Marcus. She started to frown, wondering what that silent look was about and not liking it at all, but she caught herself before her projected confidence could waver in front of the crew.

"I know that you're afraid," Rori said, making sure her voice was strong and clear. "I'll admit, I am too. I thought I'd die before I let another ship take me through these waters."

She looked up then, following the lines of the rigging to where Xander perched. Now that the wind was calmer, the riggers had reclaimed their vertical territories. Xander in particular had always preferred to sit above the crowd, watching things unfold with clear, unobstructed sight. He met her gaze now, and in the quickly fading light, gave her a strong nod of encouragement.

"But I returned willingly," Rori continued, "because I have all of you with me. This crew does not run in the face of fear, and more importantly, this crew stands strong together. So I stand before you now, as your navigator and as your crew mate, and swear by every god above and below, I will see you safely home no matter how you vote today. You are my crew, and I will never lead you astray."

There were no cheers or hollers when she finished speaking. She had not expected them, but she was very aware of the lapping of the dark waves against the hull of the ship and the cold stars taking over the sky as she stepped back down to the main deck. She took up her place at the railing again, and tried to find somewhere to put her attention that would not scald her further. She settled on the captain, and was surprised to see the woman looking at her with open pride. She gave Rori the faintest of smiles, and then drew herself up and called for the crew's attention once more.

"A little wind," Captain Arani said, her voice clear and strong, "and a few red skies. As our fine navigator said, we've faced far worse than that." When she fixed the crew with a challenging stare, the effect was almost invigorating. Rori felt a rush of relief and gratitude for that. "We've come this far, and I, for one, know that this ship and her brave crew can go even further." The captain grinned then, a feral and intoxicating thing. "This is not the first legend we've chased. Who's for seeing this one to the end?"

The ayes that came were stronger than Rori had hoped, and even when the considerable nays were tallied, the vote still carried in favor of continuing west. Jim Greenroot and his gunners were openly dis-pleased, but it was done. And the closer they came to the Vanishing Island, the closer they'd be to the greatest treasure of their lives.

Rori only wished she could feel genuine excitement alongside the people who had shouted their ayes the loudest. There were no shackles on her wrists and she was free to move about the ship she loved surrounded by people she could trust, but there was a pit in her stomach, and she did not know how to seal it up.

No one needs to die this time, she told herself. The

next thought came like a lightning strike: *But they so easily could.*

Rori shook her head, trying to clear it away like a nagging bug. She wasn't going to do what she'd done last time. There was no need, and these people were her family.

She glanced over to where Jim Greenroot and his gunners were whispering darkly to each other.

Most of them.

When a hand came down on her shoulder, Rori was startled enough to upset Luken. The bird gave her a hard nip on her earlobe for her transgression before diving belowdeck for his stabler perch in the berth. She rubbed at the pained spot as she turned to face Captain Arani.

"Now that the vote has been decided, may I have a word regarding our heading? I think the chart we need is in my cabin."

Rori followed Arani down into the private room, and was surprised to see both Dax and Novachak already waiting at the table inside. The captain gestured Rori into a seat before taking her own at the head of the table.

"You did well," Arani said as she shrugged out of her coat and carefully draped it over the back of her chair. "But all three of us are equally concerned about what you just did."

A lump rose in Rori's throat. She glanced at the quartermaster and boatswain and saw them looking back at her with grim expressions. "I'm sorry," she said. "I had to speak before they voted to turn east."

Captain Arani waved her hand dismissively. "It's not that. You did exactly what was needed in that moment, and I applaud you for it."

Dax and Novachak did not look like they shared Arani's admiration, but neither man said anything.

"The issue," the captain continued, "is that you just explained in great detail what the next three signs of the Vanishing Island are."

Rori blinked, confused. "Is that a problem?"

"In this particular circumstance," Dax said, "it very well may be."

Rori frowned at the three officers. "I don't understand."

Novachak mirrored her expression. "The boys didn't tell you?"

Something unpleasant churned in Rori's gut. "Tell me what?"

"The other night," Captain Arani began, "Nate went topside by himself, and used his Skill."

From there, the captain recounted Nate's discovery of the suspected messenger bird, and the dangerous implication that had when there was so much unrest among the crew. Dax and Novachak agreed, and supplied their own stories about their fruitless search for a lodestone that could be guiding the bird to the *Southern Echo*.

"That's actually what we and the boys were discussing before the commotion brought everyone out of the woodwork," Novachak finished.

"And while that 'commotion' won't go unacknowledged," the captain said with a hard look at Dax, "the bigger concern is that there very well may be a mutiny brewing, and one that involves outside players."

Stunned, Rori could only stare down at the table, her mouth hanging partly open.

It can't be, she thought. *Not in this crew. Not on this ship.*

She shook herself and said as much to the officers.

"It can," Captain Arani said grimly, "and there's a very good chance that it will. Especially now that the vote was to continue west."

This is all your fault, a vicious voice whispered in Rori's mind. *You brought them here, and because of you, their blood will spill.* She thought of Jim Greenroot and Theo Yellowwood and all the others who had voted no, and then looked so upset when the ayes had carried. Would they really rise up and mutiny with the crew so divided?

Not if you kill them before they can. Drown them all.

Rori shot to her feet, trembling, and was very aware of all three officers looking at her with open confusion and concern. She tried to hide the revulsion she felt at her own thoughts under a show of false confidence. "We're going to the Vanishing Island," she said vehemently. "I can get them this treasure." She slapped her hand against the table, harder than she'd intended. "I swear on my family's name, I can give them this."

"None of us doubt that, Miss Rori," Novachak said gently. "But we haven't been able to find the lodestone, and whoever is sending messages with that bird, they now can tell their friends where to go and what to look for." He removed his cap and ran a hand over his balding head. "We have to assume that we're not the only ones heading for the Vanishing Island."

"They won't get there," Rori said. "It's not possible."

The officers paused, fresh worry coming into their expressions.

"Any worthy ship can reach the Vanishing Island," Rori said, "but to get to the beaches, there's a price that must be paid. A blood price." She watched the officers' worry give way to horror, and forced herself to keep speaking. "The captain of the *Godfall* wanted to offer the Lowwind from the crew, and then me, if that wasn't enough. He thought that the magic in our blood would make for a more compelling sacrifice." She shuddered, remembering the glint of a sword beneath a crimson sky and the wild, desperate need to survive howling inside her heart. "When I destroyed the *Godfall* and drowned everyone on the ship, the price was paid. And then, when I just swam away from the island, I..." Rori shut her eyes, trying to push the rushing roar of water and the dying screams of the *Godfall*'s crew out of her ears. She failed.

Monster.

She did not open her eyes again until she felt a warm hand rest gently on top of hers.

"They told you that you'd be welcome to return," Captain Arani murmured. She gave Rori's hand a light squeeze. "You paid the price, and now we don't have to."

Rori nodded.

"What happens if a ship approaches, and the crew doesn't know that they have to pay?" Dax asked.

Rori winced. "There are very powerful currents around the island." She made herself meet the quartermaster's gaze. "Strong enough to tear a ship apart."

"Ah," was all the quartermaster had to say to that.

"Miss Rori," Novachak said, "you're certain the *Southern Echo* will be safe?"

"As long as I'm aboard," Rori said.

If you don't kill them all first, the voice whispered.

The boatswain blew out a hard breath and turned his pale eyes to the captain. "A lovely place you're taking us."

Arani made a thoughtful sound. "We knew what we were getting into, although perhaps not the true depth of it." She sat back in her seat. "Thank you, Rori. You may leave now."

Rori stood and turned to go, but stopped before she'd taken more than three steps. "You said it was a lodestone you're trying to find?" she asked.

Dax and Novachak both nodded.

Rori unclipped her compass from her belt and

placed it on the table between the two men. "Be a lot easier with this," she said. "The needle should spin if you bring it close to a lodestone. I'll use the spare compass in the navigation room until you find it."

Dax and Novachak both stared at the small wooden box for a long time.

"This," the boatswain finally said, "would have saved me from so much agony."

And in spite of the gravity of everything they had just talked about, Captain Arani began to laugh, and even Dax couldn't help but chuckle.

Rori wanted to believe that she felt a little lighter as she left the room, certain that things would turn out all right in the end as long as she was on this ship and with this crew, but she kept hearing the screams from the *Godfall* in her ears.

I won't hurt this crew, she swore to herself. *I won't.*

But they had to keep going.

CHAPTER FOURTEEN

One Last Message

AS THOUGH EAGER TO make up for the horribleness of the wind wall, the gales filling the sails now were steady and almost tame. The riggers resumed their work without complaint, and as their spirits lifted, some of the others' were buoyed as well. AnnaMarie and Liliana were both cautiously excited about the Vanishing Island now that the *Southern Echo* was making better headway, and they made a game out of imagining the most lavish purchases they could make with their cuts of the treasure, always trying to outdo each other. A few others joined in, and by the second day after the vote, many people seemed to have forgotten about the fight that had nearly exploded on the main deck.

Others, Nate included, would not so easily forget it.

Especially not after the captain and the boatswain had finished doling out punishments with the flogging stick. Nate was left with a sore spot that made it difficult for him to sit down. Marcus, Eric, Xander, Jim Greenroot, and all of his gunners shared the same problem.

Dax had not escaped, either. His near loss of control had not gone unnoticed. Nate overheard Arani haranguing him in her cabin the night after the almost-fight, threatening to give the crew the chance to vote in a new quartermaster. Nate had not heard how that heated argument had ended, but Dax was the perfect image of a sailor the next day, focusing hard on his duties and overseeing the others alongside Novachak without so much as a bitter glance at Greenroot or his gunners.

Nate couldn't understand how, even after part of the crew had almost openly rioted on the ship, Arani and the other officers still wanted physical proof before acting. The lodestone search continued—aided now by a compass that Dax and Novachak traded off when their respective turns to search came up—but no one found anything.

Although Nate had promised Arani that he would not use his Skill, he could not sit idly by when he had the means to help in a way that no one else could. Especially not after the ship had passed through the wind wall. So every day and every night, he jumped into the wind and ranged out off the *Southern Echo*'s stern, searching for a shadow of any sort coming in from the east. He did not go as far as he had on the dragon hunt. He wanted to, but he knew that pushing himself to the point of exhaustion would only make him useless if a fight did break out, and then his training would have been for nothing.

Of course, on the dragon hunt, he'd also had a general direction to narrow his search to. This bird, he realized, could come from almost any direction, and unless Nate was lucky enough to be on the main deck when its shadow passed in the wind, he was unlikely to find anything at all.

So Nate started finding reasons to be topside as much as he possibly could. He volunteered for the resumed shifts on the night watch, which were difficult enough without hours spent earlier in the day working with the riggers to find the best winds. That work was becoming easier as his arms and shoulders strengthened, but still left him exhausted by the end of his shift. More than once on the night watch, Nate nearly nodded off under the stars, only to jerk awake when the ship rocked violently beneath him, her nightly aquatic companion making its presence known as it lunged after its next meal. As soon as the ship had steadied and Nate's heart was back under control, he would range across the open sky, hoping he'd find something in the wind. He found nothing at all.

A week passed, and Nate got so little sleep, he nearly collapsed into his breakfast after coming off his final dawn watch rotation.

"Easy there," Eric said, catching Nate just in time. "At least try to eat some of it before you use it to paint your face."

"Or better yet," Marcus added around a mouthful of stale biscuit soaked in broth, "give it here."

Eric slapped the stout Darkbend's reaching hand away and made sure Nate successfully navigated his way to the berth before heading off to assess the previous night's damage from whatever massive thing had decided to scratch its head against the *Southern Echo*'s keel.

Nate slept for a few uneasy hours, then dragged himself topside once more.

He found several people at the bow, pointing ahead and talking with either excitement or dread. He could not tell which, and he was not certain that he cared as he joined them to see what new thing the Forbidden Sea had to offer.

He squinted, rubbed his eyes, and squinted again, but that did not change what he saw.

Ahead of the *Southern Echo* and only coming closer was what looked like a patch of glass on the sea. Waves did not disrupt it, although they surged right up to its edge before dying silently. Nate experimentally tasted the faint wind coming in from the west, and found that there was nothing particularly special about it that might have impacted the water in such a way. He could not explain why the sea had gone mirror-smooth up ahead. No one could, and when the *Southern Echo* glided into the patch, the ship did so with the slightest of shudders, and then settled into such a gentle rhythm, Nate had to look for the wake to be sure they were still moving.

"Third sign," AnnaMarie mused. "Just like the Goodtide said."

By mid-afternoon, the *Southern Echo* was firmly into the glassy water, and there were no waves to be seen. It was a little after then that everyone realized the carnivorous fish had disappeared, and hadn't been seen since the ship had crossed into the deathly calm water.

Nate wasn't the only one who peered over the railing, although he did not share Xander's adventurous spirit and chose to keep a tight grip and his boots firmly on the ship's deck instead of climbing up into the rigging and leaning out, trusting the ropes to hold his weight without trouble.

"Nothing but blue straight down," Xander called. "No fish or sharks or anything."

"Let's hope it stays that way through the night," Eric remarked dryly. "The hull could use a rest after the battering it took from the giants."

"The hull, or you?" Xander asked as he jumped down and landed next to the Darkbend.

"Either," Eric said. "Both. What do you care?"

Xander smirked and went to talk to the other riggers about the positioning of the sails, and Eric drifted away as well. Nate remained at the railing for a long time, looking out over the flat water and wondering if Eric and Arani had been right, and the promise of a finished treasure hunt really was enough to quell a mutiny.

The thought followed him into his hammock that night, and it stole a good part of what was supposed to be his first full night's sleep in a while. The ship was eerily quiet without the lapping of the waves or the shifting creaks of the hull, and Nate had the feeling that he wasn't the only one lying awake in the dark, listening for the absent sounds that had been the pulse and breath of the *Southern Echo*.

He did not know how long it took for him to finally drift off, but the crack of a gunshot woke him with a violent start. He nearly fell out of his hammock and landed on Marcus below him, but the Darkbend sat up so fast he cracked his head against Nate's hip.

"Wha'sat?" someone called out blearily from the other side of the berth.

No one answered, but nearly everyone surged to their feet and ran for the stairs. Shouts came from above, followed by another gunshot, and then another.

Nate did not bother with his boots. The wood was hard and unforgiving beneath his bare feet, but he scrambled up the steps and was one of the first ones on the main deck, cutlass drawn and ready.

The sun had not yet risen, and the morning was gray and unremarkable, but there was still enough light to see the flat, empty sea all around the *Southern Echo*. There were a few people gathered along the starboard railing, pointing spent weapons into the north and calling for fresh guns. The faint smell of smoke from the fired pistols and rifles lingered in the air, but it was too late.

Against the pale sky, Nate saw the black speck of a bird flying away from the ship.

He did not waste any time. His magic surged through him as he plunged his awareness into the wind, ranging out after the bird. The winds had already whipped its trail away, but Nate had seen it with his own eyes, and he knew where to look. He shot perpendicular to the gales, the ring on his hand beginning to grow warm as he ranged farther out, but he was determined to follow that bird to the end of the world if he had to. He saw a spark of light up ahead, large and swooping, almost ungainly compared to Luken's tidy wingbeats, and Nate lunged after it, fighting to keep it in sight even as the wind smeared its trail into nothing.

He fell sideways when something hard slammed into his body back on the ship, and his connection to the wind snapped. Nate's head spun terribly when he opened his eyes back on the *Southern Echo*'s deck, but there were hands on his arms and shoulders, keeping him upright.

"—too far away now," someone was saying heatedly, "and you just broke the Nowind's concentration."

That was Xander, then.

"Well, if you hadn't missed the shot when it was closer," the sour voice of Jim Greenroot retorted.

With a groan, Nate turned back to the north and squinted into the sky. It was changing from gray to blue, and as empty as the sea around them.

The bird was gone.

"I may be able to find it again," Nate mused, "but I need everyone to back up and—"

"There's no need for that," Captain Arani said. Nate turned to see her staring grimly in the direction the bird had gone. "We can't catch it now, and I won't have you destroy yourself trying to follow it."

"Captain," Nate began, but Arani held up her hand.

"Whatever message that thing is carrying, it's going to be delivered," she said. Her gaze passed from Nate to Xander and the others who had been on the final stretch of the night watch. "Tell me, exactly, what happened."

"Greenroot saw the bird flying away from the ship," Xander said. "He called it out, and I was the first one to take a shot at it. It was going fast, and I didn't have enough time to take proper aim." His mouth turned down as though he was tasting something bitter. "I missed."

Nate heard the low scoff from Jim Greenroot, who seemed a little too pleased by Xander's failure. Arani had also caught the sound, but rather than looking contrite beneath the captain's stern gaze, Greenroot puffed up his chest.

"Not such the crack shot you've been bragging about, are you?" the gunner sneered at Xander.

Nate glowered at the man, daring him to say anything more as Xander ducked his head in shame.

"I'm sorry, Captain," the Grayvoice said.

"What's done is done," Arani said, but she did not take her eyes off of Jim Greenroot for a long time. Nate thought that she was finally going to call the gunner out, but then she turned to Dax beside her. "I think the time for subtlety has passed."

"Aye, Captain," the quartermaster responded darkly. He stepped forward, drawing himself up to his full height, and sent his voice booming out across the ship. "Everyone line up in the middle of the ship, away from the railings. We're going to search you. *All of you.*"

Nate was ushered into a line alongside everyone else, from Novachak all the way down to the lone cabin boy. The boatswain looked distinctly unimpressed as Dax patted down his clothes and rummaged through his pockets, but the moment he was declared clear, Novachak turned and began to search the person behind him. Captain Arani began in the middle of the line, and Dax moved to start at the other end. Between the three of them, they finished the search in minutes, and they had come up empty.

The officers exchanged dark looks, and then Arani rounded on the crew.

"All weapons are to be turned over to the quartermaster immediately," she barked out. "No one is allowed even a pocket knife from this moment on. We know what you're carrying, so don't even try to hide something from us. All tools will be kept under lock and key, their use for necessary tasks overseen by the boatswain alone. If you are found with so much as a *spoon* after this, you are going under the keel."

Several people shifted uneasily, but from their expressions, Nate thought that came from their confusion more than anything else. Still, everyone came forward and deposited the weapons they were carrying on to the deck, creating a small, haphazard pile at the quartermaster's feet. When that was done, Dax stepped forward to address the crew once more.

"Someone on this ship is using a messenger bird to betray us all," he said frankly. "We know there is a lodestone somewhere on the *Southern Echo* that the bird is using to find us. All duties are suspended until the lodestone is found, and you all are ordered to remain here on the main deck unless the captain, boatswain, or I tell you otherwise."

Stunned confusion met these words, but Dax cracked them out again and pushed people into small, unlikely groups that divided up the usual friends. Several of those groups were made to sit on the deck beneath Dax's hawkish glare. The few others, which included Nate and Eric, were told that they would be assisting the captain and boatswain as they searched the ship once more. Eric went off with Captain Arani and two of the riggers to dig through the hold, while Novachak took the next group to the berth. Nate was instructed to go with AnnaMarie Blueshore and the cook, old Steven Brownsand, to search the gun deck, and then immediately return to the main deck whether they'd found something or not.

"Do either of you have the faintest idea what's going on?" Blueshore asked as they descended into the gloom.

Brownsand shook his sun-weathered head. "Dax said something about a message and a traitor," he ground out in his gnarled voice. "And the captain wants us looking for a rock?"

"A lodestone," Nate corrected. He slid his eyes between the gunner and the cook, wondering if either of them were involved. He decided it was unlikely, given that they had both voted to continue west, and Brownsand especially seemed uninterested in the wants of the crew beyond keeping everyone fed. The old cook went where the *Southern Echo* carried him, and he did so without protest.

Still, Nate did not know if he could trust either of them. He certainly did not know them well enough to understand what could turn their hearts, so he said nothing more as they stepped on to the gun deck.

They waited a few moments for their eyes to adjust to the gloom, and then they began the search. Nate knew they wouldn't find anything as this deck had already been gone over by him, Xander, Dax, and Novachak at least two times each. Nate remembered Eric suggesting that the traitor could have been moving the lodestone, however, and he forced himself to go over each cannon carefully, using a ramrod to explore the interiors of the cannons and listen for anything that might have been pushed down their mouths before dropping to the deck to sweep the rod under their bellies. It was a mechanical motion for Nate by then, and half of his attention was on Brownsand and Blueshore as they picked through bundles of wadding and carefully secured cannonballs. He twisted and turned the things he knew about both of them around and around, and found his understanding of the two wanting.

What would turn their hearts? Nate wondered.

He knelt on the deck and swept the ramrod under the next cannon as he tried to answer the impossible question. The ramrod jolted lightly against the deck, and then there was a skidding sound as something dark and hard shot out from under the cannon.

Nate, Blueshore, and Brownsand all went still as the stone rattled over the deck and came to rest. For a long moment, they all simply stared at it, and then all three of them were moving.

AnnaMarie reached it first. She scooped up the rock and held it in her open palm, not protesting in the least as Nate and Brownsand came up on her sides to peer at its polished surface.

"Is that it?" Brownsand asked.

"It must be," Blueshore answered.

Nate was dimly aware that his mouth was hanging open.

We searched this deck so many times, he thought numbly. *That wasn't here before.*

But that did not matter now. They had the lodestone, and Nate bounded after AnnaMarie as she carried the rock up to the main deck and turned it over to the quartermaster.

All doubts as to whether or not this was the lodestone were destroyed when Novachak was called up and brought out a compass. The needle shuddered as it came near, and then began to spin freely, first one way, and then the other. Novachak snapped the compass closed and tucked it away, not once taking his eyes off of the small black stone resting in Dax's hand.

"That's it, then," the boatswain said. "Such a tiny

thing, to be causing so much trouble."

Dax closed his hand around the lodestone. He pulled AnnaMarie aside to speak with her, and Novachak tugged Nate around before he could hear anything.

"Best go find the captain," the boatswain said. "She'll want to put an end to this now."

Nate did as he was told.

Arani did not say much when he informed her that the lodestone had been found, and she remained quiet as the crew regathered on the main deck, forming a ring around her. She stood in the center of the ship rather than on one of the elevated decks at the stern, the lodestone cradled in her hand. The wind was the only thing that spoke for a long time.

When Arani raised her head and looked out at the crew, taking in every face around her, her eyes blazed with so much anger, it was a wonder no one burst into flame.

"I did not want to believe it," she said, low and dangerous and with enough force to make Nate's heart stumble in his chest, "but I can no longer let it pass in silence. The seeds of mutiny have been sown. They will not grow.

"We may not know who is at the heart of this yet, but I promise you, it's only a matter of time." She lifted the lodestone, turning slowly so that everyone could see it glinting in the sun. "To the would-be mutineers, I only have this to say: even if your next incoming message does not reveal who you are, you have just lost your one way of communicating with your outside allies. It doesn't matter who they are. The crew of the *Southern Echo* does not suffer traitors. Once you are found out—and make no mistake, this is not a question of if—justice will be swift."

Nate picked out Jim Greenroot from the crowd,

standing on the other side of the circle. The gunner was frowning at the lodestone in Arani's hand, as though trying to understand how she had it. His frown only deepened when she tucked the black stone into an inside pocket of her coat.

"I could throw the lodestone overboard right now, and stop that bird and its handlers from ever finding us," Arani growled, "but that would be too easy of an escape for you. I want to know what your allies have to say, and now, their words are going to be delivered right to me.

"So now, I offer this single chance for anyone involved to come forward and confess," Arani continued. "If you do, I will show mercy, and give you a clean, painless death with a proper burial. Your fellow traitors will not be so fortunate." Her eyes blazed as she took a firm grip on the saber at her hip. "They will be whipped, doused in hot tar, and keelhauled, their corpses left to feed whatever monsters roam these waters."

Nate swallowed, sickened by the thought of such a fate, but it was no less than what the code demanded, and what a mutineer deserved. He gazed at the people around him, and waited for someone to come forward and throw themselves on the captain's mercy as they revealed the rest of the traitors.

No one moved.

"All right, then," Arani said after a moment. She began to stalk around the edge of the circle, and people recoiled instinctively. "When that bird returns, I will have the mutineers, and I will get the name of the leader even if I have to cut it out of their followers' throats." Captain Arani stopped pacing, and her wrath washed over the ship like a tidal wave. "Mark me now, I will hang the leader's head from the bow." The captain resumed her prowl across the deck, and for the first time, Nate understood why Arani had been afraid of herself, of what she could become. "Pray to the gods above that they show you mercy and kill you before that bird comes back," she snarled, "because if they don't, I'll deliver your souls straight to the gods below."

CHAPTER FIFTEEN

Lockdown

RORI HAD NOT WANTED to believe that there really could be a traitor among the crew, but the cracks in her life ran deep, and they did not care what she believed.

As Arani had ordered, the confiscated weapons were turned over to Dax, who locked them in heavy sea chests down in the hold. He kept the keys with him, and randomly checked the chests to ensure that the contents had not been removed or shifted. The tools went to Novachak, which included the sextant and the other instruments Rori needed for navigation, leaving her unable to perform her tasks.

"We're sailing west," the captain growled when Rori approached her. "We don't need guidance beyond the sun and that damned star." She focused a harsh glare on Rori. "Unless there's something else you've neglected to mention?"

"No, ma'am," Rori said and retreated.

Anyone who had to work belowdeck was supervised by one of the officers, but idle hours were strictly regulated to the main deck, where everyone could be easily observed. The officers watched everyone in the crew with harsh suspicion, and the crew watched each other in equal measures.

This was not how it was supposed to be.

I brought them here, Rori thought with tears stinging her eyes. *I did this to us.*

She waited for that steady, clear voice to tell her to keep going and make her feel like she was on the right path, but it did not return. There was so much dissent and mistrust among the people she'd been so determined to keep together, and she did not know how to make it all go away.

Drown it.

She vehemently shook her head and tried to clear the thought, but she couldn't dissipate the feeling that it would be the simplest, cleanest solution.

I won't hurt them, Rori promised herself over and over again. *This is not the* Godfall.

And she was right; there had been no traitors on the *Godfall*, except maybe Rori herself.

The thought haunted her all through her now-empty hours, and it was becoming harder and harder to ignore the unwanted ideas that kept spilling across her mind, spewing forth from some dark corner that had cracked open and could not be patched shut.

Her agitation spilled over into Luken, or at least exacerbated his own. The bird wanted to stretch his wings and fly, but if he could be coaxed off of Rori's shoulder at all, he only made tight, irritated circles before diving back and sinking his talons through the fabric of her shirt, all the way down to her skin. He would not be soothed by offered treats or gentle petting, and he pecked at his food and Rori's hands with equal bad temper.

And throughout all of this, singing through her pulse like the steady currents beneath the ship, was a new and infuriating song at the edge of her mind. She could not hear it even when she strained, but it came from the west and pulled her towards the beacon star that refused to fade even during the day, just as it had done when she'd been aboard the *Godfall*.

They were so close. Rori knew it without any doubt,

just as she knew that, in her desperation to keep her world together, she'd found the exact thing to tear it apart.

She did not want to be alone with her own thoughts anymore, but her friends had gone off on some secret search without her, and the two men and one woman she trusted more than anyone were all waiting for the smallest reason to put someone to death. Even if Rori had wanted to, she could not sequester herself away in the navigation room while everyone was under lockdown, so she took herself to the railing and stared down in to the deep, dark waters of the Forbidden Sea.

The last time she'd sailed these waters, she had not been allowed anywhere near the railing, even with her hands bound behind her back. There was nothing of interest in the mirror-smooth water disturbed only by the *Southern Echo*'s passage, but Rori made herself look, simply because this was something different.

She watched her own reflection dance in the ripples thrown by the hull, and wondered why she'd ever thought that she could save her crew.

She did not move when another reflection joined hers down in the water.

"Thinking about a swim?" Xander asked as he leaned his arms over the railing. His shoulder brushed hers, which could only have been intentional.

It annoyed her, but Rori did not pull away.

"It *would* be the one place you couldn't follow me," she told him, her voice soft but firm. "You never really learned to swim."

"I know," Xander said, and she was surprised that there was no resignation in his voice. "I just saw you looking a bit forlorn over here, and thought I'd come stop you before you got it into your head to throw yourself overboard."

"I wasn't going to do that," Rori said hotly.

Xander made a noise somewhere between a snort and a whine. "I know you," he said, "and I know that you're currently blaming yourself for a lot of things going on right now that are not your fault." He shifted a little, pressing his shoulder more firmly against hers. "I'd like it very much if you'd stop doing that."

Rori looked at him, but Xander kept his eyes trained on the horizon. There was no trace of laughter on his face. He was, for the first time in a very long time, completely serious.

"Do you feel it?" she asked. "The pull from the west?"

This time, Xander whipped around to stare at her. He nodded slowly. "Like something in your soul, asking you to come?"

"More like telling," Rori murmured. "Commanding, even."

"I don't let people command me," Xander said. "Or strange feelings coming out of a tear between our world and the realm of the gods."

Rori gave a small snort of halfhearted laughter. "You let Captain Arani and Dax and Novachak give you orders," she pointed out.

"Sometimes." Xander smirked. "If their orders happen to line up with what I wanted to do, anyway."

Rori shook her head and bumped him with her shoulder, but it was even weaker than her laugh had been.

Xander sighed and leaned the other way, putting space between them. "If you won't do me the favor of not blaming yourself for gods know what, do it for yourself, then. Be selfish for once." He looked at her, open and frank and without any of the traces of the fear or uncertainty she was used to seeing in other people's faces when they were confronted by her Goodtide tattoo. "Gods below, Rori, we're on a ship heading straight for the Vanishing Island, and we're all here because of you."

"Thanks for reminding me," Rori grumbled.

"I mean it," he said, turning towards her more fully. "You think anyone else could have led us this far? You think anyone else could see us to the end? This ship needs you to go all the way."

"You have no idea," she murmured.

Xander chuckled. "You see? You've got it in you to be a little selfish. So quit feeling sorry for yourself, because we need you to take us to that treasure."

"You know," Rori said, "for a second there, I thought you were actually trying to be supportive."

"You knew what I was before you decided to like me," Xander shot back with a smirk. It faded when she did not return the smile, and after a few moments, he walked away.

Rori intended to let him go, but found herself turning to call after him, "What animal can you speak to?"

He stopped, and fixed her with a stare for several long moments. Then he gave her a more relaxed smile, one that was devoid of calculations and cleverness, and Rori felt something around her heart ease. "Cats," he said, "but only when the moons are full."

Rori cocked an eyebrow. "Is there some special connection between cats and the moons?"

"Nah," Xander said, "that's just about how often the haughty bastards will deign to talk back."

Rori shook her head as Xander walked away, but she was finally smiling, and feeling just a little bit better.

CHAPTER SIXTEEN

The Serpent

NATE DID NOT UNDERSTAND why no one came forward to reveal the mutineers. As Arani had said, it was only a matter of time before the truth was exposed, but though the *Southern Echo*'s sailors were eyeing each other with open suspicion and speaking in whispers, that's all there was: suspicion and whispers.

"No one's tried to speak with you at all about the dragon hunt?" Nate asked Eric the next morning, when they stole a brief moment of privacy at the ship's railing. He wasn't worried about being caught talking to Eric; there were no accusations anyone could levy against them. Nate still lacked the proof he needed to destroy the mutiny once and for all, but he was determined to find it.

"Why would they?" Eric said in response. "Far too dangerous for them to do that now."

"Dangerous, yeah," Nate agreed, "but they have to be desperate by now. Wouldn't they be trying to rally enough support before the messenger bird returns?"

Eric hesitated, thinking. "That's what I'd expect," he finally said, "but the fact that it hasn't happened..." He raked his gaze over the people on the main deck. "I think the mutiny died before it ever really got any traction."

"How could that be?" Nate pressed. "Someone sent that messenger bird out, and we found the lodestone on the ship."

"Maybe that's not tied to a mutiny on the ship, though," Eric mused. "What if it's one person, and not a whole part of the crew?"

"How could one person have kept the lodestone hidden from us for so long?"

Eric did not have an answer for that. "Where did you say you found it, again?"

"Third cannon on the starboard side of the gun deck."

Eric was quiet for so long that Nate had to prod him to share his thoughts.

"It's just such an odd place to find it," the Darkbend finally said. "We checked around the cannons gods only know how many times, and for it to be that particular one..."

"What about that one?" Nate asked. "Why is that cannon special?"

Eric hesitated, and then reluctantly said, "That cannon is assigned to Jim Greenroot's gun crew."

Nate's heart leapt into his throat. "That's it!" he said. "We've got him!"

"We don't," Eric said firmly. "You found a rock under a cannon. Anyone could have put it there, or it could have fallen and rolled into that spot. What's more, only a perfect idiot would hide something like that with his own equipment." He frowned and traced a knot in the grain of the ship's railing. "Could be someone is trying to frame him."

"Or," Nate said, with what he thought was far more patience than the situation deserved, "it could be that he really is that stupid. The man openly talked about going after the dragon again, even after the vote to continue west. The only thing that shut him up was the discovery of the lodestone."

Eric paused. "I just think that we would have found

it a lot earlier if he was the one holding on to it. Finding it now, under his cannon, just does not make any sense."

Nate threw up his hands. "So even though we found the lodestone, we have nothing. What else could we hope to find at this point?"

Eric fixed him with a hard look. "A round robin with his signature included, a piece of correspondence from the messenger bird, something that puts it in writing, but you're not likely to find anything like that. If they'd ever existed, they would have been destroyed by now."

"Maybe," Nate mused, "but maybe not. Maybe this happened so fast, they made a mistake. There must be somewhere we haven't looked." He stopped then, and realized that there was one place no one had checked.

"Nate," Eric began.

"No," Nate said, already turning away. "Whoever this is, they don't get to get away with this."

"Where are you going?" the Darkbend asked, but quietly, so he wouldn't draw anyone else's attention.

Nate did not answer. All he saw as he crossed the deck was that shadow pressing down on his friends. He could not just sit by and wait for the darkness to swallow them. Nate had to do something to protect them, and fast.

Stealing into the berth to paw through everyone's possessions was risky at best, and if he was caught, the code would demand a far worse punishment than a few strikes from the flogging cane. He wished he had a better idea, but other than the crew's personal possessions stowed in the berth, he could think of nowhere else to look that had not already been scoured over by half a dozen pairs of eyes. If he was going to find any evidence of the traitor, it was going to be in the berth, and Nate needed a lookout.

He could not ask Eric or Marcus, as they would never agree to it, and Nate did not like the idea of potentially getting them into trouble. Dax and Novachak were both out of the question, and the only other person that Nate could imagine helping him undercut the code, violate the crew's privacy, and find the evidence he needed to kill the mutiny once and for all was Xander.

Nate found the Grayvoice by the bowsprit, staring into the west and idling away his time.

"I have a proposition for you," Nate said as he came up next to Xander. "It's risky, but if we pull it off, we'll get what we need to stop the traitor. I know that you and I haven't exactly patched things up, but that's going to have to be okay, because you're the only person I can trust with this. The officers can't know, and we can't let anyone else..." He trailed off as he realized that Xander was not listening. The Grayvoice had not even blinked.

What is so fascinating out there? Nate wondered.

He got the answer when he followed Xander's gaze and saw a jagged fin racing towards the ship, moving so fast it cut foam into the still water. In no time at all, the fin was less than a stone's throw away from the bow of the *Southern Echo*, and that was when it slid beneath the surface, leaving only the ripples of its passage to lap against the hull. Nate took a step forward, craning his neck to peer over the edge of the ship, and then he yelped and fell back as a gaping maw full of teeth erupted out of the water, sending a spray of glittering drops into the air and on to the deck.

Nate landed hard on his elbow. Jarring pain echoed up his arm, but he barely felt it as he scrambled backwards, away from the serpentine body that twisted itself around the bowsprit. The *Southern Echo* bobbed in the water under the weight of the serpent's sinewy muscle, and Nate thought that he heard the wood of the bowsprit groan as the creature twisted its head around and regarded him with beady yellow eyes.

The sea serpent wasn't as big as the leviathans that prowled the south. Those were said to grow so large, they could bite an unwary rowboat in two, and swallow a grown man whole. But in that moment, with the leviathans a world away and this smaller serpent gurgling and hissing through its teeth mere steps away, this was easily the more terrifying of the two.

Nate was vaguely aware of people shouting somewhere behind him as he stared at the serpent.

It was an ugly thing, all dripping black coils with a head that blurred into its body and that jagged fin running along the length of its spine. Its jaws were stretched tight with serrated teeth, the mouth running so far back along the head it looked like someone had taken a blade to its throat and carved it open. Its nostrils flared as it tasted the air, and it gave that gurgling hiss again as footsteps thudded on the deck.

Nate realized that Novachak was shouting for Xander to get clear, and he glanced back to see that the boatswain already had a rifle aimed and ready to fire, Captain Arani a step behind him with her pistol in her hand.

"Xander!" Novachak shouted again, but the Grayvoice did not move.

It figured that they'd finally found something Xander was afraid of, just in time for him to be eaten by it.

Nate squeezed his eyes shut as the serpent drew back, and he waited for the sickening sound of teeth tearing into flesh, or gunshots as the officers desperately took whatever shots they could, probably hitting Xander along with the serpent, but there was only that horrible hissing sound again, and then silence.

"By the frozen goddess," Novachak murmured.

Nate opened his eyes to see the serpent coiled around the bowsprit, its mouth hanging open to reveal its slimy maw... and Xander standing in front of it, smiling. The serpent hissed again, and then Xander made the same impossible sound with almost no effort at all. The Grayvoice and the serpent stared at each other for a moment, and then the sea serpent abruptly jerked its head to the side and lunged, mouth open and going right for Xander's arm. Xander snatched his limb away before the teeth could close around his flesh. He slapped at the serpent's head and laughed as the creature retreated back to the bowsprit.

"Someone mind bringing a chicken for our friend here?" Xander called over his shoulder, without taking his eyes off the serpent. "She's quite hungry."

No one responded.

As Xander and the serpent traded more hisses, Nate slowly picked himself up from the deck, freezing whenever the sea serpent's yellow eyes flashed to him. His entire body screamed for him to get away from the bow, but he dared not draw the creature's interest with sudden movements. He did not take his eyes off of Xander or the serpent until he felt the boatswain's hand close over his shoulder and gently move him aside.

Finally away from the serpent, fear washed freely through Nate in cold waves, leaving him clammy and shivering. His knees felt weak, but he managed to keep his feet.

Xander, somehow, was still grinning at the sea serpent.

"Gods below," someone said, and it took Nate a long time to realize that it had been his own voice that had shaped the words.

Frantic footfalls suddenly slapped across the deck, and Nate turned his head to see Rori pushing her way through the crowd that had gathered in the middle of the ship. She broke through and halted, her eyes going wide. "What are you doing?" she nearly shouted, and then she surged forward.

She was around Captain Arani and dodging Novachak's reaching hand before Nate could blink.

Rori stopped when she was past the boatswain, Xander between her and the serpent. "Come away slowly," she said, but Xander raised a hand to warn her off.

"It's all right, Rori," the Grayvoice said. His smile had taken on a hard edge, and he still had not taken his gaze off of the serpent. "Stay back."

The sea serpent wove its head to the side and looked at Rori with clear interest. It hissed, and Xander responded. The creature did not advance further, but it kept Rori in its line of sight.

"I'm serious about that chicken," Xander called to anyone who was listening. "Eggs won't do it, and I don't think we're ready to give up the dairy goat yet." When no one moved, Xander gave a visible sigh. "Unless someone wants to volunteer a limb as a meal," he said, as though instructing a group of particularly reluctant children, "you'd better find something that will bleed for this pretty girl."

The serpent gave another gurgling hiss, and Nate wasn't sure if it was his fear coloring his perception, or if the creature actually sounded hungry.

"Get a chicken," Captain Arani said softly.

Footsteps receded as someone moved to carry out the order. Nate was still staring at the serpent, but he heard the gentle clucking of the chicken as it was brought up from the galley. The serpent hissed and wriggled along the bowsprit at the sight of the bird, which alerted the chicken to its fate and sent it into a panicked frenzy. It squawked and frantically beat its wings, sending a few white feathers into the wind. It managed to break free and fall to the deck, but Xander was already there. He caught the chicken and flung it over the side of the ship. The sea serpent uncoiled itself from the bowsprit with alarming speed and dropped into the water.

Nate turned away, but he still heard the splash and crunch, and then the sudden silence that follows death.

"She's happy, now," Xander said from the railing. He was leaning dangerously far over to watch the serpent's meager feast. "Let her finish, and then she'll show us the way."

Nate wasn't certain if the Grayvoice was completely unaware of the way the crew was shrinking away from him, or if he did not care. There was no tightness to Xander's posture, but he did not turn to face anyone behind him.

A quiet exchange between the captain and Rori drew Nate's attention away from the Grayvoice.

"I thought you said the blood price was already paid," Arani was saying. She looked even grimmer than she had when she'd only needed to contend with a possible mutiny.

"It was," Rori murmured back. She was visibly troubled, and had not taken her eyes off of Xander. "The serpents didn't do that last time."

"What was that, then?" Arani demanded.

"A courtesy," Xander cut in. Evidently, he'd been listening, too. "That serpent came a long way to meet us. Didn't seem right to let her go hungry."

The captain did not have a response to that. Neither did Rori. Jim Greenroot, however, did.

"Fitting that you've got snake lips," the gunner said as he pushed his way towards Xander. He glared at the Grayvoice over the rims of his spectacles. "You're not stupid enough for sheep, but you slither with the worst of them. You poisonous like a snake, too?" Greenroot bared his teeth in a sneer. "Maybe you're the traitor crawling around the ship."

Xander went rigid then, but he still did not turn around, not even when Arani snapped at Greenroot to stand down unless he wanted to lose his tongue.

"I'm not accusing him," Greenroot said, "but it would be fitting, wouldn't it?"

Nate's fear slowly warmed to anger at the sheer audacity of the gunner, but Arani chased Greenroot off. When he was gone, Nate stepped to his friend's side. "We'll get him," Nate promised.

Xander did not respond. After a moment, he turned his back on Nate and stalked away. Nate moved to follow him, but Rori was already there, and he watched her chase after Xander with a strange feeling in his gut.

CHAPTER SEVENTEEN

Open Hearts

RORI CAUGHT UP WITH Xander at the bottom of the stairs down to the hold. He ignored all of her calls, but he stopped when she got close enough to grab his arm. He did not turn to face her, but she could plainly see that all of the usual bravado and swagger had drained out of him.

Rori took a firmer grip on his sleeve as she stepped in front of him, but it took her a few moments to find the right way to begin the conversation.

"Snakes, is it?" she finally asked, making sure her voice was gentle.

"Sea serpents," Xander said, still not looking at her. "Snakes a bit, but with them, it was always like trying to talk to someone underwater."

"But sea serpents you can speak to?"

Xander fixed his gaze on a point somewhere over her head and nodded.

"All right, then," Rori said. She let go of Xander's sleeve and brushed the wrinkles out. "That's not so bad. Terrifying, but not bad."

The ghost of a smile twisted Xander's lips for a moment. "They don't keep sea serpents at the animal speaking academy," he said, and the bitterness was a heavy stain on his voice. "Just a few small snakes and a whole lot of other animals they'd rather be able to talk to. Sea serpents are too uncommon outside of the

Leviathan Sea for anyone to even try to communicate with them. So much easier to just kill them, if they ever show themselves to a ship."

Rori paused, her hand still on his arm. "You'd have been marked a Clearvoice if they'd had a serpent, wouldn't you?"

"Probably," Xander said. "I'll never really know. I'm not exactly planning on going back there to retake the assessments."

"But you *do* know," Rori said. "You know what your magic can do."

He finally dropped his gaze to meet hers, and gave her a long, silent look.

She sighed and lowered her hand, trying not to notice the way Xander's gaze flicked after it. "So you didn't tell anyone," Rori said, "because you were worried about..." She thrust a thumb towards the deck above them, where the voices of Dax and Novachak barked out orders and Jim Greenroot was hopefully going to receive a few lashes for what he'd said. "About all of that happening. You know it doesn't matter that—"

"It does matter," Xander cut in. "*You* know that."

Rori tentatively reached out and touched his arm again, pressing firmer when he did not pull away. "I know that you're no traitor," she murmured.

Xander's hand came up and closed over hers.

"You're selfish to a godly level," Rori said, earning another faint smile, "but you're not a traitor."

Xander's eyes were very dark as he looked back at her. This was the closest they'd been in a long while, and with everyone else preoccupied on the main deck, it was a stolen moment alone. Xander leaned down, closing the distance, and then there was no more space between their lips. His hand came up to press against the small of her back, drawing her even closer, and for a moment, Rori shut her eyes and let him, drinking in the simultaneous familiarity and strangeness of the kiss. They'd shared many kisses before, but this was the first time on the ship, and Rori almost let herself fall into the warmth.

But she thought of Xander in his entirety, of the cutting words he could fling as easily as knives, of his coldness and his calculations and all the small promises he'd broken before he'd shattered the biggest one and voted to keep the dragon, and Rori remembered why she only ever let him kiss her on land, away from the steady presence of the *Southern Echo*. On land, she could pretend that he was someone else, because he had more room to spread the bad things.

Gently but firmly, Rori extracted herself from Xander's embrace and stepped back. "No," she said, "we're not doing that."

"Now?" Xander asked, an odd note straining through his voice. "Or ever?"

Rori folded her arms and looked away.

"Right, then." Xander drew himself up, instantly shedding the tender warmth he'd shown only a moment ago. "Can't say I'm surprised."

"Xander," Rori began, but he shook his head and took a step away.

"It's fine," he said. "We all do what we need to."

Then he disappeared into the gloom of the ship, and Rori let him go.

CHAPTER EIGHTEEN

The Mutiny

JIM GREENROOT WAS GIVEN three lashes for his slanted accusation of Xander, leaving him with thick welts across his back, but he did not even cry out when the braided leather struck him. Rather than the vicious cat o' nine tails with the metal beads at its tips, Novachak used the standard whip for the punishment, which was what Arani had suggested and Nate personally found inadequate. It was worse than the cane, but it was not enough.

Greenroot had to pay, and Nate knew there was only one way that could happen now.

Xander was withdrawn and sullen in the wake of the accusation and the reveal of his true Skill, but his eyes gleamed with intrest when Nate found him and asked, "Want to send that bastard straight to the sixth hell?"

The next chance they had, Nate and Xander stole down to the berth. The Grayvoice stood watch while Nate picked through private possessions as quick and quiet as he could, starting with Greenroot's.

The bespectacled gunner had a pack hanging over his hammock, and a small sea chest beneath it. The chest was locked, but the pack was easy to dig through. Beneath a change of clothes, Nate found an old whistle, three copper marks, and a carved wooden bird not at all unlike the one Nate had left back on Solkyria, although it was even more worn down than Nate's had been. There were no papers of any sort, and without the key to the chest, Nate's efforts were thwarted.

"Where do you think he keeps that key?" Nate wondered.

Xander snorted. "Probably somewhere on his person. That's what pretty much everyone with one of those locking chests does."

"Think we could distract him long enough to knick it?"

The Grayvoice shook his head. "If I so much as look at him too long, he'll run to Arani and claim assault."

"I could do it," Nate offered.

Xander snorted again, this time with a wry smile. "No you couldn't," he said. "You still can't tie a halfway decent knot. No way are you picking anyone's pocket and not getting punched in the face for trying."

Nate bristled a little, but had to admit that Xander was probably right on that front. He couldn't give up, though. The man had insulted Xander, and been horrible to Rori, and put Nate in danger. Those things could not go unanswered. Nate swore that they would not, but he had to put them aside for the moment as he continued his search.

Even if he's not part of the mutiny, Nate told himself as he moved on to the next pack, *I'll make sure he pays for everything he's done.*

The promise helped propel Nate along, even as his search turned up nothing but his own guilt for pawing through his crew mates' privacy.

He made himself think of Rori and Eric and Marcus and even Xander each time a new wave of shame washed over him. He saw that dark and terrible shadow of a still unknown enemy looming over them all, and he kept digging. By the time Xander hissed a warning about the amount of time they'd spent below, all Nate had to show for his efforts was a handful of various wooden carvings, a small silver flask filled with something he could not even begin to identify, a few decks of playing cards, and one crude drawing of several naked bodies.

Nate quickly stuffed the possessions back into the last pack he'd been able to search, then ducked out of the berth and followed Xander topside.

"Nothing?" the Grayvoice asked as they slipped back into place among the riggers and prepared for their next shift on the sails.

Nate shook his head.

Xander shrugged. "Maybe there's nothing to find."

Nate could not accept that. He kept seeing that cold shadow over his friends, and swore he would find something, *anything*, that would shed light on someone's guilt.

Nate spent all day searching, dipping into every nook and cranny of the ship whenever he had the smallest excuse to go below. He couldn't return to the berth without a lookout, but he did not let that deter him.

A round robin, Eric had said, or something written.

Nate would not be able to read anything he found, but he'd gotten Eric to describe what to look for, and the image of signatures arranged in a ring so the leader could not be found burned in his mind's eye. Nate resolved to gather every scrap of paper with writing on it that he could find and present them to the ship's officers, but by the time the sun had set behind the bloody wound in the sky, all he had found were a few discarded scraps from Rori's navigation calculations, and what turned out to be a particularly awful love poem someone had started writing for Liliana.

"Now, see, this is just sad," Novachak said when he'd finished reading the pitiful attempt at poetry. "If this poor fool has any hope of wooing the girl, they'll need a better rhyme for her name than 'banana.'" He crumpled up the paper and tossed it over the railing before rounding on Nate. "As for you, don't waste my time with anything like that again, and stop trying to fling your crew mates into an early grave."

Nate glared at the boatswain, frustration erasing his caution. "Someone on this ship is trying to mutiny."

"I'm well aware of that," Novachak said coldly. "As is the captain. She has the matter in hand. Or at least she will, when that bird returns."

"So after everything," Nate spat through gritted teeth, "she's just going to sit and wait?"

"What would you rather she do?" Novachak asked. "Round up everyone and put them to the whip until someone confesses?"

"Yes!" Nate said.

"Then I suppose you're volunteering to go first."

Nate did not have a response to that.

"Did you think you wouldn't be included in 'everyone?'" the boatswain asked, one bushy eyebrow cocked. "It's all of us, or none of us, boy. You don't get to pick and choose who gets the captain's wrath simply because you don't like 'em. If that was how we ran things on this ship, we'd have a mutiny every other week." Novachak hooked his thumbs into his belt. "This is no tyrant's ship. If you wanted that, you should have stayed in the empire."

Nate felt as though he'd volunteered for the whip after that conversation, and he retreated.

But his entire body itched with anxiety and the need to do something before someone got hurt. The thought that anyone could get away with betraying this crew based on whether or not a bird returned with a damning message was enough to make Nate's blood boil. But without the proof he needed to outright accuse someone, Nate turned to the one thing he alone could do, and thrust his magic into the sky.

The winds were empty around the *Southern Echo*, and Nate knew that if he ranged out, he'd only exhaust himself searching for a pinpoint trail in the open air. This wasn't like the dragon hunt, where there were numerous creatures for him to stumble across. This was one bird in the wind-smeared void.

Nate jumped from gust to gust around the ship, waiting with excruciating patience for a wind shadow to brush across his awareness. He hated that he could not actively seek it out, just as he hated the traitor for ruining so much with their selfish moves against the captain and the crew. They were on the cusp of a legendary treasure, but for someone, that wasn't enough. They wanted more. Nate was determined that they should not have it.

Nate spent the better part of an hour prowling through the winds around the ship before he felt the flicker of a shadow in the wind. He seized on the trail immediately, and went plunging after the source. He forced himself to slow down when he felt the heat in the ring on his finger, and wait for the bird to come to him. Its shadow grew stronger with each passing moment, the imprint of its wings clear on the wind, and flying much lower now that there was no wind wall to overcome. Nate watched it long enough to be sure that it was heading directly for the ship. When he pulled himself back, the stars overhead were bright in the moonless sky, but they all paled in comparison to the signal star that hung over the western horizon.

But in the east, coming ever closer, was the messenger bird.

Nate sprinted off to find the captain.

Arani waited on the poop deck alone, the lodestone in her hand. She stood in full view of the crew gathered on the main deck. Though a few yawns escaped here and there, no one spoke as they waited for the bird to arrive.

Lights were lit throughout the ship, bathing the normally dark decks in golden warmth, and everyone had their eyes trained on the captain. Everyone, except for Nate, who darted his gaze across the crew, not daring to blink for fear of missing a single move. His attention finally settled on Jim Greenroot.

I hope it's you, Nate thought. It was an ugly wish, he knew, but it would have cleared up so many things.

The gunner was with his usual crew, gathered up by the mainmast. None of them had been on the night watch, so they all had bleary, sleep-starved looks on their faces, equal parts exhausted and bewildered after being woken up in the middle of the night. Nate's dark hopes fell as he observed Greenroot. If he had been involved with the mutiny, then the man should have been sweating profusely now that his damnation was winging ever closer. Instead, he was rubbing the sleep from his eyes, as if a night out of bed was the worst he had to worry about.

He's either innocent, Nate mused, *or a phenomenal actor.*

He did not know which was more plausible, so Nate made himself look away.

He did not need his Skill to know that the bird was close. A few people lifted their arms and pointed at the circling silhouette against the stars, tracing the messenger's path as it slowly descended to the ship and landed on the railing in front of Arani. Its claws made a scrabbling sound as it gripped the wood, and memories of the nights Nate had woken to strange sounds immediately flooded his mind.

That bird trying to find its balance was exactly what Nate had heard.

The messenger bird was a big, ugly thing, with dark feathers and a head with a heavy beak hunched between ungainly wings. Its naked feet were gray in color, with long talons that scraped along the railing. When it was finally settled, it cocked its head at Arani, blinking at her fiercely with one pale eye. It did not squawk or utter even the slightest of sounds, not even when Arani slowly reached forward, towards its leg. The messenger bird blinked at her, or maybe at the lodestone she held, and then obediently stuck its leg out and allowed her to retrieve the slim roll of paper from the carrying tube secured against its gray skin. Then it waited as Arani took a step back, held the paper up to a lantern, and began to read.

Nate held his breath.

Captain Arani looked up, and waved Dax forward. The quartermaster climbed the steps to her side, and they spent several long moments staring at the paper in silence. When Dax raised his head, his eyes ran across the gathered crew, pausing on a few different faces, including Nate's.

Confusion welled up inside of Nate. Where was the proclamation of guilt?

Instead of speaking, Arani drew the pistol from her sash and slowly made her way down to the main deck. Nate lost sight of her among the sea of heads, but he heard her calling out names as she threaded her way through the crowd.

"Lucien Scorvani," she said as she drew closer, and the named sailor stiffened.

"Julian Redpool."

Another name, and another tense spine.

"Marcus Darkbend."

Nate blinked. *Marcus?*

"Xander Grayvoice. Esmerelda Durmanti. Steven Brownsand. Liliana Blackriver. Jim Greenroot. Eric Darkbend."

The person in front of Nate stepped aside, and there was Captain Arani, terrible in her fury, and terrifying in the impassive way she stared at him.

"Nate Lowwind."

Nate had no idea how—or if—he should respond.

Arani regarded him for a silent moment, and then raised a fist into the air. "Everyone named is to move to the bow immediately. Everyone else, stay back."

The crew began to shuffle to their designated spots, but Nate felt as though he was rooted to the deck. He did not know what was happening, but he had an uneasy feeling growing in his chest.

"Captain," Nate began.

"Move," Arani said, and Nate did not have a choice.

At the bow, Nate ended up standing between Marcus and Liliana, both of them equally bewildered but also looking a little afraid. Nate tried to mask his own fear, but it cracked under Arani's glare and the confused scrutiny of the crew behind her. Dax and Novachak had made their way towards the bow to stand between Arani and the rest of the crew, and over their shoulders, Nate picked out Rori straining to get through the crowd, her arms wrapped protectively around Luken. There was a flutter of graceless movement up on the poop deck as the messenger bird hopped from one railing to another, watching the happenings on the deck below with clear interest.

"All of you standing before me have something in common," Arani said, her voice sharp and clear. "Do you know what that is?"

Nate risked a small glance down the line. There were men and women of all ages, Solkyrians and Veritians, gunners and riggers, a cook and a carpenter. He had no idea what Arani was getting at.

"We all sail on the *Southern Echo*," Jim Greenroot tentatively offered after a moment.

Captain Arani did not smile. "The time for loyalty has long since passed, Mr. Greenroot." She slipped her pistol into her sash and raised her open hand, and Dax slapped the rolled up parchment into her palm. She kept her eyes on Nate and the others as she unrolled the message and turned it so that they could see.

On the paper, rough sketches had been scratched out in charcoal. Some of them had smudged a little, but even in the sparse lantern light, Nate still recognized the dragon head eating the sun. It was the same symbol that adorned Arani's flag. There were other images scrawled on the page, but Arani crumpled the paper into her fist before Nate could get a good look at them.

"Not one of you," the captain said, "can read or write."

Nate understood then. The message had not been written in words but pictograms, meant for someone illiterate. Arani had picked out everyone from the crew who had not learned to read. That included him, Xander, Marcus and Eric, of course. The Skill academies had focused entirely on their magic, and they're supposed places within imperial society. Rori had learned to read during her childhood at a civilian school, when her magic had been kept secret, and Dax had learned sometime after joining the crew, though before or after he'd been elected quartermaster, Nate did not know. Eric had learned numbers for measurements and basic arithmetic, but was illiterate beyond that. The Veritians in the lineup were unsurprising, given that colonials rarely had access to the same resources as Solkyrian citizens. As to why there were any true-born Solkyrians who could not read or write,

Nate did not know, but it did not matter.

Jim Greenroot was in the line.

Nate's uneasiness evaporated under a surge of anticipation, and he had to dig his nails into his palms to keep himself from smiling.

I know it's you, Nate thought as he looked to the gunner. *Gods below take your soul, you horrible bastard.*

But Arani did not call Greenroot's name. She did not call anyone's name, and when Nate turned back to her, he saw her eyes skimming over each person in turn, her mind running through all the reasons she had to suspect them, and the ones she didn't. Her grim expression did not change when she did the same for Nate, and if the sinking feeling in his stomach had left any room for another emotion, he might have felt affronted at the very idea. He was relieved when Arani looked away from him.

She spent less time looking at Marcus than Nate, and longer on Scorvani before passing on to Greenroot. Nate waited with his heart in his throat.

Arani looked away from the gunner.

Nate could not take it anymore. "Are you really not seeing it?" he burst out. "It's all right in front of you!"

"Stand down, boy," Arani growled, her hand tightening around the paper in her fist.

Nate stepped forward instead and thrust his finger at Jim Greenroot. "Everything is pointing to him! You know it is, Captain!"

Greenroot gave a cry of outrage. "What are you saying, Lowwind?"

"Is it not obvious?" Nate asked, rounding on the gunner. "You're the traitor!"

"*Stand down,* Nate!" Arani shouted, but Nate pulled out of her reach.

"All this time, you've been talking about turning

around and going back to the dragon hunt," Nate snarled. He advanced on Greenroot, and the gunner moved to meet him.

"It's my right to say what I want," Greenroot spat.

"Like words of betrayal and mutiny," Nate said.

"I'm no mutineer, Lowwind." The gunner was so close to Nate now, his breath washed over him in sour waves.

"The proof is there!" Nate gestured wildly at the paper still closed in Arani's hand. "You can't read!"

"So what?" Greenroot snapped, his face growing heated. "Neither can you. Why are you innocent?" The gunner rounded on the stunned people still standing in the lineup. "Or the Darkbends? Or better yet, the Snake Lips! If anyone was going to betray us, it was always going to be one of you Skilled bastards."

Nate swung his fist into Greenroot's cheek, anger burning through the abrupt pain in his knuckles. The gunner stumbled under the blow, then lunged for Nate, and then Arani and Dax and Novachak were there, trying to pull them apart, and the night was suddenly filled with more shouts than stars.

CHAPTER NINETEEN

What Turns a Heart

ANGER ERUPTED ALL AROUND Rori, and it was all she could do to shield Luken from the surge of bodies pressing towards the bow. The captain and the quartermaster were shouting and trying to break up the fight while Novachak tried to stem the flow of people angrily surging forward, trying to get to Nate and Greenroot. In front of it all, the beacon star burned hungrily in the dark sky, as though feeding off of the violence and chaos.

I never should have brought us here, Rori thought.

It was far too late now. All Rori could do was throw her shoulders into the people fighting to get around her, and let them push her towards the port railing. Someone's elbow cracked against her ribs, and a hand grazed the side of her head, ripping her hat off, but she grit her teeth and pushed her way out of the worst of the crowd. Luken screamed in her hands and pecked at her fingers, but she bent over him protectively and tried to speak a few soothing words to him over the shouting of the crew.

No matter where she looked, all Rori saw were the angry faces of people arguing and shoving. The thought came to her like a lightning strike that this really and truly was so different from the *Godfall*.

This was so much worse.

Rori stumbled into the railing, catching herself with

one hand, the other still holding tight to the screaming Luken. She gazed helplessly at the warring crew—*her* crew—and was ashamed of what she'd done to them. Her eyes were hot with threatened tears, but she made herself draw in a few deep breaths.

Fix this, she told herself furiously.

But she had no idea how.

Drown them, the vicious voice commanded, and her magic rolled through her like it wanted to obey.

Rori stamped it down.

Behind her, one of the shoving matches escalated into another brawl, and she heard the solid collision of a fist with a face. Someone fell into her, hard, and Rori stumbled and lost her grip on Luken.

The bird immediately took off, still screaming as he ripped into the night. Rori pulled herself along the railing, trying to follow the flashes of Luken's blue pennant feathers in the light from the ship. Something heavy whooshed over her head, and Rori watched in horror as the predatory messenger bird chased after Luken. It was so much bigger than him, and would shred him to feathers and bones in a matter of minutes.

Gods above, no, Rori thought, but she was on the ship and the birds were in the air and there was absolutely nothing she could do.

Luken screamed again and began to cut back and forth, trying to shake his pursuer. The messenger was nowhere near as agile as him, but it was faster, and quickly caught up again each time Luken dodged its talons. Rori's nails dug into the railing, and she might have screamed too, but then there was a gunshot and a dark burst of feathers, and the dead messenger bird plummeted into the sea.

The world fell into a stunned silence.

Rori did not try to stop her tears as Luken came

arrowing back to her. He shot straight into her arms and trembled against her, and did not seem to mind when a few tears fell on to his back.

"Is he all right?" a familiar voice asked.

Breathing hard, Rori looked up at Xander, and nodded. He had the spent pistol against his shoulder, barrel pointed into the sky.

"Thank you," she whispered.

Xander did not smile, but he nodded back to her.

"Xander Grayvoice," the captain's said, her voice cutting clear across the quiet. "Where did you get that pistol?"

Weapons were confiscated, Rori thought numbly. Luken chirped softly, and she bundled him closer.

Xander turned to the captain and saluted her with the gun before tossing the pistol to her. Arani caught it, bewildered, but that quickly gave way to outrage as her hand went to the sash around her waist and found it empty.

"Things were starting to get ugly," Xander said calmly. "Figured I should do something before anyone got hurt." His eyes flicked past the captain, to where Jim Greenroot stood holding his broken spectacles and Dax had managed to restrain Nate, whose nose was streaming blood. "Anyone important," Xander amended.

"You could've killed someone," Dax growled as he pushed Nate away.

Xander shrugged dismissively. "Only if I'd been aiming at them."

Rori winced, feeling the cracks in her world grow even sharper. At least Luken was safe. She had that to hold on to.

"So now your aim is good again?" Greenroot spat, the words thick around the swelling from Nate's first punch.

"My aim was always good," Xander said.

Something twinged in Rori's mind, and she frowned as she tried to understand it. Her heart was still in her throat, though, and Luken felt so fragile in her hands, and her roaring blood was making it hard to concentrate.

Greenroot scoffed and stomped forward, dropping his broken spectacles to the deck. "Why'd you miss the first time, then?" He advanced on Xander, who did not step back. "The light was better and the bird was flying in a straight line." He stopped when there was less than a hand's breadth between the two of them. They were of the same height, and glared directly into each other's eyes. "Did you *want* to miss the first time, Snake Lips?"

Rori's blood froze in her veins, and the world went dead in her ears as she realized the same thing the gunner had: Xander Grayvoice was one of the best shots among the crew, maybe *the* best after Roccani had died in the fight with the navy. Xander would not have missed a clear shot like Jim was describing.

Not unless he'd wanted to.

Because he'd wanted the messenger bird to get away.

Because Xander was the traitor.

Rori's hands went limp, and she barely felt it when Luken fluttered away. "What did you do?" Rori asked, and her voice was quiet and cracked.

Xander did not look at her, but his mouth quirked into a flat smile. Then there was a flash of metal as a dagger appeared in his hand—the very same one he'd taken as a prize on Spider's Nest after shooting ten bottles at thirty paces—and something warm and wet and dark splashed across Rori's face as the blade slashed through Jim Greenroot's throat.

Someone screamed, and Rori thought that she

heard the captain shouting, but then Xander was on her, and his fist slammed into her gut. The breath rushed out of Rori as the pain washed in, and she doubled over in shock. Xander caught her and pulled her against him, and he might have murmured in her ear before he leaned back and pitched them both over the railing. The wind rushed around Rori, and then she slammed into the sea, and it was all she could do not to gasp water into her lungs as the water closed over her head. Her magic surged, but all she wanted was air, and it could not help her. Something rough brushed against her, and then she was pinned between it and Xander, and then they were moving fast through the cold water, and Rori had to put everything she had left into trying not to drown.

After what felt like hours but couldn't have been more than several minutes, the sea serpent slowed its relentless pace and thrust its dorsal fin above the surface, finally giving Rori the chance to take more than a quick gasp of air. She coughed and retched against its scales as it glided along the surface of the unnaturally still water, seawater and bile coming out of her in small jets.

Behind her, Xander was coughing too, but he hadn't been short of breath when he'd pulled them overboard. His hands were worn and bleeding from gripping the sea serpent's fin, but he kept his arms locked around Rori, pinning her against the creature as it pulled them along. Rori turned her head to look back the way they had come, but the sea was dark and empty all around them. The only light came from the stars and their pinpoint reflections in the mirror-smooth water.

Fear spiked through Rori, clean and sharp as a blade, but behind it came fury.

Xander had betrayed them, had betrayed *her*, and now she was out in the middle of empty water, clinging to a sea serpent and headed gods only knew where. The *Southern Echo* was gone, and the cold water was sucking the warmth out of her body, but Rori's heart began to pound, steady as the current running beneath them.

Her magic waited faithfully in her blood, and stirred when she called. She reached for the current, feeling its strength and steadiness. It did not want to change its course, but Rori pulled with the little strength she had left, and the water shuddered all around her.

Xander felt it. "Don't—"

Rori yanked as hard as she could, and the current twisted in her grasp, lunging towards Xander like a snake striking at prey. She did not care that it would hit her, too. She only wanted Xander to pay for what he'd done.

Drown him.

For a moment, Rori almost gave into the temptation. Xander could not swim on his own, and it would only take a few minutes of holding him under to end it all. But Rori's hold on the current broke the moment she had the thought, and she did not fight to regain control.

It was too late to stop the magic, though. The swell came and crashed down on them, shattering Xander's grip on the serpent and sending them tumbling apart in the dark water. Rori let it take her, let it spin her around and around, until she did not know which way was up. She picked a direction and began to swim.

Her head broke the surface into the night air, and she coughed and sputtered again. Her arms and legs were weak and only growing more so as the cold leeched into her body. She looked about, and did not see Xander's head breach the water.

Monster, she thought, and she might have wept if she wasn't so exhausted. Instead, she looked up at the stars, and tried to ignore the whisper that was still in her veins, calling her further into the west.

Come, it said, once more in those warm and welcoming tones. *You are welcome on our shores.*

Rori hesitated, wondering if it would just be better if she let herself die in the Forbidden Sea.

Come, the voice said.

She started swimming.

She did not get very far when the sea serpent burst out of the water in front of her, hissing and gurgling and looking very much like it wanted to eat her. Xander clung to its back once more and hissed urgently at the creature. The sea serpent thrashed its head and snapped its jaws, but it turned its teeth away from Rori at the last moment. Its scales grazed her as it swam past, and Xander reached out and snatched her against him once more.

"I'll give you that one," he panted as the serpent turned itself into the northeast, "but next time, the serpent bites you."

Rori jammed her elbow into Xander's ribs and was glad when he gave a soft grunt of pain. He pressed her harder against the sea serpent in response, and the scales scraped through her clothing to the skin beneath. Rori shuddered, but she did not let herself cry out.

"How could you do this?" she asked after a few minutes of silently cursing Xander in every way she could think. "Everyone trusted you." She twisted until she could see the curve of his cheek. "*I* trusted you."

His throat bobbed as he swallowed. "You shouldn't

have," he murmured. "You knew better."

"I thought I knew you," Rori said.

"You did," Xander said. "You knew what I was the moment you met me. It's not my fault you decided not to believe it."

Rori pushed against the sea serpent, but the body was too slippery beneath the water, and Xander's grip was too strong.

"You're not going anywhere," he told her flatly.

"I'm going wherever you're taking me, apparently," she grumbled.

Xander made a disinterested noise but offered nothing more.

Rori fumed in silence as the serpent swam on. It did not dive beneath the surface again, but that was a small relief. She shivered violently, and though she wanted nothing more than to pull away, she pressed her back firmly against Xander's chest, taking some of his warmth. He let her do it without saying a word.

She knew it was not done out of affection. Whatever scheme Xander had, he needed her alive to complete it.

She remembered the last kiss they'd shared, the one aboard the *Southern Echo*, and how she'd been the one to pull away. Of course she'd known that he would hurt her. She'd just never thought it would happen like this.

"Why did you betray Arani?" Rori asked.

She felt Xander shrug against her.

"I once said I'd follow her to the end of the world, but that was back when she was the only one heading that way," he said. "After she let that dragon go, I knew I couldn't trust her anymore."

"She did it to save Nate's life," Rori said softly.

"One life," he said, "and she threw away the Thief's treasure for it."

"So this is your revenge?" Rori asked hotly. "It's not going so well, since you grabbed the wrong person entirely to help you follow Mordanti's trail again."

"We don't need the Nowind," Xander said, and he did not keep the bitterness entirely out of his voice.

"I'm not going to help you," Rori snapped. "You'd have to beat the information out of me, and even then, I don't remember the maps well enough to follow them."

"I know," he said simply. "You didn't care about them, so you didn't study them. But we're not going after the Thief's treasure anymore, and as the serpent told me, it doesn't matter if you're willing to help us or not. All we need is for you to be present on the ship when it crosses into the Rend. If you want to throw yourself overboard after that, I won't stop you."

Rori swallowed hard. "Who's 'we?'" she asked tightly. "What ship?"

"You'll see soon enough," Xander promised.

CHAPTER TWENTY

To Truly Know

NATE STOOD AT THE railing, staring down at the ripples in the water. They were the only sign that Rori and Xander had been there mere moments ago, but they were already settling back into the unnatural smoothness of the far west Forbidden Sea.

I didn't protect her, he thought numbly.

Nate strained his eyes, searching further out, but he saw no sign of them, or of any sea serpents. All there was beyond the *Southern Echo* was Luken, flying in frantic circles as he searched for Rori, his pennant feathers streaming out behind him.

When Nate flung himself into the wind, he knew that there was nothing for him to trace, and even with the sea this calm, the water disrupted his magic if he strayed too close to the surface.

Rori was gone, and there was nothing he could do.

I didn't protect her.

Nate came back into himself and stared out at the horizon, and he kept staring long after Luken had given up and returned to the ship, huddled trembling and forlorn on one of the rigging ropes. Eventually, someone came and pried Nate away from the railing. They took a firm grip on his collar and stood with him as Jim Greenroot's body was removed from the deck. Nate watched as the corpse was wrapped in a hastily cut bit of canvas. Greenroot's eyes were open and unseeing, the gash across his throat impossibly red against his skin. His clothes and the deck were soaked with blood. The wet, rusty patch that was left behind drank in the light from the lanterns, as though it refused to be anything but a void.

Just like the one Xander had pulled Rori into.

I can still save her.

"We have to go after them," Nate said abruptly, but his voice was weak and only the person holding him by the scruff of the collar heard him.

They gave him a gentle but firm shake. "Easy, lad," came the boatswain's voice.

Nate stared into the slowly drying patch of blood and tried to remember how to breathe.

Rori was gone, Greenroot was dead, Xander was the traitor, and there was nothing Nate could do.

No, he thought, *there must be something.*

But there was a horrible ringing in his ears and he could not tear his eyes away from the blood on the deck. He was vaguely aware of people around him speaking, some frantically, others calmly, and he did not understand any of it.

There has to be something I can do.

A voice broke through the noise in his head, and Nate heard Captain Arani say, "We keep the current course."

No! Nate thought, and this time, he managed to shout his way out of his own stupor. "We have to follow them!" He started to turn towards Arani, one arm raised and gesturing in the direction the serpent had gone, but Novachak gave him another shake and yanked him back.

But the captain heard him, and she looked at Nate coldly. "We keep the course," she repeated. "After the boatswain is finished with you, report to my cabin." She turned away.

"You can't—" Nate started to snarl, but Arani rounded on him with such fury that he staggered back into Novachak.

"My orders are final." She cut her eyes over Nate's shoulder, to the boatswain. "Use the whip, not the cane. Do not be gentle, but five lashes will suffice for now. His punishment has only just begun."

"Aye, Captain," Novachak said.

Nate's mouth went dry as Arani turned her back on him. She fired off orders to the crew to get the ship sailing on a clear path forward, and the crew leapt to obey.

"Come on, lad," Novachak said, giving Nate a small push towards the foremast.

"This isn't right," Nate protested, but his feet moved under Novachak's firm guidance.

"Aye," the boatswain said, "you deserve far worse for what you've done tonight. Best accept the captain's mercy quietly."

"Mercy?" Nate put weak venom behind the word.

"A traitor murdered a man and kidnapped our navigator," Novachak said. "We're essentially at war now, and that means the captain's word is law. You just tried to undermine her authority. What's more, you falsely accused a man of mutiny without any evidence, and then struck him. Code says you should lose your tongue *and* hand for that alone. So yes, the captain is showing you mercy. For now."

Nate opened his mouth to speak, but the words dried up in his throat. He'd been so determined to stand between danger and the people he cared about. How had it all gone so wrong?

He did not have an answer by the time the cabin boy came running with the coiled whip in hand. Novachak released Nate to take hold of the handle, and told Nate to remove his coat and shirt.

"Five lashes," the boatswain called out so the whole crew could hear, "for insubordination." He took a step closer to Nate and dropped his voice low. "I'll make it as quick as I can. Keep your eyes on the horizon, and try not to scream."

The whip had not drawn blood, but Nate's back felt like it had been cut to ribbons, and his shirt was agony against the welts. Once the initial pain had passed, however, all Nate could think about were the scars on Rori's back. He couldn't imagine how that must have felt, let alone how she'd managed to survive it. Now she was gone, and Nate's back was on fire, and Captain Arani was looking at him tiredly from where she sat at the long table in her cabin. She'd offered Nate a seat, but even if he hadn't just endured the lashing, he would have been too agitated to sit. As it was, he kept fidgeting on his feet, and wincing when his back reminded him of what it had just endured because of his rashness.

Arani scrubbed a hand across her face and sighed. "I don't even know where to begin with you," she said.

"I do," Nate said quietly. The whipping had been horrible, and he'd finally understood what Novachak had meant about the captain's mercy, but each lash had been a thunderclap of clarity across his mind. There were still glaring problems before them, and Nate's anger with Arani had gone cold. "Tell me why you're abandoning Rori."

"I'm not," the captain said.

"You are!" Nate insisted. "You gave up the black mimic and Mordanti's treasure for me, but you'll turn your back on her?"

Arani slowly leaned back in her seat. "Be careful what you say to me, boy. You already owe far more than what the boatswain made you pay with the skin on your back."

Nate stood his ground. "You released the dragon and stole aboard a navy ship for me. Why won't you do the same for Rori now?"

"It's a very different circumstance."

"It's not!" He took a moment to regain control of his voice, bring it back down from a shout. "I don't understand you at all."

The captain studied him for a long moment, looking as tired as she had the night he'd come to tell her about the messenger bird. "You know," she finally said, "when I met you, you were terrified to look me in the eye."

"A lot has changed," Nate said.

"Yes, it has," Arani agreed. "I'm not sure it's all been for the better, but one thing that has not changed at all is my devotion to this crew."

Nate snorted, not even trying to hide his disbelief. He and Arani were alone in the cabin, and he wanted answers to all the questions that had been burning holes in his heart since the ship had first crossed into the Forbidden Sea. "If that were true," he said, "you would have acted sooner on the mutiny."

He said it to make her angry, but to his surprise, Arani only gazed at him, the silence broken by the slow tap of her fingernail against the wooden table.

"It wasn't a true mutiny," she finally said.

Nate threw his hands up, wincing when his back raged with fresh pain. That only stoked his anger further. "We were betrayed!"

"By Xander Grayvoice," Arani said. "Not Jim Greenroot."

"He was clearly planning something!" Nate said, his

voice rising again. "Xander killed him before he could act, but that message was for Greenroot, and his accomplices are still walking the ship."

Arani shook her head. "He wasn't planning anything," she said, and her calm certainty made Nate want to break something.

"How do you know?" he demanded.

"Because I knew Jim Greenroot," Arani said, "far better than you did."

"Not as well as you think," Nate grumbled.

Arani folded her arms. "Do you know the reason why Jim Greenroot, unlike so many other Solkyrian citizens, was illiterate?"

"Too stupid to learn?" Nate quipped.

The captain pressed her mouth into a thin line. "Don't disrespect the dead on my ship, boy. You did not know the man."

"I knew enough."

"Oh?" Arani suddenly stood up. "Then I suppose you know that Jim Greenroot's mother died when he was barely seven years old, leaving his father to care for him and his four younger siblings." She paced to the windows at the back of the cabin, each step slow and deliberate. "And I suppose you also know that Jim's father suffered from chronic pain, and drank heavily to numb it. After the Greenroot mother died, the father fell into a deep depression, and the drinking only got worse. He kept working, but Jim had to leave school to take care of his younger siblings. Gods above know his father couldn't do it." Arani stopped in front of the windows. She half-turned back to Nate, but kept her gaze on the night outside. "Eventually, the father stopped working altogether, and Jim lied about his age so he could take his father's place on the docks. Jim was always a big one, even when he was a child. No one questioned it, although he always suspected that they knew.

"Jim spent a few years working on the docks. He saw all kinds of sailors and ships, and he swore that he'd be on one of them someday, too. By the time his youngest sibling had aged into school, he figured it was too late for him to go back, so he stayed on the docks, and he eventually tried to join the navy. He lied then, too, claiming that he had finished school and could serve as an educated citizen. That did not go well, as I'm sure you can imagine. He was ultimately allowed to join, but he suffered so badly under his officers that he deserted the first chance he could.

"I met him on Spider's Nest, after he'd spent the better part of two years wandering from island to island. He was deeply drunk when he told me all of this, but he was desperate for a captain who would let him speak his mind in exchange for his sworn loyalty."

Arani paced back to the table, her gaze now pinned on Nate. "Jim Greenroot was not a good person," she said. "He picked up all kinds of terrible ideas from his time on the docks, and the navy destroyed what little empathy might have been left in him. He simply wasn't all that pleasant to be around. I myself did not like him." She halted in front of Nate, forcing him to either meet her gaze or step away. "But for as long as I knew him, Jim Greenroot was an honest man, often to a fault. He did not hide things from anyone, even when he knew that they'd get him into trouble. For all of his flaws, none of them made him a traitor to the crew. That's something I had to understand and accept a long time ago, and it's a rule that applies to everyone who sails with me.

"No one on this ship has clean hands, Nate. Most of us have cheated and lied. Many of us have killed. We'll all do it again before our time in this world is done. It's why we sail under a black flag that belongs to no country or kingdom. Just us, and us alone."

Nate did not have a response to that. Arani left him floundering for one, but she turned away again rather than watch him struggle.

"As to Rori and Xander," she said before he could form some semblance of a thought, "we'll never find them if we try to follow them. That serpent left us to take Xander to wherever he's going, and they're dragging Rori with them." Arani glanced over her shoulder, searching Nate's face for signs of understanding. "He took *Rori*, Nate. Not you. That means whoever Xander is working with is heading for the Rend and the Vanishing Island. If we want any hope of seeing that girl ever again, that's where we have to go."

Nate felt like the world had been ripped out from under him, but he clung to Arani's words like a lifeline. "We can get there on our own?" he asked.

"From what Rori told me," Arani said, "we'd have to blindfold ourselves in order to miss the Rend now." She hesitated, distracted by a sudden thought, but then she shook her head and her determination returned twofold. "If I have to fight the gods themselves to get to that island," she growled, "so be it."

Relief washed through Nate, chasing away some of the shame he felt for how wrong he'd been about everything. Not all of it, but some. "Did you...?" he started to ask, but broke the idea off before he could say anything else foolish.

Arani nodded for him to ask the question anyway.

"Did you ever suspect Xander?" Nate asked.

Arani sighed. "No," she said, flat and candid. "I should have, but I didn't. I knew that he was angry after we released the dragon. Honestly, I was expecting trouble from him back on Spider's Nest, but he came with us into the Forbidden Sea. And then, when he took Rori... I never thought that he'd do something like this. Not to her." Her eyes narrowed as she glared down at the table. "I did not know Xander Grayvoice as well as I should have, and Rori and Jim had to pay the price for my mistake."

"I didn't know him either," Nate said quietly. "He fooled us all."

Arani made a thoughtful noise that came out almost like a growl. "He won't do it again." She shrugged into her coat and placed her hat on her head at a neat, determined angle. She did not hesitate when she reached for the saber. When the weapon was belted around her waist, she once more became the pirate captain Nate had chosen to follow.

She's really not giving up, Nate thought, his heart lifting. *Neither am I.*

"They have to be on a ship, right?" Nate asked.

"Unless Xander intends to swim all the way to the Vanishing Island, yes."

"I can track it, then."

"Oh, you will be," Arani said, giving him a hard look. "You're going to use your magic to tell me every movement that ship makes. Consider it replacement punishment for not losing your tongue."

Nate was certain that she was not joking.

The captain moved to step past Nate, but she paused to place a hand on his arm, well away from the welts from the whip. "We're going to get her back," Arani said, "but it is not going to be easy. Neither is finding and tracking that ship, now that there's no bird to follow back to it. I want you to try your best anyway, but don't you dare try to push past what you can handle. I need everyone ready and able to fight when the time comes. Understand?"

Nate nodded, and Arani released him.

"Captain," he said before she could move away, "it sounds like you may know who's been following us."

Arani grimaced. "I have an idea." She moved to the door and opened it, gesturing Nate through. "Unfortunately," she said, "I'm dead certain that I'm right."

CHAPTER TWENTY-ONE
The Dragonsbane

R ORI WAS EXHAUSTED. IT was all she could do to keep her head above water, even with Xander locked around her. She could feel his arms shaking, and while it wouldn't take much to break his hold now, she knew that she'd never be able to make it back to the *Southern Echo*, let alone find the ship again. And that was if the sea serpent did not bite her in half before she drowned. Her hands were raw from holding on to the creature's scaly body, and as badly as she wanted to let go, she wouldn't let herself. Not yet.

When dawn came and began to lighten the world, Rori looked up to see that they were approaching a ship. It was larger than the *Southern Echo*, and she recognized it as a frigate from its three masts. Dully, she wondered whose ship it was, but the thought fled when she saw the sea serpents in the water all around it.

They churned the sea angrily, dorsal fins cutting harsh lines back and forth along the hull. Every so often, a serpent would launch itself out of the water, throwing its thrashing body against the side of the ship before falling back with a heavy splash.

That was how it had been with the *Godfall*.

Rori shuddered as they drew closer to the unfamiliar ship. Serpents turned and swam towards the one towing her and Xander along, and Rori couldn't help releasing a small whimper of fear.

"It'll be all right," Xander croaked. His lips were as cracked and dry as hers, but determination burned in his voice.

Rori did not respond. Instead, she tried to make herself as small and unappetizing as she possibly could as Xander's serpent swam for the ship. Its fellows came uncomfortably close, and Rori shut her eyes rather than watch all those teeth flash in the water. She heard the gurgling hiss of a serpent, and it might have been Xander who responded. She did not care. She just wanted to be out of the water.

After a few minutes, Xander jostled her until she opened her eyes. They'd reached the ship, and there was a rope ladder hanging down to the water.

"You have to climb," Xander told her.

Rori stole a glance at the serpents milling behind them, and then reached shakily for the ladder.

Hauling herself out of the water was the hardest thing she'd ever done. Her hands and arms did not want to cooperate, and they threatened to give out and send her plummeting back into the sea with each agonizing step she took. The sun was above the horizon by the time she was halfway up. She had to stop to rest, clinging to the ropes and hating the cold, unfamiliar wood of the ship beneath them.

Her magic rose with her anger, and Rori took one hand off of the ladder and reached towards the sea. But she was so tired, and even that small gesture made her arm shake, and all she could call up was a small wave that set the ship gently rocking.

A few steps beneath her, Xander shot a warning look up at her, but it lacked any real force.

That was more than made up for by the sound of a pistol being cocked from the deck above.

Rori glanced up, and saw what was either a very

large man or a partially shaved bear leaning over the railing, glaring down at her.

"Don't do that again," the bear-man rumbled.

Rori groaned and pressed her forehead against the side of the ship. After a minute, she felt Xander tap her boot, and she forced herself to resume climbing.

When she finally reached the top, she had just enough time to wonder how she was going to find the strength to get herself over the railing. She needn't have worried; the bear-man snatched her up and hauled her on to the deck. He let her fall to her knees, and Rori did not try to fight gravity. She was so tired, and her hands were raw and stinging, and everything was wrong.

She heard voices around her, and they only grew louder when Xander flopped to the deck somewhere behind her. He was the first to clamber to his feet. Rori let him have the honor. She was content with her seat on the deck.

The bear-man, however, was not. He grabbed Rori's arm and dragged her up, and then began to tie her wrists together in front of her.

Memories of chains stirred in Rori's mind, and she tried to thrash away.

The bear-man slapped her hard enough to make her ears ring, and by the time her head was clear again, he'd finished the last knot.

Rori felt sick as she finally raised her eyes to see where she was, and who surrounded her.

There were no friendly faces. Most were the gruff, weather-worn ones of sailors, and Rori noticed that there were very few women in this crew. Those that were there were viciously scarred and glowering, thick arms crossed over their chests and absolutely no room in them for mercy, pity, or anything of the kind. By the mainmast, a single anemic Lowwind stood with his arms raised, pushing wind into the sails. His was the only Skill mark among the crew, other than hers and Xander's.

Rori swallowed, and tried not to look afraid.

"I see you actually made it," a deep voice rang out, and the crew parted to allow a tall, thin man to stalk his way forward. He wore a black coat trimmed in silver and a large black hat with a massive gray feather stuck in the rim. His boots were polished to a mirror-shine, and the heels clipped the deck with authority as he strode past Xander. His eyes were so dark they barely seemed to reflect any light, and his face was creased with lines. He had an aquiline nose and a strong jaw beneath his neatly trimmed beard, and his Solkyrian skin had been burnished a deep bronze by the sun. There was a sword at his hip and three pistols strapped across his chest, each adorned with a simple blue ribbon, just like the one that held back his salt-and-pepper hair.

Rori knew exactly who he was long before he stopped in front of her and swept off his hat in a mocking bow.

"Miss Goodtide," Captain Blackcliff said in a poisonously charming drawl, "welcome to the *Dragonsbane*."

He offered her an equally venomous smile, which Rori answered with the nastiest glare she could muster.

"Now, now," Blackcliff chided as he replaced his hat. "There's no need for hostilities. In fact, you could show a little more appreciation for our hospitality. We've gone through all the trouble of getting our best cell ready for you."

A low chuckle ran through the crew, and Rori was very aware of every eye on her.

"As long as you cooperate, you won't be harmed,"

Blackcliff continued. He abruptly dropped the false smile and rounded on his crew. "They've all been ordered to leave you be. No one is to touch you without my say."

A reluctant murmur of agreement went through the crew.

Rori's skin crawled. "I'm not your property," she growled.

Blackcliff turned back to her and cocked an eyebrow. "Be a lot safer for you, if you were," he informed her. "I promise you this, Miss Goodtide. The *Dragonsbane* is nothing like that pathetic little dinghy run by the Veritian bitch. You do as I say, or you bleed."

Rori held Blackcliff's gaze, but she did not speak again.

Satisfied, the captain nodded and gave a dismissive wave of his hand. "Take her below," he ordered, and two men came forward to push Rori towards the stairs.

The last thing she saw before she descended into the gloom was Blackcliff shaking hands with Xander, who had an unusually cautious look on his face, but not a trace of regret.

They gave her a blanket, which was more than what the captain of the *Godfall* had done, but that was the smallest gesture of decency Captain Blackcliff was willing to offer. Rori sat huddled in her cell, the blanket pulled around her shoulders as best as she'd been able to manage with her tied wrists, and tried to track the time by the intensity of the light leaking in from above.

For all of Blackcliff's disdain of Arani, he could not say that he kept the *Dragonsbane* in the same condition as she did the *Southern Echo*. There were gaps in the deck from bad upkeep, and with the way the ship was riding in the water, Rori suspected that it had been a long time since Blackcliff had careened the *Dragonsbane* and gotten rid of the muck and growth on the hull. That harried Lowwind she'd seen was probably being forced to compensate for the drag. It was amazing he'd survived this long, especially if Blackcliff had set him against the wind wall.

Maybe there was another wind worker at one point, Rori thought, but she tried not to dwell on the idea.

There was a guard posted outside her cell, but he was only there to make sure that she did not try to hurt herself, or start gnawing on the ropes around her wrists. If she rested, Rori might have been able to use her Skill to summon a wave strong enough to capsize the ship, but with her arms bound together, she was more likely to get a bullet in her skull before she could even send the *Dragonsbane* rocking.

Rori had to settle for making herself as comfortable as she could in the cell while she tried to find something to occupy her mind other than frustration and depression. She contented herself with highly unlikely but soothing fantasies of the *Southern Echo* catching up to the *Dragonsbane* and blasting Blackcliff's ship into oblivion.

After what she thought was a little more than two hours, the anemic Lowwind was brought down and locked in the cell next to hers. He'd been worked to the point of total exhaustion, and he collapsed the moment his captors were no longer making an effort to hold him up. He did not stir after they'd left.

Rori wondered when the Lowwind had been abducted by Blackcliff's crew. He had the starved, haunted look of the Lowwind that had served on the *God-fall*, suggesting it had been maybe a year since his conscription, although Rori could only guess how long he'd been in service on his original ship and what those conditions had been like. Either way, with Blackcliff working the Lowwind like a Solkyrian merchant would, Rori did not think he would last another few months.

The guard was completely uninterested in the Lowwind's health, and while Rori couldn't do anything to help him, she still watched his prone form closely, looking for the shallow rise and fall of his chest that proved he was still breathing. He was out cold, but he was alive, and that was the best either of them could hope for.

The sounds of the *Dragonsbane* and its crew were strange and unfamiliar, but with enough time, anything could fade into the background. Rori tried to follow the shouts of the crew for a while, hoping to piece together the ship's speed and position, but what she heard was garbled at best, and she gave it up.

She drowsed a little, her head against the cold wood of the ship's side, but in spite of her exhaustion, she could not sleep. She was probably as safe as she possibly could be down in that cell, but her nerves were stretched too far to let her relax.

She was given food and drink, and was surprised to find it on par with what she'd expect the rest of the crew's rations to look like at this stage of a voyage. The Lowwind, too, was given food, but he did not wake when his cell was opened, and his bowl and mug were left on the floor, which allowed for a couple of rats to come scurrying out of the shadows and devour his share. Too tired to do anything about them, Rori chewed her own hardtack and dried meat and tried not to pay the rats too much mind.

This, too, was how it had been on the *Godfall*.

Drown them all, a voice insisted in Rori's head.

Maybe I will, she thought, and she was too tired to be afraid of how easily that response had come.

Rori passed a full day down in the cell. The Lowwind was roused twice from his stupor and brought topside again to work the wind, although the second time required the use of a bucket of what Rori desperately hoped was stale water, but very likely was not. Once awake, the Lowwind offered no resistance and went stumbling after his captors. They did not use any sort of restraints on him. He was too broken to fight.

No one bothered Rori. It seemed Blackcliff had the respect of his crew, taken through fear if not earned through camaraderie. Either way, the day wore into night, and the only time anyone approached Rori was when they came to give her another bowl of food.

That lasted until Xander came to see her.

He waited until after nightfall, when a good part of the ship was asleep. The Lowwind was passed out on the floor of his cell, and the guard lounged on a chair and picked at his nails with a knife. There was a soft creak on the floorboards, and the guard was immediately out of his seat with the knife raised.

"I want to talk to her," Xander said from around the corner.

The guard scoffed but sank back into the chair and resumed cleaning his nails.

Rori shifted until her back was to the cell door. For her part, she had no wish to speak with Xander.

She heard him step in front of her cell, and knew that he was purposefully making noise. He could be silent as a stalking cat when he wanted to be, and as the quiet stretched between them, Rori would not have been surprise if she turned around and saw that he had disappeared. She wished he would do just that, but knew that he hadn't, so she glared at the wall and waited for him to be the first to speak.

"You don't have to be a prisoner," he finally said. "I know you must hate it down here. If you agree to cooperate with Blackcliff, he'll let you freely walk the ship."

"There's nothing free about this," Rori spat, still facing the wall. "He'd be a fool to release me."

"True, you couldn't be alone," Xander said after a moment. "Or unbound. I'd be your escort, though."

"I'd rather claw my way through all six hells and back."

Xander was silent long enough that she hoped he'd taken the unsubtle hint. She wasn't so fortunate.

"I'm sorry," he said, and he sounded just genuine enough for fury to stir inside her heart.

Rori pushed herself to her feet, letting the blanket pool around her ankles. She stalked to the cell door and glared up at Xander. "Not yet, you're not," she snarled. "Someday soon, you're going to find out just how badly you messed up, what you threw away. You had everything you needed with Captain Arani."

"Maybe," Xander said, completely unfazed by her rage. "But it wasn't everything I wanted."

"And what is it that you want?" Rori asked. "More importantly, do you think you're going to get it here, from Blackcliff? You're in for a nasty surprise, if you really believe your life is that secure."

"I know it isn't," he said simply. "I'm going to be watching my back for the rest of my life, but with Blackcliff's crew, at least I know where I stand. He knows that I've betrayed one captain already."

"Only one?" Rori scoffed.

"That he's aware of," Xander amended.

Rori thumped her elbow against the iron bar of the cell. "And you're okay with this?"

Xander shrugged. "It's too late for anything else." He wrapped his hands around the bars of the cell, leaning in a little closer. "I really am sorry that it came to this."

To her surprise, Rori believed him. "As much as someone like you can be," she said, and took a step back.

"I do care for you," he said. A deep frown creased his brow, cutting across the black Grayvoice tattoo on his face. "You know that, right?"

Rori laughed, breathy and scornful. "Maybe, in your own way, but never more than you've cared for yourself. You've always been like this, Xander. It's why we never..." She trailed off, but he was angry now.

"Say it," he growled. "But say it all. Say that you could never be with me, the dirty animal speaker, and you dropped me the moment you had another weather worker to play with."

"You'd love for it to be that simple, wouldn't you?" Rori said. There was no heat in her voice, but the truth put force behind the words. "One more thing for you to blame that isn't yourself, but you know what really happened. You know that it was always you and all the lines that you crossed that did this." She turned away and went to retrieve the blanket. "I wanted so badly to believe it, but I'm done pretending that you're a better person than you really are. This is the last line you'll ever cross, because my forgiveness is not going any further. Not now, and not ever again." Rori struggled with the blanket, somehow managing to get it back around her shoulders. "I was stupid enough to trust you," she whispered, "but you're the one who broke it all."

Xander did not say anything, but she could feel his fury rolling off of him in waves. She wasn't surprised when, a few moments later, she turned back around and saw that he had gone.

Two more days passed, marked by the strength of the light seeping through the deck overhead and the red color that soaked the evenings, and Xander did not come to see her again. Rori ate the food Blackcliff's men brought her, watched the anemic Lowwind for signs of life, and felt the way her heart pulled in her chest, evermore into the west as the *Dragonsbane* sailed towards the inevitable.

Sure enough, the time came when the light leaking into the hold was all wrong, too red for late morning. The bear-man who'd pulled Rori aboard the *Dragonsbane* came for her, and ordered her to go topside with him. Rori did not fight. Instead, she calmly walked out of the cell and climbed the steps into the fresh air.

The sense of foreboding slammed into Rori like a hammer and her magic rose to meet it, but she somehow managed to keep herself from staggering. She still needed a moment to collect herself, and swallow the bitter nausea that rolled over her with the same rhythm as the waves lapping against the hull of the ship. The bear-man made an unimpressed noise as Rori paused, but judging by the way he was staring at the western sky, he himself wasn't feeling too brazen.

When she had her footing back and her heartbeat had calmed in the wake of the sudden surge of her magic, Rori picked her way to the bow of the ship, where Blackcliff waited. He stood silhouetted against the bloody wound in the sky, watching its edges weep crimson into the world as the sea turned black.

For the second time in her life, Rori stood before

the Rend.

She turned her gaze to the east, searching in vain for some sign of the *Southern Echo* behind them, but there was nothing on the open sea.

"All right, Miss Goodtide," Blackcliff called, dragging Rori's attention back to the tear in the world. "This is where you bring us safely through." His dark eyes glittered in the red light, daring her to put so much as a toe out of line.

Rori looked at the Rend, growing larger and redder the closer they sailed, and for a brief moment, she hoped that she'd been wrong about the blood price, that Blackcliff would fail to pay and the gods would strike the *Dragonsbane* down. Then the wind changed, becoming whispers in her ears, and she swore that they said, "Welcome back."

Her heart sank as the realm of the gods opened to her. She turned east once more, desperately wondering how the *Southern Echo* would be able to cross without her, but Blackcliff closed his hand on her shoulder and tugged her back around.

Up ahead, Rori saw an island flicker into sight on the red horizon.

CHAPTER TWENTY-TWO

Reunion

NATE WORKED AS HARD as he could alongside the riggers, trying to coax as much speed out of the *Southern Echo* as they possibly could. The ship responded willingly, and Nate kept up with the more seasoned riggers without his arms and shoulders burning in protest, but without a weather worker who could put more wind in the sails or quicken the currents, they were limited to what the steady breeze could give them. The frustration that sat in Nate's chest was all too familiar, and a nasty voice in his head told him that he truly was useless, after all.

He ignored it as best he could and set himself on the other task Captain Arani had given him: finding the *Dragonsbane* in the wind.

She was certain that it was Captain Blackcliff who had followed the *Southern Echo* into the Forbidden Sea. Arani could think of no other captain who would chase after them like this, and especially no one who would dare conscript one of the *Southern Echo*'s own right under her nose. Her anger was a palpable thing, but she turned it west and poured it into the horizon, spending each day either at the helm or at the bow, one foot up on the bowsprit and glaring at the sky.

Each day, Nate had to report his failure to her. No matter what he did, he could not find the *Dragonsbane*—or anything—in the wind, and his frustration with himself only grew.

"It's all right," Arani told him every time. "We'll catch them at the Rend."

It's not all right, Nate wanted to reply. *Nothing is all right.* He kept the thoughts to himself and tried to focus on his work, but he knew that so much of this was his fault.

He'd been so fixated on Jim Greenroot as a traitor that he'd blinded himself to the truth. What was more, Nate had so badly wanted to believe that the rift between him and Xander had been healed, but he'd only made it worse.

"Xander is a complete bastard," Eric said firmly after Nate confessed these thoughts one night, finally unable to hold them in any longer. "What he did is unforgivable, but you can be sure that the captain will make him pay." Eric glowered at his dinner and shredded the salted meat with his hands. "We all will."

Marcus nodded in silent agreement, for once not interested in eating.

The one good thing that came out of Xander's betrayal was the reunification of the crew. Everyone wanted to see justice done for Rori's kidnapping, even more so than Greenroot's murder, and they threw themselves into their tasks with none of the protests or bickering that had clouded the air mere days ago. Those who mourned Jim Greenroot's death worked hard at their tasks, and the ship sped along.

Still, Nate floundered in the wind, searching in vain for the shadow of another ship, but he always came back to the *Southern Echo* with nothing but a pounding headache and a burning ring on his finger.

The one comfort to Nate was that Arani clearly had the ship's course well in hand, even without the sea serpent to guide them. The red tear in the sky was lingering longer each day, and even without Rori to confirm it, everyone knew that they were getting close.

They simply did not realize how close until, one early afternoon, Nate felt a sickening shift in the wind. It did not change in direction or intensity, but the air suddenly felt wrong, like it did not belong in this world. It left him with a queasy feeling that thankfully passed, but he could not shake the uneasiness that came with it.

Dax suffered, too. He nearly collapse on the main deck, completely overwhelmed by the sudden strength of all of the heartbeats around him. "They're so loud," the quartermaster said as he pressed a damp cloth against his forehead. "I can even hear the rats in the hold."

"A pleasant thought," Novachak remarked mildly, but his icy eyes skimmed past where Dax and Nate sat recovering from the magic surge, searching out Marcus and Eric. When he found the Darkbends, they confirmed that they, too, felt unwell, but they had not been hit anywhere nearly as hard as Nate or Dax.

"There's something... poisonous about the light," Eric said. "I don't know how to describe it."

"It hurts," Marcus said. "That's how you describe it."

"Bad enough that you need to rest?" Novachak asked.

The Darkbends looked at each other for a moment, squinting in the sun, and then shook their heads.

Not long after that, the sky split open in the west, and red light began to pour into the world.

"This is it," Arani called from the bow. She had her sword drawn and ready. "Whatever happens, we will not stop."

Nate stood with the rest of the crew behind Arani, staring through the hole in the world to the black sea on the other side. The wind still felt wrong, but not unbearable, and Nate took courage from Arani. He made himself stand tall as the *Southern Echo* sailed on. It was hard to ignore the cries from the main deck, however.

They'd gathered the remaining chickens and the dairy goat from the galley, and their distressed clucking and bleating filled the air. The animals thrashed against the hands and cages that restrained them, and Nate couldn't help but pity them as the ship drew closer to the Rend.

Arani had warned them all about the blood price that must be paid for the ship to cross into the realm of the gods. She hoped that the animals would suffice; if they didn't, she intended to fight her way into the Rend. Nate had the terrible feeling that a few chickens and a goat wouldn't be nearly enough to appease the gods, but if anyone could cut their way out of the mortal world, it would be Captain Arani.

She wouldn't be alone. Weapons had been returned to the crew in full, and the red light glinted off the hard edges of swords and pistols all around the ship.

"Steady," Arani called, lifting her sword into the air.

The Rend reared before her, open like a bloody maw, and Nate tightened his grip on the cage he held. The chicken inside pecked at his fingers and threw itself against the sides of the cage as the ship sailed to the cusp of the Rend, but Nate would not let go. Beside him, Novachak stood with a dagger in his hand, ready to reach in and do what he needed the moment the signal came from the captain. The two of them were at the railing, ready to spill blood into the sea, one pair in a line of people and doomed animals that stretched back to the stern. Beyond Novachak, Nate saw Marcus and Eric with a cage of their own, and AnnaMarie Blueshore and two of her subordinates holding the dairy goat.

"When you cut," Dax had told them all earlier, "make it certain, and make it clean. There's no reason these animals should suffer by our hands any more than they have to."

Nate stole a final glance at the chicken in the cage he held between himself and Novachak. The poor thing looked terrified.

I'm sorry, Nate thought.

Then Arani roared, "Now!" and her sword came down.

Mercifully, it was over fast, the animals' fear cut short by sharp blades. The carcasses went over into the water, which turned black with their blood. Nate held his breath as he waited, his gaze locked on the looming tear in the world and the red horizon that lay on its other side.

The bowsprit pricked the Rend first, and for a brief, hopeful moment, it seemed that the animal sacrifice had been enough.

Then the entire ship shuddered, a vicious wind came tearing out of the Rend, and the waves lashed the ship so hard, the *Southern Echo* pitched sideways.

Over the panicked shouts of the crew, Nate distinctly heard something snarl, "Unworthy."

Nate clung to the railing as the ship was slammed by another wave, turning her broadside to the onslaught and her bow away from the Rend. Another hit, and the ship would capsize. Nate found himself praying that would not happen, but if the gods chose to answer him, they did so cruelly. Instead of another wave, a massive fin broke the surface of the water, and it arrowed straight towards the *Southern Echo*.

"All of you, get back!" Arani shouted as she ran across the deck, her saber still drawn. Her eyes were locked on the fin racing towards the ship, and Nate knew beyond any doubt that she really would fight whatever monster had come for them from the realm of the gods.

Nate scrambled back and the captain skidded into his vacated space. Novachak remained where he was, one arm raised to catch Arani and keep her on balance. The boatswain's fear was plain to see, but he stood beside the captain all the same as she readied her sword. Dax appeared on her other side, no weapon drawn but with his hands raised and a look of steady concentration on his face, the same look Nate had seen him wear whenever the quartermaster had used his blood-working Skill.

"If this thing has a heart," Dax growled, "I'll stop it."

Nate did not hear the captain's reply, but whatever she said, it made the quartermaster smile.

Then the monster was upon them, rearing up out of the sea and baring its terrible fangs at them all. It was a serpent, far larger than the one that Xander Grayvoice had spoken to, maybe even larger than the leviathans of the south. Nate swallowed hard as it lunged for the ship, mouth open and ready to close on Arani even as she lifted her sword to meet its teeth. People cried out all around Nate, and he felt his own heart lodge itself in his throat as he watched this terrible thing fall towards their captain.

The *Southern Echo* gave a violent shudder, strong enough to knock Nate off his feet. As he fell, he heard the sound of splintering wood, and he wasn't the only one who gasped as the boards of the deck began to ripple. A wave ran through the wood from the bow to the port railing, and it reared up in front of the three officers, upsetting their own footing and driving them back.

The splintering sound grew louder, and without warning, a massive figure erupted out of the wood, long arms reaching to rake jagged fingers across the serpent's face. It hissed and withdrew, and there came a fearsome scream that sent a bolt of pain through Nate's head and threatened to split him open like a ripe melon. He slammed his hands over his ears, barely aware of the others around him doing the same, but even over the pain, Nate heard that piercing voice, and felt the echo in his soul.

MINE!

And then a silence fell, sharp and violent, and the pain receded as quickly as it had come.

Slowly, Nate uncurled himself from the fetal position he'd fallen into. He sat up and looked around, just as dazed as everyone else. Some steps back from the railing, Arani, Dax, and Novachak were picking themselves up, and Nate pulled in a stunted breath when he saw the sea serpent still rearing, its head well above the *Southern Echo*'s deck. One side of its arrow-shaped face had three deep furrows cut through its scales to the raw flesh beneath, and the serpent gave another angry hiss. Between it and the officers was the figure Nate had seen earlier. It was now perfectly still, its arms thrown wide as though to shield the three from the serpent. It was such a meager defense, and Nate held his breath as he waited for the serpent to strike again, for those teeth to close around the ship and the captain and tear them both into the sea.

Instead, the serpent turned and sank back into the water, vanishing from sight. The sea grew calm in its absence, and even the wind quieted to a whisper.

Nate frowned, realizing that was *exactly* what the wind now was.

And it kept saying, breathy and joyful, "Daughter."

Abruptly, the figure at the edge of the ship melted back into the wood, and the deck rippled again as a wave shot towards the foremast. Several people shouted and scrambled away, retreating to the stern, but Nate froze when he heard something even stranger than the wind speaking.

It was laughter, and it was coming from Captain Arani.

Nate wasn't sure if that meant they were safe, or if the captain's mind had cracked. The latter was probably a safer bet, based on the stunned look the boatswain was giving her, but Dax was smiling too, and then he and Arani were running for the foremast.

If Nate had not been so shocked, he might have screamed when he turned and saw the face that had appeared on the foremast, the very same face carved into the figurehead of the ship.

No, Nate realized, this *was* the figurehead of the ship.

And it had moved from the bow to the railing to fight off a giant serpent, and now it was in the foremast. Arani and Dax were there, reaching out to touch the mast, their face bright with genuine happiness.

And the figurehead *smiled*.

CHAPTER TWENTY-THREE

Beyond the Rend

"So the dryad is real?" Eric asked. "That wasn't just a story?"

Nate, Marcus, Liliana, AnnaMarie, and several others stood with him near the mainmast, gathered around the boatswain. For the past several minutes, the *Southern Echo* had been stalled at the edge of the Rend, and Novachak had been shaking people out of their stupor and answering the inevitable followup questions while Dax and Arani spoke with the dryad like it was the most natural thing in the world.

"Dax told all of you about the dryad when you joined the crew," Novachak said as he hauled Theo Yellowwood to his feet.

"But we didn't know he was serious!" Liliana protested.

Novachak quirked an amused eyebrow at her. "Well, now you do." The dry humor melted out of his expression as he surveyed the open Rend just beyond the ship. "And it's a good thing for us he was serious. That dryad saved our lives."

"Why, though?" Marcus asked, his voice hushed with awe.

"More importantly," Eric cut in, "*how?*"

The boatswain held up his hands. "I don't have all the answers here." His gaze darted briefly to Dax and Arani, both still talking with the dryad and looking more serious now. "Might be as simple as this is the dryad's ship as much as it is ours, and she was protecting it, along with her crew. As to the how, I'd guess she woke up because of all the magic leaking out of the sky."

Nate, Marcus, and Eric all stared at him.

"Since when did you gain an understanding of magic?" Eric asked.

Novachak gave him a flat look. "I'm from the North, boy. I may not know how your southern magic works, but I've seen things that would freeze your blood." He gestured to the Rend and the empty red horizon beyond. "You three and the quartermaster all had some nasty reactions to the Rend opening, and you're our magic users. A dryad drawing power from the hole in the world isn't exactly a far leap from there."

Eric eyed him suspiciously, but any argument that might have followed was cut off by another shudder running through the ship. The *Southern Echo* began to turn, angling her bow into the Rend once more as Dax came to join them.

"Good news," the quartermaster said. "Dryads are children of the gods, which means our dryad can grant us safe passage through the Rend. She's agreed to take us to the beach."

"What beach?" Novachak asked.

Wordlessly, Dax pointed into the Rend. The boatswain followed the gesture, and then gave a startled jump. "Definitely magic," he grumbled.

Nate turned to look, and heard the gasps around him as the full crew took in the island that had appeared out of nowhere. It flickered, as though it was trying to decide if it really wanted to be there at all, and then solidified into a dark mass against the red sky.

"We're going to the Vanishing Island," Dax said firmly, drawing everyone's attention back to himself.

"Keep your wits about you when we cross the Rend. None of us know what to expect, but if we've made it this far, then the ship carrying Rori must have, too. We want to find the *Dragonsbane* before Blackcliff has the chance to find us. Yes, Marcus?"

The stout Darkbend lowered his hand. "If the dryad is real," he said, "does that mean she was the one fixing the holes in the ship back on Spider's Nest?"

Novachak gave Marcus a hard look, but the quarter-master's mouth curved into a smile.

"I would imagine so," Dax said.

"How come she's never made repairs before?"

Dax's smile faltered. "I don't think she had the strength for it, before the fight with the navy." He cast a sad look at the deck beneath their feet. "Blood is a powerful thing. Never forget that." He turned and started back for the foremast.

Nate stared at the quartermaster's retreating back, and then blanched when he realized what the man had meant. "Gods below," Nate gasped.

"Wait," Eric said, rounding on Marcus, "you were *right* about the dryad drinking the blood?"

A heavy silence fell, and then several people moaned and skittered uncomfortably across the deck, breaking for the stern.

"All of you, relax," Novachak said. "The dryad isn't going to hurt you."

"How could you possibly know that?" Liliana shrieked.

"Because she'd have done it already," Novachak said calmly. "Besides, where are you going to go on this ship where she can't reach you?" He winced as soon as he finished the words, and genuine regret crossed his features as Liliana gave a low, frightened moan. "That wasn't anywhere near as comforting as I thought it would be before I said it out loud," he admitted apologetically.

"All hands to your stations," the captain's voice suddenly rang out. "We're ready to cross."

Nate looked past her in time to see the ripple of wood move from the foremast back to the bow. From the splintering sound near the front of the ship, it seemed the dryad was reclaiming her place as the figurehead. Nate did not have time to linger on that thought, as Novachak tapped him on the shoulder and sent him off to assist with the rigging.

Soon enough, everyone was preoccupied with their duties, and the fear they'd felt earlier melted away under the familiar rhythms of the work.

When the *Southern Echo* glided over the threshold between the two worlds, Nate looked up to see the divide in the sky, where it went from pale blue to deep, undying red. The ship passed into the crimson realm of the gods, and without even the smallest of warnings, the Rend snapped closed, and the blue mortal world vanished. The winds were silent and the sea was still and there was nothing but the bloody horizon behind them.

"No turning back now," Novachak breathed.

Nate shuddered as a feeling of wrongness closed around his heart. There was power here, so much power, but Nate knew down to his very core that it was not meant for him. "We don't belong here," he murmured.

"We don't," the boatswain agreed, "but they let us in all the same." He nodded to the island that reared up in front of the *Southern Echo*, solid and steady as though it had not flickered into existence mere minutes before. "Best mind how we step."

The Vanishing Island was dark with growth that reached all the way to the top of its single mountain. Compared to Solkyria, it was a gentle, diminutive rise, but to Nate, it looked unscalable. At its top, perched at the very edge of a cliff and silhouetted against the red sky, was a temple. Nate could not tell if the light was making it difficult to see, or if the temple had been built out of rock so black it threatened to swallow the sun.

A cry came from the crow's nest, where Liliana had somehow gathered the courage to climb up and take the lookout station. "Ship ahead!"

Nate dragged his eyes down from the temple and saw that there was indeed a ship anchored just off the beach. Its sails were furled and the wood of its hull was darker than that of the *Southern Echo*, nearly blending in with the vegetation of the island, but it was there, and Nate's heart leapt into his throat. He ran to the bow, where Captain Arani had a spyglass raised and her mouth set in a hard line.

"That's the *Dragonsbane*, all right," she said as she lowered the spyglass. Her eyes were murderous in the red light. "Set our course for that beach," she called back to the helm. "I want the cannons ready to blow Blackcliff and his traitorous bastards all the way to the sixth hell."

"Aye, Captain," came the unified response, but before anyone could scurry off to their tasks, the *Southern Echo* gave a shudder, and then the ship began to turn.

"What are you doing?" Arani shouted to the helm, scaring Luken off her shoulder. "They're off our starboard bow, why are you turning away?"

"I'm not, Captain!" the helmsman replied. He strained at the wheel back on the quarterdeck, but despite his best efforts, the ship continued to veer away from where the *Dragonsbane* was anchored. "The ship is fighting me!"

The sound of splintering wood came again, and

Arani swore under her breath as the boards beneath their feet rippled. The dryad ran in a wave from the bow to the quarterdeck, fast and hard, as though desperate. Nate just barely managed to keep his footing this time, but he nearly fell anyway when the figure he'd seen earlier burst out of the ship's wheel.

The dryad's body nearly enveloped the helm, but her arms dropped down to the deck, fusing with the wood and forming a living chain around the wheel. When she had the helm firmly encased and it was impossible for anyone to so much as think about turning the wheel, the wood of the ship stopped surging, and Nate finally got a good look at the dryad.

Her entire body—from the end of her torso where it joined with the ship to the crown of branches upon her brow—was the same warm brown as the rest of the *Southern Echo*, polished smooth but textured with the same woodgrain. When she opened her eyes, they glowed an eerie green that seemed so out of place in this red realm, but she looked about with certainty and purpose, and her eyes glowed brighter when they alighted on Arani. The wooden mouth opened, and the dryad spoke in a slow, rustling voice that made Nate think of the wind brushing through the leaves of a tree.

"Thou cannot shed blood into this water, nor upon this land," she breathed.

Captain Arani was already moving to stand in front of the dryad's new roost. "I very much can," the captain said, seeming completely at ease despite the fact that she was talking to part of her ship. "In fact, you'd see that I'm more than capable of it, if you'd be so kind as to release the helm and the rudder, and let us sail to that beach."

"No," the dryad said.

Arani's hand curled around the hilt of the saber at

her hip. "They took one of our own," she said. Anger seethed beneath the words, but Arani kept her voice calm.

"The girl who makes the waters dance," the dryad said, sounding almost mournful.

Arani nodded. "I'm going to get her back."

The dryad mirrored the gesture, sending gentle ripples across the ship as if it were the surface of a disturbed pond. "Thou shall have thine chance," the dryad said in her whispering voice, "but this land is hallowed ground. Thou must not spill blood without the blessing of the gods."

Nate frowned, unsure what to make of that, but Arani's face briefly twisted with fury.

"This isn't a game," she said, still fighting to keep her voice calm. "You may not care that they took her, but I—"

The dryad's eyes flashed. "*MINE*," she hissed, and the word seemed to echo through Nate's bones, all the way to his soul.

His heart stuttered in his chest, and he gasped as though something heavy had suddenly dropped over him. It vanished a moment later, replaced by a deep sense of warmth, and he could breathe again.

He knew immediately that he wasn't the only one who'd felt the sensation. The entire crew, Arani included, had their hands to their chests, and they were breathing hard, as though they'd just run a great distance.

Captain Arani's expression softened. "Yes," she said, taking a step closer to the dryad. "We are yours, as you are ours." She raised her hand and placed it against the edge of the quarterdeck, just below the dryad's form, and held it there.

The dryad shut her eyes, and another shudder ran through the ship. "If thou spills blood on this island," the dryad said, "thou will be claimed. I shall not let thee go."

Arani was quiet for a long moment. "I'm going to that island," she said. "If I have to swim, I will."

The entire ship shuddered again. "I will take thee," the dryad said sadly, "but thou must not—"

"Spill blood," Arani finished. Then she cocked an eyebrow. "Unless I have the blessing of the gods?"

The dryad did not answer. Instead, she melted into the wheel, and then there was the creaking and splintering of wood again as she rushed back to the bow. The *Southern Echo* shuddered once more, and then began to turn back towards the island, although the bow was pointed well away from the beach where the *Dragonsbane* was moored.

The captain stared at the enemy ship with open hunger.

"Best heed her warning," Dax said, loud enough for the crew to hear.

Arani ran her thumb over the pommel of her sword. "Our lives are not a game," she said, more to herself than the quartermaster or anyone else. Then she turned to face the crew. "I will lead the shore party. Who is coming with me?"

"I am," Dax said immediately.

"As am I," Nate called out. He thought that he felt another small shiver run through the ship, but the dryad was silent.

Arani looked at him in surprise. "I think," she said after a moment, "you'd better stay here."

Nate shook his head. "So much of this is my fault," he said. "If there's even a small chance that I can help make it right, I'm going to take it." He drew himself up and stared Arani dead in the eye. "And I'm not going to sit here when Rori needs us."

Arani looked to Dax for help, but the quartermaster

only shrugged. "It's as you said," Dax told her, looking faintly amused. "They took one of our own."

The captain gave a deep sigh before relenting. "All right, Nate. You're with us." She turned to the rest of the crew. "Who else?"

Several hands went into the air, although the boatswain did not raise his.

"I'll stay here," Novachak said. "If you don't come back, I'll do what needs to be done." He cast an uneasy look over his shoulder, to where there was no blue tear in the sky. "If there's anything that can be done," he muttered.

Arani put her hand on the boatswain's arm and gave him a light shake. "We're coming back," she said firmly, "and we're bringing Rori with us."

"I hope so," Novachak said. He looked at the captain sadly. "In the North, there are places that are not meant for humans. Places we do not go unless we mean to forfeit our lives to the Frozen Goddess." His icy eyes slid from Arani to Dax, and then to Nate, and they looked so strange beneath the red sky. "There's no snow, but this is one of those places." He looked back to the captain once more. "I really hope you come back."

"We will," Arani promised.

When the dryad had finally brought them close enough to the beach that they could climb down the side of the ship and wade their way ashore, the *Dragonsbane* was no longer in sight. Captain Arani was the first one over the railing, followed by Nate and Dax, Marcus and AnnaMarie, and a few others from the crew. The rest stayed behind, Eric included. The Darkbend stood holding Luken, and he and Novachak watched with clear trepidation on their faces as Nate and the others followed Arani to the beach, and then into the jungle beyond. They set off on what should have been the edge, right along the coast of the island, which would have taken them to the *Dragonsbane*. But the ground kept sloping up under their feet, no matter how much the captain tried to lead them around the mountain, and Arani finally gave up.

"Seems we're wanted at the top," she growled. She adjusted her grip on her sword, and turned more fully into the mountain. "Let's go."

Nate felt that clinging sense of wrongness, but he drew in a deep breath, and followed his captain. The others were close behind. The incline increased under their feet in earnest as they began the long, winding climb to the temple, Arani's red coat a beacon in the gloom as they went.

Hold on, Rori, Nate thought. *We're coming.*

CHAPTER TWENTY-FOUR

Circles

THE ONLY SOUNDS IN the jungle were their own footsteps and heavy breathing as they trudged up the slope, retracing their last path and trying to understand how they'd gotten turned around again. Rori's hands were still bound, and Blackcliff had attached a lead to the ropes before they'd left the ship. He did not tug on the lead, but it was clear that he was not giving Rori any chance to escape.

"Why is this godsdamned temple so hard to find?" Ed the bear-man growled from behind her. "There's only one hill, and all we have to do is go up."

"Quiet," Blackcliff said, and that was the final word on the matter.

As Rori followed Blackcliff, however, she found herself wondering the same thing.

They'd been traipsing up and down the small mountain for the better part of the afternoon, and somehow, they had not come across the temple yet. Blackcliff was leading them, but he was taking a slow, methodical approach to navigating the jungle, not charging off in whatever direction suited his fancy. And yet, every path had brought them back to the beach and the *Dragonsbane* and the questioning looks of the people still aboard, no matter how much time the small group had spent climbing. Rori was sweating and her legs were burning, but it was a little easier to endure the fatigue knowing that Blackcliff, Xander, Ed, and the rest of the sailors from the *Dragonsbane* were finding nothing but frustration in the silent jungle.

Blackcliff paused at a tree they'd seen several times before, notable for the way the trunk had split just above their heads. They'd gone left the last time they'd come across this tree. Blackcliff studied it for a long moment, as if he'd found a map within the whorls of its bark, and then set off to the right. The incline increased under their feet, and Rori ducked her head as they trudged up the slope. She did not look up until she nearly ran into Blackcliff, who'd come to an abrupt halt ahead of her.

The same split tree rose in front of them.

"Gods below," one of the men swore. Whiteleaf, if Rori had his name right. "I'm gonna burn this miserable island to the ground."

"This island," Blackcliff said, "would probably kill you for that." He slowly turned and focused his heavy frown on Rori. "How do we get to the temple, Goodtide?"

Rori shook her head. "I don't know."

"The Grayvoice said you've been here before."

"To the edge of the Rend," Rori said. "I never set foot on the island, let alone in the jungle."

Blackcliff's gaze bore into her before sweeping over her shoulder to Xander. "You said this girl was the key."

"She got us to the island," Xander said, panting shallowly. "I never said she'd take us further than that."

Blackcliff made a thoughtful noise as he focused on Rori again. "I'm beginning to think she may be hindering us."

Rori met the captain's stare and tried not to seem afraid.

"Legends about this treasure say that it takes the form of what one desires most," Blackcliff mused.

"Makes me wonder, whose desire takes precedence? The man leading the way..." He jerked hard on the rope, and Rori went stumbling forward. Blackcliff caught her with one hand around her bicep, his calloused fingers digging into the muscle and threatening to bruise. "Or the little bitch who wants to see us wander this jungle for all eternity?"

Rori swallowed hard, unsure of what to say.

Ed the bear-man snorted. "You think this girl has that much sway with the gods?"

Blackcliff drilled his gaze into Rori's, cutting deep as death. "I think she bought their favor when she gave them all those lives from the *Godfall*." He gripped her arm even harder, and Rori couldn't stop herself from wincing. "Tell me I'm wrong, Goodtide."

She couldn't, and so she said nothing.

"You want her back at the ship?" Ed the bear-man growled. "Whiteleaf, take the girl and—"

"I'm not letting her out of my sight," Blackcliff cut in. "One slip up and she could destroy the *Dragonsbane*."

Ed sighed tiredly. "So what, then? Cut her throat?"

He said it so calmly, it put raw panic in Rori's gut. She struggled against the captain's grip, but he held her fast, his black eyes glittering in the red light.

"I do wonder," Blackcliff said, dragging her a step closer, "what *your* blood is worth to the gods."

"Make her lead," Xander said abruptly.

Blackcliff's attention snapped to him, and Rori felt the fear that had been gathering in her heart wash through her in a cold wave.

"I fail to see how that would help in the slightest," Blackcliff growled.

Rori looked back at Xander, who gave her nothing more than a fleeting glance.

"If she wants to live, she'll take us right to that temple," Xander said. He sounded almost bored, but Rori saw the tightness in his shoulders. "If she doesn't, kill her then."

"Or we kill her now," Ed put in, "and save ourselves a bit of trouble."

Xander shrugged. "Unless she really does have the favor of the gods, in which case, they may not like it if you kill her without any real reason. At least this way, we'll all know if she actually wants to live or not, and that will probably figure in to whatever happens to the person who spills her blood."

No one spoke for several long moments, until Black-cliff pushed Rori ahead.

"Walk, Goodtide," he said, "or I'll have the Grayvoice kill you now."

Rori fought the urge to turn around and see how Xander reacted to that. It would have been nice if he'd been horrified by the idea, but after everything he'd done, Rori knew that he likely had not even batted an eye. She did not particularly want to see his face in that moment, anyway. It would do nothing but anger her. So instead, she chose a direction and started walking.

Dark trees loomed all around Rori as she picked her way through the underbrush. The footsteps of Black-cliff and the others followed her, and she tried to hold on to the thought of taking them in endless circles, or better yet, right off a cliff, but as much as she hated to admit it, Xander knew her too well; she did not want to die yet.

She did not want to lead Blackcliff to the temple, either.

What she really wanted was to see Captain Arani again, and Luken, and Dax and Novachak, and Nate and Eric and Marcus and the rest of the crew. She wanted to be on the *Southern Echo*, leaping across the waves of the clear blue sea and far, far away from this red world. She didn't need to understand her magic, and she could carry the deaths from the *Godfall* with her for the rest of her life, if only she could return to the ship she loved with the crew that was her family once more.

Rori held the image of her crew and the *Southern Echo* in her mind, and kept walking.

She could not tell if she brought them anywhere new. They'd turned around and retread the same paths so many times that all of the markers she'd picked out on the first trek had scrambled in her head. The ground kept sloping up under her feet, though not as severely as before, and she hoped that was a good sign.

She pushed past a plant with massive, rubbery leaves, and found herself staring up at a structure made from rock so dark, it looked like a hole in the world.

We knew you'd come, a voice whispered in Rori's head.

Her heart sank as Blackcliff came out of the jungle beside her.

"Seems you've earned yourself a little more time alive," Blackcliff said. There was a smile in his voice that made Rori's skin crawl. "Come on, then," Blackcliff called to the others. "Our greatest desires await!"

And then they were hurrying into the temple, the rope lead tugging Rori after them.

Inside the temple, it was as black as the rock the building had been hewn from. The excited voices of Blackcliff's crew bounced off the stone walls, and Rori shivered as the temperature dropped.

"We need light," Ed said. "Who's got the torches?"

No sooner had he finished the words when flames burst into life along the walls, filling the temple with a startling amount of light. There were several gasps, and Rori shut her eyes against the brightness. When her vision had adjusted, she cracked them open to see Blackcliff and his men staring in awe.

Around the entire perimeter of the temple, flames danced and illuminated the walls, which were painted with strange beasts and lands that Rori had never seen before. Overhead, the roof of the temple was lost in complete darkness. In front of them, the room descended several steps into a wide open stretch of gleaming white floor, partially ringed by massive stone pillars that reached into the dark. Small tendrils of white mist crawled along the bases of the pillars, but Rori was distracted by the stone itself. There was something odd about the pillars' carving that she could not quite place, and as she peered up into the darkness, she couldn't help shivering again. She felt like something was looking back at her.

Her attention was dragged away from the blackness overhead when someone gasped, and then there was a low moan of fear.

Rori looked into the sunken room just in time to see the white mists rush into the center of the floor, swirling together and rising up to coalesce into the semi-solid figure of a young man. His skin, hair, and clothes were all completely white, his smile was too wide, and where his eyes should have been were gaping black pits, but Rori recognized him immediately.

Tim Redsand, one of the sailors from the *Godfall*.

She felt her heart stop in her chest as Redsand turned his head towards her. For a moment, all Rori could see was his face as it had been in his final moments of life, screaming and terrified before the wave she'd called ripped across the ship, dragging him and many others beneath the sea and never returning them to the surface. Rori had made sure of that.

But Redsand looked away, and with a start, Rori realized that this spirit, if it really was Redsand, did not recognize her at all.

"Travelers," the spirit said, its voice weak but somehow still carrying clearly to her ears. "We welcome you."

Rori did not like that the spirit had said 'we,' but Blackcliff had a different matter on his mind.

"We've come for the treasure," he said. He held himself tall, but Rori noticed that Blackcliff did not step forward, and he had a pistol in one of his hands, as if that would protect him from the dead.

The spirit cocked its head. "This is your desire?"

Blackcliff nodded.

"Then come," the spirit said, beckoning him to the center of the room.

The captain hesitated, a small glimmer of excitement stealing across his face. But before he could move, another voice rang through the temple, achingly familiar.

"BLACKCLIFF," Captain Arani roared.

Rori's heart leaped as she turned to see Arani and several others from the *Southern Echo* storming inside the temple, armed with swords and guns and coming on fast.

Arani pulled up short when Blackcliff turned his pistol on her, but there was no fear in her eyes, only rage. "Release Rori," she snarled, "and give me the traitor."

"You're in no position to make demands of me," Blackcliff said calmly.

"I don't care," Arani growled. "I'm not leaving without my navigator."

Blackcliff arched his eyebrows and tugged lightly on the rope lead, bringing Rori forward. "You mean this?" he asked. "I've no need for another navigator, but a Goodtide would go nicely with the Lowwind we picked up on our last hunt. She needs some training, but I'll break her out of that rebellious streak soon enough."

Chuckles from Blackcliff's group crawled across Rori's skin. They were met with angry growls from the *Southern Echo*'s crew, none louder than Nate's. He hefted the cutlass in his hand and looked ready to charge Blackcliff all on his own. Over her shoulder, Rori heard Xander scoff.

She thought about the dagger that Xander always carried, and wondered if she'd be able to get it off of him.

"As to the treasure," Blackcliff continued, "you're too late. I've already made my claim on it."

"I don't give a damn about the treasure," Arani snapped. "You're going to release Rori and give me the traitor, or I will kill you where you stand, gods willing or not."

Blackcliff gave her a slow smile and knocked the hammer of the pistol into place.

Then he froze, his eyes going wide as white mist curled up his body and along the length of his arm. It dripped off of the gun to pool in front of him, coalescing into another all-too-familiar face from the *Godfall*.

"This is your desire?" the spirit of Olivia Bluetwig said, her voice the same weak whisper that still managed to echo in Rori's ears.

Captain Arani did not recoil from the spirit, but it took her a moment to answer. "It is."

Dax leaned over the captain's shoulder to murmur something in her ear, but she shook her head and took another step forward.

"I was warned not to spill blood here without the gods' blessing," Arani said, "but I will stain these floors redder than the sky outside if anyone tries to stand between me and my crew." She leveled her saber at Bluetwig's spirit. "I do not wish to hurt you, and I don't know if I even can, but you are between me and one of mine. It would be best if you moved."

In the silence that followed Arani's words, a low grinding sound began deeper inside the temple, as though the ceiling were beginning to collapse. Rori looked up, expecting to see cracks of sunlight cutting through the dark, but instead she saw several pairs of pale, glowing lights, and she could not shake the feeling that they were focused on her like eyes.

She went very still when she realized that the lights *were* eyes, and that the columns ringing the sunken room were massive statues. The limbs were exaggerated to the point of being unrecognizable, the feet obscured by the white mist that still swirled around them, and the heads and torsos were lost in the darkness above, but it was too easy to imagine that grinding sound coming from the heads as they turned to look at the two groups fighting below them, their eyes open and hungry with interest.

Sheer coldness washed across Rori's side, and she whipped around to see more white mist sliding past her. Xander recoiled from it the same as her, and there were uneasy murmurs from both sides as it formed up into another spirit. Rori was relieved not to know this one.

"The divine have taken interest in your conflict," the third spirit said, his voice more like falling sand than a whisper. "They will allow a duel to the death between two blades."

Rori could have wept with relief. Captain Arani was a fine duelist on her own merit, and there were few who could stand against her when she was truly angry.

Arani did not smile, but she flexed her shoulders and made to step forward.

Tim Redsand's spirit blurred into the space in front of her. "No," the spirit said. "First claimant chooses his champion."

Captain Arani's eyes narrowed, but she said nothing.

Rori's heart felt tight in her chest. She knew that, no matter what happened next, this would all be over soon.

"Who will duel until death?" the third spirit asked Blackcliff.

Captain Blackcliff did not immediately respond. He returned his pistol to the sash across his chest, then ran his hand thoughtfully over the pommel of his sword. His gaze swung around to focus on Rori, and she realized with a cold spike of horror what he was thinking.

"You try to send me," Rori growled, "and I'll fall on my own sword. Then my spirit will come back and haunt you until you throw yourself into the sea."

"You're more trouble than you're worth, girl," Blackcliff muttered. He faced Arani again. "Seems to me there's quite a bit riding on this little duel," he said, projecting his voice clearly. "Let's make sure you and I have the stakes clear. First, if you win, you get your Goodtide back."

Arani did not speak, but her glare made it obvious that she intended for that to happen whether she won or lost.

"Second, since this is a duel to the death," Blackcliff went on nonchalantly, "seems only fair that whoever is left standing gets to claim the treasure for their crew."

Blackcliff's men tensed, but no one said a word.

"Third," Blackcliff said, moving to stand next to Xander, "you said you wanted the traitor. I know he's done a grave injury to you. I'm a just man, so I'll let you have him." He placed his hand on Xander's shoulder. "But with his life on the line, it seems to me that he should be the one to fight for it." Blackcliff shoved Xander forward, clean through the third spirit.

Xander came out trailing wisps of mist and gasping from the cold. Rori saw fear flash across his face, but he quickly smoothed it away before glancing back at Blackcliff.

"It's your life, Grayvoice," Blackcliff said. "Earn it, if you truly believe it's worth anything."

The spirit reformed from the agitated mists, obscuring Xander behind a semi-opaque curtain of white, but Rori saw Xander's face harden with rage. When he turned to face Captain Arani again, his spine was straight and his shoulders were back.

In spite of everything, Rori felt a cold surge of dread. *Why?* she wondered. *Why, Xander, did you ever think this was right?*

"And now," Redsand's spirit said, "the other duelist."

Arani adjusted her grip on her sword, and took a step forward. There was another grinding sound, and Rori felt the bright eyes of the statues pass over her.

"No," the third spirit hissed. "The divine will see the duel between the two who desire it most."

Arani frowned, mirroring Rori's own confusion, but the spirits were moving again, and they were circling up around Nate.

"No," Rori breathed. "They can't."

But they could. White mist flared up around them all, wrapping them in bone-chilling cold. When it cleared, Rori was standing with Blackcliff and his crew on one side of the sunken floor. Arani and Dax and the others from the *Southern Echo* were on the other, too much distance and a large stone dais suddenly stretching between them.

In the middle of the polished dais, Xander and Nate stood facing each other, and there was a long, wickedly curved sword in each of their hands.

CHAPTER TWENTY-FIVE
A Heart's Desire

NATE DID NOT KNOW what had happened. One moment, he was at the entrance to the temple, standing behind Captain Arani with the others, waiting for the smallest signal to charge in and do whatever it took to save Rori. The next, he was shivering as white mist cleared away, and he was standing alone. His cutlass was gone, replaced by a heavy sword that Nate had no idea what to do with, but seemed like it could cut him if he looked at it wrong. He had to use two hands to hold it up.

Several paces away, Xander stood wielding the same weapon. He frowned at Nate, equally as disoriented, and then he flinched when a spirit coalesced next to his ear. The Grayvoice froze as the spirit began speaking. His expression hardened, and Nate felt a pit of fear open in his gut.

"He betrayed you," a voice said in Nate's ear, clear as a bell on a winter morning. Coldness radiated off his shoulder, and he did not have to look around to know that he had another spirit whispering into his own ear. "He made a fool of you a hundred times over. He could have been your brother in arms, but he cast you aside, just as your true brother did, Nathaniel Nowind."

Nate shuddered, and his fear began to boil into rage.

"He knows the name suits you," the spirit said, "not because you cannot control the wind, but because you are nothing. You blinded yourself to the truth, and now a man's death is on your hands. You failed your captain, you failed your friends, you failed yourself, because you are nothing."

Across the way, Xander's snarl gave way to a sudden and familiar smirk, and Nate realized just how much he'd always hated that smile. His grip tightened around the handle of the sword.

"Will you prove him wrong?" the spirit sneered. "Will you finally be strong enough, or do you truly deserve the name Nathaniel Nowind?"

Xander was the first to move, but Nate was only a step behind. Their swords came together with a jarring crash that Nate felt all the way up to his shoulders. He and the Grayvoice glared at each other, lips curling back from their teeth, and then Xander shoved forward. Nate was forced back several steps, but he managed to keep his guard up and catch Xander's next blow on the flat of his blade. He felt the Grayvoice's strength in that strike, all the ways Xander was bigger and stronger than Nate, but in that moment, Nate did not care about any of that. Metal rasped as he twisted his sword, forcing Xander's wide, and then he slashed the edge across the Grayvoice's chest.

Xander managed to pull back just in time, and Nate pressed his advantage.

Through his fury, some of Nate's training managed to surface in his mind.

Keep calm, he told himself. *Wait for your chance... there!*

He lunged with the sword, but Xander dodged away again, and the tip of Nate's blade only grazed the Grayvoice's sleeve. Nate did not let up, though. He knew that Xander was stronger than him, and his only real hope now was to land the first blow, before the Grayvoice could gather himself and launch his own attack. There was no grace to how Nate swung the blade as he drove Xander back, but he put all of his frustration into each blow, as though he were striking at the mistakes and failings that had marked his entire life like stepstones. Nate was determined that they would stop here. He was not going to let his captain and his crew down again.

The swords clanged and rasped, and Nate saw a flash of actual fear in Xander's eyes as they came back together.

In that moment, Nate knew that this wasn't right. He did not want to kill Xander. But when he hesitated, that was all Xander needed.

The Grayvoice shoved with a savage fury, sending Nate stumbling. It was all Nate could do to bring the curved sword up and block Xander's blade as it came down in a glittering arc towards his head. Clashing metal rang through the temple, and then Xander was swinging fast and wild, and Nate was the one falling back.

The fear was gone from Xander's eyes now, re-placed by loathing. Between each clashing ring of the swords, he snarled, "I'm not... losing... to you... you arrogant... bastard... Nowind!"

Nate grit his teeth, braced for the next strike, but Xander shifted at the last moment, and he lashed at Nate's legs. Nate stumbled back, just managing to turn Xander's sword aside, but he almost tripped over his own foot and had to catch himself. That gave Xander time to swing the sword around again, and Nate had to throw himself out of the way before the blade took his head off. Nate felt the wind from the attack, and his heart went tight with fear as he rolled back to his feet.

Xander was on him immediately, showing none of the uncertainty Nate had felt. "You wormed your way into the crew with nothing but a promise," Xander growled. He swung the sword again, and Nate's arms trembled with the sheer amount of effort it took to block the blow. "I had to fight for it, and prove my worth every single day. They still looked at me like I was no better than the rats."

The blade hissed through the air again, and Nate cried out this time when he swung his own up to meet it, his arms protesting the movement.

"You think that because your tattoo is blue instead of black, you're special, and deserve better," Xander spat. "And everyone agrees!" His next strike cracked like thunder against Nate's blade.

Nate's sword went spinning out of his hands, and Xander landed a ruthless kick to his chest that sent him flying. Nate landed hard on his back, the breath fleeing from his lungs.

"Your only worth was finding that dragon," Xander snarled as he stalked towards Nate, "but Arani let it go, like you meant something more. You don't!"

Nate rolled over on to his hands and knees and tried to crawl away. Xander kicked him again, driving more air out of his chest. Nate coughed and curled up on the ground. Faintly, he heard someone screaming, but he could not tell who it was.

"No one needed you to find this place," Xander spat. He shoved his foot against Nate's shoulder, forcing him on to his back again. "No one needs you at all." He raised the sword over Nate's chest, eyes blazing beneath the simple black tattoo on his brow. "Especially not Rori."

Fresh anger bloomed in Nate's heart, but it wasn't enough to save him. He could only watch as the sword came down.

It caught on another blade, thrust forward just in time to turn it aside and send it into the ground rather than Nate's chest.

"ENOUGH!" Captain Arani roared. She slammed her own boot into Xander's ribs, and the Grayvoice stumbled away.

Nate heard her sword crash against Xander's three times before a blade went clattering to the ground, and then Arani was there, pulling Nate to his feet. She pushed him towards the edge of the dais, where Dax and the others beckoned him over. Nate stopped before stepping off the edge, arms wrapped around his aching chest, and watched Captain Arani brandish her sword at the agitated spirits swarming around her, and then up at the inky blackness overhead. Glowing eyes stared back at her from the abyss.

"I suppose this is entertaining for you," she shouted up at the darkness. "Two mortals fighting, trying to kill each other for your pleasure." She pointed the tip of her saber at each of the spots where the statues' heads should have been. "Our lives are not your game, but if you are so desperate for someone to amuse you, try me." Arani bared her teeth in a dangerous smile. "Just know that if you want to toy with me, you'd be better off killing me. If you don't, I'll come back here, after I've learned what it takes to kill a god."

Arani's words echoed off the walls as the spirits around her went still. They turned their eyeless white faces up, and they actually looked terrified.

A rumble came from the darkness, and then a voice spoke in a bass so deep, Nate felt it reverberate through his chest.

"You would defy us, mortal?"

Captain Arani spread her arms. "I don't know how much clearer I could be."

"You are not afraid of us," the voice ground out, and it was not a question.

"No," Arani snarled as she adjusted her grip on her

sword, "but you're about to be very afraid of *me*."

Another silence followed those words, and then the rumble returned, steady and rolling. Nate felt very small beneath the sound, even before he realized it was laughter.

"We know what you fear," the voice said.

The white mist returned, wrapping around Nate in blinding coldness. When it cleared, he found himself standing on a high platform in the center of the room. His head swam with vertigo, but he froze when something rough chafed against his skin.

Rope.

It was wrapped around his torso, thick and heavy and not about to let him go. He looked up to see the rope extending up into the dark before tumbling back down to the ground. There was a second rope next to the one that connected back to Nate. In front of both stood Captain Arani.

"A choice," the god rumbled, "for the captain who does not fear her own death."

Dazed, Arani traced the ropes with her eyes, and froze when she saw the platform. Just behind her was Blackcliff and the men from the *Dragonsbane*, looking equally as disoriented and shaken. Xander was among them. For once, there was no sly smirk on his face. Nate turned and glanced over his shoulder, looking down from the dizzying height to see Dax and Marcus and the others from the *Southern Echo* huddled further away, off the dais and so very far out of reach.

Nate had no idea what was going on, but he did not like it.

When he looked back to Captain Arani, the white mist had coalesced into a spirit next to her.

"You came here seeking treasure to repair your breaking life," the spirit said. "But you insist that it does not matter. The divine have chosen to test your resolve." The spirit turned its white face up to the platform. "You must pick one to save."

Nate looked to his left, and his heart stopped when he saw Rori next to him on the platform.

"This is the captain's choice," the spirit said. It turned back to Arani, and a wide smile split across its face. "What is it you *truly* desire?" the spirit asked. "The chance to right the wrong done to the legacy of your people and your hero, or the treasure you so desperately need to fulfill the promise you made to those who depend on you?" The spirit circled Captain Arani, gleeful as a child. "Choose the boy, and you will leave here with the means to follow Mordanti's trail once more, but the girl will die. Choose the girl, and you shall take her and the treasure owed to your crew with you, but the boy will die."

Nate swallowed. He desperately wanted to live, but he could not see Arani picking him over Rori and the treasure. Not this time. Still, Arani looked torn as she stared up at the platform. Nate glanced at Rori, and saw his own terror reflected in her expression.

"We'll be all right," Nate said. His voice was rough with fear.

Rori shook her head, eyes wide.

"Make your choice," the spirit said, "or lose them both."

With that, the platform that Nate and Rori stood on began to tilt. It was slow but persistent, and Nate felt his boots start to slip against the smooth surface.

"Hang the treasure," Arani snarled, reaching for both ropes. "Give me my people. That's all I want." But before she could touch the ropes, she cried out in pain and pulled her hands back.

The spirit grinned even wider. "That is not the choice before you. One captain, one child. Choose."

Arani's gaze flitted between Nate and Rori as the

platform tilted further, and they both began to skitter towards the edge. Nate gasped, and Rori gave a small moan of fear.

"Take her!" Nate shouted before he could think. "Take Rori!"

"No!" Rori screamed. Her breath hitched, ragged and wild. "Captain, no."

Arani stared at them both in open anguish, then cast her gaze desperately about the room. Nate could practically see her thoughts churning in her head as she took in the unyielding gazes of the gods and the spirits, the impossible distance between her and Dax even as he clambered up on to the far side of the dais, the undeniable tilt of the platform as Rori and Nate slid closer to the edge.

Nate wondered if Rori would be spared if he jumped, but his feet shied away from the edge even as gravity clawed him closer.

Arani turned, and her gaze alighted on Blackcliff behind her, and she went still.

Then Arani lunged at the captain of the *Dragonsbane* and snatched him by his coat, hauling him back to the ropes.

"Another captain," she shouted, and flung Blackcliff at the rope that led to Rori. "We each take one."

Blackcliff stumbled to a halt just before the rope, clearly surprised.

Arani threw herself at the rope that held Nate. "Together," she barked at Blackcliff. Her gaze was desperate when it raked across Nate and Rori one last time, but it twisted into anger and promised vengeance when she turned to the man beside her.

The platform tilted further, and Nate's feet finally slid out from under him, unable to keep him perched any longer. He landed hard on his hip and slid clear off the edge of the platform, Rori in free fall beside him.

Someone screamed, and Nate felt the rope around him jerk tight, and then there was nothing but the cold white mist all around him, and the faint sound of laughter. The rope vanished, and Nate had just enough time to wonder what that meant before the mist suddenly cleared, and he was no longer falling but standing on the beach next to Arani, the *Southern Echo* before them and the crew all around.

Nate felt his stomach give an unpleasant twist and leap. There was cold sweat on his skin, and his heart was slamming against his ribs. He took several shaking breaths to convince himself that he was still alive. Then he looked at the faces around him, and his battered heart lurched.

Rori was not with them.

Nate turned to his captain.

Without a word, Arani drew her sword and walked back into the jungle.

Nate followed her, Dax and the others only a step behind.

CHAPTER TWENTY-SIX
A Gift from the Gods

WHEN THE MIST CLEARED, Rori was left shivering on the beach in front of the *Dragonsbane*. The ropes were gone, her heart was pounding hard with terror, and she was completely free. The dark ship loomed before her, and her magic stirred and quickened in her blood.

She could tear this ship apart, just like the *Godfall*.

The currents around the island churned with un-shed violence, and Rori felt their power wash over her between each beat of her heart.

Just like the Godfall, she thought.

"Where is the treasure?" Ed asked from somewhere behind her. The sand shifted as the bear-man began to pace. "The spirit said the girl came with the treasure." He halted, and Rori heard him grab ahold of someone and shake them hard. "Where is it, Grayvoice? Or is your little lady friend here supposed to be our com-pensation for all of this?"

Tear it apart, Rori thought. *Drown them all.*

She shivered again.

Next to her, Blackcliff stared up at his ship and made a thoughtful noise in his throat.

"Take your hands off of me," Xander said coldly.

Ed scoffed. "You think that little pocket knife of yours scares me? I'll pop your head off your shoulders before you can even scratch me."

Blackcliff turned and gazed up at the temple on the

mountain behind them.

Rori stared at the *Dragonsbane*, or maybe it was the *Godfall*, and her magic flooded her chest. She felt like she herself was going to drown if she did not release it, if she did not kill the captain and his entire crew, if she did not force them beneath the sea and never let them go.

Drown them all.

But she recognized that voice in her head now, and the last thing Rori wanted to do was obey a god. She shut her eyes and fought against the riptide of her magic.

Ed gave a cry of rage, and someone went stumbling across the sand.

"I'd say that's more than a scratch," Xander said. "Touch me again, and I'll flay you alive."

The bear-man growled deeply, and Blackcliff's men began to stir, and then there was a small splash as something landed in the water.

Rori opened her eyes to a world gone still. Blackcliff and all the others stared at the ripples from the disturbed water just in front of the *Dragonsbane*. Another splash sounded out, this time on the other side of the ship, and then another, and then there was the sound of something hard striking the deck. Rori looked up and saw hail falling from the sky, winking in the red sunlight. Those still aboard the ship yelped and ran for cover as it began to fall all around the *Dragonsbane*, and there were several cries of pain as the hail struck flesh, but they were drowned out by the thunder of it slamming into the decks or crashing into the water.

It wasn't hail, though. It was too shiny, each piece too regular, and when one landed on the beach in front of Blackcliff, the man began to laugh.

Rori looked down to see a brilliant gold coin sitting in the sand.

Blackcliff snatched it up and turned to show it to the men behind him. His grin was sharp and feral. "Looks like we got what we came for, after all."

The crew looked from the coin in Blackcliff's hand to the ones still raining down from the sky. Their eyes went wide and smiles began to split their faces, and even Ed forgot to staunch the bleeding wound in his arm.

"Half of it's falling into the sea!" one of the men yelled, and the glee changed to panic as the men charged into the water.

Drown them now, the malicious voice of a god whispered in Rori's head.

It would have been so easy, but Rori balled her hands into fists, and kept them firmly at her side.

"The Veritian bought your freedom, Goodtide," Blackcliff said, and Rori turned to face him and his cold smile. "Best be going before the price goes up." He swept his hat off his head and dipped into a mocking bow. "Thank you kindly, for your service." He laughed again and started towards the water line, but he flicked the gold coin to Rori before he went.

Reflexively, Rori caught it. The coin was heavy and cold in her hand, but nowhere near as much as her heart. She turned away from the *Dragonsbane* and its hated crew, only to find Xander in her path. His hand was pressed to his head, and there was a dazed look about him underscored by the coldness she knew all too well.

"Rori," he said, reaching for her.

Rori hurled the coin at his head and sprinted into the jungle.

Go back, the voice commanded. *Kill them.*

But that wasn't what Rori wanted. She ran through the trees, tears blurring her vision. Twice, she stumbled over roots and went sprawling, but she pushed herself back to her feet and took off again. Trees loomed all around her, the canopy forming a thick ceiling nearly as dark as the one inside the temple. She kept seeing flashes of light through the leaves that looked like eyes tracking her, and she ran harder. She kept running until she heard what she was after, and then she arrowed towards the voice calling her name.

"I'm here!" she shouted back.

A patch of red stirred between the trees ahead, and then Captain Arani was there. The relief was clear on her face when she saw Rori, and she sheathed her sword and held her arms open. Rori ran into them without hesitating, nearly knocking Arani over with the force of the collision.

"You're all right," the captain murmured into her ear. "You're safe now. I promise."

Rori nodded, but she couldn't stop herself from shaking.

Gently, Arani disentangled herself from Rori, and then removed her coat. She draped it across Rori's shoulders. Rori huddled into its warmth as the captain began to steer her through the jungle. They came to Dax soon enough, and he let out an audible sigh when he saw them. Nate was with him, and his eyes shone when he looked at Rori.

Kill them, the voice of the god snarled. *Obey me.*

No, Rori answered.

She did not trust herself to speak aloud. She nodded to Dax and Nate as Arani guided her past, and then to the others they collected on the way back to the beach. When they hit the sand, Rori looked up to see the *Southern Echo* anchored just off the shore, and her eyes welled up with tears.

Then white mist flooded on the beach and gathered into a tight spiral before them.

Arani moved fast, pushing Rori behind her and unsheathing her sword in one fluid motion. She had the saber at the ready long before the spirit coalesced, and she lunged as soon as the white form had taken shape.

The spirit of Olivia Bluetwig was completely unbothered by the sword that went through her gut. In fact, she might have been amused by it. "Not all of the divine enjoyed your trick in the temple," the spirit said, ghostly smile plastered in place. "But you've won some of their favor today."

"I think I'd rather not have it," Arani said as she pulled the sword out of Bluetwig's stomach. Mist swirled into place, and the hole disappeared.

The spirit's impossible grin widened even more. "It is not your choice."

She held out her hands, and more mist came to swirl through the space above them, taking on an odd shape. Bluetwig thrust the mist towards Arani, who had no choice but to catch it against her chest. The moment the captain touched the white mass, the mist blew away, revealing a large, old drinking horn in its stead.

The horn was elegantly curved, the shape familiar but not something Rori could immediately place. Its tip was wrapped in silver with filigree patterns swirling across the tarnished metal, ending in a wicked point that would easily go clean through someone's hand if they were not careful handling the horn. The drinking end was similarly decorated, but instead of filigree, the worn image of a dragon wrapped around the rim.

"A gift," the spirit said with a bow, "for the captain who amused the gods." Then the spirit dissolved into tendrils of mist on the breeze, leaving them in total silence.

Arani stood holding the drinking horn for a long time. Then she sighed, slung the horn's thin chain over her arm, and reached for Rori again. "Let's get off this island," she murmured.

Rori wanted to run for the ship, but she made herself walk next to the captain. That turned out to be the right choice, for as they stepped into the shallow water around the ship, the dryad figurehead suddenly moved. Rori froze, not even her heart daring to beat, and the air fled from her lungs when the glowing green eyes fixed on her. Then Captain Arani gave her shoulder a comforting squeeze.

"It's all right," Arani murmured. "She's a friend."

The dryad smiled, and a calm, warm feeling washed through Rori's chest, easing the coldness around her heart. With a loud creak, the dryad reached down and lightly touched the top of Rori's head.

"Mine," she whispered.

Rori bowed her head, and tried not to let anyone see her tears. She kept her head down as the captain led her aboard the *Southern Echo*, even as people surrounded her. She flinched, waiting for that malicious voice, but it did not return, and no one told her to drown her crew even as she wished they would step back.

She had no idea what to say to anyone.

Captain Arani moved in to push away the crush of bodies. "I want this ship ready to sail in record time," the captain barked as she guided Rori across the deck. "We're leaving."

"Aye, Captain!" came the shouted response, and the crew dispersed.

"Wait," a soft voice said, and Rori felt as though a knife had been driven into her side. Trembling, she made herself turn and face Eric Darkbend.

He stood looking at her impassively, no trace of joy or sadness or even anger on his face. That hurt more than if he'd struck her. When Eric raised his hands, Rori almost hoped he'd do just that, if only to release the tension lingering in her heart. But there was a flutter of wings and a frantic chirp, and Luken came shooting out of Eric's grip to land on Rori's shoulder and bite her on the earlobe, just hard enough to let her know that he was upset with her for leaving him. Rori's breath hitched in her throat, and her fingers shook as she reached up to stroke Luken's brilliant blue feathers.

Arani's hand came to rest on Rori's other shoulder, gently turning her away from Eric. "There will be time later," the captain said.

"Aye," Eric answered. "Later." His eyes were still impassive, and Rori had to look away before that gaze could cut her any deeper.

Arani brought Rori down to her private cabin. She sat Rori at the long table, deposited the drinking horn on an empty seat, and then went to get something out of her sea chest.

Rori stared at the drinking horn, and she kept staring at it long after the captain had pressed a small glass of whisky into her hands. Rori turned the glass idly in her fingers, barely seeing the amber liquid shift out of the corner of her eye.

Arani sat down in the chair next to her, and waited.

The tears returned to Rori's eyes as she faced her captain. She thought of the life she'd lost on Solkyria, of the lives she'd taken from the *Godfall*, of the whispering inside her head, of Xander's betrayal and Greenroot's spilled blood. She'd wanted to keep her crew, her *family*, together, but she'd nearly torn them apart by bringing them to this horrible place at the edge of the world. She'd put them through so much to chase after a whisper in her head and a tug in her heart, and she'd given them nothing in return. How they must loathe her now.

Monster.

This time, the word came from Rori alone, and she had to force herself to look up at Captain Arani, the woman who had given up a legendary treasure to her hated rival for the chance to take Rori back.

"It wasn't worth it," Rori murmured as the tears began to spill down her cheeks. "You should have left me there."

Arani shook her head. "My choice," she said. "I'd do it again in a heartbeat."

Then she opened her arms, and Rori let herself fall into their steady embrace as she began to cry.

She did not stop for a long time.

CHAPTER TWENTY-SEVEN
What Remains

THEY LEFT THE VANISHING Island as quick as they could. Captain Arani was absent for the initial push off, but she came topside not long after the *Southern Echo* set sail. They headed back the way they had come, lingering only just long enough to confirm that the *Dragonsbane* had left ahead of them.

"Good riddance," Novachak spat, but no one asked the obvious question of where that ship was. They could not find it anywhere on the bloody horizon, and Nate sensed nothing in the wind.

He thought about reaching further with his Skill, but something told him to keep his magic contained while he was still in the red world beyond the Rend. Nate did not know why, but he had the feeling that something was reaching for him, like it was testing the very edges of his mind or his soul. He held his magic close, and as the ship left the island, he felt that probing reach recede.

The *Southern Echo* turned east, heading towards the unending line between the red sky and the black sea. It wasn't long before a rip in the sky appeared, and the familiar and soothing blue of the mortal world stretched out before the bow. The ship crossed the Rend once more, into waters that were choppy and untamed, and then the tear between the worlds closed behind them, taking the Vanishing Island and the realm of the gods with it.

The moment the Rend was gone, there was a soft sigh from the bow of the ship, and then a long creak of wood. The ship shuddered and settled, and the captain ran to look at the figurehead. She was considerably subdued when she returned.

"She's asleep again," Arani said, a clear note of sadness in her voice.

Despite his unease around the dryad, Nate felt a pang of sympathy for the captain. It was never pleasant, losing a friend.

But then Dax said, "I don't know about that." The quartermaster frowned hard at the deck. "Something's... different."

"How so?" the captain asked.

Dax lifted his eyes to hers. "Can't you feel it?"

Arani hesitated, casting her gaze about the ship. Her expression clouded, and she slowly walked to the foremast and placed her hand against the wood. She held it there for a moment, and then drew back in surprise. "It's never been that clear before," she said.

"No," Dax agreed. "It hasn't."

Nate looked between the two officers, and then at Novachak as the boatswain bent down and pressed his palm against the deck. His bushy brows arched in surprise.

Nate reached for the ship's railing, Marcus and Eric and all the others doing the same, and he felt the familiar warmth of the wood on his skin. Beneath that, faint but steady, there was a pulse.

"She's restless," Dax said solemnly.

Nate looked around to see the captain nodding. "What does this mean?" he asked.

Dax and Arani exchanged a long look.

"I don't know," the captain finally said. "But I imagine we'll learn soon enough." She turned her attention from the ship to the blue world stretching all around them, and her frown returned. "I don't know where we are," she said, "but we'd better keep heading east until we figure it out."

Dax nodded and went to put the crew to work.

Nate lingered by Arani's side. "Where's Rori?" he asked.

"Resting," Arani said. "She needs it."

Nate nodded, and then went to help the riggers.

It took several hours, and no one quite believed it when they spied the first island off the *Southern Echo*'s bow, but they did learn where they were. Arani and Dax and Novachak took turns staring at the island through a spyglass, and all three of them looked equally perplexed when they lowered the instrument.

"Unless I've completely forgotten what it looks like," Arani told the crew, "that's the westernmost island in the Coral Chain. We're barely a day's sail from Spider's Nest."

"How is that possible?" Eric asked. "We sailed due west for over a month."

Arani shook her head, but there was an uneasiness in her expression.

"Magic," Novachak grumbled. "It's always magic."

Nate wasn't entirely certain how he felt about the ship and all her held lives being deposited wherever a few otherworldly powers felt was appropriate, but he was glad they were so close to port. They all needed a chance to rest away from the water, Rori especially.

Nate did not see her for the rest of that day. Dax kept a firm watch over her, letting no one but the captain approach and speak to her, but the next morning, Nate found Rori on the poop deck with Luken on her shoulder and a haunted look in her eyes as she stared off the stern of the *Southern Echo*, into the west.

"Are you all right?" Nate asked as he came up beside

her.

"No," Rori said.

A long moment passed.

"I'm glad you're back," Nate said.

Rori looked at him vacantly. Then she turned and leaned over the railing, buried her face in her hands, and began to cry. Luken twittered and fluttered to the railing, tilting his head and hopping closer to Rori as she sobbed.

Nate wrapped an arm around her shoulders. "It's all right," he murmured. "I'm here for you. So are Eric and Marcus, and Arani and Dax and Novachak, and everyone. We're all here for you, Rori. We're not going to leave you."

She trembled against him, but she did not pull away. "I trusted him," she gasped.

"We all did," Nate said. "We won't make that mistake again."

Rori shook her head, her tears falling into the sea. "This is all my fault," she said. "I sent us into the Forbidden Sea. If I hadn't done that, Greenroot would still be alive, and Xander wouldn't have..." She couldn't finish the thought, and ducked her head in shame.

Nate shook his head. "Xander was always going to do what he wanted. You couldn't have stopped him, but that wasn't your responsibility. He made his choice, and we made ours."

"And we came back with nothing," Rori murmured.

"Not nothing," Nate said. "We came back smarter—"

"Don't," Rori said savagely. "Don't talk about trials by fire and pain making us stronger." She folded her arms and huddled into herself, drawing a soft chirp from Luken. "I don't feel stronger."

She pulled away. Nate let her go, but he followed her. He did not think that being alone was what she really wanted, or needed. Not after what she had just been through.

"Maybe not," he said softly, "but you're not a monster."

Rori turned to face him, tears streaming down her face.

"It's okay not to be okay right now," Nate said, his heart aching for her. "No one should have to go through what we went through. What *you* went through. It's okay not to be strong after that." He stepped closer and put his hands on her shoulders. "But this crew is not broken, Rori, and you are *not* a monster. I promise you that."

"How can you be sure?" The words shook as they left her. "You didn't hear the voice in my head, telling me to use my Skill to drown everyone."

Nate blinked. That was certainly alarming, but something didn't fit. "You didn't do it," he pointed out quietly. "You only ever used your magic to save us."

Rori buried her face in her hands again. "But it kept telling me to do it, and I almost did."

"But you didn't," Nate said firmly. He reached out to draw her hands down, but stopped when he thought of that faint, probing touch he'd felt in the Rend, like something was reaching for him and trying to grab him through his magic. Nate gently placed his hands on Rori's shoulders. "That voice in your head," he said slowly, "was it *you*, or was it... something else?"

Rori froze. When she lowered her hands, her gaze was flooded with confusion and dread.

"It wasn't you, was it?" Nate asked.

"It may as well have been," Rori said. "I answered."

Nate shook his head. "That doesn't make it *you*."

"How can you be so sure?" Rori asked.

"Because I know you," Nate said. "Maybe not completely, but I know enough. I know what you've been through, and I know that you're scared of yourself, but more than anything, I know that you're not alone. I'm here, and I'll be here for as long as you'll let me. I promise."

Rori looked at him in silence, her eyes red. Then she stepped forward and pressed her head against his shoulder. Nate held her tight, even over Luken's twittering protests, for as long as she needed. When she finally drew back, her breathing had calmed and there were no fresh tears on her face. Then her eyes slid over his shoulder, and she went rigid just as Nate heard footfalls on the deck.

He turned as Eric came striding up to them, Marcus trailing behind and darting nervous looks between him and Rori. Nate knew both Darkbends well enough to recognize genuine trouble when it came from them, and this time, Eric was the source.

"Eric," Nate began, slowly raising one hand to hold off whatever was coming, but Rori tugged on his sleeve. She took a deep, shaking breath, and stepped around Nate to meet the Darkbend.

For a moment, neither Rori nor Eric spoke. They simply looked at each other, Rori with genuine fear, and Eric with the stoic blankness Nate had come to associate with a pained kind of anger the Darkbend kept locked inside.

Rori was the first to speak, in a quiet, cracking voice. "I'm sorry," she said, "for everything. I shouldn't have taken us out into the Forbidden Sea. I shouldn't have put you all in danger, I shouldn't have trusted Xander, I shouldn't... I shouldn't have..." She broke off as her breath caught in her throat. "You should be angry," she managed to scrape out. "You should scream at me, tell me I'm horrible, hit me, *something.*"

Nate's heart gave an uncomfortable squeeze. He reached for Rori, but she shrugged him off and moved closer to Eric.

"Please," she said. "Speak, yell, scratch, hit, do *something*. Don't look at me like you don't care and do nothing. *Please,* Eric, just—"

Eric lunged then, startling everyone and drawing a cry from Luken. But Eric only wrapped his arms around Rori and held her tight. After a stunned moment, Rori hugged him back just as fiercely. Marcus let out a relieved breath, and Nate felt his own muscles relax.

"To be clear," Eric said as he broke the embrace and held Rori at arm's length, "I haven't completely forgiven you."

Rori nodded and scrubbed the heel of her hand against her cheek, wiping away a tear.

Eric's gaze softened. "But I'm so glad you're back." He pulled Rori in again, and for once, Luken remained quiet. "You're my family," Eric said firmly. "Nothing is ever going to change that." He grinned as he drew back. "Not even if you keep beating me at Liar's Farm, although I'll *never* forgive you for that."

Rori laughed then, the sound weak but genuine, and Nate's smile mirrored hers.

Nate was glad that he'd been right; they weren't broken. Battered and scarred and maybe more than a little scared, but not broken. He did not know what the future held for any of them beyond the next day. They were going back to Spider's Nest, where Captain Arani intended to sell the drinking horn she'd received on the Vanishing Island. It had come from the gods, and Spider would pay whatever he needed to get his greedy hands on something like that. And after that, maybe Nate would have a conversation with Arani about tracking a certain pirate ship in the wind, and following the *Dragonsbane* until they had the chance to blast that ship into oblivion. They may not have known where Blackcliff's ship had gone, but once the drinking horn was sold, they would have the means to find out.

Nate shifted closer to Rori, and said none of these things to her or the Darkbends. There would be time later to talk and to scheme, to avenge their wounds and find their way forward. This, though, was a moment that Nate wished would last for a year.

Rori leaned into Nate and rested her head on his shoulder as Eric and Marcus settled in on her other side. They all stood shoulder-to-shoulder at the railing of the ship, watching the islands of the Coral Chain slip by. The *Southern Echo* was warm and familiar all around them, the faint pulse of the dryad beating steady as a drum throughout the ship. Overhead, a black flag snapped in the breeze, proud and free against the blue sky, and that moment was perfect.

But like all moments, Nate knew, this one too had to pass.

Catch the next voyage of the *Southern Echo*:

<u>A Silence Falling Dark and Deep</u>

Coming 2024

Sign up for the newsletter so you never miss an update or release and get a FREE Iris Arani prequel story!

Scan the QR code below to sign up:

About the Author

K.N. Salustro is a science fiction and fantasy author who loves outer space, dragons, and stories that include at least one of those things. When not writing, she can be found drawing and painting, designing and crafting plushies, and trying to play video games while her cat paws at the screen.

For updates, new content, and other news, visit:
www.knsalustro.com

Acknowledgements

WHERE TO EVEN BEGIN.

This turned out to be the hardest book I've written to date. Not because of the content, but because of all the things that happened in my life surrounding it. I jokingly told a few people that I felt like this book was cursed, as every time I went to work on it in earnest, something awful would happen, and that would either physically stall my progress, or just make it near impossible to continue emotionally. Fortunately, I have people in my life who helped me through the worst, and reminded me that I still have the best to look forward to. Poor Rori may not have felt stronger after her world broke, but I do, and I have the following people to thank for helping me get there.

First and foremost, my family. Mom, Dad, and Jacki, your unconditional support and encouragement means the world to me. Thank you for your love and for your respect. I'm so grateful to and for you all, and that feeling only grows stronger every day. There never would have been a very first book without you, and there certainly would not have been this one. Thank you.

A huge thank you to my extended family, too, both by blood and by choice. You all also gave your words of love and support, and I can't thank you enough for that. There are, quite honestly, too many of you to name, and I'll never forgive myself if I try to do it here and accidentally leave one of you out, but you know who you are, because I have grown up calling you my aunts, uncles, cousins, and friends.

Next up, the wonderful Housemates (on three, ready?). It's been a long time since we actually were housemates, but sometimes it only feels like a day has passed since then. Your friendship is truly invaluable, and I'm so happy that you all are still in my life.

The enduring game crew gets another shout out for their tenacity and remarkable collective ability to flirt with disaster and still manage to skate by in every campaign. You all have provided me with some much-needed laughs and escapes, and I can only hope I've been able to do the same for you. Onwards, crew!

Another massive thank you to my editor Susan, who was beyond patient with me while I was working on this one for far longer than we initially thought it would take me. As always, it was fantastic working with you. Thank you for asking all of those questions that never occurred to me, for sharing my excitement and joy over this project, and for helping me make this book the best it could be.

Finally, thank you, reader, for coming on this journey. A lot has changed since the *Southern Echo*'s first voyage, and there's still a lot more to come. I hope you'll join me for the next one.

Books by K.N. Salustro

Southern Echo

The Roar of the Lost Horizon
A Whisper from the Edge of the World
A Silence Falling Dark and Deep*

*Coming 2024

The Star Hunters

Chasing Shadows
Unbroken Light
Light Runner

The Arkin Races

Cause of Death: ???

Tales from 2020